Return to Faërie

***

Book Two

A Delicate Balance

Return to Faërie

A trilogy comprising the following books:

Moonrise
A Delicate Balance
Windy Hill Prayer

www.return-to-faerie.com

Copyright © 2021 Jane Sullivan

All rights reserved (including all forms of reproduction or adaptation of text and images, in all forms, in all countries)

Jane Sullivan
www.calligrafee.com

ISBN: 9798558825237

Table of Contents

A Delicate Balance

1. Lily's Secrets 1
2. Hastening Home 27
3. The Poet-Prince of Dawn Rock 47
4. A Spiral of Stars 71
5. Moon-Music of Shee-Mor 91
6. Sweet Flight into the Rainbow 117
7. Yellow Writing on a Red Page 139
8. The Lake of Lily-White Stars 171
9. Sapphires and Potpourri 197
10. The Key of the Ghostly Chapel 229
11. Magical Beings 255
12. The Seven Arches and the Seventh Gate 281

13. The Deepest Dell in Aumelas-Pen 305

14. Straying in the Salley Woods 325

15. The Sunder-Stone of Kitty Kyle 349

16. Rendez-vous at Castle Davenia 373

17. The Longings of Far-Flung Fairies 399

18. Turning Fear to Light 429

19. The Offerings of the Summer Solstice 459

Index of Characters 485

Maps 487

Chapter One:
Lily's Secrets

aelys Penrohan was written in a flowing script on the top of the first page of the little journal that Eli's father had given her. The name, followed by a concise address: *Los Angeles, USA*. And a little further down, in faded pencil lines, there was a skilful sketch of a beautiful flower, a lily-of-the-valley, and below that --- still in pencil --- another two words: *My Secret*.

Her mother's journal. Except that Maelys Penrohan, or Lily, was not her mother. And now Eli knew this.

This was the very private, well-hidden journal that Lily had kept, year after year, throughout her daughter's childhood at home and all her unsettled adulthood as well, completely unbeknownst to Eli. It was her secret, just as it had been a secret to Eli for fifty years that this wonderful woman was not, in fact, her true mother.

In the beginning, that had been a secret to Lily, too. It wasn't until the day when Leo, a young poet from Santa Barbara, had come to ask this struggling artist to illustrate a book of his poetry, that Lily learned the truth. From that meeting with Leo had sprung the greatest miracle of Lily's life. Well, perhaps she would have said that meeting Sean Penrohan had been the most miraculous and romantic event of her life, and losing him so soon to a sudden and inexplicable illness the most tragic. But then *this* miracle had

1

come. A poet, who turned out to be an enchanted creature from another world.

Not an angel, but every bit as good as one, in Lily's eyes.

In wonderment Lily discovered that Leo was in fact Leyano, a Prince of Faërie and guardian of one of its Portals, called Dawn Rock, opening onto the rocky heights above a white-walled monastery in Santa Barbara. The doorway on the 'human' side of the Portal was known to the fairies as Eagle Abbey, and Leyano, youngest son of the royal family of his shee, had made the journey from this hidden doorway to L.A. to bring Lily a message, disguised in the words of the poem he read aloud to her that day, that an oft-told 'fairy-tale' had come true in her own life: the King of Faërie had ventured into the realm of humans, taken a wife there, and had even orchestrated the exchange of their own child for a fairy-changeling.

Lily, suddenly, had found herself living a dream, not unlike the dream that Eli had now stepped into, discovering that she herself was that changeling babe.

As Eli cradled the little volume in her lap, fingering the worn corner of the first page and smiling to see the smudged sketch of the modest lily-of-the-valley, she prepared herself to read her 'little moon's' account of this meeting with Leo, and then --- braced for the extraordinary event by this preliminary encounter --- of being reunited with her husband, whom she had buried ten years earlier. And not reunited in some ghostly vision, but visited by the real and very-much-alive King Aulfrin, clearly recognisable as her beloved Sean.

But this was not exactly how Lily told the tale.

Everything has changed. All the most important 'truths' of my present situation have been turned on their heads! Thirteen years ago I fell in love with a wild Irish musician named Sean, we married and then, after only a couple of precious years together, he became ill and died of a mysterious malady, leaving me alone with our only child, a beautiful little red-haired toddler.

But now I have been given another explanation, another version and vision of those events.

For Sean was not Sean, or rather he was merely disguised as Sean. He was not a wandering Irishman, but a wandering fairy --- in fact, a King of the Fairies. He died, but only as Sean, for his true self, the king that he truly was and is, could not die a human death. From the eerie underworld of a human graveyard, he travelled --- still 'disguised' in the body of Sean but en route *transformed once again into himself --- through a liminal land of roots and fungus, to return to his kingdom. An amazing tale indeed, but I now know it to be the real and veritable story, rather than what I believed to have happened...*

Added to this is another layer of revelation: the little girl whom I believed to be my *child, our child, is a princess of her father's fairyland. She was exchanged with our baby, the true child of my marriage with Sean, at birth. I saw her, my own daughter, for only a second --- just as she was born. When I awoke from the charmed sleep that followed, my baby was gone and the princess of my husband's fairyland lay in her place. A fairy-changeling, just as in the old legends! For twelve years I have raised her, loved her, as my own child, our child... for until now I thought that Eli* was *our own daughter.*

It is strange to find myself writing this news, and to reread my words: scribbled words on paper, the bare facts of the story. But, although it's all correct and I know this because Leo and now Sean himself have explained it to me, it was not --- is not --- really like this in my heart.

First of all, I never lost Sean. How could I? My love, our love, was so great, so magical, that it could not leave me. I **did** accept that he had died, but the flimsy curtain of death was less 'true' to me than the sure and solid connection of love. "Love is strong as death," says the Biblical Song of Songs. Stronger, I would say. I've always felt him with me, beside me, a part of me. When Leo, lovely dark-eyed

Delicate Balance

Leo, told me that my husband wished to come back to visit me --- it did not seem very strange at all. Of course, it was a miraculous and mystical twist in the tale, but no stranger than falling deeply in love in the first place, or than witnessing Sean fading and finally dying, no stranger than watching Eli grow and become more and more her wonderful self and at the same time seeing so much of her father reflected in her, no stranger than my own inner voice telling me, all along, that Sean was still alive. All miracles, of one kind or another...

Of course, it was extraordinary to discover that my Sean was a king, and a king of the fairies what's more! But he had always been a king to me, and so unlike any other 'normal' man. I have always known that fairies and spirits exist, so why I should not meet and fall in love with one?!

And Eli? I wept when Sean told me that our own baby had been stolen at birth, but immediately my heart protested. My maternal love had been kindled that night in March 1960, as the full moon was eclipsed and my months, my years, of waiting ended. From the moment I awoke and Sean passed the little bundle into my arms, I believed --- naturally --- that Eli was my child. Perhaps my heart knew better, but I think not; in any case, it adopted her with unconditional love. That she is not the child of my own body, I do not mind, not at all in fact. Ah, I would love to see our true child --- she is called Brocéliana, a beautiful and mystical name! But she has also been adopted: by a marvelous land where she is part of her father's royal family in the realm that he refers to as Faërie. I am deeply happy for her. Eli is my girl now, my little girl now growing into a woman. One day she will learn the truth, but not while I live. This, as Sean has explained to me, is the law in Faërie.

If you are reading this now, my Eli, my daughter in all but mere flesh and blood, know that I love you --- as ever, and _forever_ --- and that I hope you have learned and gracefully accepted the truth of your identity, as Sean told me you would. I hope you have not just happened across this journal too soon by mistake! But I believe it will be as it should be. If you are just now learning, from my words, who and what you are, then be courageous and filled with faith and *love. Believe, and continue to live your human story with joy! If I am gone when you come into possession of this journal, as is planned, then I can tell my tale to the Princess of fairyland, and your ancient wisdom and regal fairy-spirit will possibly be yours already, and you will have found again your father --- so you will be living an enchanted tale as well. Just as I am now...*

Eli closed the little journal. She couldn't continue reading through her tears; but they were sweet tears.

She was sitting in her tattered arm-chair, pulled up beside the open window of her small apartment in Saintes. She had left the Abbey of Ligugé earlier this morning, just after the office of *Laudes*, to be home by mid-morning. She knew what she must do. First: brew a pot of strong Irish tea. Second: sip slowly and begin reading Lily's Journal. Third: play her harp, Clare. And so far, she had only done the first two...

Eli dried her tears, and rose, replacing her empty mug on the kitchenette-counter at one side of her studio-cum-sitting-room. She ran her hand down the graceful sweep of Clare's smooth upper-curve where the strings were wound around their pegs with stubby little levers beside them to adjust the semi-tones of each note. Eli had had Clare with her at the Abbey, but she had not played her harp since returning to the world of humankind, late yesterday morning, following her adventures in Faërie.

Now she settled herself behind her instrument, leaning Clare's golden wood against her body, encircling her harp with her arms, exhaling deeply and closing her eyes. Gentle glissandos, up and down, up and down ---- barely audible --- sent their tingling vibrations into Eli's ears and fingers, arms and chest. And then soft notes, plucked with tender finger-tips or, Eli preferred to think, *released*. One of her harp teachers had expressed it in those terms: *"You don't pluck or pull a harp-string: you hold it with intention on the pad of your* *finger, and then you release it, <u>liberating</u> the sound and freeing its voice!"*

A melody took form, 'liberated' from the strings, but not one that Eli had consciously intended to play. She smiled as she cradled Clare in her arms, rocking gently with the rhythm of the piece of music that was now pouring out of her fingers and coming to life on Clare's strings. She was playing an air she knew well, and had loved for many years, the haunting Scottish song, "The Water is Wide".

*The water is wide; I cannot get o'er,
And neither have I wings to fly.
Give me a boat that can carry two,
And both shall row, my love and I...*

She had often found that the lyrics of this song tickled her with an unanswered question: *what was this ocean too vast to cross?* Was it our life's journey, or a great romance or even Love itself, or was it something even more mystical and divine? And in the song, the prayer is for a boat that will carry two: 'my love and I'. Eli thought of her own homecoming adventure now, and of the strange vision she had been sent when meditating in the abbey's side-chapel, where she had found herself rowing a tiny boat across tempestuous, grey waves --- following the luminous path of starlight or moonbeams shining across the surface of the choppy seas before her.

And now, knowing that she was being recalled to her life as a fairy and being offered three magical Visits in order to make her final decision of whether she would ultimately return to Faërie or not, Eli was inspired to play this tune and to contemplate the riddle of its poetry. Why had this Scottish air come to her now? And who was the belovèd that she needed, in order to row her boat to the far shore of her voyage? She wondered, of course, if it were Reyse. Hadn't Muscari told her that his shee had portals opening into Scotland?!

Or did she really *need* anyone else, in order to cross this vast ocean? Were the 'two' in the boat, in fact, one and the same in her case: her own double-identity, as Eli and as the Princess Mélusine?

The improvisation that Eli now skilfully elaborated became stronger and surer. She breathed very deeply, filling her lungs and her whole body with air, with aliveness, with connection to this life and to the life of that other world. She closed her eyes. Aloud, almost sung to the notes of the rolling chords, she heard herself asking: "When may I return, go back for my second Visit? When may I go home, again?"

Her fingers stopped on the topmost notes of a rising arpeggio. She exhaled, and opened her eyes, surprised and shivering with a sudden sensation like a rogue wind shaking a tree. She had heard the answer. She had heard it as if spoken by a familiar and commanding and yet so loving voice.

"Summer," it said simply. And then it added, "Your birthday".

The room was very silent. Golden and silent. It was Saturday, the 1st of May, late morning, with a sky calm and clear and pale sapphire blue.

"But my birthday was in March," thought Eli. "It's not in the summer!"

Then she smirked to herself. For the answer was obvious.

"My birthday as Eli, as a changeling baby placed in the crib of Lily and Sean's new-born Brocéliana, *that* birthday --- which I've celebrated as mine for these past fifty years --- was at the lunar eclipse on the 13th of March, in 1960. But I am not *only* Eli; I am also Mélusine. And Mélusine is over six hundred years old, and I have no idea of the exact date of her birth.

"Or have I?"

Eli brought Clare back against her shoulder, and her fingers descended the strings, retracing the same arpeggio in the other direction. But the words she heard were the same, and every bit as firm and assured. "Summer. Your birthday."

And she knew that this was the answer. Mélusine was definitely born in the summer, and she could even add that it was surely at the Summer Solstice: the 21st of June. She knew it now, with sudden and unequivocal certainty. And that was the answer, the date when she should go back again. In just over seven weeks...

Eli felt there was nothing more to be said, to be decided, just now. The details would come. She had seven more weeks to remain in this world, in her more mundane life, and then she would go back for another three weeks' Visit to Faërie. How it would happen would be made clear later. She felt no doubt or anxiety, and she knew that the plan was in place.

The hardest thing now was simply to navigate her life in the present, balancing herself between Faërie and the human world as best she could. She had the amusing image of having her feet in two different canoes, gliding down a wide, swirling river ---- and hoping the boats would not drift apart, and that there were not too many rapids ahead!

Meditation, or music? That was the only question. Well, there remained a nice slice of beautiful morning before her in which to do one or the other: and she chose the second. She had been missing Clare for three weeks while in Faërie (although it had been only three hours in human time), and she wished to play her again. So she pulled out sheets of 'not-yet-memorised' music that would require her to concentrate and occupy her mind as well as to enjoy her harp. This was *not* the moment to idly amuse herself with improvised pieces or ones that she knew well by heart!

Later, she would perhaps continue to read Lily's journal, and then she must prepare her work for next week: the usual round of classes to give, and then on Monday afternoon she had a presentation of the folk harp at a local elementary school. That would be nice work: children always loved meeting Clare, hearing a few simple tunes, stroking the harp-strings and making waves of vibrating sound, discovering the little painted dragons and the colourful Celtic interlace on the soundboard.

Eli did not read much more of Lily's journal that day, nor indeed all the weekend. It was as if she needed a 'retreat' *following* her retreat at the Abbey of Ligugé; or more to the point, following the intense and amazing three weeks of stolen time spent in the kingdom of Faërie.

She spent the weekend walking through the pretty public gardens of Saintes, or even further along the River Charente, sipping coffee or a glass of wine in a sidewalk café, strolling and shopping in the Sunday morning market, praying and meditating in her favourite churches: cool, quiet, smelling of old stone and years of incense and candles.

Monday morning she had a harp student and a private lesson in English conversational skills and then, after lunch, she went to the school for her little recital and talk about harp music.

Indeed, all the twenty or so youngsters in the class she visited adored meeting Clare, for most had never seen an Irish harp before. Some had glimpsed a big concert harp in an orchestra and one or two had heard a harp in recorded music, and several had seen harps in paintings or illustrations. But aside from one little girl who had been with her family to a Celtic music festival in Brittany, none had ever had the chance of seeing one close-up, or of touching its strings, or of learning a little about the technique of harp-playing.

Such delight in her ten and eleven-year-old audience was not unusual or unexpected for Eli. But something much stranger occurred during her presentation.

A little boy in the front row, considerably smaller than the others, had spent the entire duration of Eli's little recital and explanation in wrapt attention, his elbows on his knees, his chin resting on his cupped hands, his eyes huge and intense behind very thick round glasses. Eli wasn't sure if he was perhaps slightly handicapped, and was leaning toward Clare in order to hear or see more clearly. It was true, his little spectacles seemed terribly heavy and thick, and his expression was rather distant and dreamy (but as for that, Eli found it normal when hearing a harp for the first time!).

When the bell rang, and the teacher ushered the children out for their recreation time in the courtyard, Eli began to neatly pull down the levers of her harp and reach for Clare's transport-cover. The teacher came forward to shake her hand and thank her, but as she did so, both noticed the heavy little spectacles left on the small boy's chair.

"That's odd," said the teacher, picking them up, "Emile has forgotten his glasses. He'll surely be back in a second --- he's not able to see much without them!"

Eli finished packing her music pages and stand, and securing the ties of Clare's cover; and with the teacher walking beside her she carried her harp to the door. But Emile had not returned. Both Eli and the teacher stopped at the open door and looked out onto the playground, where all the children were running and shouting, hop-scotching or skipping rope in the sun. The teacher was very quiet for a moment, and then she whispered to Eli, "I don't understand this at all. There he is, there's Emile. He's running and playing ball with those two other lads. He *never* plays ball. And he hasn't his glasses..."

She called to the little boy, who finally left his joyful game and ran up to her. "*Oui, maîtresse?*" he querried, his face flushed and his eyes sparkling.

"Emile," began the teacher, "you forgot your glasses...in the classroom. Don't you need them?"

There was a strange moment where the face of the little boy looked puzzled, as if he were trying to remember his multiplication tables. And then he smiled gleefully once again. "No," he said simply. "No, I don't need them."

When Emile had run back to rejoin his comrades, the teacher simply looked at Eli for a moment. Eli said nothing, but she felt an odd shivering sensation ticking her all up her back. It wasn't at all unpleasant.

"Well, that really is *very* odd," concluded the teacher, politely bidding Eli good-bye but with a perplexed expression on her face still. "Very peculiar."

Eli glanced once again at Emile, and then she carried Clare out to the parking lot and carefully loaded her into the car. She then decided that a cup of something at her favourite café in town would be in order, before heading back to her apartment.

Lily's journal was tucked into Eli's shoulder-bag, and as she settled herself at a corner table on the *Musardière*'s terrace she pulled it out. She ordered herself a cappuccino and watched the swallows dipping and diving in the warm air high above the old stone walls around her. She opened to the page where she had stopped reading, and continued.

I did not begin to keep this journal from my very first meeting with Sean, re-united after so many years. I'll probably go back to that amazing and exciting moment when dear Leo ushered Sean back into my life, and then I will recount all of the details of our conversation and the joy of our finding one another again perhaps. But for now, I want to write about what we discussed today --- and this is already Sean's third visit to me.

He does not come too often. He says that he always asks one of his musical instruments before visiting me: it seems that they advise him and confirm his own intuition, on many subjects. This was always true when he was with me before: his flute or his dulcimer were his counsellors and guides. But since he has taken this audacious step of contacting me and coming back to see me from his fairy kingdom, he tells me that they often urge him to go slowly and not to make the voyage too frequently.

Well, I realise that he cannot live here with me always or be my husband in the world again. But it seems there is some risk about his journeys here too. Perhaps he should not leave his kingdom often or perhaps crossing the threshold between the worlds is dangerous even for a king.

He is very real when he does come: it is not as if he is a spirit or phantom appearing in a white mist, a harbinger of otherworldly fears! Not at all. When he is with me, he is solid and we can even touch or kiss. But we do not **make love** --- or have not done so. We both have some hesitation about too much contact, at least yet. Perhaps his harp or flute tells him to be distant as regards physical intimacy, or my own heart is holding back a little. In any case, I will accept how it evolves. This is only, as I say, his third visit.

It is late June. Sean told me that he must not come when the moon is full --- and tonight it will be just past the full, what he calls a waning gibbous. I rather like that word! But he says that a waxing crescent is also a good time ...

In any case, we spoke today about music, and about his instruments. I asked about the wisdom and guidance that they offer, and also if he still had the little wooden flute he was buried with. Immediately he took it out of his pocket, and played our own precious love-song to me once again. And then he kissed me.

He had kissed me once before, just before he left me on his second visit, over a month ago. But his kisses are not as they were when he was my 'human' husband. To touch him, especially to feel his lips and breath, or to be embraced by him, sends a powerful sensation all through me, like an electrical shock. It's not the shivering delight at the kiss or touch of one's lover; it's quite exceptional... I would say that it is the <u>opposite</u> of being drunk, but just as intoxicating!

After our flute-song-kiss, I told him how very sad I was that his beautiful painted dulcimer had been stolen, oh about five years ago now. But, marvellous news: it was not stolen, or rather it was stolen by Sean himself! He explained that our own daughter, Brocéliana, who had just turned seven at that time, was clearly possessed of a great musical talent. He wanted her to have his dulcimer, and he sent a pixie to whisk it away one dark night.

Then he told me that his favourite instrument for gaining insight or seeking the answer to a difficult question was his harp. I did not know that he played the harp. He told me he would not be able to bring his own lap harp into this world to play for me, for it was a very enchanted creature, and would probably be neither visible nor audible to me, as a human. (Evidently, his flute is much more down-to-earth!) But he did ask that I find a way to expose you, Eli, to harp music and encourage you to learn to play, for he said that you would be able to hear its musical voice for guidance and insight too.

I told him that would be very easy, for our Eli was always drawing mermaids playing harps, all up and down the margins of her school notes --- and it was infuriating her teachers! He laughed, and said that was quite normal, for she had learned to play the harp beautifully, as the young Princess she truly is, hundreds of years ago; and, he added, her music-teacher was a mermaid.

"There are <u>mermaids</u> in your kingdom?!" I exclaimed.

"There are many marvellous beasts, my little moon," he replied with his customary laugh and his eyes sparkling like green jewels. "There are mermaids, and flying-horses, and friendly little green dragons. But there are also much more menacing dragons, huge and white, with glowing red eyes. And there are giant cats, much larger than lions or tigers. And," he added, almost in a whisper, "there are ghostly unicorns, *rare and wonderful.*"

Eli paused in her reading, and sipped her cappuccino. "Unicorns," she mused, murmuring the word under her breath. "My nickname was 'unicorn', but in the language of this country where I now live. *Licorne,*" she said to herself, very very softly. "*Licorne…*"

"Licorne!" a voice echoed. At first she thought it was coming from her heart, rather like when she heard a message from Clare as she played. But now the voice repeated the word, or greeting, and it was louder and coming closer. Eli looked around the crowded terrace of the *Musardière*.

Luckily, she had replaced her cup in its saucer, for if not she would have surely spilled its contents as she jumped with surprise.

"Liam!" Eli swallowed as she caught her breath, and then she shook her head. "*Liam?*"

The man had reached her table, and placed both his hands on the back of the empty, wrought-iron chair facing her. He smiled warmly.

"Reyse..." said Eli slowly, still in shock. "You're Liam again! But, oh my, the thirty years since Kilkenny and Cork have been kinder to you than to me: you've hardly aged a day!"

Reyse pulled out the chair and before he seated himself he reached for Eli's hand, kissing it rather than shaking it. He sat down and laughed, almost nervously.

"Not too disturbing, seeing me turn up here?" he asked after a moment or two of scanning Eli's turquoise eyes for her reaction to his presence. "Yes, well, though older than you, my dear Eli, as the Lord Reyse, I have chosen to use the same age-charm and disguise as I did for our brief affair in the early 1980s, thus I am a dashing human of about, hmm, what would you say? Thirty-five-ish?!"

Eli had to laugh. "Yes, yes, I think that would be about right! And how wonderful to see you again!"

"I'm relieved to hear that," he confessed. "I hoped I would not imbalance your foot-hold, now that you must live in the two worlds at once." And then, in a more serious and sympathetic tone, he added, "I know how strange it can be, to come back into the human realm when one knows that Faërie exists. I thought you might be finding it quite hard."

Eli, still smiling, replied, "No, not too hard. It is a balancing act, I suppose, but I'm happier than I've ever been, I think, knowing that I belong to Faërie and have just *chosen* to have this experience, this *educational* experience, here. It makes such sense to me, and so believing it is easy and really a great relief."

"I'm very happy too," nodded Reyse, "very happy to see you again, my Lady Eli." After a moment's silence, in which Eli felt the terrace come slightly in and out of focus, he continued, "May I offer you another drink? An Orion Nebula perhaps?!"

Laughing again, Eli shook her head. "It's a lovely café, the *Musard*, but it's not *The Tipsy Star*! And I think coffee suits me better than beer, or I may become as tipsy as the *Star*. Do fairies become drunk?" she inquired light-heartedly.

"Never," conceded Reyse. "We are rather immune to alcohol, owing to the fact that we are intoxicated by Life itself. We sense the jovial nature of a well-brewed beer, mind you, or the warmth of an old brandy or the glad and festive beauty of a good wine, but it cannot go to our heads. Nothing goes to our heads because everything stops at a fairy's heart, and that is a riotously mad garden of delights already, so inebriation holds no charm for us!"

Reyse rose with Eli, and they walked together down the long avenue of shops. "Speaking of gardens," he said, offering her his arm, "may I suggest a walk around the pretty *jardin public* here in Saintes, on the other side of the River Charente?"

For many days and nights, Eli would remember and re-live the half hour of this unexpected reunion with Reyse, as they crossed the arched foot-bridge and entered the gardens.

It became very clear to Eli, as they wandered arm in arm, that she was being invited to fall in love. Whether invited by Life, by her own heart, or by Reyse, she was not sure.

But she also knew that she was a human still, with her human past of emotional roller-coaster rides and tempests and illusions, needs and desires and romantic idealism, and all sorts of other psychological baggage and scars. She was no longer the youthful Eli of her first encounter with Liam in Kilkenny, and she was not the Princess Mélusine again either. She wondered if, as Mélusine, she and Reyse had also been lovers. Somehow, she thought not.

They passed a rather sombre fish-pond, not at all reminiscent of the fountains of Fantasie, and some sad, caged animals: a goat, and a peacock, and some poor ducks. Eli wished she could see an end to any and all cages, on the spot. She thought of Jizay's poem. Suddenly the notion of complete freedom and of honouring the fact that all creatures had the birth-right of living life according to their true destiny and instincts (and even their impetuosity) became paramount to Eli. Reyse felt the tension in his companion's spirit, and led her away from the miniature zoo.

As they passed beside a particularly radiant group of rose bushes, he stopped and turned to face her. Eli clearly remembered Liam, in Kilkenny, years and years ago. And this was a re-enactment of Liam's first kiss of that first affair. His hands were on her shoulders, his wavy hair was shining a deep chestnut red in the afternoon sun, his deep brown eyes were intense and tender.

She sighed, and took one step backwards. Reyse's eyes became questioning and slightly sad.

"So much has happened, Reyse," she said, "and so much is happening at the moment in my life… Today I am Eli, not Mélusine, and I will soon have to decide which one of those women I will truly be for the years, or centuries, to come. Fairies are drawn to fairies, you told me once. It is clear that we are drawn to one another, but to me it is not clear exactly *why*. You stir my longing, perhaps, for my fairy-life --- as you probably did when we met in Kilkenny. But is it *you* I long for, or Faërie itself? You must give me time to know the answer."

Reyse reached for one of Eli's hands, and she allowed him to take it to his lips. He nodded, and he smiled a little. Then before he released her hand, he squeezed it and said, "You are still and ever *full beautiful* and *a faery's child*, dear Lady Eli of my heart. But your eyes are no longer wild. They are wise and searching and inviting, but no longer wild. You have grown up. May I continue to befriend you, and see you sometimes, although you reject me as your lover at this time?"

"I think that would be alright, Reyse, but give me a little time...even for that?"

He assented with a nod, still smiling. "When do you return to Aulfrin's kingdom for your next Visit?"

"In June."

"May I see you while you are still here in the world, perhaps in a fortnight's time?"

"I don't know --- yes, probably that will be alright. I don't know yet."

Reyse nodded once again. "I will try to send you word beforehand, and if your answer is 'no' I will respect it. As I will always respect your decisions, my Princess.

"But," he added, about to turn now and walk away, "don't be surprised if I continue my quest for your heart!"

She had to laugh a little, and Reyse did also. He bowed his head, and briefly laid his hand on his breast, then turned and walked away among the trees beside the river.

Eli thought he looked every bit the noble lord of an enchanted land; he was so full of dignity and so worthy of love and respect.

But she knew she had been right to refuse him.

****

Later in the evening, back at her apartment, Eli took out the little journal again. She opened it to where she had read that morning in the café.

I asked my darling Sean to tell me more about unicorns, but he said that he would have to go as delicately into that subject as he had gone into his desire to see me again --- and that decision had required years *of hesitation! He said that he would consider telling me more, but later... on another visit, perhaps.*
And I accepted this.
It's strange how acceptance is so liberating. I think I have taught you that, my darling Eli, but I want to remind you of it... for it may be of help in all you are facing now. I have had much to accept, to learn *to accept. Widowed twice over, first by Yann's death when he was only a very young man, and then by the loss of my Sean, I have nonetheless never grieved in anguish or with 'chagrin'. I have grieved as a woman will do, when she is no longer in the arms of her beloved. But as I do not fear death, neither for myself nor for my loved ones, I cannot plunge my heart into sorrow because of it. And so I* accepted *those 'separations' --- and then came the 'reward' for my calm and my interior peace, for my Sean came back to me!*
I have accepted that I will never see Brocéliana, and because of my serenity --- finally --- in the face of that loss, I was blessed with a deep and truly maternal love, forever, for you my Eli. Ours was a difficult life in the early years after Sean's death: not difficult to love you (for then I thought you to be my true child), but to accept our situation together and its precarious lack of security. However, I have always thought that Helen Keller was quite right, when she wrote: "Security is mostly a superstition. It does not exist in nature, nor do the children of men as a whole experience it. Avoiding danger is no safer in the long run than outright exposure. Life is either a daring adventure, or nothing." *I have always loved those lines...*
Leaving our beautiful little canyon cottage to live in a garage --- all I could afford! --- was a foolish solution, I now believe. But I had little choice. I was very naïve and trusted that humans were as good, at heart, as Life itself. I'm afraid I still like to believe that, even in the face of all evidence to the contrary. But I misjudged, very

generously misjudged, those 'friends' whom I thought were trying to help me and my little girl.

Ah well. You will remember it Eli, as you read this perhaps. The garage we rented belonged to a couple I had met at my life-drawing classes, and they seemed so sincerely desiring of doing good. I soon found that the man's intentions were not quite so noble. Alas for his wife, for I was not the only object of his philandering and his constant and irritating flirtations.

Not long after I had refused him, for the fifth time I think, he determined to put us out of our very miserable home, which for me --- at that time --- would have been very dramatic, for I had no money to rent anything else. My only remaining close family, if one could call it that, was Morvan, Yann's child in France. He was only about twenty-seven years old then, and was pursuing his own rather risky life-choice as a sailor. His adoptive family who had raised him were Yann's relatives, of course, but we were no longer in close contact, and so I was reluctant to return to France and seek help or lodging from them. In any case, the price of such a voyage was utterly beyond my means.

Sean said that he thought the 'gold' he had left me would help me through: dear man! He was not very accustomed to the modern world, for his previous visits to meet human women --- yes, he has confessed to an inclination in his character towards the fair sex of humankind, and several interludes! --- had been long, long before the twentieth century. A pocketful of large gold coins was as much use to me as the proverbial crock of gold found at the end of a rainbow! And fairy gold is unmarked, and eventually fades into the cracked and withered leaves from which it is made... (I often wondered how he had secured our pretty canyon-cottage, but I have not yet asked him about that.)

When the lascivious and lecherous man, the landlord of our garage-home, was on the verge of putting us out in the street, a knife attack by the irate husband of one of his 'conquests' left him mortally injured. He died later the same day. Our problems and sorrows were far from solved, though, for his wife soon replaced her husband with a lover of her own, but a violent one. Not violent to her, as far as I knew, but on one occasion sexually violent to her daughter, then only twelve or thirteen. So horrible. You did not know her too well, I imagine, my Eli, as you were so much younger. The poor child: unable to put her life back together after the incident of rape and possibly other brutality, she chose suicide when only sixteen. It was a gruesome environment, I'm afraid, in which to bring you up. Oh so different from the simple, old-fashioned and rural life Sean and I had expected to live in Brittany.

I struggled to protect you, Eli, from the ugliness of our immediate surroundings; I encouraged your imaginary world to blossom and I was glad to see that there were many happy and solitary hours of curiously complex make-believe games to fill much of your time. We read and drew together, too, do you recall? And you followed me willingly, in your tastes and your later studies, into a love for the Middle Ages and for a chivalrous and distant culture. And you were devout, also, as I was, in the Christian faith. It is good, I have always said, to believe. *And* that *belief has been my greatest strength.*

But I believed, too, in the world of folklore and legend --- and I have now been proven right!

When Sean told me about his dulcimer being given to our daughter Brocéliana, it led me to ask more about her, how and where she lived in his kingdom, and what other talents and tastes she had beyond music. And so it was that Sean told me more and more about mermaids, for Brocéliana was being taught to play her dulcimer and also to master other arts by an ancient and revered mer-woman, called the Lady Ecume. I liked her French name: the 'Lady Sea-Foam' I translated it, in my now thoroughly American dialect, and I asked Sean to tell me more about her. She is a harpist too, I understand, and very skilled. But she and her sisters play the dulcimer also, and Sean tells me they have long white hair made of feathers. Amazing!

He also told me that Brocéliana loved to speak with rabbits --- what a sensible girl! He says that she will probably be drawn to do her first 'Initiation' in their company. Now, I have no idea, as yet, what that means --- but no doubt he will eventually tell me more.

All he has told me about where she lives delights me: for she dwells in a marvellous city called Fantasie where seven Great Trees are venerated and there are more grass and flowers and silver fountains and winding streams than there are buildings or houses. How very at odds with the life we live here in this land of concrete and materialism, speed and aggression. I am so happy for her, and so I cannot mourn her loss or wish her here, really.

We will continue together, Eli my dear one, you and I, and now I have also the occasional visits of your father to fill my heart with undreampt-of joy! We will manage here, and perhaps we will improve our situation soon. Everything changes, and I am convinced that God's design is that changes are always for the best --- even if it is not too clear to us at the time. So we shall see what comes next.

Ah, you will be home soon from your riding lesson, so I must hide this secret journal of mine. (How thrilled you were that I could afford that summer treat for you, of horseback riding. That was a blessing, thanks to a recent commission from the owner of the stables, allowing me to negotiate a few classes for you --- and it has left me with some afternoons here on my own, so that Sean could come to me behind your back!).

Bless you, my Eli…à bientôt.

Eli closed the little journal once more, and held it fast against her heart for many minutes. But suddenly she found her thoughts turning back to Reyse, and so she decided to have a quick salad dinner and a glass of red wine, and then read a little more before going to bed. She really did not want to dwell on her past interlude with Liam or on the proffered present one!

However, as she finished preparing her salad and opened the kitchen cupboard to take down a wine-glass, she had that now-not-unfamiliar feeling of someone watching her, from inside her own head or being. With a foot in each world, she concluded, her intuition and extra-sensory skills were becoming somehow sharpened, perhaps.

How did she know this? Why could she feel this 'winking watcher' with her now?

Now she thought: "Messages were sent to me a month ago to ease me back into an awareness of who and what I really am. I've been told that they were sent by my father, and by Reyse, and by the Lady Ecume. If they could contact me and perceive the right moments to communicate with me, then they have some kind of access to my mind or to my life, even when I think I am completely alone. I suppose this is all part of being a *changeling*, but it feels rather disquieting. But let me think. Reyse is here in the world, probably, still. Can he perceive me, or send me messages now? Or was he only *allowed* to do so at the one specific moment?"

She decided not to have that glass of wine after all. A clear head seemed to be more vital than the relaxation she would derive from a *Côtes de Blaye*!

No, she decided, her romantic wonderings about the noble Lord Reyse were coming from her own heart, no doubt about it --- and not from some exterior or psychic suggestions. But her desire to read more of Lily's journal, normal as such an idea and such an activity would be, seemed to come from somewhere else. She could almost hear the journal *asking* her to open it again....

Yes, she insisted to herself, water instead of wine!

As she took her bowl of salad to her armchair and began to eat, she placed the journal on the small, adjacent table. Not wanting to risk staining it further --- this time with olive oil and balsamic vinegar --- she simply reached over and opened the little book at random, letting it fall to whatever page it wished. She didn't look at it right away, but took a couple more bites of her dinner in mindfulness and gratitude. And then she looked.

The notebook had opened much further on than where Eli had read to so far. She could not see a date, but the left-hand page was decorated with a sketch of her father's painted dulcimer. It sent a rippling, rising surge of poignant joy up Eli's back. Yes, that was the instrument! She could even imagine the colours now, just as she had seen them when a child of six or seven, before it was retrieved (as she now knew) by a pixie of Faërie. A caption of a few words was written beneath it. Eli leaned a little nearer, and read: *Sean's dulcimer, from memory but also with his help to get the details right.*

The dulcimer sketch took up most of the page, but below it was another little drawing, much less confident. It didn't actually look like Lily's hand had done it, in fact. Eli placed her salad bowl on the table, exchanging it for the journal now. She studied the spidery sketch and read the finely written lines that Lily had added beside it.

It was a tiny mermaid. She was sitting on a rock in a bay or at the shore of the sea. Her scaly tail was curled into the water indicated in the foreground, and her hair was a blowing mass of scribbled feathers. One arm was outstretched around a lap harp with a sort of sea-horse design on the highest point of its top curve. But with the other hand the mermaid was reaching out towards the surface of the water before her. Floating on the water was an ornate key, filled-in with pencil lines so that it was very black.

Lily's handwriting gave this explanation: *The Lady Sea-Foam, drawn by Sean as he tells me about her. I will write more later... Oh! She is lovely, and I am so grateful to her! And to you too, dear poet Leo.*

Eli froze, and then she took a sip of water. She wondered if she were even breathing. It was the image she had seen while listening to the music of the harp at the *Inn of the Smiling Salmon*. It was the mysterious floating key, and the mermaid whose regard had seemed so forceful as to be almost dangerous.

So, this was the Lady Ecume. Who and what was she? And what was the importance of this key which seemed to be intrinsically associated with her?

On the facing page, Lily's journal entry continued.

Sean has left me again now, for this visit. He will try to return before the close of this year, so he says. He will send me word, as usual. Fairies, I have discovered, are indeed marvellous creatures. All of them.

As we spoke today of what had happened to you, Eli, Sean comforted me with tales of your true youth, as the Princess Mélusine, in Faërie. In those days, many centuries ago now, the lovely dulcimer that he has helped to draw again here was in his palace, the King's Tower it is called, in his belovèd capital city. When Mélusine was eight years old, all her family was about her still: her three brothers, and both her parents, and even the other Princess whom Sean thought was his own child. Mélusine's mother, her real mother and the Queen of Faërie, would be banished a year or so later. But at that tender age of innocence, the little Princess, now you my Eli, was loved and safely guarded.

I could not do so much for you as a human child, at eight, under my protection. Oh, but this news is lying so heavy on my heart. Sean told me not to grieve and not to feel the guilt that all my motherly love is forcing upon me. For Eli Penrohan is my child --- the child of my heart. How could this have happened?

Sean insisted, I must not tell you the explicit details of what I have discovered. The memories have been buried now, in your youthful mind, for they were too distressing and incomprehensible for a child to 'digest'. He agreed with me that this dramatic experience, only now come to light, this childhood trauma when you were only eight, will likely leave some scars in the form of inexplicable fears or even anger as you grow up. But, he insisted, I must remember that you are living a brief experience as a human, and one day you will return to the world from whence you came --- and in that world, you knew only love and respect.

The painted dulcimer, he now realises, had been a great protection for us both; and he, in his turn, feels guilty having sent for it. But as I drew it, I could hear its melodies once more, and he said that they would resonate now in my heart, and rekindle the protection that had been lost for these past seven years since it was taken back to his kingdom: we could not have imagined, either of us, how vulnerable you would be without that instrument nearby, even in its silence.

You are fourteen now, and will begin the graceful transformation, gradually, day by day, into a woman. I fear for the fragility that is sown in your young psyche since this tragedy; I fear that it is not so deeply buried that it will not come to haunt you as you mature.

But Sean has told me of another protection that you will have, and that he has negotiated with a being who loves you dearly in his kingdom. As he spoke, he began to draw the little design at the bottom of the page where I drew the dulcimer. The mermaid. The Lady Ecume, or Sea-Foam, as I call her. I asked how <u>she</u> would protect my dear Eli, but he did not answer immediately, continuing simply to sketch the feathery hair, the long tail, and the pretty little harp. "This is the harp," he said at last, "which Eli learned to play, when she was the Princess Mélusine, and studying the art of healing music with this most ancient and magical of the mermaids of his realm. It is called the Harp of Seven Eyes."

"But how will this heal her heart and protect her in her life here, as a human?" I asked, still very worried for my precious girl.

He was quiet again for a moment, and busied himself with the final detail of his sketch: a dark key, floating miraculously on the surface of the water.

"The Lady Ecume holds the Black Key," he said slowly. "It is, perhaps, the most powerful treasure in all of Faërie. I have spoken with her about what I learned had happened to Eli, six years ago now, here in this violent and dangerous world that she chose to come into. And I asked the Lady Ecume if she could use the Key as a form of protection, a charm, a blessing for my daughter."

The Mermaid replied: Mélusine chose this course in freedom and from the depths of great wisdom and long, long years of study and silence and great, perilous adventures here. She understood the risks." *This was the first remark of the Lady Ecume. But then she added:* As Eli, yes, she will bear the scars of this crime and violence, all of her human life, whether she recovers the actual memory of the event or not. But before the close of her human changeling adventure draws near, I will most probably give this renowned Key into her keeping, as I gave it briefly once before to another noble fairy, and it will open the hidden door --- as it did for him --- whereby she may regain her kingdom and her true being, crossing the threshold of cleansing fire --- of yellow flame it was for him, of a rich garnet-red it will be for her --- to be purged of all dross and demons that have darkened her path.

"*I do not yet know, my dear Lily,*" Sean continued, "*how or when this will take place. We must wait, long years I think, before it will come about. But find comfort in the pledge of this greatest of mermaids. For I believe that the wonders of the Black Key brought my youngest son, the Prince Leyano, back to me through darkness and despair. And now, as you yourself have seen, he is a joyful and regal fairy. Eli, when she comes home, will cross the threshold of Faërie to re-inhabit the body of Mélusine, and she will hold her head high and her heart will be filled with pure joy!*"

Eli turned back to the illustrations once again. She stared blankly at the drawing of the mermaid, and also at the dulcimer. And then she raised her eyes, and stared at nothing at all.

She could not make herself turn back to a previous page that *might* refer to what this 'tragedy' had been; and she could not read any further ahead. She had no memory of the event being alluded to, and she was not sure she ever wanted one to come back to her.

She wondered if she would find the courage to read any more of Lily's secrets --- ever.

****

Chapter Two:
Hastening Home

But *I cannot go back* to Faërie on the 21st of June!"

It was already two days since she had played at the local school, and had met Liam (or rather Reyse). And several days had passed since she had returned from Ligugé and had begun reading Lily's journal, and had asked her harp when she could hope to return for her second visit. And Clare had clearly said to Eli's heart: "Summer. Your birthday."

Eli's intuitive 'hearing' seemed unambiguous and decisive: As the Princess Mélusine, she had been born, she was now certain, at the Summer Solstice. She was being told to return on the 21st of June.

"Impossible," she repeated to herself, sitting up in bed. She had startled herself out of sleep --- just as dawn was tinting her thin, lacy curtains with a pink and pearly light --- with this sudden realisation. "It's not possible to re-enter Faërie on the 21st of next month, because I'm sure it will be almost the full-moon again. And I'm not allowed to be in Faërie when the moon is full. What did Clare mean, then?"

She jumped out of bed, wrapped her silky, flowery house-coat around herself, and went into her sitting-room-cum-kitchen. The calendar on the fridge door gave the phases of the moon --- information Eli was well in the habit of following --- and she ran her finger over the remaining dates in May and then into June. Indeed, the moon would be full on the 26th of June.

"It was the 1st of May, four days ago now, when I came back here to Saintes, and the last full moon was the 28th of April. I went into Faërie on the 30th of April, just as the moon was beginning to wane --- and I was there for three weeks. Now, on the same date (strangely), the 28th of May, there will be the next full moon. And the full moon in June is the 26th," she muttered, looking over at her harp, and pursing her lips as though reprimanding Clare.

"Oh dear, but no, that isn't right. But it must be! Oh, let me think: I was there for three weeks, and the moon continued to wane and then it was dark, and then I saw the *new* moon before coming back here.... But, in fact, the three weeks in Faërie amounted to only *three hours* in this world. I'm living those days again now, of course. How exactly is this possible?! It was May Day when I returned to Saintes, and opened Lily's journal, and met Reyse... It was Beltaine, again!" She sighed, and blinked sleepily.

"I need a cup of tea," she concluded.

Eli stroked Clare as she passed her to put on the kettle, shaking her head and almost whispering her apologies.

"How does this work?!" she laughed. "My goodness, it is very confusing stepping out of time. Rip Van Winkle has all my sympathy!"

She held the warm mug with both her hands, and sat by the window. She had to laugh out loud. Her apartment's two windows looked out over the little street winding up to Saintes' Roman *Arc de Germanicus* (like a modest 'arc de triomphe'), and both windows faced east. At this early hour, the rising sun was still hidden from view by the buildings facing her, but in the tilted skylight-window of the house just across the street, at the level of her own apartment, she could see the reflection of the westering moon, a half-moon almost at the third quarter, ghostly --- and quite probably, she imagined, giggling at her! She chuckled back at it, then heaved an over-dramatic sigh, and began calculating again.

"So, let me see… if I go back to Faërie on the 21st of June, I will only be gone *three* hours, and it will not yet be the full moon. Then maybe that's alright. However, maybe not, for if I begin my Visit there on that date, and I live the three following weeks there, as I did on this first Visit, it will coincide with the full moon *there*, and that is not permitted.

"Is that right?" she asked, looking vaguely at the moon's reflection, and then at her harp, almost expecting a reply.

Just as she asked the question, a sharp sound surprised her, but it was not a lunar or even a very musical voice answering her, as she had hoped. It was her door-buzzer.

Eli rose and pressed on the intercom button. Who would be ringing her door-bell at six-thirty in the morning?

"I know I said I would see you in a couple of weeks' time, but I cannot wait so long. Dear Lady Eli, it's only been a couple of days, but may I come up and talk with you?"

Eli smiled, and even laughed softly to herself.

"Hello dear Reyse, and good morning. Well, give me five minutes, and then I'll open for you!"

It was, she had to admit to herself, a lovely feeling. She liked Reyse very much; perhaps she even felt love for him --- she wasn't yet sure. But, in any case, it was very touching to be courted by a noble fairy-lord. All of her over-romantic dreaminess was rising to the surface. There was, at the same time, however, the far-off sound of alarm-bells as well as door-buzzers!

She dressed hastily, brushed her long red hair and twisted it up into a coil at the nape of her neck, and went back to press the 'open' button for the downstairs door.

She stood at the door of her upstairs apartment as she heard Reyse's graceful footsteps jogging up from the ground floor. He arrived at the landing with, of course, a small bunch of lily-of-the-valley in his outstretch hand. Eli felt her cheeks flushed and a school-girl smile of springtime love-in-the-air stealing over her face!

Tall and slender and strong-limbed, Reyse smiled a little sheepishly back at her. The jewels that Eli had seen in Faërie, set into his ear-lobes and ear-points, shimmering little moonstones she thought, were no longer there, and his ears themselves were normal, rounded and human-ish. His curly brown hair was not quite as long as he wore it as a fairy lord, but his merry brown eyes --- sometimes a hazel-nut colour and in other lights a deep mahogany --- were dancing with stars.

"It's a few days late for the French custom of offering these flowers on the 1st of May, in token of friendship," he confessed, "but then, I am still dreaming of becoming much, much more than a friend. However," he concluded, "I'm not here to force my suit any further on your sensitive and somewhat hesitant nature today. I have received an urgent message and must return to my shee, and I wanted to see you before I left."

Eli took the charming little bouquet, and gestured for her fairy-visitor, now in human disguise, to enter. She put on the kettle, and Reyse went immediately to Clare, greeting the little golden-wood harp as he would if it had been Eli's child.

The teapot was topped up and two steaming mugs were poured. As Reyse took a seat on a wooden chair beside her small round dining table, Eli herself sat once again in her armchair. Reyse stirred a spoonful of honey into his tea, and then casually asked, "Do you heal people with Clare?"

"Pardon?" Eli's eyes were wide, both at the question and at Reyse knowing the name of her harp. "Do I what?"

Reyse sipped his tea, and glanced back --- with great respect, it seemed --- to Eli's harp before smiling and commenting, "This is tea from Cork, is it not? I like this beverage very much. We rarely have blends of black tea leaves in Faërie, either in Aulfrin's realm or in my shee. In the Sheep's Head Shee they sometimes smuggle teas from the human world into their kingdom, and --- I must admit --- even stronger drinks! Wonderful shee, the Sheep's Head. Now, what were we talking of, my lovely Lady Eli? Ah, yes. Healing with Clare. I can feel her lovely name and her profound gift: it is very potent her healing-skill. Of course, that would be natural for you to find a harp with that power, given your own studies with the Lady Ecume..."

"So it's true that I learned to *heal* people with harp music?" inquired Eli, open-eyed and now smiling. "And that I learned the skill from a mermaid, from the Lady Sea-Foam?"

"That's surprising, to translate her name into English, my dear....*Licorne*! You were, as Mélusine, given more to great ceremony and respect in regard to your harp-teacher and mentor, even when only a small --- and irrepressible --- fairy child of eleven!"

Eli did not tell Reyse where the name, in that form, came from. Her father had instructed her to keep Lily's journal a secret from other humans, but she felt it prudent to extend the restriction to other *fairies* as well.

She simply said, "I suppose it *is* a little too informal for the greatest of mermaids --- or so I have heard her described. I don't recall ever meeting her, I'm afraid, not yet. And I don't know much about healing with the harp; though I must admit the skill would interest me." She was lost in thoughts of the little boy Emile, and his abandoning, with great joy, his thick glasses. Had that truly been her skill, or Clare's, that had miraculously improved his vision?

Reyse looked a little sad. It was clear to Eli that he, like her, was between two worlds here. He almost expected her to remember her fairy life, but at the same time he was aware that she was still a human. He nodded to himself, with good-humour. Then he continued.

"Yes, yes, the Lady Ecume is certainly the most miraculous of mermaids. When you were in my charge, as a wild-willed child of eleven and twelve, I often escorted you to your lessons with the great mer-harper. You were always playing, and quite beautifully playing, my own little harp, to my great annoyance. Do you recall?"

Eli was laughing now. "No, I don't remember that! And I didn't know that you were a harpist, Reyse!"

"We say 'harper', not harpist, my dear. And yes I do play the harp, but not very *seriously* or very often. I prefer the *vielle* --- I learned to play it in the early Middle Ages, from a charming troubadour here in France, in fact. I had both my *vielle* and my small lap-harp with me in the White Willow Isles when I was your tutor there: the former you loved to listen to, but showed little interest in leaning to play. But the pale little willow-harp, with a dove on the fore-pillar, you had great difficulty in keeping your fingers from touching that! I at last asked your father if I could arrange a meeting with the Lady Ecume, and thus your own talent on that instrument was confirmed by her, as well as her discovery that you possessed the added gift of being able to cure certain illnesses and especially troubles of vision. Natural, in a way, that you exhibited that blessing --- or perhaps received an added charm from the ancient mermaid herself --- for the harp you learned on was none other than the powerful sea-harp that the Lady Ecume herself plays: the Harp of Seven Eyes, it is called."

Eli was silent now, for her thoughts were taken up with Emile, so absorbed by her presentation of the harp at his school and then amazing his teacher by no longer needing to wear his glasses. At the mention of this mighty Harp of Seven Eyes, she looked at Clare for a long moment, and sighed, hearing an echo of Lily's words about the Lady Sea-Foam.

When she looked back at Reyse, he was regarding her intently and with great affection. She felt herself blush.

At last she decided to change the subject. "You say you must return to your shee, Reyse? There is no great problem, I hope."

He placed his mug on the table, rose and walked to the window. The sun was now peeping over the facing buildings, and Eli could see it illuminating Reyse's tanned and handsome profile. She noticed that his eyes were wide open, and looking directly into the golden light. He finally turned to her, and Eli saw that his sparkling eyes were filled with what she could only characterise as unspoken poetry.

"Not so much problems as duties --- and surely some delights," he said. "My shee, the Shee of the Dove, has portals opening into Ireland and also Scotland. And another very, very far away from those two. My riders are planning to go through the Scottish portal into the Highlands and perhaps south into Northumbria, and they are anxious that I return to plan our voyage into the human realms. Alas, I do not play with time, as your father was wont to do on his visits, you see! I am not a 'royal fairy' as he is. When I am here, time passes in both worlds. I came here to see you again, my dear Eli, but I shall have to hope to renew that pleasure later; perhaps it will be in Faërie when you return. Do you know yet when you shall be making your second Visit?"

"It was just *that* which was troubling me when you arrived," confessed Eli. "And it's really a question of all this time-lapsing and time-charms. I don't really understand how they work. I've asked my harp when I should return next, and I clearly heard that it was to be in the summer and at the time of my birthday. Well, it must be my birthday as Mélusine, for my human birthday is in the spring. I seem to somehow 'know' that my fairy-birth was at the Summer Solstice..."

Reyse nodded. "Quite right, June the 21st. I'm sure your father would be delighted to have you in his kingdom to celebrate that with you. You were born on such a lovely summer's day, I remember it well, six-hundred and fifty-three years ago --- yes, I believe that's right. But, of course, in fairy-age you're only thirty-three, even younger than you would be in normal fairy-calculations, given that you have traversed the Great Charm. But we always celebrate our annual birth-dates, even though we don't count our ages from them. Time, and age, cannot ever be reduced to mere numbers, can they?"

"I suppose that's very true, and even more so for fairies than for humans! But it's true for us too," remarked Eli thoughtfully. "But it's that very subject which is puzzling me. I cannot be in Faërie when the moon is full, and that will occur on the 26th of June. I'll only be gone for three human hours, but I'll live *three weeks* of fairy-time. So how can I go on the day of the solstice?"

"Did Clare say that you must 'go' on that day, or be there *for* that day?" Reyse asked. This stopped Eli short. She thought again about the very brief message of her harp: only three words, vibrating in her ears and in her heart. *Summer. Your birthday.*

"In fact, that's probably it, Reyse. She said "summer" and she said "your birthday", but she didn't say that I should travel on the actual date of my birthday itself."

As Eli spoke this last phrase, a sudden breeze wafted into the room from the open window, making the light curtains billow like the banners over the City of Fantasie. The gust of wind found its way into the resonating form of Clare by the oval sound-holes in the back of her hollow body, and it stroked her strings as well. A soft series of sounds, like gentle laughter, came from the harp.

"Aha!" grinned Reyse, moving closer to Clare, and laying his hand on the sweep of her upper curve. "I don't think she *exactly* agrees with your solution to her riddle!"

"What do you mean?" whispered Eli.

"Well, I will tell you what *I* heard, if *you* did not translate the sound so easily. She says that you should, indeed, travel on your birthday… but not going. Coming back, it seems."

"Did Clare say that?"

"Play her, and listen," suggested the rich voice that Eli could now recall and recognise as the voice of her tutor when she was a child-fairy. Or was it reminiscent of her father's voice, encouraging her to ask questions of her harp? She was not sure...

Reyse moved aside, and Eli went to her harp and sat on the stool draped with a woven shawl, long-ago made by Lily, even before she had met and married Sean. Eli's arms encircled her harp as she leaned it delicately against her right side and shoulder. Another draught of cool morning air swept into the room, and as Eli began to play she could almost imagine that this was some sort of duet being improvised between herself and the morning breeze.

After many minutes, she lowered her arms and the sounds of the last sweet notes continued to vibrate. She opened her eyes and looked up at Reyse.

"Were you playing, or was I?" she asked, bewildered. "I didn't feel the music was coming from me at all. Did you enchant me?" she concluded, but with a smile rather than in any accusatory tone.

Reyse laughed, but there were tears on his cheeks. "I wouldn't need to charm the Princess Mélusine to make her create glorious music on a harp," he assured her. "That was beautiful, and it was the music of Faërie, and *not* the music of a human-wrought harp, or of a human harper. Whether it was you as Eli, or you as Mélusine, or Clare herself composing the melody, I do not know. But tell me if you heard the answer to your question --- or anything else."

Eli leaned her head against Clare's golden body. She looked puzzled still, almost incredulous.

"I felt myself asking if I should go back *before* my birthday, and so come home well before the full moon. It was very clear, Clare's instruction: Twenty-one days, from the 1st of June to the date of Mélusine's birthday on the Summer Solstice. I must leave Faërie in the early evening of the day of the 21st --- so I would indeed be travelling on my birthday, but coming back, not going. But there was something else..."

Reyse raised an eyebrow. Eli continued slowly.

"I asked if I might go, not by the Fair Stair from Ligugé, but from Gougane Barra in Ireland, thus arriving at the Portal held by my brother Finnir, in Barrywood."

"Did you, now?" interjected Reyse. "So *that* was the modulation I heard, poignant and longing and almost sorrowful, into the Lydian mode. You wish to meet Finnir? Or to see the unicorns of the ghostly Glens? Or to look upon the Inward Sea and the isle of Windy Hill?"

"Yes, or rather, I don't know," stammered Eli. "I had never really given it any thought, where I should enter Faërie on my next Visit. The question just came out, came from my heart, or --- I thought --- perhaps as a suggestion from you?"

"I would not suggest that, or anything so bold to you, my lovely Lady. Your life's journey as a changeling and even your fairy-life, they are part of *your* path, not mine. But to go to Barrywood, on only your second Visit and still more human than fairy, that would be either very impressive bravery, or utter foolishness --- if you are really asking my opinion."

"It seems that Clare agrees with you, Reyse. I at once retracted the question and said I would be happy to go via the Fair Stair again. But she disagreed with that too. *Eagle Abbey*, she said. *Eagle Abbey to Dawn Rock*. But that's the Portal of Leyano...

"And that's in <u>America</u>," concluded Eli, her brow furrowed. "How would I get to California by the 1st of June, and why would I want to? I've *never* been back to the States since I left at the age of twenty-nine."

Reyse had no further insight or counsel to offer to Eli on the subject of her return to her father's realm by its American portal. He only smiled very contemplatively and commented on it being 'appropriate' that she be directed to *Eagle* Abbey while he was with her... It seemed to her that he said this with an almost wry glint in his eye, knowing and amused and rather sentimental all at once. She stood and faced him as he prepared to depart. After a silent and still moment regarding one another, they both went out to the stairway and walked slowly down together.

"I wonder when, and where, we may meet again, dear Reyse --- but I'm sure it will be soon," said Eli, bidding her visitor farewell at the street-door. "And I wish you a good adventure in Scotland and Northumbria."

The tall fairy-lord (clearly recognisable as such despite his human disguise) regarded Eli for a moment, still quiet and thoughtful. He seemed to be memorising her face, framed by wisps of wavy, red and silver hair that had fallen loose from the chignon at her neck. Her green-blue eyes were a little hazy, clouded by her own preoccupations and questions. Her pale skin, with only the faintest beginnings of age showing in fine lines here and there, was rather rosy, almost flushed with the emotion (he hoped) of his early morning visit. He kissed her hand, bowed his head again as he stepped back, and smiled --- but only slightly.

"Farewell, dear *Licorne*," he said, turning. And he walked off, towards the river and the ancient *arc de triomphe* of Saintes.

Eli returned to her apartment, gathered up her coin-purse and Lily's journal, and descended the stairs once again. She bought a croissant at the bakery which was the first place to be waking up to a new day of normal business and activity on her street, and she went to eat it under a long line of sleepy trees beside the river, sharing her shady bench --- and her breakfast --- with two plump pigeons.

She decided to deliberately avoid the part of her little moon's journal that had spoken of some awful event, discovered by Lily and by Aulfrin when Eli was fourteen, but which had occurred years earlier when she was about eight. It seemed all too obvious that something sinister and probably sexual had darkened her childhood, and been consigned to a locked room in her mind almost immediately: her young psyche's only device for protecting her --- perhaps aided by the blessings of the mermaid...

Eli fingered the pages of the little notebook, admitting to herself that she had not the courage to read the details of what had been discovered (if any were there). She shook her head, continuing to hold the book closed now, and sighed gently.

"Nothing ever arrives by chance," she murmured. "If I have been given this journal now, and if I have come across this information, it is because it's the time to deal with it. I should consider it a 'compliment', from God, that he deems me ready. And the truth, so they say, shall set us free..."

She opened the notebook, somewhere in the middle, and began to turn back the pages to look for the entry of Sean's third visit, and more about the event alluded to. But as she flipped through the slightly yellowed leaves, a double-page fell open with a little text and the image of a pool of water surrounded by stones, huge stones. There was a short waterfall, and above it a stone propped over the source of the fall, making a dark, triangular sort of cave-mouth. The water in the pool had been painted in a light, watercolour wash: sea-green with a rich turquoise blue for the shadows. The illustration took up all of the right-hand page, but on the left there were a few lines of writing in Lily's flowing hand.

My darling Sean has brought me to visit 'Eagle Abbey'! This is the wonderful pool amid the Seven Falls, far up in the foothills above the charming little monastery where we are staying. We met Leo here, but oh he looked so different! I think I have seen him now as he truly is. He only stepped over the threshold of the hidden door for a moment, but it was wonderful to see him again --- though no longer a young, bohemian poet: he was like a dream of fairyland, proud and powerful, filled with radiance and enchantment. I could only look at him for a moment, and then I had to close my eyes and simply squeeze Sean's hand. When I looked again, he was gone --- and my Sean was laughing merrily at me!

Eli could not turn any more pages. She could hardly breathe. She knew this place; something in her deepest heart and memory recognised it.

Eagle Abbey. Yes, yes that image was Eagle Abbey. But Eli could feel herself looking through the paint and the sketchy pencil-lines to a land on the other side of that dark triangle, on the other side of the Portal.

"My memory is returning," she said, softly and with amazed gratitude. "I can see through my little moon's drawing, into Faërie, to Dawn Rock, to the Portal of Leyano on Mermaid Island. I have been there, on both sides. I remember it…

"And I'm going back. I'm going through that door. It will open for me; it is waiting for me. I know where it leads, and I know I will be there…very soon."

Eli closed the journal.

"And now I know where it is. The Seven Falls. I must go to the monastery in the hills of Santa Barbara, and be there for the 1st of June, so that I can make the final leg of the journey up to the Seven Falls. It's completely crazy, but I know I must go, and I know it will be possible.

I must go back to *California*!

****

For weeks to come , Eli would recall the 'affirmation' she had uttered that Wednesday morning, sitting under the old trees of the *Sentier des Courlis* along the river near the public gardens. It occurred to her that she had, perhaps, **proclaimed** her formal request, or decision, with those words. And she began to think that the Universe had pricked-up its ears!

On the following Monday morning, the 10th of May --- a lovely and symbolic moment, Eli thought, because she could see the tiniest sliver of the end of the moon's waning in the clear sky --- she received a call from the teacher at the elementary school she had visited.

"Could you stop by, Eli, perhaps after school today?" the voice inquired. "If so, I'd like to arrange a little *rendez-vous*... with the parents of Emile." Eli agreed, of course.

Later that afternoon, the four adults and one happy child were gathered in the school office: Eli and the little boy's rather incredulous teacher, Monsieur and Madame Camiade, and Emile. An Emile *without* glasses.

"We wished to meet you, Madamoiselle Penrohan," began Monsieur Camiade. "We just, well, wanted to make your acquaintance."

"And see if you knew, hmmm, if you were aware of your .....gift," added his wife.

"My musical gift? My harp-playing?" asked Eli.

There was a short silence, as the parents of Emile looked at one another, and at their son's teacher, and then at their son. And then they all looked back at Eli.

"Not exactly, well, er, in a way, yes," replied the gentleman, biting his lip a little nervously.

"We've tried everything, ever since he was born," interjected his wife, rather more loudly and emotionally than she had intended. It made the teacher jump with surprise. But then it was she that nodded to the enthusiastic mother, and offered to elaborate.

"You see, Eli, Emile has not been quite the same since your little presentation here a week ago. In fact...well, how shall I say this? He hasn't worn his glasses since, and his parents have taken him to his ophthalmologist and there just isn't any explanation. His vision is fine. Just perfect."

"And he keeps humming this same tune, all the time! Especially when he goes to bed. He says it helps him to sleep." Madame Camiade was trying not to be too exuberant or tearful, but it was obviously not easy for her. "We're so very grateful!" she added, now sobbing happily.

Monsieur Camiade put a steadying hand on his wife's knee as she pulled a handkerchief from her bag.

"It's a problem he's had since birth," confirmed her husband, speaking very slowly and nodding his head. "From birth."

Eli looked back and forth between them for a moment. She could feel her nervousness transforming into another feeling, as incredulous as the teacher's (whose expression was one of wonderment and yet somehow delight as well). There was a little silence, and Eli broke it at last by turning to the grinning Emile.

"What's the tune you like to hum?" she asked the little boy. "Can you sing it for me now?"

Emile jumped up and clasped his hands behind his back, placed his feet squarely apart and lifted his chin. Then he began to hum one of the pieces that Eli had played: a little composition of her own, in fact; or was it a tune out of very ancient memories of her life as Mélusine --- perhaps learned on the Harp of Seven Eyes?

Eli closed her own eyes, and could not help allowing a "thank you, dear God, and thank you Lady Ecume" to escape her lips.

"Then it *is* that, that music, that melody, that has healed our son?" whimpered Madame Camiade, but with great happiness in her rather dramatic tone of voice.

Eli opened her eyes, and hesitated for a moment. And then she replied, as calmly as she could.

"It's not impossible. I suppose that it *could* be that the vibrations, the resonance of the harp, were able to heal Emile's problem of vision." She could not help but smile. "Or it could just be a miracle!"

Monsieur Camiade's eyebrows shot up rather high into his forehead, but he had no time to comment. His wife spoke first, with a quite passionate outburst accompanied by both of her hands seizing Eli's.

A Delicate Balance

"I *do* believe in miracles!" she nodded fervently. "I always have! I was raised as a Catholic, although we really are no longer *practicing* Christians, Bernard and myself. But I've heard of faith-healings, and I think they **are** possible..."

"I don't think it was exactly that," interrupted Eli, smiling broadly now. "I think that harps are, and have always been, enchanted instruments. And I think their vibrations are, well, powerful and calming, *aligned* --- if I could put it that way --- and filled with wisdom. And so I suppose they could possess rather miraculous healing powers as well. Many cultures, all through history, have used music to heal people."

Monsieur Camiade was set upon being sensible and down-to-earth. He now asked, "Mademoiselle Penrohan, did you *study* this somewhere? Did you *learn* to heal with your harp?"

Eli was almost inclined to laugh, but with very good humour. She decided to limit her remarks and her answers to her human life only.

"No, I'm afraid I have no diploma in this art," she admitted. "But, come to think of it, I have heard of someone --- what was her name? Oh my, I've just recalled a lecture-series or a workshop or something of the kind, where was it? Ah! I remember now: I heard about this harpist playing at hospitals and nursing homes --- yes, I found her web-site when I was looking at gentle and sort-of *alternative* therapies for hospice patients, just before my mother passed away. Yes, yes, that was it. There is a woman, in the States, in Northern California in fact, who's been using harps as a sort of therapy in hospitals.

"That's funny. I'd forgotten all about that, until this afternoon," added Eli, feeling that strange sensation, once again, of someone invisible winking at her. She was almost speaking to herself as she continued, softly: "When I found her web-site it was when my dear Lily, my 'mother', had her accident, and I wanted to learn if anything could be done to sooth her. Of course, I played for her at her bedside, sort of applying what I had read about this Californian harpist's work, and the tonalities and cadences she recommended *did* seem to ease her into a quieter death. Her injury wasn't something 'curable', and somehow I don't think she really wanted it to be. She was a very devoted Christian, and she was ready for her death, and almost welcoming of it, I think."

There was another silence, and it was much longer than the last. But this time it was broken by Emile.

"I *know* that it was Eli's harp that took my glasses away," he said. "I know it was Clare."

His mother regarded him with an inquisitive stare. "Why do you say that, *cheri*?"

"Because Clare told me," Emile retorted simply.

His father was staring now too. And the teacher reached over and turned the child 'round to face her where she sat. "What did Eli's harp, Clare, tell you?"

"To take off my glasses."

"Now, son," said his father, trying to speak with some sort of authority in his voice, "you know that harps can't talk. Did you hear an imaginary voice, a voice you made-up?"

"No, papa. I heard *Clare's* voice. It was in my head, I guess, but I didn't make it up. I didn't make up the tune, either, or knowing for sure that I should sing it all the time. *Clare* told me to take off my glasses, because I didn't need then any more. And she told me to keep singing her song, too."

"That's quite enough, Emile," reprimanded his father now. "Harp's don't have speaking-voices. But I will admit that something clearly happened. Perhaps it is, hmm, something *vibrational*, a sort of scientific sound-effect phenomenon…"

"Or perhaps it's a miracle," offered Madame Camiade.

"Or perhaps Eli really does have this gift of healing with her harp, that the Californian harpist she heard about has also," contributed the teacher. "Does this American harpist do this for a living, Eli? Does she *teach* it?"

"Well, let me try to think," said Eli. "Yes, I think she *does* sort of teach it: that is to say, I believe she helps other harpists to develop their inborn gifts, and to use their instruments in hospital settings and the like. Yes, I think I did see some reference to workshops or coaching on her web-site."

Monsieur Camiade straightened up, and then he said --- or rather *announced*: "We are very, very grateful, dear Mademoiselle Penrohan. However it happened, and whatever was at work, we are *most* grateful to have our Emile's vision restored. The doctor has no explanation, but I think we will just have to accept that something, well, *extraordinary* has taken place. And we would like to thank you. We would like to offer you something to show our gratitude."

It was Eli's turn to raise her eyebrows. "I don't want anything more than your very kind thanks, and to know that Emile has received this grace, this healing I mean."

But the gentleman was determined and firm. "We would like to make a gesture of appreciation to you, dear Mademoiselle. You say that this American harpist gives classes or holds some kind of programme of study, to develop this skill? Well, I suggest that we offer you an airline-ticket to go to visit her, to meet her and maybe to take one of these classes …. if you think that this would hone your healing skills even further, and perhaps help you to help others, and that if it would give you pleasure."

"But that is **so** generous of you!" Eli exclaimed. "You would pay for me to go to California, to meet and study with this harpist? Are you serious?!"

"I happen to be a travel-agent, my dear, so it is something that springs easily to mind," replied Emile's father with a warm smile. "In fact, I had thought of offering you a holiday ticket, somewhere tropical perhaps. But if you can find a workshop or secure a private tutorial or short programme of study with this *healing harpist*, then I think that would be the ideal gift to propose to you."

"It would indeed, dear Monsieur and Madame Camiade. I would be just delighted! May I go…soon?"

Hastening Home

"I have some great offers on pre-peak summer get-a-ways!" chortled the happy father. "And I even have a last-minute cancelation --- if my memory serves me --- for a flight to San Francisco before the end of this month. Would that work out well for you, and for her, do you think? It's not too close a date? Could you meet her from there?"

"'I'll contact her right away, dear Monsieur Camiade, but I somehow feel it would work out just splendidly, for us both," said Eli, swallowing hard and trying not to weep with joy. "I think it is, quite probably, *meant* to be."

Everyone kissed each other on both cheeks, except Emile, who hugged Eli around the waist and asked her to say a special *'merci beaucoup'* to Clare for him. And then Eli went home to contact the hospital harpist she had found on internet several months earlier, to see if a meeting and some classes together could be arranged.

But she had absolutely no doubt at all that it would not only be possible, but quite simply perfect. She knew that she would be in California in late May and part of June, with her tickets all paid for thanks to the miracle of Clare and her magical melody.

And she would find her way to Santa Barbara, and Eagle Abbey, on the 1st of June, to step across the threshold of her brother Leyano's Portal and back into Faërie.

****

A Delicate Balance

Chapter Three:
The Poet-Prince of Dawn Rock

Leyano's hand remained lightly curved around the stem of his chalice on the glassy table before him. His fingers were long and graceful, thought Eli, and his smile like that of a meditating Buddha.

He had told Eli that he had aged only two years, obviously (obvious, is it? Eli had retorted in her own head) in the fifty years since he had last seen her. But on that occasion, he had reminded her with a grin, she would not remember him for she had been a tiny newborn baby, swaddled in gossamer tapestry-blankets and cradled in the arms of Reyse. In any case, he admitted, he was now turned forty-one.

"And so," he laughed mischievously, "my age, my appearance-age as we are wont to call it, is now eight years ahead of you, rather than four. For you were born in the year 1357, and I in 1353; but you began your Initiations later than I did, and you then undertook the Great Charm --- it all adds up, you see, or rather subtracts! And here in Faërie you fell asleep on Scholar Owl Island in the year 1959, and you were thirty-three. You have not aged, as the Princess Mélusine, during your waiting sleep. You'll awake at that same age when you come home. If you come home."

"You never saw me, when you visited Lily, as the poet Leo?" asked Eli, "when I was a child, in Los Angeles?"

A Delicate Balance

"You were off riding horses, as I understood from our father," laughed the beautiful Prince. "They were, alas, not Half-Moon Horses --- the theme of your second Initiation and a passion of yours here --- and they were not flying-horses, like your beautiful Peronne --- but I suppose, even as a human, your devotion to all things equine was still present in your spirit. As was your talent on the harp."

Eli took up her own chalice again now, and then Leyano refilled them both from a giant *Californiconus* seashell-decanter. The chalice of Leyano was made, it seemed, of very pale gold, with a tracery design of spirals and wave-motifs, fine-point-punched interlace and knot-work sea-serpents meandering between inlaid crystals and black pearls. Eli's was not much simpler: its stem was a spiral of alternating strands of silver and green glass, and its cup was a round, deep shell of some mysterious mollusc --- perhaps a kind of *trocca*, several shades of turquoise and rose on the outside and pearly-white in its interior cusp. The wine they were drinking, if it was wine at all, was rather like champagne, pale pink and delicately perfumed, with bubbles that tickled the nose.

The high terrace where they sat faced south, and was semi-circular. Their panoramic view included the south-west coast of Mermaid Island, the waters of the Sound to the west lapping against the toes of the rocks far beneath them and undulating between Leyano's island home and the shores of mainland Faërie some thirty miles distant. To the east was the high plateau of Dawn Rock, about seven miles from the Castle and now drenched in the red rays of the setting sun. Behind the high peaks of Dawn Rock with its hidden Portal, one could glimpse the shadowy stretch of the eastern half of the Island and beyond that the immeasurable distance of Sea-Horse Bay with one or two craggy isles deep pink and gold and sombre blue on the horizon.

"Speaking of flying-horses..." began Eli, catching the eye of her dashing yet serene brother and feeling a slight wave of surprise at the darkness and depth of those eyes. They were like over-ripe black cherries, incredibly dark but glinting with playful crimson and plum-purple highlights. Amazing, thought Eli, how beautiful my brothers are! She continued with her question.

"I thought that I would meet my, I mean *our*, father here --- if not at the threshold of the Portal, then here at your Golden Sand Castle; my goodness, this gorgeous edifice really *does* seem to be constructed of sunny sand! And I thought that he would be offering me, on this Visit, my own flying-horse. I had a *vision* of riding Peronne, but I imagine the reality of such a phenomenon will far surpass that wonder. Do you know when I will see the King, and my magical horse?"

"He will be joining us here at the half-moon, in three days' time, my dear sister," replied Leyano. "I do not know if he will be bringing Peronne with him then, or taking you to meet him elsewhere. My only instructions were to keep you amused until he arrives."

"Amused?!"

"Yes, and re-educated into your true life here. On the subject of harps, for instance, I think I can assure you of a delightful *amusement*, or perhaps I should use a more profound word. This evening, after our dinner, we will go to the northern shores of Mermaid Island to listen to harps played under the light of the late-rising moon. A fine 'diversion', or educational experience for my sister who is re-learning her skills as a healer on that instrument, don't you agree?"

"Harps? Played by ....mermaids, do you mean?"

"Just so."

"Oh how marvellous, and how very **very** good to be back here in Faërie!"

"I hope you will continue to feel that way, dearest Eli. And that you will choose to come back for good, after your final Visit. I think you have much, still, to experience and to offer in this blessed and beautiful realm.

"But, then, that is probably true for you in the human world as well."

Eli regarded Leyano in silence, thoughtful and with that nagging, interior question haunting her once again. Yes, much to do, to experience, to give, to contribute. Here, perhaps --- she could not judge that yet --- but *there*, in her human life, yes, she *knew* it to be true.

Before hiking up to Seven Falls in the grey foothills above Santa Barbara on that afternoon, Eli had been to visit the 'healing harpist' whom she had discovered on internet when Lily had been taken to hospital with her fatal injury. The brief contact, two days ago now, with this fellow musician had confirmed Eli's desire to work with her to develop her own skills, now as a human rather than a fairy harpist that is, in the domain of musical therapy and soothing, melodious care and --- just maybe --- many more 'miracles' such as that which had occurred for Emile. Eli had, undoubtedly, now found a new and passionate direction in her own career, and she knew that this was not by chance, as she was still and ever committed to her philosophy that such a thing as 'chance' did not exist.

No, there was no coincidence in her finding Janet living just south of San Francisco, and as she was already, evidently, a mighty 'healing harpist' in her life as Mélusine, she could only conclude that she had things to accomplish among *human beings* with this newly re-discovered, latent talent of hers.

So there it was again: the ultimate and perplexing question-mark. Should she seek to help others with the development of gifts she possessed as a fairy, and which were somehow still accessible to her? Should she use what she was re-learning of the fairy philosophies of harmony and respect for nature, and freedom and beauty to try to help, or educate, or enlighten a human population on the verge of ecological disaster, or perhaps at the dawn of a new era of consciousness and change? Was she being given the choice of retreating back into the comfort and privilege of her life as a Princess in an enchanted kingdom, or of making some sort of saintly self-sacrifice and remaining in a struggling world of violence and ignorance and selfishness and greed?

"You know," a soft voice somewhere in the back of her head interjected, "nothing is ever, ever so *black and white*. And the whole idea of worrying about it is, to say the least, premature. You're not at the point of making that decision yet, because this is only your second Visit, and it's only just begun. Give it the time to ripen, this dilemma of yours, and you will probably find that, when you come to the end of your third and final Visit, the answer will be crystal clear, and you will have the courage and the confidence to act upon it."

On that sensible note, exhaling in the calm that was rippling out from her wise little conversation with herself, Eli nodded to her noble brother, and said, "I'm sure I'll know, when the time comes. For now, I'm basking in the golden joy of this astounding adventure. And just now, in the pleasure of meeting you again, dear Leyano."

"Yes, I'm sure you will know, when you need to," he agreed. "Let us go in to dinner now. I hope you will enjoy what we eat here --- but then I think you are an eater of plants and grains and even seaweed in your human experience too."

"Yes, yes, teetering on the brink of veganism; at least I've been a fervent vegetarian for many, many years already."

"It's a pity you did not get the chance to dine at the monastery in the hills below Eagle Abbey, though; you would have enjoyed the small community of monks. And they kept an excellent table. I used to go, in my poetic disguise of Leo, to stay there for a day or two --- when I crossed the threshold, for a little escapade of my own."

"I was so disappointed not to be able to stay there," agreed Eli. "I had planned to. What devastation the brush fire wrought! It was two years ago now, I believe, but it's still a sad and dramatic scene. Practically nothing remains of the monastery, and I think the brothers have taken refuge near the old Spanish Mission in the city. I was looking forward to being on retreat there, for a day or two anyway, before coming here. And, yes, Benedictines usually have a flare for a very good sense of *cuisine*!"

"Indeed those of my white monastery had," laughed Leyano as he led Eli back into the amazing Sand Castle, and towards the candlelit dining room whose walls were inlaid with seashells and whose floor paved with yellow, pink and pale green calcite and silvery cassiterite. "They had a rather rotund brother who was their *chef*, and I remember thinking, after one particularly copious and delicious mid-day meal on a saint's feast day, 'well, if <u>this</u> is 'poverty', I wonder how they interpret 'obedience', and what *'chastity'* resembles here!' But I never dared ask the Abbot!"

Eli burst out laughing, and followed her wonderful brother to a small round table just beside the western window, which was wide open and filling the room with the songs of waves and the last, sleepy cries of the gulls swirling back to their craggy, shaggy beds on the cliff face below.

****

The moon was just rising over the northerly slope of Dawn Rock, the Portal being a little south-east of Leyano's Castle, when he and Eli had finished their delightful meal. They strolled around a circular balcony accessible from their dining-room, and stopped to admire the moonrise. It was evidently several miles, by land, to the small promontory where the concert was to be held, but to Eli's great delight her brother proposed to take her there by boat.

"It will prove a swifter road, the sea-route, and pleasant to meet the mermaids, first, in their own element and at close-hand. And if we go by boat, another meeting awaits you also," Leyano added.

Spiralling staircases wound down through the heart of the sandy edifice, and finally brother and sister emerged by an arched passageway onto a little landing-pier at sea-level on the Castle's western side. At the end of the short pier was the crescent-moon barque of Brocéliana.

"Ah!" exclaimed Eli, "It's my dear moon-child sister; Brocéliana is there!"

The hooded figure, who had been arranging cushions on the small bench within her slender boat, climbed up onto the driftwood pier and pulled her hood back. Her smile and bright blue eyes shone in the faint moon-and-star-light and also in the glow from the swinging lantern hung over the little craft.

"But why didn't she dine with us?" inquired Eli of Leyano as they walked towards her.

The Prince cleared his throat, smiled, and pointed to the far end of the pier. "Because she had a private dinner engagement this evening, a picnic at sea, I believe, as she and her escort came here from Curious Cove."

Eli strained her eyes to see beyond the circle of lantern-light so she could identify the form at the pier's far end. But she had already guessed, of course. She sighed happily.

"Young love. How nice! And how glad I will be to meet Garo again, too."

"Only a short meeting tonight, my dear Eli," commented Leyano as they reached Brocéliana and the two sisters embraced. Garo was striding up, now, to join them too.

"Hello, hello!" cried Eli warmly, as she kissed her sister's cheek and inclined her head to Garo, who graciously returned the gesture with a broad smile. "But are you not coming to this mermaid concert of moonlit harps?"

"Already, perhaps, somewhat tired from their voyage here from the Cove, I have imposed yet another duty upon them for this evening," explained Leyano. "They must remain here in my Castle to play host to other visitors arriving shortly. But you will have time to talk with everyone tomorrow, Eli, so do not worry that this is only a brief greeting as we take the place of these sailors in their swift dolphin-boat."

"Are we to be pulled by *dolphins*?!" squeaked Eli, too excited to refrain herself from a completely childlike glee. All the company laughed.

"By far the most elegant way to arrive for a harp concert," asserted Brocéliana, looking --- Eli thought --- as happy as true love was ever reputed to render a maiden. She was radiant and shimmering; and once again tears came to Eli's eyes to be so forcefully reminded of Lily by every detail of her facial features and expression.

"We wish you a magical and moving performance, dear Lady Eli, and my dear Prince-Poet," said Garo, helping Eli down into the swaying boat. There was just room for her to sit and for Leyano to stand at the prow. Barking and laughing dolphins, three of them, were popping their heads out of the water before him, helping him to adjust their diaphanous reins and harnesses.

"It will be a pleasure to have some time with you tomorrow," Garo added, tossing the mooring rope to Leyano. Eli waved breathlessly as the dolphins splashed off, pulling the dancing boat out into the dark waters of the Sound and off to the north.

Again and again that night, Eli repeated the same words inside her head, spinning with wonder: "I will never forget this; I will never, *ever* forget this!"

As they rounded the most north-westerly point of Mermaid Island, the gently curved cove where their concert would be held came into view. It was peppered with rounded rocks, their heads just above the undulating swell, and phosphorescent wavelets were breaking in strange herringbone diagonals all along the narrow, silver beach.

At first, Eli thought there were many other dolphins, breaking from the surface of the water far out to sea and making splashing, sparkling arches of droplets in the cool air.

Perhaps some *were* dolphins, for the sweep of the Sound around Leyano's Island and the coasts of Vivonny was home to many members of that race. But Eli soon saw that most were other creatures swimming towards their places on the protruding rocks. And these were mermaids.

Their skin was luminous in the moonlight, their eyes were shining like diamonds or stars, their hair was crinkled and long and of many hues: yellow-gold, dark platinum, raven-wing blue-black, fiery red, but also pearly white, brilliant turquoise, the crimson of a humming-bird's throat, the green of a new spring leaf. Their tails were long, much longer --- in proportion --- than those of fishes of the same size. Some had clearly defined individual scales, pointed or rounded, laid one over the other and flapping as they swam. Some had smoother tails with delicate silver salmon-mail or the rainbow colours of trout, and some had stripped tails like tigers or zebras, or tails spotted like an ocelot's coat. Their ears were either singly pointed or with multiple tips and webbed, or they were like exotic flowers with just two or three petals; and most wore long garlands or necklaces while others had bracelets of gold or tiny, stranded shells. And when they took up their instruments, Eli could see that all their fingers were webbed.

They made no sound with their mouths, but Eli thought she could hear voices speaking or laughing or singing. She supposed it to be the mermaids, and in that case she was hearing their voices with her heart.

Before each mermaid took her place, leaping or sliding gracefully up onto a stone, she reached into the gurgling wavelets and into a hidden hole or tiny cave concealed underwater, just beneath the sea's surface, to pull forth her harp.

No two mermaids were the same, and no two harps! These multiform instruments came in every possible shape: stubby and wide, slim and pointed, clearly triangular or strangely lopsided, made of flat or slightly rounded wood, shell, silver or gold ... Eli could not really tell how the harps were constructed or of what material. Nor with what fibres or cords they were strung.

But oh, the sound! *That* she could certainly hear, and clearly.

Mingled with the constant ocean-drone, the sudden kisses of wave on stone, the breaking waves on the shore behind their backs where they had moored the small crescent-craft in the shallows and clambered onto an arm of smooth rock jutting into the bay, were the mesmerising sounds of the twangling and chanting of perhaps thirty or forty mer-harpers. If stars could sing, if starlight on the crests of waves could serenade, if tears were musical notes, if heart-break had a voice, if longing could take form as crooning, if dreaming woke up to find it could trill and troll, then this --- thought Eli --- would be the symphony of those sounds.

Did the mermaids play for an hour, or for many? The moon wandered over the starry sky, cocking its ear at the concert no doubt, shining her spotlight of diffused silver over the scene. And finally, one by one, the harpers fell silent, and only the waves continued to chant and carol.

Except... no --- was there *one* harp still ringing? Eli strained her ear, and tried to distinguish the rippling arpeggios and glissandos from the humming 'whoosh' of the waves. Yes! There was still one harper playing, she was sure now. But where was she?

Leyano placed a strong hand on Eli's shoulder, perhaps to stop her from leaning any further forward on her slippery stone. And then he pointed far out across the water to where the waters widened into the expanse of Sea Horse Bay. It was much too far for Eli to see the exact form of the mermaid, but the sound of her exquisite playing was wafted over the swell to her.

And suddenly, as if someone had adjusted the definition on a camera's zoom, the far-away, lonely outcropping of stone with the twenty-mile distant mer-harper on it, came into view. Eli felt she was being flown out over the Bay's surface to be brought right before this mighty musician, just for an instant.

But she had not moved. It was a magical change in her eyesight, in her night-vision, so extreme and astounding, that she cried out with a gasp. And there she saw her. Youthful yet ancient, proud, noble, queenly and at the same time humble and simple and softly maternal: the Lady Ecume. Just as Eli had seen her in her vision at *The Smiling Salmon*, just as Aulfrin had sketched her in Lily's journal. Only there was no Black Key floating on the water beside her, and her webbed hands were both busy with the pale, moonlit strings of her sea-horse harp, the Harp of Seven Eyes.

She continued to play, and Eli continued to gaze, and then she could hear a voice, the Lady Ecume's voice, speaking or chanting or intoning slow, liquid words.

"In twenty days it will be your birthday, Mélusine. And I have a gift for you. Meet me on the *inish-beg*, the tiny Island of the Archangel, before you return by the Portal of Dawn Rock to the world of men. We must meet there, and speak, before you go back. And I will give you a precious birthday gift. May the blessing of the Moon, queen of the night but also serene in the sunlight, be with you."

The harp of the Lady Ecume fell silent, and Eli's vision returned to normal. She could not even see where the ancient mermaid had been, for the sea's colour had deepened to a dark ultramarine which blended with the night-sky. The Moon had lost itself behind a bank of shadow and cloud and the wind was very chill.

Leyano tugged at the ropes to draw the boat close to them, helped Eli into it, and wrapped her long cloak tightly about her as they began their swift dolphin-drawn voyage home to his Sand Castle.

****

A Delicate Balance

When she awoke, to sunlight streaming through her bedchamber windows like rich but transparent caramel, Eli still had the music of the mermaids' concert playing in her ears. Only now it was accompanied by two other sounds: the wild crying of the gulls --- many hundreds of them, it seemed --- and an impatient tapping on the door of her bedroom.

She climbed out of her soft, swaying hammock, and threw a long, light dressing-gown over her loose pyjamas.

"I'm coming, I'm coming! Who is it?" she called softly, expecting a reply from a fairy-in-waiting, or perhaps from Leyano himself. But there was no answer.

Eli opened the door a crack, but saw nothing. Until she looked down.

There was Periwinkle, his arms akimbo, a mock expression of exasperation on his perky, rosy face.

"Piv!" cried Eli, delightedly. "Piv, you're here! I'm so glad to see you! When did you arrive, and what time is it?"

The pixie pursed his lips, shook his head, and then doffed his little green beret as he bowed.

"Welcome back, once again, my darling little Mélusine," he chirped in his piccolo voice. And then he laughed heartily. "And in answer to your string of questions, I arrived when I got here, and the time is porridge-and-*buicuri*-biscuit-time. Dress yourself, my lovely Lady, and come down one flight of stairs, please, to the great Breakfast Room, for everyone is waiting for you."

And with that he turned his tiny, bright green wings into a buzzing blur and rose into the air before Eli's bemused and smiling face. He pirouetted in mid-air, leaned toward his friend, kissed her forehead and tidied one strand of her disarrayed red hair with a shake of his curly head, and then flew along the corridor and disappeared down the winding staircase.

Eli found she had a wardrobe in one corner of her bedroom with an assortment of lovely gowns, comfortable trousers and long smocks in it. She choose an ensemble of the latter two, in sea-green flecked with white, hurriedly splashed her face in a basin of cold water scented with subtle spices and perhaps algae, and bound her long hair in a single braid down her back. She slipped her feet into a pair of woven-cord sandals and went downstairs.

Leyano, Garo and Brocéliana were facing her across the long table as she appeared at the doorway of the bright room, one wall of which was simply a row of tall, curved windows like an elegant arcaded boulevard. The high ceiling dotted with oval sky-lights seemed to let in as much golden sunshine as the soaring arcade which presented a view of Dawn Rock, purple-silhouetted against the intensely bright rising sun.

It was early, by Eli's reckoning, in this clock-less world; and it had been a late night, so she was rather sleepy-eyed. She smiled, still a little dazed, and then the other three fairies, whose backs had been toward her, one at a time turned to rise and greet her.

She had been hoping, in some secret corner of her heart, that Reyse would be among the guests, but in fact he was not there. Her disappointment had no time to flow over her, however, for the tall gentleman-fairy who met her eye first was known to her, and she felt a thrill of pleasure in seeing him again. He touched his heart and lowered his curly, strawberry-blond head of hair.

"Aindel, how very nice to meet you here," said Eli, lifting her hand to her own heart and smiling back. And immediately her pleasure redoubled, for the first of the women-fairies to turn around was familiar as well. It was Muscari, as ever dressed in various shades of blue with green trims and trappings, her pale ash-gold hair in two long tresses over her shoulders, her cerulean eyes glinting with merriment and wisdom.

"Greetings! We meet again, dear Eli," she said with a slight bow. "Master Periwinkle was becoming very impatient for you to join us. I hope we did not awaken you too early?"

A Delicate Balance

"Piv was becoming impatient to sample the *buicuri*, to tell the truth!" commented Garo. The pixie, who was helping himself to a foamy-crisp wafer from where he had alighted beside the young dragon-lord, quickly dropped his biscuit back onto the plate and folded his chubby arms once more.

Eli was arrested in mid-laugh, however, for now the third fairy at last slowly turned completely to face her. A wave of strange, truly otherworldly energy climbed into the air between them, and rolled over Eli like a towering wave collapsing onto a Pacific-coast beach. But the strikingly beautiful woman fairy was smiling, very like Leyano's sublime expression of enlightened and peaceful inner joy, which somehow put Eli more at ease. In fact, this fairy resembled Leyano in many of her features: in the shape of her mouth and the structure of her cheek-bones and chin, and also in the darkness of her huge eyes, which in her case were even a deeper blue than the ocean had become last night. Her loose hair was jet black and hung thick and luxuriant over the bodice of her simple gown and short cape; her skin was dark also and she was almost as tall as Aindel, and almost as muscular and athletic, Eli thought, as Garo.

Leyano then introduced her. "This is another of your half-sisters, dearest Eli. May I present Alégondine, who has sailed here from Quillir to join us. A long voyage, but one that such a skilled and seasoned mistress of the ocean seemingly enjoyed greatly!"

"Truly, I did enjoy my voyage here, for I passed by the northern seas and crossed the mouth of Moon Mad Bay: wild and glorious waters that I had never before encountered. I had many adventures and unexpected meetings in fact, but the most pleasant meeting is the last, to be re-united again with my sister, or half-sister, as you say Leyano. We were very young when we last saw one another, Mélusine, for I was only five and you perhaps nine or ten when our paths were sundered by our mother's banishment."

"I wish I could remember the days we shared in our childhood, but I have little of my fairy memory as yet," Eli said. "But I am very pleased to make your acquaintance now, for I feel extremely blessed to discover that I have a family, and quite an extended one. In my human life, I was such a solitary child."

"I, too, am very solitary, dear Mélusine --- or should I call you Eli? It is rare for me to come into contact with other fairies outside of Quillir, except on voyages to visit our exiled mother. It is a joy for me also to discover my siblings, whom I hardly know: you and Leyano and also Garo. For we all four share a parent --- three of us have the same mother, and two of us the same father! And Brocéliana is half-sister to two of you as well. Strange, is it not, that the web and woof of our family's weaving should have so many, and so varied, threads?"

"Strange and beautiful, I think," agreed Eli. "And where does the tapestry of fathers and mothers, and more distant ancestors ever stop, really? We are all, ultimately, connected, and if not by blood then by soul and heart, if we choose to see it that way."

Eli stopped herself, slightly embarrassed by her words, and wondering why she had let herself become so carried away. But Leyano applauded her sentiments.

"Exactly, dearest Eli, exactly. And precisely what our council is convened to discuss, in fact. For it is the greater 'family' of Faërie that is our business today, and our dream and our hope."

"And our challenge," added Aindel, ushering Eli now to her seat and holding her chair for her. "But before we delve more deeply into these weighty matters, let us break our night's fast with fruit and tea, porridge and foam biscuits!"

"Here, here!!" cried Piv with pent-up emotion; and so all the grinning gathering turned to their bowls and mugs in good cheer.

A Delicate Balance

****

When the cool teapots and empty bowls had been cleared from the table, the high golden-sand arcade of windows was suddenly draped by a cascade of flowering vines tumbling from a roof garden or spontaneously growing from some hidden flower pots along the Castle walls. Eli had not seen any plants outside before, but now there was a curtain of starry blue flowers with yellow centres, shading the room from the sun which was rising higher into the summer sky.

"Ah," she thought, "I've seen that flower in Ireland. Lily had it in her garden: I remember her buying the young plant from a garden centre where we'd gone for a morning coffee. *Solanum crispum* ....'*Glasnevin*', or some such name, I think it was. I liked the Latin part of the name; it made me think of a crazy translation like *crispy cracker that must be eaten in the sunshine*, rather like the *buicuri*..." But Eli said none of this nonsense aloud; she just enjoyed the spectacle of the fragrant climber installing itself all over the arches, clearly in order to graciously keep Leyano's visitors cool and refreshed.

"What a very polite and considerate plant," she confirmed inwardly, with a grin.

Leyano had wiped the last traces of his breakfast biscuit from his chin with a rough-woven serviette (while Piv was busily gathering all of *his* remaining crumbs from the tablecloth with the help of a rather sticky, jam-coated finger), and the Prince now nodded to Aindel and Alégondine, inviting them to commence the meeting. Aindel had a bag slung over the back of his chair, rather like an archer's quiver. From this he pulled a roll of paper or parchment, and opened it in the centre of the table.

Alégondine held down the curling corner of the scroll nearest her, and pointed with her other hand to each form drawn on the beautiful map: most of the parchment was painted or stained a deep blue, but the irregular shapes traced here and there, of varying sizes, were mostly coloured in many greens and ochres, although some were a burnt or raw sienna or a slatey grey. They seemed to be islands, or perhaps continents, of some mysterious world unknown to Eli from any course of geography she had ever attended. One by one they were named by the dark and stately Princess of Quillir.

"The Shee of the Dove, here; and there the Great Shee, one of its closer neighbours; the Sheep's Head Shee, here on the other side; and the Little Skellig Shee; the Shee of the Red Lizard; the Shee of the Bull; the kingdom beyond the Falls of the Seven Sisters which is called the Shee of the Red-Eared Hart; the Shee of the Giddy Goats; the remotely distant White Kangaroo Shee; far to the south, the Shee of the Dragon-Bats; and right over there, so tiny, SheeBeg --- or the Shee of the Bells. Eleven in all. The mystic number, the great constellation, the spiral of stars."

Her indigo eyes closed softly, as if she were ending with a silent benediction. And then they re-opened, and Eli saw that she had wept. Aindel now spoke.

"Dear friends and fairies, travellers and dreamers, Sun-Singers and Moon-Dancers, this is our prayer and our project: the unification of the eleven shees in peace and collaboration. It is our only hope, we feel --- Alégondine and myself together with the twins of the Stone Circle Belfina and Begneta, who could not be with us for this council --- our only hope, as I say, if we wish to bring the knowledge and help of Faërie to the world of humankind."

"But *where* is *this* shee, where is Faërie?" interrupted Eli, so transported by the great map and by Aindel's words that she spoke aloud before she could check herself. "Oh, excuse me; it is perhaps impertinent of me to speak in the midst of your important discussions, but I'm trying to understand and to follow them..."

"Not in the least," Leyano reassured her empathically. "You do not recall, perhaps, my dear sister, but this our noble plan was the very reason you undertook the Great Charm, in the year 1625. You avowed then --- and surely the world of men was not yet facing the dangers it has generated for itself since --- that you would find a means to help mankind to learn more of our ways and our beliefs, help them to accept this knowledge and wisdom, before it was too late. Three other fairies of our number had consecrated themselves to the rigours of the Great Charm, also, before you did so; but their goals were perhaps not so particular in this respect."

"But as to your question of the whereabouts of Faërie," interposed Alégondine, raising her hand to suspend Leyano's revelations, "*all* of the eleven islands constitute that realm. This is the map of 'Greater Faërie', if you like; but all fairies refer to their own mother-shee simply as Faërie in common language. This island we inhabit, the kingdom of Aulfrin, is here --- she indicated the largest of the islands --- and it is called the Shee Mor, the Great Shee."

"I see," nodded Eli. "But what you say about the Great Charm intrigues me. It is something which I did, expressly *for* humans? It is some sort of school, or order, or test of courage, which can forge a bond between mankind and fairies, or help a fairy to accomplish such a goal?"

"Not exactly, or at least exclusively," said Garo, speaking softly and slowly. "It can be undertaken with such a goal at heart, or at least a goal to diffuse fairy-lore and fairy-wisdom to some other race or into some place or situation in need of healing and guidance --- a land ravaged by war or pestilence, a natural drama such as an earthquake or the eruption of a volcano --- but it can also be a means of taking a fairy's own soul, his or her very being, to a higher or more refined level. In that way, a fairy can become a seer, or a great sage, a shape-shifter and a worker of miracles and magic, a protector or a king...or a queen. I myself dared the Great Charm, even before you did, beginning in the year 1444. But my goal was not to reconcile our fairy-world with that of humans, but to bring greater aid to their animal kingdom, enslaved at times in their cruel and perverse society.

"It was only when I had come to know this princely poet, the brave Leyano, that I began to think that my skills, gained in my own three-hundred-and-thirty-three years of Charm challenges, could perhaps be of use to men as well as the creatures fallen under the shadow of their dominion. And now I have met Brocéliana, fair and free and open-hearted with a generosity of love outshining even a true fairy's --- for she is but half-fairy in fact --- and my pledge has been renewed with her at my side, my vow to the three Princes of our shee to stand beside them and to work in union with them."

Eli's eyes were growing wider and wider in astonishment, but somewhere in her heart a light was also kindled, and growing. She was beginning to recall, she thought, certain things. She had a sudden vision, only a fleeting image that flashed through her mind, of a whirlpool of water and a tremendous surge of music and song, a blazing sun and herself gazing up into a sky of brilliant constellations that she knew and could almost 'read'. Her body felt as if it were glowing with warmth and gradually expanding. Was this a memory, coming vaguely back to her, of her Great Charm? She glanced quickly at the vines of *solanum crispum* dangling down over the open arcade, and she started, for suddenly she could see creatures among the flowers and leaves: tiny fairies or sprites with near-transparent wings beating fast like those of dragonflies. She blinked, and they were gone, lost in the shimmer of the sunlight.

She looked around the company of noble, wonderful fairies. Her family, her friends and allies. They were all smiling gently and lovingly. She asked one more question.

"How many of us are there? You mentioned the twins, who could not be here today. We are eight around this table this morning, so with them it would be ten. Is that a sacred number, like eleven for the island-shees?"

A Delicate Balance

"No, there is no set or sacred number, not for our Alliance, dear Eli." It was Muscari speaking now. "For our company is growing all the time, and there are many 'ordinary' fairies, neither royal nor noble by birth, who are also among our ranks. But there are other *very* great fairies who were not free to come to this meeting today. The Princes Demoran and Finnir, for instance, hold honoured places in our movement --- but they were required to remain at their Portals. The former lover of the Lord Reyse, Ceoleen, works with us also, though she dwells for the most-part in the human world; just as is true of the two daughters of Grey Uan, for they --- half-fairies, like the Princess Brocéliana --- reside in the same lands as Ceoleen, and offer us an invaluable contact with humans.

"The Lord Reyse, himself, is of course also counted among our number, and is very active in our plans, but he is with the King today and tomorrow --- and will arrive here on Mermaid Island with him in two days' time, bringing you your winged-horse, Peronne. But he must not find us still here, not while he is in company with the King, for Aulfrin does not yet know the full extent of our goals, and neither does Erreig, the Chieftain of the White Dragon Clan. We are trying to win them over, but it is a delicate and sensitive task. This is also the case in regard to other nobles of several of the shees you see before you on this map: some are counted among our allies, some we are seeking to encourage into our ranks, and others remain, alas, still hostile to our ideas. For the moment..."

Muscari was now silent, but another member of the assembled continued.

"There is another name to include, a member of our alliance and perhaps the greatest among us. But he may not come to this or any other of our meetings --- at least not above ground --- unless it could be on Star Island itself, which is impossible and forbidden." It was Garo speaking once again now, still in a hushed voice. "It is my master, the mighty magician whom I have been promised to, as apprentice and scion. The Sage-Hermit."

"Maelcraig?" whispered Eli. "The Sage-Hermit of Star Island is part of this wondrous endeavour?!"

There was a brief silence, and the golden air of the wide breakfast room seemed charged with tingling energy. And then a voice more gentle and reserved even than Garo's said, "His name is not Maelcraig, dear Eli, for that was the *previous* Sage-Hermit."

The tender, musical voice was that of Brocéliana.

Garo's hand was laid over hers on the table, and their fingers now interlaced. She added, "The present Sage-Hermit, whom my beloved Garo will be required to replace in two years' time, is of a softer and warmer and *deeper* nature even than Maelcraig, his predecessor. He is an ancient fairy, one who has passed through death and utter silence, tempest and tumultuous waters, and who knows the passages beneath plain and mountain and forest. He is the Sage-Hermit and he is also the Mushroom Lord, as I believe you have learned already, on your last Visit. But his true fairy name was, and is, Aulfrelas. He is our grandfather, Eli, the father of our father."

Fairies, Eli discovered --- or now remembered, or felt in her own being more and more --- were very attuned to the slightest of changes, be it in the weather and the seasons, in the wind and the light, or be it the sentiments and sorrows, longings and love in the hearts of creatures around them. The eight members of this council of family and friends in the Sand Castle of Leyano fell silent with one accord. Even little Periwinkle sat quietly, cross-legged on his comfy place-mat of dry-woven sea-grass, stroking the zebra-striped wings of a large butterfly which had just alighted on his knee.

Eli thought of Demoran's tale, of their grandfather's body disappearing into Sea-Slumber Bay from the shores of the Great Strand: *A burial, or another life,* her brother had said. *For 'death' is only a doorway, even less substantial than one of our Portals, into another verse of the great, unending poem of seasons and tides and days and nights. May he, our good and kind and wise grandfather, be blessed...wherever he is!*

Clearly, the King, and also Reyse, did not know that Aulfrelas had replaced Maelcraig. Why was this, and what purpose did it serve? Would the ancient King Aulfrelas reveal himself to his son one day, when Aulfrin was ready to learn the truth? And why had his own father seemingly acted against the present King, working a counter charm to Aulfrin's own spell controlling time and its passage, forcing him to return to Faërie shortly after Eli's birth?

There was no sound in the room for a long time.

And then Brocéliana slowly arose and walked to a small sea-chest at the far side of the chamber. She opened it and returned carrying a colourfully painted instrument. It was a dulcimer.

Eli felt hot tears rising to her eyes.

Garo reached down between the legs of his chair, where he had left his own instrument, a *bodhrán* with a Nordic-looking emblem of a stag's head emblazoned in its centre, surrounded by a circle of knotwork in grey, yellow and orange. Brocéliana laid the dulcimer across her knees and began to strum it with the fingernails of her right hand, pressing the strings to make the chords with the fingers of her left. Garo used his own rugged and ruddy fingers to tap intricate rhythms or to brush the surface of his *bodhrán* with graceful caresses. Their music was so tender that one could hear the deep breathing of the listeners, each breath taken in time with the cadence of the sad, sweeping, hopeful or exulting melody.

The tune was played so sweetly and near-silently that it was no more than a clear and natural harmony when the Poet-Prince Leyano began to speak, or rather to chant, his verses.

Spiral of stars, eleven isles,
Seven kingdoms, and one and three,
Separate, distinct as lovers' eyes
Filled with their longing and destiny.

Old, more than old, are our yearning dreams,
Heady as kisses of nightshade-sleep.
But lovers must waken and so must we;
For dreams, sown by others, are ripe to reap.

The lovers' eyes may look with love
Yet they shall never be one, until
Their gaze is turned towards the skies,
And together the Sun and Moon fulfil

Their dream of joining all to all.
For of that union shall be born
A single realm of light and dark,
Midnight, mid-day and dusk and morn.

We who are Singers of the Sun,
We who are Dancers of the Moon,
We now awake, we now unite,
Before the trees are each one hewn,

Before the waters are troubled with plague,
The fishes are fossils, the birds are flown,
The beasts are caged, the portals locked,
Apocalypse come and the trumpets blown!

Lovers awake! Join hand in hand:
Single your eye, your dream, your fate.
Both worlds, be one, oh stars recall -
Recall the truth, for the hour is late:

A Delicate Balance

Eleven stars, one spiralling dream.
And lovers true, though many, are one.
You will see the Moon forever full,
When you look at last with the eyes of the Sun.

****

Chapter Four:
A Spiral of Stars

he company conversed throughout much of the morning. But before their luncheon was served on a balcony terrace on the western side of the fantastical fortress, all descended to the rather triangular-shaped cove on this coast of Mermaid Island.

Far over the waters of the Sound, Eli could see the estuary of the Jolly Fairy River, pointed out to her by Brocéliana. Muscari stood beside them as the gentlemen fairies, Periwinkle, and also Alégondine, walked further south along the shore of the small bay.

"My home, Curious Cove, is further to the north, dear Eli," said her half-sister, "and you probably cannot see it in the midday haze. I have *almost* a true fairy's vision, but even to me it is blurred by the distance. However, facing us there, and quite visible to you I imagine, are the whirlpools and strange criss-crossing tides where the River of the Jolly Fairy meets the Sound. That river winds in and out of Barrywood, so they say; but I have never been permitted to follow its course. It is enchanted and enchanting, and I have heard that fairies who wet their feet in it when crossing, risk remaining inebriated by its crazy joyfulness forever!"

"And there are legends," added the poised voice of Muscari, her eyes fixed on the far coast-line, "that an ancient breed of white horses, who used to run over the plains of Mazilun near to where the Jolly Fairy leaves Shooting Star Lake, once came to the bewitching river under the tiny horn of a new moon, and they drank deep in the shallow, swirling, silver waters. They **all** became very intoxicated and immediately began leaping and dancing and executing mezairs and cabrioles, pirouettes and courbettes! At last, they dashed under the eaves of the woods and became lost between the river and White Hart Head Mountain. They never emerged again, and eventually, so it is recounted, they inter-bred with the small herd of ghostly unicorns in the great Glens. Thus it is that some of the unicorns of Barrywood are said to be real horses, not phantoms, and can --- in theory at least --- be ridden. I have never heard of anyone actually doing so, however. But that is touching another legend, and we will not have time for our swim, if I begin recounting all of the folktales of Faërie!"

The rest of the fairy-folk had wandered far out of sight, presumably to find private pools and rocky inlets in which to bathe. Brocéliana, Muscari and Eli, laid their clothes on the sunny stones beside a small, rounded basin naturally formed by the tide at the very foot of the high pinnacles of the Sand Castle behind them. Here they all three swam and washed and relaxed, with beautiful and brilliantly coloured fishes playing around them.

The bells summoning them to their mid-day meal and the continuation of their Council sounded too soon for Eli, but she obediently came back to the golden beach and was dry before she had taken the few steps to reach her clothing on the stones. As they walked back to the exterior and zigzagging staircase in the rock-face up to the Castle, leading them to their lunch, Eli spoke softly to her sister.

"Your love-story has blossomed swiftly, it seems. For in fairy-time --- if I understand correctly how that works! --- I only left a week and a half ago; and I left *you* at Demoran's castle, and *Garo* at the Stone Circle. I know you had...well, briefly glimpsed one another a few days earlier, but Garo must have left Castle Davenia that night, I suppose, and I do not think he was there when I returned and visited the Great Strand with Demoran before I left. Or was he? I hope you don't find me too inquisitive, asking you?" she added, a little nervously.

Brocéliana laughed merrily. "Not at all, my sweet Eli! How could I mind your loving curiosity? I can hear only tenderness for me and blessings for us both in your kind voice. And you are quite correct, it has been less than a fortnight since you passed through the Portal of the Fair Stair and went back into your human world, in the time of this realm.

"And it is as you surmise, for I did not see Garo again until quite recently, after I had left our brother in Davenia and returned to my little boat to sail to Curious Cove. The King our father deemed that I would be quite safe there, rather than obliging me to go to Fantasie out of fear of any 'aggression' from Erreig. Well, Curious Cove *was* my initial destination, and supposedly my final one, in our father's thoughts... Oh dear, it all seems a little too secretive, doesn't it?!

"I sailed, with the companionship of dolphins but not pulled by them --- for there was a nice, gentle wind and I was not in need of great speed --- close along the northern shore-line and across the wide mouth of Moon Mad Bay. That was the first day and night of my trip, but on the second morning, only three days ago now, I came within sight of Not Quite Point, the western and highest lookout over Blue Harpers' Bay. The lands on the other side of that Bay, a wide estuary filled with the waters of the River Nazzy that flow around the White Willow Isles, are much lower hills. As I left Not Quite Point behind me, I could see the silhouette of a noble stag on the little rise of the facing shore where it reaches out into the sea. The late morning sun danced in my eyes and the salt breeze made them water. I closed them for a few moments, and when I opened them, and had sailed even nearer, the stag was gone and Garo was standing on the low sea-hill. It was the tide itself that bore me to him, and into his arms for the very first time!

"We had both been invited to this Council of Leyano's, unbeknownst to the King, and so we continued our journey together. My heart is so full, my dear Eli, that I have no words to tell you more of my, of our, love. It is all so new, but it feels a very old story as well."

"You don't need to tell me more, not yet or ever, my dear Brocéliana, not until you wish to anyway. I'm just so pleased for you, for both of you. And I wish you both such great happiness, always."

"That will be a challenge, that 'great happiness', I think. We have so short a time left to us until Garo must take up his role as the student and inheritor of Aulfrelas, on Star Island…alone. And I may be leaving Faërie even before that," she added, candidly but with no resentment or self-pity in her tone of voice at all.

Eli sighed, but could not answer. They had nearly reached the balcony where Aindel, Alégondine and Leyano were already assembled. Muscari, chatting with Piv who was flying along beside her shoulder, was just coming up behind them on the last flight of the staircase.

They ate, for the most part, in silence and calm; all seemed to have been lulled by their swims and now happy to concentrate on their lunch. There were salads of sea-shore herbs, twisted boiled yellow tubers and crunchy miniature lettuces, tiny blue and purple grapes or possibly they were peas of some strange maritime vine-like plant, and delicious cakes of barley and pink pepper and sweet berries all baked together.

They remained in this, their dining-and-council-chamber, long after their meal, to talk until late into the evening.

Eli learned much about their plans and dreams, their designs for an Alliance of all of the shees and the hope that such a federation of fairies would also be prepared to mingle with the human world in what they deemed was a very acute and urgent need. She wished that she could recall more of her own

Great Charm and her obviously long-held desire to be a major protagonist in this movement. But, alas, she was still more human than fairy, although she could now recognise that she had more and more subtlety in her understanding and perceptions, and could see more of the fairy-life around her. Although the *solanum crispum* had receded once again from its curtaining of the arcade, there were sea-lavender and jasmine now appearing, swiftly growing around the base of each soaring arch. And in each plant, Eli could discern minuscule beings, most with wings like huge, furry moths, in tones of mauve and blue and grey.

She did not like to ask too many questions, but contented herself with listening to the discourse of her comrades and family, and trying to piece together more and more information and understanding. It seemed that the eleven shees were all very different, and very far-flung. Seven had kings or queens, or both, evidently; three were not ruled or governed by anyone in particular, as far as she could gather, but just lived in harmony and mutual comprehension; and one seemed to be populated by a single family with a mother, or matriarch, at its head --- rather like a mixed community of monks and nuns with an abbess to guide them, for it sounded as though this was a shee with particularly spiritual practices or rituals.

The map remained open on the table all the time, and Eli enjoyed studying it even when the conversation eluded her a little. Once or twice she caught Leyano looking at her, smiling and almost winking, as he had done in her meditation-vision when she had knelt in the chapel of Ligugé, the vision of their father striding into the great circular room after his dragon-battle, and she --- as a little girl --- restraining herself from running into his arms! Yes, it was the same brotherly, knowing wink; even though this Leyano was no longer a young adolescent, but a mature and regal Prince. His deep red hair hung in three long braids on each side of his tanned face, falling across his broad chest, and the tresses were studded all along with turquoises that shone bright blue, veined in gleaming green, twinkling in the light from the two great candles now standing in ornate shell and coral bases on the long table, one at each end of the map-scroll. The evening light began to colour the room with violet and rich blue streaks and shadows, except for the golden glow cast by these candles.

It surprised Eli to realise that, until now, she had not really *noticed* the jewels that Leyano wore. For there were some very extraordinary ones, more remarkable than the turquoises. But she had only seen his eyes, really, until now.

As Alégondine was speaking, very slowly and sedately, the tiny pink and grey pearls in her own hair modestly glinting from time to time, Eli found herself scrutinizing Leyano more and more, and seeing --- as if for the first time --- all the details of the rich prizes he had won in his Initiations.

His ears, not covered at all by his thick, braided hair, were quite pointed; but it was in their lobes and not their points that he had other jewels set. These were like the stones in Aulfrin's silver circlet: not the larger emeralds of the King's crown, but the smaller, though equally bright, peridots. Eli had always loved that gem, and those in Leyano's ear-lobes were very fine indeed. Each ear had one large peridot-jewel, round-cut and smooth with a star shining deep in its centre, and then there were four others of diminishing sizes going up towards his ear-points.

But the most striking of all was the incredible stone set into his forehead, just a little higher than the level of his red-brown eyebrows. Eli knew it to be a diamond as soon as she concentrated her gaze on it: it was not terribly large, but it was a curious oval shape that seemed to suggest a beetle. It was of such a sweet, innocent yellow hue that Eli found herself on the verge of tears.

Immediately, and instinctively, she knew that she was not crying because of the colour, or the beauty of the diamond, and certainly not for its worth or price in the world of men. She knew, absolutely and simply, that these precious stones had no value here in terms of wealth. But they spoke of something much more moving. As she stared at the yellow diamond, Eli began to see a landscape, very like that she had hiked through to reach the Portal of Eagle Abbey at Seven Falls in Santa Barbara only the day before. There was no image *in* the diamond, but looking at it made the picture take shape in Eli's mind, or in her heart.

There were huge grey rocks, and water in pools, waterfalls and pine trees. And wheeling overhead were mighty birds of prey: falcons and strange white amber-eyed hawks, and immense eagles with their wings held wide and the fingers of their feathers spread out to navigate the hot winds. For the winds were very, very hot and there were sparks of red fire blowing about the diving, soaring eagles.

Was she seeing the ravaging brush fire that had burned the monastery near Eagle Abbey two years earlier?

She knew the answer before the question was fully formed in her mind. No, this was not a scene from recent times. The years were roaring out and streaming forth, or backwards, as if time itself was being rewound. Years, long years ago, many centuries, *that* was when this diamond had learned its song and first told its story. *This* was the moment when Leyano had won his prize. The red sparks were cast from unseen fire, but it was not a brush fire ---- however destructive and tragic --- in the hillsides of human lands. It was mightier, and more menacing, than that.

Dragons, huge and horrible. Not little green, portly fellows pulling *wyrm-chars*! Dragons whose throats and chests, like blazing furnaces, where almost transparent and kindled inside with red and orange flame. There was an odour of charred flesh and hideous cries, and the air was shadowy but at the same time lit with bursts of flame roaring out from the giant jaws of these monsters. How many were there? They flew too quickly to count them. Their broad, leathery wings beat slowly

A Delicate Balance

or arched to hold their enormous bulks in the air as they manoeuvred over the jagged peaks and boiling waterfalls. But when they flew, they flew fast! Like bolts of lightning.

Darker and darker the skies became, clouded with the reek from the dragons' burning gusts of flame and the kindled pine trees. Were the trees wailing? Eli felt she could hear them, in pain and anguish. The images in the scene were all deepening to ruddy crimson and gold-tipped black, like embers. Only one colour truly contrasted with the darkness: at the centre of each blast of flame from the mouths of the dreadful dragons, there was a glow of pure light, so pale and pristine a yellow that it was almost white.

It was the colour of Leyano's diamond. Exactly.

"We must conclude now," said a gentle voice. It was Aindel's, and he was carefully rolling up the long map. We will meditate on a blessing-melody before we go to our beds, if you are all in agreement with that idea?"

Eli began to breathe again, wondering if everyone had noticed her so shocked and staring, falling further and further into the story of Leyano's diamond. But as she glanced quickly, nervously, around the table, it did not seem that anyone had witnessed her being lost in her terrible vision. With the exception of her brother. For Leyano was looking into Eli's eyes with deep understanding. And he was smiling his calm, Buddha-like smile once again.

Then he looked away from Eli and rose and went with Brocéliana to the sea-chest. She took her painted dulcimer once more, and Leyano reached in and extracted a lovely lute, also beautifully decorated. Muscari had produced a small flute like a delicate Irish whistle from the pocket of her robe, and Garo had again taken up his *bodhrán*. Aindel delighted Eli by going to a curtained alcove beside the unused fireplace at the room's far end, and returning with a rather tall yet narrow harp, made of twisted, silver-white drift-wood and strung with fine golden strings. Eli wondered if Alégondine would produce an instrument, and of what mystical or magical type it would be; but she did not.

However, as the musicians began to play (and Piv to blow into his cupped hands as if they were a sort of harmonica --- producing sweet bird-calls and cooing cascades of notes) and all the impromptu orchestra began slowly weaving a tapestry of liquid and glorious melody, Alégondine did, indeed, join the medley. But hers was a contribution of song. She chanted, in a language that Eli could not recognise, but which reminded her of the twelfth-century plainsong compositions of Hildegard of Bingen. But this was not Latin, and certainly not any form of Gregorian chant.

As Eli's mind had conjured, or seen revealed, the dramatic scene of the dragons and the diamond, now she was transported elsewhere. Green waves undulated endlessly, eternally, and the breeze licked their crests into lace and white butterflies of spray. Flowers and trees were sown or planted, and grew, and counted the cycle of seasons a hundred times, or a thousand, and then passed into oblivion, or into soft, warm light. Or perhaps serenely into the green sea with its rolling, rippling, white-tipped waves.

The sun rose, and set, and the new moon glistened against the palette of twilight colours in the west. And then it was a full moon, and a dense crowd of stars exploded into the deep velvet black of the summer sky. Some of them were moving, and Eli felt herself falling into them, up into the infinite universe, into the spiral of moving stars. Sun and moon were merging and the stars were singing, or was it the voice of Alégondine?

Or was she asleep, and dreaming?

How had she come here?!

For as she opened her eyes, just a crack, she could see the stars blinking and laughing at her, filling all of her open, seaward window. She snuggled down and pulled her soft blanket over her, and the sea-breeze gently rocked her hammock to and fro, to and fro, until she fell back to sleep.

****

Alégondine and Aindel had left Mermaid Island by the time Eli arrived for breakfast the next morning. Piv sat near Eli and told her that he had seen them off early, in Alégondine's marvellous boat of pale pink abalone and white mother-of-pearl, deep purple coral and star-like crystal.

"I would have liked to see it up close," commented Eli, sipping her tea from a deep and rustic pottery bowl.

"You've seen the Princess's boat before, but at a distance?" inquired Piv, his eyes wide.

"I think so, yes. When I was visiting the Sweet-Faced Flower Beds with Brocéliana. But she was still asleep when Rapture bore me up to the coast and we looked out towards Scholar Owl Island. I saw a marvellous boat, sailing towards the east, and from how you describe it, I think it could have been the sailboat of Alégondine."

Eli said nothing of having seen *two* boats on that occasion, for now she wondered curiously about the sight of Aulfrin, in Brocéliana's crescent-moon craft, pulled-up alongside the larger sailboat. Had he met, once again, the fairy whom he had thought to be his own daughter and who had been taken back to her true father's province of Quillir when she was only five? Had they ever met, before that, in the intervening years? And, if it was indeed Alégondine sailing eastwards along Faërie's northern coast, where was she bound? Was she simply taking her time --- a very long time --- to arrive here, for this Council?

But Eli's ruminations were curtailed by the gentle voice of Brocéliana.

"That was the Point of Vision, I suspect," she said, softly and with wonder in her voice. "I knew you had looked out to Scholar Owl Island, but I did not know you had seen other things. There is one magical place that allows the gift of a very special sight, and I have been there once, also. It was Rapture who showed you the spot, perhaps --- for the animals know it well and it is necessary to be invited there by one of them in order to see any vision or miracle. But nothing that the Point reveals is ever false; they are not dreams or trickery. Sometimes they are out of their own time, or space, and one is permitted to witness what was, or is to come, or something that is happening elsewhere."

"How on earth does this work?!" laughed Eli in bewilderment and amusement. "Are there any rules here, natural rules and laws, about time and space?!"

Leyano cut open a giant, exceedingly prickly fruit and served a large spoonful of its creamy white interior to himself and to Eli. He laughed a little too. "My dear Eli, those *are* natural rules and laws! But perhaps they do not work quite like that 'on earth', as you say. I believe that, in the human world --- which I have only visited rarely, it's true, but quite recently, so I know a little of their modern beliefs and even their sciences --- it is now conceded that time is rather an elastic and multifaceted thing. It is 'relative', I believe they say. It is good that humans have at last come to that clarity of thought; for the concept of time as something *linear* is quite absurd, really. That way of perceiving time has always seemed to our fairy-race as an odd invention of the mind of human-beings, for it really doesn't seem to us to reflect any working of nature or clear model of creation. And space is the same; it's 'relative' and quite elastic too! The closest they seem to come to this very basic comprehension, on earth, is to speak of *infinity* and *eternity*."

Eli smiled, trying to digest this idea. But she found it easier to digest her delicious fruit. She turned back to Piv. "Where were they sailing, Alégondine and Aindel? Back to Quillir?"

"To the Morning Star Shoals, sixty or seventy miles southwest, on the coast of Mazilun. They have another meeting to attend there, to share all we discussed last evening." Periwinkle would have continued, but his mouth was now very, very full of the sweet, white fruit. So, as Eli looked highly inquisitive, Leyano took up his explanation.

"And the Shoals are only about twenty or thirty miles from the eastern eaves of Barrywood. They have gone to bring news to our brother Finnir."

"And I will be taking the news to the Prince Demoran," added Muscari, as she entered the bright breakfast-room with Garo. She smiled, and laid a hand on Eli's shoulder. "No, no, don't get up --- continue with your meal, dear Lady Eli. We shall meet again, soon I hope. I must return to Davenia to bring details of all our discussions to your other brother. My horse awaits me in the lands of the Singing Bee-Hives, just north of the Queen's Ride, the river that marks Vivony's borders. I must leave you all now, and begin my long journey back to Davenia."

"And how do you reach your mount, dear Muscari," asked Eli. "Do you have a boat too?"

"No, dearest Eli. But I have wings! I won't fly all the way to the west, though, but only as far as the plains of Vivony where my steed and three of my companion horse-lords await me. They, in their turn, will carry messages to others in our Alliance. You see, star by star the night sky turns into a diamond-studded work of art. You just have to keep looking up!"

Eli hesitated, but she could not restrain herself. "May I, could I, watch you take off?" she asked slowly and almost in a whisper.

The others all grinned. Periwinkle was the only one *not* too smile. "You see *me* fly all the time! Why is it so special to see my darling blue Muscari take flight?"

Eli gave her pixie-friend an apologetic look from under her eyebrows. "It's of course always marvellous to see *you* fly, dearest Piv, and I don't mean to make any comparison. It's just that I thought it would be, well, very interesting to see what Muscari's wings were really like."

Piv seemed placated, and flew over the table to serve Eli one more scoop of fruit. "You're quite right, too, my curious little Eli-een," he said, hovering in the air before her. "My Muscari has very lovely wings, as blue as her pretty eyes. I hope she will let you watch her whirl away over the Sound."

"Indeed I will, and with pleasure," agreed the laughing Horse-Lady. "But take your place at the window now, for I have left my cloak and a package of *buicuri* for our friend Eochra in the room just below us, and I'll depart from there in only a few minutes."

Eli was not disappointed. She went to the western window and waited only a moment or two, with Piv on the sill beside her, and then she saw the marvellous apparition: from the small balcony protruding from the Sand Castle walls one storey below them, Muscari soared out over the shores of Mermaid Island. Her dark blue tunic and loose trousers were covered by a long cloak that flapped and billowed about her. But her clothing was not seen in any detail by Eli, whose attention was wholly concentrated on the wonder of her friend's large butterfly-like wings. They were iridescent and veined in gleaming green, but mostly they were a multitude of blues, dark and light and subtly striped or shadowed.

Eli watched until Muscari was barely visible, seemingly as small as a real butterfly in the distance.

"What must that *feel* like…?" she mused to herself. "How incredible that must be…"

When she turned back to the room, Garo had joined Brocéliana and was now turning to gather his *bodhrán* and her dulcimer and wrapping both instruments in richly embroidered cloths. They were obviously preparing to depart as well. He was already wearing a long cape over his brown and grey travelling clothes, and Brocéliana was standing beside him, simply watching him with tenderness in her eyes.

She too was in comfortable clothing suitable for a sea voyage. Unlike the long white dress she had worn yesterday, stitched with bobbles of seeds or grains of creamy yellow dried corn kernels, she now had close-fitting leggings of very pale blue overhung with a long shirt-dress in beige linen, fastened all up the bodice with criss-crossed laces of blue cord.

"Are you sailing back to Curious Cove so soon?" asked Eli, quite sad not to have the day before them for further conversation, and perhaps another musical interlude.

"My lovely lady, Brocéliana, is returning to her home, yes," replied Garo, coming to Eli and taking both her hands in his. Strangely, Eli no longer felt the rushing and tingling sensation, like electricity, when a fairy touched her, as she had on her first Visit. She seemed to be becoming more and more fairy-like herself, or at least better able to receive the charge of energy from these enchanted people.

"But I will be bidding her farewell there, and galloping swiftly on over the land and leaping over streams and rivers, for my journey will continue far into the west; I will be racing the stars in their sky-course!"

Garo's eyes, a brighter blue than Brocéliana's, were directly before Eli as he stood just at arm's length from her. Their hands joined. He was not so tall as her brothers, and certainly far from Aindel's height, but he bore himself so uprightly --- though without haughtiness --- and carried his broad shoulders with such a commanding posture, that he always seemed to be towering above everyone else. He had not yet wound his sandy-blond hair into its customary knot at the nape of his neck, but then, neither had Eli. Hers hung long and red down her back, and his long and yellow, behind his shoulders. The early sun-light was streaming through the arcade, and the starry flowers had not yet trailed over the opening to shade the room.

"You are glowing with the colours of the banner of Faërie, my dear ones!" announced Leyano. "But your clans are reversed!"

"It's true!" cried Brocéliana in delight. "Garo is a Sun-Singer, and a dragon-lord; he should be the *red* half of the face. And Eli should be the *yellow* moon, for she is a Moon-Dancer. How wonderful that you have exchanged your roles!"

"And with your hands clasped, what a perfect symbol you make to conclude our conference," beamed Leyano. "You are the two faces of Sun and Moon united, but also interchanged. You will be our emblem, to seal the 'pact of the spiralling stars', to keep in our hearts --- just we four!"

"Five!" squeaked Piv, at that instant flying back in from the western window where he had escaped for a moment to play with the diving sea-gulls in their morning aerobatics.

"Five, I beg your pardon, Master Periwinkle," agreed Leyano.

****

Leyano, Ei and Periwinkle walked down to the slender pier where Brocéliana's crescent-moon boat was moored. There they bid their farewells to the lovers, and watched as the silvery craft, joyfully led out into the Sound by its three dolphin-guides, left the cool morning shadows cast by Dawn Rock and glistened like a sea-borne star as it turned to the north.

"They make a very handsome couple, and a very sweet one," said Eli, still gazing after them even after their forms could no longer be clearly distinguished. The Sound was undulating in the crisp breeze, and clouds of gulls were swooping and crying, or perhaps laughing and singing sea-shanties, as the trio returned to the Castle. "But I am sad for Brocéliana that she has fallen in love with the next-in-line to the Sage-Hermit. Their love affair is doomed to be quite short, I suppose, in that case."

"And not only for that reason," Leyano commented, walking beside Eli up a wide staircase of the Sand Castle which would eventually lead them back to the broad balcony where they had spoken together in private on Eli's first evening here. "It is perhaps even more imminent, their separation. For you have only one more Visit here, and then you will confirm your final decision to return to us, or to stay in the world. If you choose the former --- as our father desires and as your family and your kingdom also hope, of course --- then Brocéliana's life among us will come to an end, and she will take up her new life in the realm of human-beings."

They were in a bright, narrow corridor which was in fact a landing of the main staircase; they were still one story below the great balcony, and there was a glassy bench against a southern window, overlooking wild and beautiful gardens and the distant coastline of the Island. Eli knelt on the bench, crossed her arms on the window-sill and propped her chin on her forearm with a loud sigh. Piv alighted beside her and sat down, dangling his short legs over the edge of the sill.

"If the hopes we cherish for the spiral of stars and the Alliance of the Eleven Shees come to fruition, and the Portals become open doors between the two worlds, then perhaps they will still be able to see one another," the pixie said at last.

Eli turned from the view of the gardens below and the sea-green waters of Sea-Horse Bay beyond, and looked silently at Piv, and then up into Leyano's black eyes.

"Is that possible?" she asked.

"Until Garo formally takes up his role as the Sage-Hermit, yes. As our father visited Lily, he could come and go many times in the two years remaining him. He could even, I suppose, cast a time charm that would allow a visit to her to last all of her human life and yet cost him only minutes or days of our time here. But *she* cannot be charmed with similar time-play while in the world. She will grow old. And she will not be permitted to return to Faërie, not if you are here. That is our law. Unless…"

Leyano's voice was very quiet as he broke off his final phrase. It was Piv that concluded the thought, also in a hushed voice.

"Unless she has access to truly mighty magic, akin to the Black Key," he whispered. "She is high in the favour of the Lady Ecume, so perhaps it is possible that such a thing could be granted her. But I do not know if she even knows of its existence. Or of even greater wonders, such as…"

"The Fourth Portal."

It was not Piv who said the words, nor was it Leyano. To her great surprise, Eli heard herself pronouncing those four syllables. Both the pixie and her brother were looking intently at her now, but she had fallen silent.

How did she know this? Where had it come from? Images were spontaneously springing into her head: the concert of the mer-musicians on her first evening here, her dream of the floating key and the magical-eyed mermaid holding her regard in a vision at *The Inn of the Smiling Salmon* and that vision 'come true' when she had seen the Lady Ecume in Sea-Horse Bay (albeit without the key), the drawing that Sean had made in Lily's journal of the Lady 'Sea-Foam' and the key on the water…

And another picture was now there, more real and more dramatic than those other memories.

She was astride Peronne, and flying high over the ocean. In an instant of incredible courage, or folly, they crashed downwards through a skyscape of clouds and were suddenly diving in a wide spiral --- not a *climbing* 'spiral of stars' symbolising the high hopes for the unity of the Eleven Shees. This was a dare-devil dive, down a breathless descending spiral of roaring air and ever-approaching tumultuous waters.

She was leaning close over Peronne's withers, and hugging his neck as they catapulted downwards. She could feel something cold and heavy clutched in her right hand and her eyes were squinting in the force of the wind and the salt-spray as she tried to see through his wildly blowing mane. There, just beneath them, drawing closer and closer every second, was an enormous whirlpool like a gaping dragon-mouth of water. And just as would be the mouth of such a monster, its spinning waters were blood-red in colour and its centre was more profoundly black than the darkest midnight sky.

Eli, kneeling and perched on the crystal bench beside the window in the golden castle of Leyano, was tensely gripping the sandy stone of the sill now. She heard herself say, aloud, "Where am I? Where am I?"

The deafening roaring, of both wind and whirlpool, stopped abruptly. Her brother's voice was rich and tender and comforting, right beside her.

"You are on Mermaid Island, my dear sister. Come back. You are with me, and Periwinkle, on Mermaid Island in the east of Faërie. You are *here*."

Eli gazed up into the eyes of her noble, gentle brother. They were almost as black as the hole at the centre of the crimson whirlpool.

"How do I know that there is *a Fourth Portal*? How do I know that it exists, and that it is hidden in the sea? And how do I know that the Black Key of the Lady Ecume, or something like it, is the way to open it?"

"I do not know the answers to those questions," said Leyano solemnly.

Periwinkle had not turned from the view and was still sitting on the precipice of the window-sill. He spoke without looking around to either Eli or the prince.

"I think it is because you did the Great Charm, my Eli, my Mélusine," he said very calmly. "You told me, the year we were together in the Dappled Woods, journeying and frolicking all over Davenia together, you told me much about your three-times one-hundred-and-eleven years. You didn't tell me all, but I guessed much. And I wondered, then, if you had found it. During your Great Charm, had you *found* the Fourth Portal?"

"What *is* the Fourth Portal, exactly? And how can a recollection of it come back to me now, even before I decide about coming back here? I'm not Mélusine again, not yet."

"Maybe, in your heart, you have already decided about your home-coming," suggested Leyano. "Or maybe you have been granted some insight or wisdom, to help you in that decision."

Eli sighed again, and looked back out into the sea-green distance beyond the margins of the Island. She said nothing but she thought, or perhaps recognised as knowledge, something more. "I recall the Lady Ecume, playing her harp on a rock far out in the Bay, two nights ago. I felt her telling me something, or sending me some blessing or reminding me of something, silently, secretly..." But all of these words were only murmured in Eli's heart, and did not take form on her lips. Eli continued to ruminate, without speaking her thoughts.

"She told me to meet her, before I go home. She told me she had a gift to give me. What could the gift be? Is it the Black Key? Will I dive through the whirlpool once again, or will others do so? Will the Fourth Portal open for Brocéliana and Garo?"

Her unspoken thoughts trailed off into complete interior silence. Suddenly her normal vision of shapes and colours jolted her, as if she was awakening from a dream. She realised that her senses had been sharpened for a time, because now they were faded and dull, as she had always known them as a human.

Only three words remained, etched in her mind and ringing there like far-off harp music. *The Fourth Portal.*

Eli swallowed hard, and stood up to mount the next staircase with her brother, Piv flying ahead of them. But now the three words changed, or were given a complementary epithet. Three *other* words were there, so clear, so insistent, that they filled her head and her hearing and her heart.

The Garnet Vortex.

The sweet, sombre music of her silent thought was chanting, deep within her soul, repeating the words as endlessly as waves rolling onto the virgin sands of a beach where no one had ever stood.

"The Fourth Portal. The Garnet Vortex."

The Garnet Vortex...

****

Chapter Five:
Moon-Music of Shee-Mor

P*eriwinkle remained* an hour or so with Leyano and Eli on the high semi-circular balcony, though he explained to them that he would *not* be able to stay for lunch. He had been invited to dine with the pixies of the sea-snails, whose interlace-patterns were of a complexity that fascinated him, so he said. Aside from that, this particular cousin-clan of his, inhabiting the far north-eastern point of Mermaid Island, was also well-reputed to have the most gastronomic-gastropod *cuisine* in all of Faërie, even surpassing the nut-butters and deep brown liqueurs of the Hazel Woods of northern Quillir. It did not seem, either to Leyano or Eli, that Piv's enthusiasm to accept this invitation was entirely artistic!

But before he left them, the wise pixie returned to the subject of the Fourth Portal. He asked Eli, "You said, just now, that it is *hidden in the sea.* I fancied you had glimpsed it, somewhere to the north of Scholar Owl Island, but I imagined it was on one of the smaller 'skelligs' scattered off the Island's northern coast. It's further out in the ocean, then?"

"I don't know, my dear Piv," answered Eli, gazing from the balcony. "I don't know."

She was now slowly allowing her eyes to make the full 180° tour of the view. It was late morning, and the summer sun was already high over the peaks of Dawn Rock to her left. She remembered stepping through Leyano's Portal, only a couple of days ago: rich and astounding days of fairies and mermaids and music and dreams. She had climbed hand in hand with her gallant brother, the youngest prince of Faërie, over the grey rocks on the Santa Barbara Seven Falls' side of the secret doorway where he had met her. He had no doubt resembled, for those brief moments, the poet Leo --- just as Lily had known him. He had then led her into this world of fantasy and sublime beauty, where she evidently belonged. Eli smiled as she relived the exciting moments, the tingling and thrilling steps across the threshold, the sudden heightened perceptions, the gentle and natural feeling of awakening, the magical liminal second when one has a foot in both worlds...

Her regard left the east and scanned around to the south, to the landscape and seascape she had seen moments before from the lower storey, and then at last to the right and the south-western triangular bay at the Castle's foot. There was the wide Sound with the distant shores of Mazilun trimmed in frothy, white-tipped breakers and outlined in a medieval tone of regal sapphire blue.

"I don't know," she repeated yet again, but more slowly and softly. "I could see it, but I have no idea where I was in my vision. Did you both know, always, that a Fourth Portal exists? Why do we speak of *three* Portals here in our father's kingdom?" Eli addressed this last question to her brother. But Piv nodded as Leyano answered her.

"I've only known of the Fourth one since I held the defence of my own Portal fifty years ago, when you were taken to replace Brocéliana as a changeling, dear Eli. While our father returned to the human world to linger with you and Lily, I was required to keep the tiny and vulnerable new-born half-fairy well-hidden and protected...and I warded off the efforts of Erreig to close Dawn Rock. Reyse would have come to my aid, but he was occupied with that protection of the babe, helping me to keep her hidden, while I defended my Portal."

Leyano's countenance paled very slightly, Eli thought, as he drew a deep breath. His voice was a little lower and quieter when he resumed.

"I fell. And it was only then that I learned many things, among them the existence of a Fourth Portal. I knew already that the Black Key, held by the Lady Ecume, was a treasure of some magical and potent kind, but I did not know its true nature nor its use, or uses."

"My people," interjected Piv now, "have always kept alive the legends of the existence of a Fourth Portal, and many of the trees know much about it. But it is sacred and secret. The mushrooms and even fungi, they do not know. And Aulfrin does not know either."

Eli looked at Piv in amazement. "The King does not know there is a Fourth Portal?!"

Leyano nodded with a curt little laugh. "If he had known of it, he would have used it, rather than traversing the underworld perhaps, to return after his human death. But no, I think Periwinkle is right; he does not know, and it seems that the Lady Ecume does not wish him to have this information.

"The Wisest Ones, they know, of course, that the Black Key is Faërie's most powerful treasure and a relic of an even more ancient kingdom than that of our eleven islands. And there may be other treasures like it. They know a little, or a great deal perhaps, of *some* of the powers of these objects, no doubt; for they surely open many locks --- not only those of doors, but also of treasure chests and magical passages within enchanted rooms, and other things....stranger and even more cunning as secrets. I was told by our father, when he returned to you and Lily, that I was to seek the Black Key from the Lady Ecume only in the event that I should have dire need of it. Strangely, he did not say what I should *do* with it! I suppose that I had imagined that the ancient mermaid would tell me, should it come to that.

"My 'dire need' did come, but I was not in a position to request the Key from her, as it turned out.

"It's quite a long story, dearest Eli. I will tell it to you at another time perhaps. For now, your Visit home should simply be coloured by joy. And to that end, following our lunch, we will make a tour of the south and east of my wondrous island-home, and then we will prepare for the arrival of our father and Reyse, and your fine flying-horse, tomorrow. You will be very pleased, I know, to be at last reunited with Peronne!"

Eli's smile was radiant and her eyes full of the anticipation of such an event; but at the same time she kept alive the curiosity about all that Leyano had learned and about his desperate efforts to protect his Portal at the time of her human birth.

Piv rose into the air, lifting his soft green cap just above his fair curls and bidding them both farewell. "I must be off! I've a forty-mile flight to reach my delicious meal --- I mean to study the sea-snails and their artistry at close hand --- and I see that your lunch is about to be served."

Eli waved to him as he buzzed out into the sunshine.

Indeed, attendant fairies now appeared with full bowls and laden baskets, an elegant green-glass bottle and two blown-glass chalices. Leyano led Eli to her place at the table.

But as her brother poured her a glass of pale golden, bubbly liquid and the attendants served her with salads and sea-weed cakes and a cold soup as turquoise as Sea-Horse Bay in the mid-day light, Eli looked inquiringly into Leyano's crimson-black eyes.

The attendants withdrew graciously, and then Eli said, "I don't really want to wait for another occasion to hear your tale, my dear brother. Couldn't you tell me now?!" The ruddy and serene face of the fairy-prince seemed to be shadowed by a passing cloud of hesitation, but in only a moment it had warmed and softened to acquiescence and tenderness.

Leyano sipped a little of his blue soup and then he took his chalice in his hand and clinked with Eli. He regarded her in silence for another minute, while they ate and drank to the music of the encircling waters of the Bay, and then he began to speak in a soft, rhythmic tone of voice, recounting for her the history of his strange adventure fifty years previously.

This is the tale of the Moon-Music Defence of Mermaid Island, began Leyano.

Our father had been living in the world of humans for many months already, when the Sun-Singers unleashed the great dragons and our worries began.

In fact, shortly after you had requested to become a changeling, following the completion of your Great Charm, Aulfrin had begun to make preliminary visits to the human lands: he ventured into France, by way of Demoran's Portal, to observe and to become at ease with the much more modern world of human-kind than that which he had known centuries earlier, on the occasion of his last...interlude! He discovered Maelys and watched her, from a respectable distance, for many weeks as well, before he finally took upon himself the disguise of Sean Penrohan in the spring of 1959.

In those days, perhaps, he did not see any reason to work a time-charm, for he deemed quite short the years he planned to be with you in the world, from the time of your 'birth' as Eli until you grew up. I don't know if he had tried *to play with the time --- and could not, for some reason --- or if he simply felt that his kingdom was stable and secure, and so he saw no danger in being absent for several decades. Perhaps he thought he would come and go, using minor time-charms if needed, such as he expected to do when he brought Brocéliana back to Faërie.*

For it was then, *when he arrived with his new-born infant, that he truly realised the extent of the danger. It was only then that he perceived the Sage-Hermit's counter-charm that forced him to make the decision to return to you and Lily for another year-and-a-half. But the trouble had begun even before your arrival as a changeling babe.*

Aulfrin, or rather Sean at that time, had received messages from the last of our folk able to escape through the Portal of the Fair Stair before it was closed. They found the King in Brittany and told him that Erreig's forces had chased the blue hounds and the great owls from Fantasie and had raised the uniquely **red** *banners of the Sun-*

Singers over the silver turrets. But, even then, it seems, he did not worry overmuch. He sent word to Reyse, asking him to support his three sons; and he probably believed that the matter would be settled swiftly.

That was near the time of the Winter Solstice, just before the new year of 1960 was ushered in. Erreig had flown to the Fair Stair and it had been sealed, and shortly after that the Portal of Barrywood also. Aulfrin had little choice, then, but to move to California --- with his wife near her time of giving birth --- so as to be near to the Portal of Eagle Abbey. I was able to send him news of his realm from that Portal, but I did not dare to leave Faërie. For by then, both Finnir and Demoran had been taken prisoner, and Erreig had turned all his attention upon me, for he was resolved to close, or control, Dawn Rock as well.

Reyse had been given the task of safe-guarding your passage from Scholar Owl Island to me, to effect the exchange of infants. What a feat it was, too! But almost a mightier deed and a more heroic tale was that of Jizay, for it was a more perilous route that he took than that chosen by Reyse for his flight with you. But that is another story.

In all of Aumelas-Pen and more specifically in the City of Fantasie there were now the dragons and bats of Quillir, save for within the confines of the garden of the Great Trees, which Erreig could not penetrate. No colours rose in waves of mist, it is said, from the circle of the Trees at that time, and only the yellow flower-ring continued to bloom, in token of solidarity with the moon-children; the blue and the white rings were withered and recumbent in deep sleep.

At last, Aulfrin stepped through my Portal with his half-fairy baby daughter, determined to hasten to the capital to engage Erreig's forces and set to rights his realm. But when he found himself once more in his kingdom, and yet unable to stop or slow the passage of time for his wife and you left behind, he was forced to turn back. It was then that he confided to me the 'sacred amber token', the sign for the Lady Ecume to release to me the Black Key. But, he said, I was only to present it to her, and to demand the Key in return, in my last and most desperate need, when all other hope was gone.

Moon-Music of Shee-Mor

As I told you, my sweet Eli, I did not know what were the powers of the Black Key, or what it could accomplish for me in the face of Erreig's occupation of the Silver City and his 'coup' of overthrowing and appropriating the two other Portals and incarcerating our brothers. I hoped that the Lady Ecume would enlighten me, should I be forced to seek it. But, alas, I delayed too long, sure of my own might and valour, confident that Finnir and Demoran would find means to escape, certain that the Moon-Dancers would rally to the clarion calls of my trumpets and to the predicament of the Dawn Rock Portal.

I do not know how much you recall of the history of our people here, my dear sister. You have heard of the division of the folk of this land, the greatest of all the Eleven Shees, the Shee-Mor. For we are destined to be united --- I am convinced of that --- but since the most hazy reaches of our past, as now, we are separated into two clans: the Sun-Singers, who in this shee have associated themselves more and more these past centuries with the proud rebel, Erreig; and the Moon-Dancers, who are loyal to Aulfrin and are content to look to him, and him only, as over-lord and king. But I wonder do you remember why we are thus named?

Eli shook her head, and Leyano continued.

No name or word in Faërie is idly used or unimportant. They may seem poetic titles, these names, but they are also truthful descriptions of our very life-force energies.

The Sun-Singers are those fairies who manifest their natural and vital force, the miraculous enchantment that is the birth-right of all fairy-folk, by song. All fairies and most creatures here can sing, and often do; but the Singers of the Sun have a particular voice that they may use to draw up from deep, deep within their very beings a flame and a power that is bright and burning and radiating and life-giving. It is beautiful and sacred, but it must be tamed and controlled. And this is why the dragon is their revered symbol.

The Dancers of the Moon, on the other hand, do indeed dance. They are a people who can move with magical grace, who sway like tall reeds or twist and turn like river-water weaving itself around *stones and roots or meandering around hills and through valleys. We are the ebb and flow of the tides, the invisible pathways of the wind, the pull of the seasons and the surge of the passions and the cycles of life in all nature. In our silent dancing --- almost always performed under the full moon --- we do as the sun-children do in their songs: we draw forth the powers hidden deep in our souls, the powers of creation, the powers of change, the powers of our destiny. So, as is fitting, the unicorn is <u>our</u> emblem.*

It was with these powers, these sacred forces, that the 'battles' of Faërie have ever been waged. In the human lands, as far as I have learned, battles and wars are fought purely by might, by strength, by cunning, and with violence. Here, we war as children of nature. For as humans speak normally with voices and fairies more with silence, we differ also in that <u>they</u> fight with exterior means, armed with weapons and even with mental concepts, while we clash like thunder in skies filled with electric pressure, or like molten rock erupting from the sea-floor to build islands. Our swords are songs, our skirmishes are dances. And they are not founded upon violence or aggression.

Yes, we will sometimes cause bodily harm --- as lightning may strike a tree and cause it to burn. But that is not the lightning's first purpose. And as the hatred and greed of humans have resulted in the creation of hideous weapons --- weapons that can never resolve the source of their conflicts, for they have their roots in fear and illusion --- our songs and dances have themselves given birth to strange creatures and even to some 'tools' to be used in our conflicts. The yellow-hot centre of sun-song is pure energy, but it has ignited the flames of the great dragons; it has not brought them into being, but it has intensified their powers. The pulsating, star-like silver that shines at the core of the moon-dance, took the form of ghostly unicorns --- and those blessed creatures became, when battles erupted, ephemeral and elusive.

We carry spears, and the gems we have won have many powers too. These are our weapons, yes, but only in the same way that the sting of a bee is his, or the claw of the eagle is hers. We all have 'weapons', should we need them to protect ourselves from some aggression. But, as for fairies, we never seek to kill. For we are manifestations of Life

itself, and so to curtail a life would be contrary to our beings, to our very natures, and to Nature herself.
But then, I suppose that the same could, and should, be said of the human race!

But to continue my tale: After our father had been forced to return into the world and Brocéliana, under Reyse's protection, had been taken to safety, I hid the amber token in a chink of my molluscarmour. I did not feel that I was, as yet, in any 'dire need'; but I knew that my duty was to remain before the Portal of Dawn Rock. Therefore, I decided that I would draw forth the 'weapons' proper to my clan. I would dance.

It was still the full moon, or so we would call it --- for we grant that title to the <u>three</u> days of the moon's visible rotundity. The night of Brocéliana's birth and the exchange of infants, there had been a lunar eclipse, a very vulnerable but very special moment for us. Symbolically, it was not without great signification, I believe. That night, our father retreated through the Portal to fly back to you and to Lily, and a fairy-nursemaid went with the Lord Reyse and the newborn half-fairy to a hiding-place in a small castle that I will show you later, for it is on this Island's southern shore.

I resolved to remain at the Portal of Dawn Rock with my small band of guards and with many of the eagles and white hawks about me too. My final Initiation had been passed in their blessed company, six centuries earlier, and they had now rallied to my aide and support.

As I say, I then danced. I danced all through that night following the full-moon's eclipse, and far into the early hours of the next morning. The most stout-hearted Moon-Dancers of my household were with me, seven fairies of great renown, who swayed and inclined like graceful lilies in the starlight; but I danced more passionately than they, with all the urgency and force and courage that I could muster.

Dawn came, and moon-set, and I finally slept in the shadow of the Portal rock, for I was very weary. My fatigue had thrown me into a dizzy dream-like state and I felt that I had emptied my spirit of its deepest reserves of challenge and resistance to Erreig, and had --- at *the same time --- radiated, like far-flung moonbeams, my calls for support and resilience and unity to all the moon-children of the realm.*

Erreig, perceiving my listless slumber perhaps, did not lose his opportunity. He had certainly felt the force of my dancing, even far away in Quillir --- for I think that is where he was at that time, rather than in the Silver City. He had clearly heard my challenge to his audacity and his treachery. He took to the skies astride Bawn, the huge matriarch-dragon of his family, to come to Dawn Rock and seize the Portal. And to imprison me also, no doubt.

I do not believe he had truly feared Aulfrin's momentary --- and obviously anticipated --- presence here, for he knew that the King would be forced to retreat immediately; he had bought (and bought dearly) the cooperation of the Sage-Hermit and the great magic that would over-ride even Aulfrin's powers. But as for the exchange of infants, he was probably quite ignorant of that. I do not know if he has ever learned of the Princess Mélusine's surprising decision to become a changeling! He knew that the King was dwelling in the world of humans, and that he had taken a wife there. He knew also, I would later learn, that a child had been born to them. But he did not guess that Brocéliana was now on Mermaid Island --- or he would have sought to kidnap her as well as me, as he had the two other Princes, for she would have represented a true treasure for him in his negotiations. It was for this reason that Reyse's protection of her was so vital.

What I believe, now, is that his greatest fear was that you, dear Eli --- or rather Mélusine --- were with me, and that you intended to defend Dawn Rock as well. I will stress this point to you, my dear sister: the Dragon-Lord holds you in some strange place of apprehension in his heart. He <u>fears</u> you, Eli.

In any case, at that time, I knew that your voyage to the human world had been accomplished in all secrecy and that practically none save my own household guard and the great Owls on your isle of preparation knew of your adventure. It is well that you are aware of this fact. But then it occurred to me that Erreig thought to find you, the Princess Mélusine, here, dancing as well. For he had rushed here in great fury but also in evident panic; so strong a challenge had he sensed that he could not imagine it to be only my own moon-force taking a stand before him!

It is five hundred miles in direct flight from the White Dragon Fortress to Dawn Rock, but he and Bawn flew here soon after sunrise, a matter of only several hours since he could have first perceived the vibrations of my dancing.

That is a fast flight for the massive dragon Bawn, and Erreig was not alone: twelve of his clan were with him (his six under-lords, plus six of his lesser-riders) mounted on white or mottled ivory dragons only slightly smaller than the mighty red-eyed Bawn herself. They arrived like an explosion, bursting through a bank of cloud high over the mouth of the Jolly Fairy River. They crossed the distance of the Sound in a matter of minutes, or so it seemed to me, as I awoke from my too-short and too-heavy sleep.

I was wrapped in my spring-time cloak, which is thick and dark grey, and I was lying against the feet of Dawn Rock's pinnacles. My seven companions were positioned in similar camouflage or dancing slowly in alternating watch among the boulders and twisted trees. Several of my eagle-friends were slumbering high overhead atop the pinnacles, though the hawk-folk had departed to be with Reyse in the south. None of us were prepared for the charge of the thirteen dragons that swept down out of the ruby-rose-painted clouds of morning.

But Erreig did not see me immediately. My cloak was the same colour as the rock shadows on the western slope of Dawn Rock where I now leapt to my feet, grasping my sea-green spear of twisted glass. As I have said, I wonder if the great Dragon-chieftain was not actually looking for you, Eli, and chose to ignore me, even though he saw or felt me beside the Portal! In any case, he whirled around the towering pinnacles of the Portal, his own white spear clasped in his left-hand, his right hand concealing the jewel set into his brown chest as he sat securely between Bawn's pinions, his knees firmly held by two of her thick, white scales. Her broad, leathery wings beat the air to either side of the champion, and together they continued to circle the pinnacles twice, then a third time. The other dragon-riders flew high over Dawn Rock and then dispersed, flying far and wide over the Island. Searching, searching... I now believe.

A Delicate Balance

I looked up, still invisible or unimportant, it seemed, to all of these intruders. The huge dragon paused in her flight, hesitating in utter stillness in mid-air like a falcon eying his prey far below, her wings outstretched, her red eyes kindled with ancient wisdom and great perception. Her rider now lowered his spear, as I gazed questioningly from the ground, and he pointed it to the highest pinnacle with which he was now aligned. He lifted his open hand from his chest, and the gem-stone that he had won and which is now embedded there since his second Initiation, over eight centuries ago, shone out with blinding light.

That stone is named Gurtha. *It is a red fire-opal, almost the same colour as the rich red-gold of the torc and arm-band that Erreig has also worn since that Initiation. In our realm, this gem, the fire-opal* Gurtha, *is known for its three-fold powers of magnification. It can triple a fairy's personal or physical strength, or his insight, or his seductive charms, or his magical skills. Erreig's second Initiation had been accomplished in the Beldrum Mountains under the guidance of one of our most spectacular waterfalls. That towering cascade marks the source of the River Siven which flows into Holy Bay, whose waters embrace Star Island before they reach the ocean. Therefore I knew that his powers over water would be very great, and I guessed in a moment what he would do.*

There is deep cave under Dawn Rock, as you know Eli, for this is the subterranean cavern which becomes the Portal itself when it is opened onto the crevice hidden in the Seven Falls in the foothills of Santa Barbara. I closed my eyes for an instant, to listen to my intuition, but now I was sure: Erreig was summoning the waters under Dawn Rock to mount through the stone's cracks and fissures, to split and explode them, and to transform the pinnacles into the seat of a new-born waterfall or gushing fountain, drowning the Portal and washing aside my brave companions. These later were already engaged in countering the swooping attacks of two of the other dragons who had remained nearby, aided in their defence by the valiant charge of twenty or thirty eagles now screaming above the flame-filled roars of the dragons and the songs of their riders. Many of the ancient trees had been ignited by the gusts of fiery breath from these tremendous beasts. The cries of those noble trees tore at my heart.

I lifted my own spear now and danced where I stood. The piercing light shining from Erreig's chest-stone onto the face of the nearest pinnacle now faltered and the great dragon and her rider turned where they hovered. The light from my own forehead was growing now, and very swiftly. That yellow diamond named **Tohtet** *had been granted me in my last and greatest challenge, at the time of my final Initiation when I was but a boy of sixteen. The eagles and falcons had been my mentors, and Reyse my tutor, but it was from the fire of a dragon's breath that my diamond had been formed. Erreig had never seen or felt this precious and powerful stone before, and I could sense his alarm.*

Erreig himself bears a powerful diamond, named **Kalvi-Tivi**, *and it is likewise embedded in his forehead; moreover, his stone was won in his own ultimate Initiation which was hosted by dragons and his marvellous gem is, like mine, the child of dragon-fire. But his were polar-dragons, and their breath is not hot and yellow, but white and blue as ice. Almost before he was aware of me and arrested by the dragon-diamond I wear, Erreig's own diamond called to mine and they both sent forth rays of intense light and vibrating power.*

His was icy and filled with blind defiance, the will to close and to seal, a desire filled with the force of his own fears. Mine was hot as the heart of a true earth-dragon, searing and opening, leaping forth into utter honesty and revelation, demanding to tear open the heart and to turn it to the heavens, to look into the eyes of the sun with the sovereignty of the eagle!

I would have gained his trust then and there, I think, had he taken the time to feel my dancing diamond-demands! But he was too rash, too fearful. He was already plunging towards me, his spear outstretched. Our roles were ironically reversed, and I saw the recognition of this in his own eyes as he bore down on me. For I was sun-fire, and he was white and cold as arctic moon-light...

But before our hearts had met, our spears had touched their targets. Mine had glanced-off a hard white scale and the point had shattered in the force of Bawn's dive; but his continued downwards and drove

home. My chest, armoured in blue crab-shell though it was, received the arrowhead of his shining white spear.
And I fell.

Although her brother had used these words earlier, it was only now that Eli truly understood what he meant. He had not 'fallen to the ground', he had *fallen* in battle. He had been struck a <u>deadly</u> blow, or so she understood the meaning of this word now.

She expected Leyano to continue, to explain, to resolve all her questions and confusion as she sat, unable to pay any further attention to the meal laid out before her. But although her breathing slowly began to become more regular and normal, the Prince said nothing more for many long minutes.

At last, when Eli thought he would remain mute and sublimely thoughtful indefinitely, Leyano turned from the view he had been staring into --- past the glistening golden and silver stone of the pinnacles of Dawn Rock and into the now hazy distance to the south-east, shimmering in the mid-day heat --- and he smiled at his sister.

"It was moon-music that caught me in its melodic and mystical arms before I drowned in the seas of death. And I do not need to convince the Princess Mélusine of the astounding healing attributes of music," he began. "When you had completed the Great Charm, you were reputed to be one of the most gifted fairies in all the aeons of the history of our race to use the harp to heal the wounds and diseases of body and of mind. You should not be surprised to hear that it was moon-music which revived me from the sleep of death, just before it had gained its victory, complete and irreversible, over me."

"What exactly is *moon-music*?" asked Eli, in a whisper, hardly daring to turn her thoughts to all the implications of what her brother had just said.

"Moon-dancers do not dance to *silence*," he retorted, his rather bushy red eyebrows raised in mock effrontery. "The ears of the moon-children hear the strains of lunar chant and the sweet cadences of the breezes that whistle past the stars. It may seem to be silence, but it is pulsating with glorious harmonies! And they are able to capture those elusive sounds, with greater or lesser success, to make even the souls of the dead, or the near-dead, to dance. Why do you think that the creatures we have manifested into being with our full-moon minuets and our circular, starlit gavottes are *ghosts*? The unicorns of the Glens of Barrywood were resurrected from the sanguine slaughter of those holy beasts in the human world beyond the Portal of the Heart Oak now held by Finnir. But the grateful souls of the first of the unicorns to hear moon-music, who found themselves returned to new life beside the Inward Sea of Faërie, were creatures from long before our brother's guardianship of the Portal. They are almost as ancient as the Smiling Salmon or the Great Trees themselves. And they could tell you, my darling Eli, what moon-music truly is, and of what it is capable."

He paused, looking deeply into his sister's wide, green-blue eyes.

"But rather than telling you more here and now, I propose to continue my story against another backdrop." Leyano rose and proffered a strong, darkly tanned hand to Eli.

"Come with me now to the southern shores of Mermaid Island, and I will conclude my tale there, where you can hear a faint echo of the music I allude to. It is not the full-moon, of course, today --- nor will it ever be during one of your Visits. But you will hear *half-moon music*, and against the background of those harmonies I will tell you how Dawn Rock was saved, and how I learned of the Fourth Portal, and how healing was miraculously granted where few had any hope that it could come."

****

A Delicate Balance

There were no horses on Mermaid Island to carry brother and sister the twenty miles or so to their destination in the south. No horses, but there were ponies.

As Leyano explained to Eli, a small herd of golden ponies, the colour of his Sand Castle home, lived on his Island: ponies descended from a sturdy little stallion, two rotund mares and their three foals, offered him by their brother Demoran when Leyano had succeeded to the guardianship of his Portal in the year 1800. Demoran had already been the guardian of the Fair Stair for twenty-three years, and he had discovered this miniature breed of coastal horse roaming on the triangle of land delineated by the two arms of the River Fraz some miles before it reached the open sea at the north-west corner of Davenia. He thought that this *double trio* of golden ponies would be the perfect gift to his younger brother, to celebrate his new title, and his age: for the Prince Leyano was thirty-three in that year, and this is a number of great import in the life of a fairy.

Once established on Mermaid Island, the six ponies had quickly become the progenitors of a beautiful family, and now a handsome herd of cheerful *frazians*, as they were called, roamed at will across the sea-grass heaths and along the white sands of the several bays and coves. They were not numerous and, as Leyano confessed, there should have been many more; but small winged-horses, from the Flying Horse Fields adjacent to the Salley Woods in western Mazilun, had alighted near Dawn Rock one spring, about a hundred years ago now, and love-stories had developed between the kindred equine clans! Now, normally, flying-horses and earth-bound horses cannot interbreed; but it seemed that an exception was tolerated in the case of these golden ponies. The result was a population, born one year later, of flying-ponies with stubby wings, but wings nonetheless well-able to support the barrel-bodied, frolic-some foals. Leyano laughed as he told Eli the tale, just as they were passing out from the lower gates of his castle into the courtyard.

"Their wings were almost transparent and oval in shape, not feathered like the wings of the great flying steeds such as Peronne. The miniature horses that had come to visit were graced with wings rather like those of giant dragon-flies, and their off-spring had wings, well, also very like insects. In fact, I often thought that they resembled, when seen from a distance, a race of large, extremely fat honey-bees! In any case, they mostly flew away over the ensuring years, to Karijan, or so I have heard. Between the Dancing Goat Plains and the Snail Woods on the shores of the Inward Sea, they seem to have found their paradise. I don't wonder, for it is a warm and sweet land, and all the creatures there are of a giddy and merry nature!

"So, come, my dearest Eli," he announced, ushering her towards the right-hand side of the large, round courtyard. "Here are the stables, and here are our happy half-horses, to take us --- very appropriately --- to Half-Moon Cove."

Eli could not have been more delighted. Two ponies the colour of late-summer wheat trotted out of the open stable-doors, their light-cord bridles jiggling with dozens of tiny bells, their long white tails swishing the ground, and their ample bellies not too far from it either! But their short legs looked as sturdy as a Shetland's, and their eyes were as dark and wonderful and kind as Leyano's. Smiling and mounted, the two riders set off at a perky gait somewhere between a walk and a prance.

In fact, had Eli realised it, the favourite gait of the frazian pony was very like that of the *tölt* of an Icelandic horse, a smooth but quick pace which offers an extremely comfortable ride. Although Mermaid Island was a stony home, their mounts had discovered pathways and trails, and the twenty or so miles were easily covered in about an hour-and-a-half.

The two riders arrived at Half-Moon Cove by mid-afternoon, and Eli was greeted by the sight of another exquisite castle, though much smaller than the Sand Castle of the Prince. The huge Cove was almost ten miles across, with brilliant white sand in a broad, rounded slice like a wedge of cheese, and gentle hills and dunes looking down upon it. On the western rim of the Cove was a grassy hill, a little higher than the rest, and on this was built a dream-like fairy-tale castle if ever there was one!

Three tapering towers of smooth, white stone were crowned with yellow, pointy roofs, from which the long banners of Faërie and the Moon-Dancers waved. Other roofs and walls were arranged in rather crazy patterns at the feet of the three towers, and medleys of flowers and fruits grew in profusion and exuberance over every surface and doorway and window sill. It was difficult to see the colour or the material of the smaller buildings, for all were decorated like the margins of an illuminated gothic manuscript, though with living and animated foliage and folly! Now that Eli had more of a fairy's vision, she was able to discern hundreds of creatures among the blossoms and leaves, the berries and grapes, the miniature trailing-melons and the heady sweet-peas and honeysuckle.

Best of all, to Eli's mind at the conclusion of their jaunty ride in the sea-air, there was a gracious welcome awaiting them, just beside the great gates of the castle. Cool drinks in tall enamelled goblets were placed on a driftwood table, and there were seats of large sea-washed stones offering views out over the Cove. Dismounting, Eli and Leyano thanked their merry mounts, and also the beautiful fairy-woman with hair the colour of the ponies and eyes as sea-green as a cat's, who had served their refreshing drinks. She curtsied to Prince Leyano, and reverently inclined her head to Eli as well.

Their table beside the walls of the castle was shaded by several parasol-pines. As they sat down, Eli could see that numerous dolphins were dancing and leaping in and out of the low waves very near the shore.

"We will enter the castle later," explained Leyano, calling for a small plate of *buicuri* and salty-sea-nuts to complement what Eli's taste-buds identified as some sort of lemonade with highlights of flowers or herbs in it as well. "For now, let us relax and talk a little more in private. You will begin to hear, as I speak, the notes of half-moon-music that I said would furnish the background to my words. Within this small castle are many fairy-musicians, for this is a place of study and sharing for those of our people enamoured of the arts of the dulcimer, lute, *vielle*, guitar and mandolin. It is where Brocéliana came to learn to play, although she also honed her skills later with one or two other particularly renowned dulcimer-players, and also with the Lady Ecume herself. I think you will enjoy meeting some of the fairies here. But for now, let us conclude our *epic tale* as they play for us!"

Eli nibbled her nuts and *buicuri*, and shielded her eyes a little as she looked across the white sand and the blue water. Shadows of great cumulo-nimbus clouds were darkening the waves far out to sea, but the dolphins seemed unconcerned for the moment, and likewise unworried was a happy family of seals, barking and frolicking like puppies on the beach below them. She then turned to look, once again, at Leyano, her expression more serious as she prepared to hear the conclusion of his story.

Indeed, as Leyano took up the threads of his tale, Eli could hear the sounds of stringed instruments, and one distant chanting voice as well, from within the castle beside them, the notes tumbling out into the breezy air and interweaving themselves into musical motifs and suggested snatches of enchanted song.

My dancing and my silent calls for help, for brotherhood, for tolerance and for the unity of our people had not gone unheeded, he commenced. *The eagles and falcons were well-awake again, of course, but so were the many stone-finches who populate the pine*

A Delicate Balance

branches and rock-crevices all about the Portal. And under the pines are holly bushes, sacred and sublime plants and servants of our cause, among whom I undertook the second of my Initiations, when I won the treasured green peridots now set into my ear-lobes. Beneath the polished and pointed leaves of the holly, within the cloistered hallows of their cool shade, are many other of my island-companions: deep-throated toads and mezzo-soprano spiders, grey mice who can cackle and squeak but who, at the time of the full-moon, can create sounds with their clever voices like tiny-tap-tapping drums or tinkling triangles. And also, during those three magical days of full-moon-music, the sea-swans from the high pools above the eastern coasts and their cousins from the far-flung islands at the very limits of our Shee-Mor's ocean-frontiers find their charmed voices, and their singing is legendary, sweetly-melancholy, celestial and transforming.

All of these singers lent their voices to my need, or so I was told, afterwards, by my faithful guards and companions who whirled in frenzied dance-steps around the scene of Bawn and Erreig above my lifeless form, mortally wounded as they knew I must be. But the strangest song of all came from another, and utterly unexpected, source. And it was not only moon-music at all, but a medley of moon and sun song...

Bawn, massive and white, lay still, near to one side of my body. One of her wings, evidently, was folded against her, but the other she held aloft, arched over me and her master. For Erreig now knelt beside me, his bare legs stained as red as his dragon-mount's crimson eyes and horny crest-points by the pool of my blood.

And it was Erreig who sang.

Not a song of triumph and victory over his slain foe. But a sun-song in the style of our moon-music, a song of power and creation, of life-giving hope and of blessed growth and change. I learned, from my friend Garo, much later, that at the time of an eclipse --- be it solar or lunar --- the sun-singers are able to link their song to the music of the moon and interpose their music's force with ours and with our dancing. I had not been aware of this genre of mystical eclipse-song before. And this is what Erreig had now chosen to do.

He chose this act, and he did not: for I believe he also did it instinctively, spontaneously, in compassion and in mourning for my mortal wound. It was as if his song was more than song, it was prayer. It was the purest of prayers, for it linked two somehow opposing fairies and their strands of melody, of moon and of sun, to forge a bridge between them, and between my life-force and my death.

Leyano paused in his tale, and seemed to bow his head as if he, too, were praying for a moment. Eli watched him, her hand raised to cover her own mouth in a gesture of complete astonishment.

She whispered, "I thought Erreig was your enemy, *our* enemy?"

Her brother's dark eyes were raised again, and the corners of his mouth belied a slight smile as he looked into her confused face.

We have no such word in our native language, here in Faërie, my dearest Eli. Even a monstrous villain cannot be an 'enemy' unless he is thus defined by another. It takes two sides to make a war; and it takes two egos to make one *of those into an enemy. Erreig is seeking to destabilise the kingdom of our father, because his ego and his fear have created a driving desire which burns him from within, worse than any dragon-fire. It is a desire to be likened to Aulfrin, to possess a part of his realm, to possess even his wife, to claim the power and the status that he believes will win him glory and high renown. But he is tormented, gravely tormented, from within. For he knows himself to be a child of Faërie and of the Shee-Mor, and he cannot escape the fact that the Sun and the Moon are* one *banner and* one *family and* one *face. He is trying to tear apart his own home; he is sundering his own heart. But he is no villain, not in his true being.*

Erreig is valliant, and gifted, and adventurous. And I imagine he is of an immense interior beauty also. If he were not, I doubt that our mother would have fallen in love with him! She would not be attracted or seduced by anything less, I'll warrant. And I have since come to know, very well, his son, Garo, and also his daughter --- our half-sister --- Alégondine. You may not know either of them too deeply, not yet, but I think you have glimpsed their shining spirits even in the brief contacts you have had so far. They have much of the dragon-chieftain's essence flowing in their veins. No, I think there is great goodness in Erreig, and if there is any 'war' in Faërie it is hidden within that complex and enigmatic 'warrior' himself. I believe he feels the conflict at the core of his own heart, more and more; undoubtedly, that day at Dawn Rock fifty years ago, he was pulled in two directions at once.

Moreover, the greatest proof I have that the beautiful side of his nature may one day emerge more strongly than all else, is that his song <u>saved</u> me. He sang wonderfully and tirelessly; he sang of eagles and dragons, of eyes that can look into the sun and of the miracle of that sun's ability to sing the great song of Life itself. He wove his clan's sun-song into our moon-music, and he eclipsed my death. I stood on the threshold of the last Portal of my life, and the rich baritone of Erreig's chant encircled me and drew me back into the light of both Sun and Moon.

When I at last opened my eyes, Erreig and Bawn were rising into the smoky skies and wheeling away. A fissure high above me in Dawn Rock's pinnacle was trickling with water, but there was no new-born waterfall and the Portal was intact. My flowing blood was now staunched, but my wound was still painful and raw. I could not move my arms.

All of my servants continued to sing, and three of my guard to dance. The four others bore me to my Castle, and laid me on the high western balcony, where the music of the mermaid-harpers and the many gulls, the dolphins and the whales, my belovèd stone-finches and a chorus of great silver spiders could continue to weave their healing charms about my body in wafting music for many hours. Until my wound was calmed and soothed, closed and cleaned, and I was restored --- very swiftly, and very wondrously, in fact --- to full vigour again.

But what actually brought me to that ultimate healing was what I heard from my bed of convalescence there on the balcony of my castle. Mingled with the symphony of loving and faithful voices about me, and now rising above it, I heard the song of the Lady Ecume's Harp of Seven Eyes. The ancient mermaid sat, far below the balcony, on a sea-weedy rock, and she played for me. But as she played, she spoke --- though perhaps only in my heart and in the sea-silences between the notes of her harp.

"The amber token, Prince Leyano, I know you have received it from the King. In exchange for it I shall, one day relinquish the Black Key. But I do not request it of you now, for it will not be used to bring you, my dear Poet Leyano, back from the realm of death. The Key will indeed bring freedom from that illusion to a fairy-lord of high renown and destiny. Ah yes, it unlocks many secrets, my Key! And it is not the only secret-key in Faërie. For, like the Black Key and its amber-token, many other wonders exist. The doors of death are myriad and cunningly concealed, but the Great and Wise Ones, they know that it is all a treasure-chest-mirage, a well-disguised chimera; they possess curious keys to turn in its apocalyptic locks! The Black Key can open some, but there are doors whose keyholes differ greatly on the two sides and those are very riddling Portals, to be sure; and none are more enigmatic than the Fourth, the most secret and capricious of all. But that threshold is not for you to traverse, Moon-Prince of the Shee Mor. Another of your kin will turn the Key in <u>that</u> sacred and perilous lock. Guard preciously the token which you hold, for it will be required of you long before the time appointed for that feat."

I was able to stand then, feeling strengthened by the graceful music of her healing-harp, if not a little confused by her riddling prophecies. But when I looked down into the bay, the Lady Ecume had already departed. My force and health had returned; I was healed by sun and moon and sea and harp-song, and I still had the amber-token, safe and sound, to bring forth when it would be needed --- though its role remained a mystery to me then, and in many ways, it still does.

I knew, with no explanations or embellishments needed, that what I had now heard about the existence of the Fourth Portal was not to be shared with others --- above all not with our father. Why or how this certainty came to me, I cannot say. And why the Lady Ecume had spoken to me of it, I do not know. But now I feel sure that it is linked to *your* discovery of that hidden doorway, and to your destiny concerning it.

Leyano rose and took both his sister's hands in his, and then he laughed.

"It is many years ago, now, that first, strange encounter I had with Erreig. And behold, I have now come to know him a little better over these past five decades. But keep what I have told you today as a sacred secret, as I do still --- for the present in any case, my darling Eli: both the tale of the Dragon-Lord's sun-and-moon song and also the reference to the Fourth Portal. On your last Visit, our father and Reyse arrived here while both Erreig and Garo were with me --- and the situation was, well, very tense to say the least. The King is aware of much, and guesses more, but some things are still in the shadow of his knowing and of his royal perception and control also. For he is inhibited in his great powers of knowledge by his own fears. Do not speak of my full tale to him, for he believes that I was healed by other means."

"He believes that you sought the Black Key, do you mean, from the Lady Ecume?" Eli's voice was low, but her eyes were bright and questioning.

Leyano nodded. "Just so, and I have allowed him to continue to believe that. For another event, after I recovered from my deadly wound, enlightened me to one of the prophecies of the mermaid about the secret and splendid power of the Key over death itself --- a 'treasure-chest-mirage' death, one could say. Our father believes that the Key was in *my* possession when that mighty door was unlocked; I think he assumes that it was *me* who held it and thus used it, to release one of our brothers from his prison and to work a miracle to match the eclipse-song of Erreig. But it was not so, for I myself never presented the sacred amber-token to the ancient Lady of the mer-harpers. That mission was undertaken by Reyse, and by his courage and by the might of the Black Key one of our brothers was liberated from his bonds, in an exceedingly strange manner.

"But I really think that Reyse, or our brother himself, should tell you that story, my sweet Eli.

"So let us go and meet the musicians of the half-moon-music you have heard only at a distance so far, and then we will come back to the shallows of the Cove to dance. For rain is in the air, and before we trot back to the great Sand Castle on the backs of our *frazian* friends, we will celebrate with joyful Moon-Dancer-dancing the cloud-burst which is coming to delight us later this afternoon!"

****

A Delicate Balance

Chapter Six:
Sweet Flight into the Rainbow

he charming fairy with hair the colour of frazian ponies was one of the loveliest dancers Eli had ever seen, but there were many others, too, exuberant and graceful and laughing, transported that evening by the strange delight that the people of Aulfrin's kingdom always took in rainfall. Leyano and Eli danced with them, and --- as before, at the sign of *The Curly Crook* --- Eli found that her feet recalled even the most complicated and dizzying steps!

The cloud-burst over Half-Moon Cove was intense, but short-lived, and brother and sister returned afterwards to the interior of the pretty castle, to dine with the musicians whom Eli had met earlier. Leyano had already introduced her to many talented fairies, and they had been offered several impromptu concerts of solos, duet or trios, as they passed from room to room.

Eli had not asked any direct questions of the musicians studying and honing their gifts of healing, insight and revelation with their instruments. It was clear that the King, and she like him, used their playing to seek answers or counsel; and he had mentioned that other fairies of his realm had this custom too. But it was also clear that these players were learning to make 'moon-music', a level of mystical musicianship above Eli's present one. Though even with her more *ordinary* musical skills, Eli was certainly now becoming

A Delicate Balance

deeply curious about her own abilities to use the harp to ease pain or alleviate disease.

Following their early evening meal, while a brief twilight luminosity filled the western skies following the departure of the last of the huge clouds, Eli and Leyano rejoined their ponies and made their jogging way back to the Castle of the Prince.

They climbed the stairs to the great semi-circular balcony for a bedtime mug of mulled juice, and found Piv swaying in a small hammock stretched between two of the slender pillars framing the high windows. He started rather abruptly from his snoring as they approached.

"Good evening, Master Periwinkle," laughed Leyano. "How was your lesson in artistic sea-snail interlace?"

Piv sighed contentedly and opened one eye. "Delicious," he replied, "absolutely and exquisitely delicious..." And he snuggled down further into his cocoon-like bed, and went back to sleep again immediately.

Eli giggled at her little friend, and she and Leyano enjoyed their warming drinks as they watched the stars swiftly coming to life and the soaring arches becoming filled with the rich prussian-blue of the late-night sky.

"Good night and sweet half-moon dreams, dearest Eli," said her brother, as he kissed her forehead at the foot of the twisting staircase up to her bed-chamber. "She is just rising now, do you see?" he added, pointing to a little oval window at the far-end of the corridor, looking east. A great half-moon was creeping up the side of one of Dawn Rock's distant silhouetted pinnacles. "And tomorrow morning, as she begins her descent into the west, she will herald the arrival of our father with the Lord Reyse and your noble Peronne. Sleep well!"

Happily arrived at her tower room, Eli washed her face in a bowl of slightly gardenia-scented water and blew out the flickering candle beside it. She pulled on her comfy pyjamas and lay into her own swaying hammock. She glanced at Lily's journal, lying on a low, shell-covered table in the corner of her

Sweet Flight into the Rainbow

chamber and glowing invitingly in the soft moon-light from her own window, but she was too sleepy to read tonight.

"That's strange," she thought dreamily as she slipped into sleep. "My window faces *west* over the Sound. How is it that the notebook of my own little moon is illuminated by that pearly light?" But she was asleep before she could trouble herself with any explanation.

****

It was a magical morning.

Rising quite early, in excitement and anticipation, Eli could indeed see the half-moon high overhead as she leaned out of her open window. The zig-zag shadow of the Sand Castle was cast over the rippling waters of the triangular Bay far below, but farther out over the wide Sound the tips of the rolling waves were glinting in the mixture of the light from the high moon, the fading stars and the breaking dawn.

She dressed hurriedly, then combed her long hair and rolled it into a coil at her neck. She pinned it in place with a sturdy branch of red coral, just the same colour as her hair, and laughed to herself at the delight of being in this, her glorious 'true' life, once again, in Faërie --- and about to rediscover her own flying-horse!

As she slipped her feet into sandals woven from silver-white sea-grasses, she was still smiling, but her expression grew slightly more serious as she lifted her hand to her chest. A tightness or a tingling sensation was there, just over her heart. She had begun to feel it at the window, when she had leaned out to catch a glimpse of the half-moon.

Not one to be anxious about her health, Eli however felt a shiver of apprehension. She decided to let it pass. It was not a severe pain; it was only a tickling...

It suddenly reminded her of the feeling she had experienced in her palm, the palm of her left hand she thought, trying to remember it clearly. When was it? Ah, yes. It was when she journeyed among the wonderful rose-bushes that she had visited with her father, on their way to the Swan's Joy River on her first Visit. When he had reminded her that one of her Initiations had been passed in the company of roses, her left hand had tingled and even burned a little.

"Well, I can't imagine what would be triggering such a recollection now, and why it would involve my heart," she mused. "I will ask my father, perhaps, if the Initiation I passed among *half-moon* horses --- I think it was my second, Leyano said --- could be the reason. But why my heart? Do I have a jewel imbedded inside me?!"

Laughing to herself and shaking her head, and feeling very light-hearted once more, she added, "How lovely that I will be seeing my father this morning! How lovely to *have* a father...again. And," she added, very softly and a little coquettishly, "it's nice that Reyse is coming too."

Leyano and Piv enjoyed their large shells filled with yellow, foamy porridge and little orange fruits like physalis, but Eli's appetite was obscured by her excitement. At last, she took her delicate teacup in her hand and went to look out the western window.

The skies were a perfect robin's-egg blue and the half-moon was as fragile and white as her pretty teacup. And then she saw them!

From this distance, it looked like two enormous eagles soaring towards her from the hazy horizon of low cliffs and scattered trees on the mainland. Leyano was beside her at the window now, and thankfully too --- for he took the teacup from her hand, just before she dropped it! She continued to stare, and her turquoise eyes grew wider and wider.

Seagulls were flying in their hundreds in the near distance; they confused Eli's vision a little, but soon they blew away, it seemed, in the ocean breeze. Or perhaps they respectfully made way for the important guests who were arriving.

First, the King came into clear view. His thin silver crown with its medley of green stones glistened on his red hair. He was dressed in dark green robes and baggy trousers, flowing and flapping in the wind, and he was proudly seated on a great winged horse. Eli wondered how it could fly, it was so powerful and solid-looking! It reminded her of a Clydesdale, only even more beautiful and majestic than any of that race she had ever seen. She vaguely associated the sight of this fantastical animal with the dream she had been sent, long ago it seemed now, of the King's aerial combat with Erreig. But then she had found little time to appreciate the horse's beauty.

Its coat was a deep grey, like last evening's rain-clouds, and its long mane and tail were both coal black. Its wings were thick and wide, shaped like a bird's and densely covered in large feathers: on top they were a rich orange colour and underneath a paler hue, like the creamy yellow of Piv and Leyano's porridge at breakfast. The marvellous horse flapped its wings very, very slowly --- or held them outstretched to glide, almost motionless it seemed. Sometimes it moved its sturdy forelegs, as if swimming lazily in the currents of the air. Its hooves were a polished, shiny black and it had long, downy grey feathers on each fetlock.

But it was when she took her eyes from her father and his mount that Eli gasped, and she lifted both her hands to her flushed cheeks. Her smile was as wide and joyful as her eyes. For Reyse, riding Peronne to give back to her, had now flown up alongside the King and had even overtaken him. He had obviously decided to slowly *parade* Eli's glorious flying mount before her!

As the King swerved gracefully aside, Reyse turned Eli's amazing horse to and fro, gliding in slow motion through the sky across her field of view; and he saluted her with a hand over his heart and a reverent bow of his head. His shoulder-length brown hair, longer than he wore it when disguised in the world as Liam, was wavy and free and as it blew back from his handsome face, the white gemstones in his ear-lobes and also set into the points of his ears, caught the rays of the sun rising over the Sand Castle.

Oh, but Peronne was gorgeous! Eli wasn't too sure if she were falling in love with Reyse, but she knew immediately that she was in love with this horse!

He was the horse she had ridden in her vision in the chapel of the Abbey, but it seemed to her now that her senses had become much sharper and her vision more acute. She remembered having seen him in that 'flash-back' scene, and no doubt something deep within her remembered him from her true fairy life, but at this moment it was as if he was coming into focus for the first time --- and in that same moment of recognition, she could simultaneously feel *centuries* of loving companionship with this animal springing up into her heart.

He was only slightly smaller than the flying-horse of King Aulfrin, and every bit as muscular and proud. The colour of his coat was grey, but a much paler and softer dove-like shade than that of the King's steed, and it was decorated everywhere with small white crescents, like tiny new moons. His mane and tail were of long, fine, crimped hair --- milky white. His amply-feathered wings, which he was lifting and dropping in exaggerated adagio tempo, as if for Eli's benefit, were a mixture of many long white, yellow, pastel and medium blue feathers, above and below.

Eli looked again at Reyse, and inclining her own head in thanks she felt her face turning even rosier and her eyes shining with pleasure. He laughed with joy at her, and blew her a kiss. Peronne whinnied and nodded his chiselled head two or three times.

Her father, now too, was lifting a hand in salute and smiling gaily. Soon both riders were circling the Castle, out of view to the north, where they were coming down to land on the soft turf and grass.

It was a very happy reunion. Leyano stretched out his hand to his sister and led her, almost running, down the stairs to the northern doorway. She jogged out onto the lawn of short, springy sea-grass and embraced her father, and even bestowed a short kiss on Reyse's cheek, which was received with surprise and gratitude and returned by one on her hand. And then she walked the two or three paces to Peronne.

Even before she could wrap her arms around his broad neck, she was arrested by his eyes. Huge and deep, deep blue they were; but most startling were the starry forms pulsating at their centres. There were white ghosts of shapes far away in his eyes, where the pupils should have been, thought Eli. They were not exactly stars --- more like flowers. They reminded Eli of something, but it was lost as she closed her own eyes to hug him, her head resting against his neck, his own head pressing against her shoulder to push her even closer into him. She stepped back to look at the marvellous creature in all his beauty, and to gently stroke his velvet-grey face and muzzle.

He lifted his head for a deafening whinny and struck the ground with both his fore-hooves in quick cadence.

"Well met, and a hundred times welcome!" The words were ringing in Eli's ears and heart, but they were not spoken aloud. She understood that they came from Peronne.

"I'm so delighted to see you again, too," she replied --- also in silence. And the magical, flowery eyes winked once at her.

"Any welcome I can give will pale beside his, I suppose," laughed Aulfrin, wrapping an arm around Eli's shoulders as they all walked back towards the Castle. Peronne and the King's mount both crossed their great wings over their backs, for they had been holding them aloft and arched, rather like swans sailing on a river.

A Delicate Balance

While the horses grazed among the patches of grass and sweet herbs nearby, the company mounted a few shallow steps to a terrace with benches and a small, gurgling fountain. They sat, enjoying the view of the two handsome horses, and talking over their plans for the rest of that day, and for the days ahead.

The King offered his apologies for not being at Dawn Rock to greet his daughter, but she assured him that Leyano had entertained her royally. He then explained that he had been required to remain in Fantasie these past few days, as he had sensed movements in and around the Stone Circle which puzzled him and alerted his suspicions.

"That is a very mysterious part of my kingdom," he confided to Eli, "though it lies so near to my capital City and to the Great Trees themselves. The Trees tell me much of what passes in Faërie, if I fail to see it all in my heart or to hear news from my instruments. But even *they* have been unable to interpret what I have seen and felt concerning the Circle. I will not worry you, though, with such allusions to my royal riddles!" His voice became more relaxed once more. "You will be ready, no doubt, to rediscover the wonder of Peronne's air-borne gaits, and to be reunited with Jizay as well."

"Jizay?! Will I be able to see him again too, on this Visit?"

"Of course, my dear girl. Your hound of joy was restored to you on your first Visit, and he will be here to accompany you on your adventures for the remaining two as well. On this, your second Visit, Peronne joins him, and that shall allow you greater scope of discovery and the possibility to venture further afield."

As he concluded, her father furrowed his brow and raised a finger in admonition --- but in playfulness as well. "I'm a little anxious about giving you *too* much freedom, as you are such a head-strong and untameable child, my sweet Eli. But this is another reason why I grant you the continued company of Jizay: with him, you will not *fly off in all directions*. He can run swiftly, but he cannot fly! Therefore, perhaps you will be somewhat restrained and prudent in your flights."

Eli laughed her agreement to this slight restriction. "I'll be very obedient and go only where you allow," she announced.

The King shook his head, almost sadly. "Ah, I would not ask you to change your nature so completely," he intoned, and then chuckled merrily. "But I will perhaps attempt to suggest certain limits, and hope that --- as you are not yet the Princess Mélusine again --- you will make the effort to respect them for the seventeen days remaining to you here, for this sojourn as a still *mostly*-human woman.

"In any case," he concluded, "for the next few days, it will be a 'guided' tour, and so I require you to stay with me, for we have important things to see and interesting folk to meet.

"Now, Reyse and I have not yet breakfasted, as we left the Silver City before dawn, so if my kind son Leyano has kept a little of his tasty tide-porridge out of the reach of Periwinkle, we will be grateful to eat as we discuss our plans. Then we will be fortified to embark on the first leg of our journey!"

Piv, in fact, had remained in the breakfast room, evidently sure that everyone would return there eventually. He had certainly not gone hungry while awaiting them, but there were still enough of all the delicacies of Leyano's table to satisfy the two newly arrived guests, and a hot pot of strong tea to share with the entire company.

****

With a small travel-bag slung across her back, containing Lily's journal and some light provisions, Eli left the Golden Sand Castle of Leyano to take to the skies with her father. For just an instant her joy was clouded by the fact that Reyse was staying behind with her brother and Piv. Eli noted, inwardly, the little thrill of sadness that this generated, and wondered if her heart was not awakening, more and more, to this fine fairy-lord.

A Delicate Balance

But Reyse assured her that they would meet again during her Visit. The days ahead were filled with excursions around the province of Vivony, according to the King's explanations, but in a week or so they would be going to the City of Fantasie, and Reyse hoped to be there at that time as well. Although Eli's head was swimming with questions and curiosity, she had decided to simply take this Visit as it came, and allow her rediscovery of Faërie to unfold before her, step by step.

Well, not exactly *steps*, as far as today's trip was concerned in any case: for now she was standing beside her glorious winged-horse, ready to mount and to actually *fly*! Reyse helped her up onto Peronne's comfortable back, and she braced her thighs under his pinion-feathers, as she recalled from her vision. Or perhaps it was just a natural movement, a habit recalled from all the years of such sky-rides.

Her eyes met Reyse's for an instant; she breathed deeply, but they said nothing to one another --- at least, not aloud.

And then Eli leaned slightly forward over Peronne's withers, buried her fingers in his crinkly mane and opened her hands on his strong neck, tightened her legs against his sides and nodded once to her father, mounted beside her on his dark grey steed.

A graceful bound forward, and Peronne's hooves danced just one measure of a short, quick cantering rhythm on the turf, and then he folded his forelegs as if to jump a small obstacle, and rose into the air like the lightest of garden song-birds.

Eli could hardly breathe. But she could definitely smile! The feathers of his mighty wings brushed her legs, covered in fine cloth leggings, and her loose tunic of deep blue embroidered fabric billowed about her and rippled in the warm wind.

Aulfrin had told her that they would be flying over the Sound in a north-westerly diagonal, up to the mouth of the Queen's Ride River. From there, they would sail over the coastal plains and make for the region known as the Singing Hives. This was a voyage of about ninety miles, and would take them only a little more than an hour-and-a-half, even flying gently, as the sea-breeze was at their backs.

Eli now looked over at her father, flying beside her at a distance of about four or five yards, and smiled even more broadly with a contented sigh. The King's eyes were sparkling with green light, and he pointed down to the Sound, about twenty-five yards beneath them. Seals and dolphins were swimming along with them, barking and singing now and then, and obviously --- Eli was sure --- wishing them *bon voyage*!

But in only a few minutes, they had left the happy creatures in the deep blue Sound behind, as the two horses climbed even higher into the bright morning sky.

Tears of joy were streaming down Eli's cheeks as the horses alighted in a field of high grasses and long-stemmed flowers, twenty miles or so inland from the sandy beaches which ran all along the rocky, wooded coast. She dismounted and hugged Peronne, with no words --- silent or spoken --- even possible, and then she turned to Aulfrin. He gathered her into his arms, wordlessly as well, and his long green cloak blew around them. As Eli felt the slight charge of scintillating energy criss-crossing her back, she turned her head to lay her cheek on her father's chest, just over his heart.

And suddenly, lines of poetry came softly into her memory:

I must fly home.

I long to hide my face in my father's robes,
And weep and weep...

Her own poem, her own words, written from the shadows of her human youth, from the 'daze-dance' of her changeling life. Now she was indeed weeping, her face hidden in the robes of her father, whom she thought she had lost forever. And they were not tears of woe or of shame or of tragedy. They were tears of gratitude and wonder and joy.

She had left the grey ghosts of the human-lands, and now she was riding home. Home. On wind-horse feet.

For here, among grey ghosts
Wandering in a daze-dance
Below the kittenish clouds,
My flight is hindered,
My path obscured.

I must ride home.
To the silver turrets of Fantasie
I must turn again my wind-horse-feet,

And homeward run,
To the arms of my moon
And my sun.

Eli could not slow the river of tears for many minutes, but Aulfrin shared her deep emotion and perhaps even cried a little himself.
****

For that day and the next three, Eli and her father explored, together, much of Vivony. They visited the Singing Hives first of all, a collection of bee-busy fields and what one might almost have called 'villages' --- filled with bees and bee-loving-fairies --- boasting wicker and wooden hives in generous cone-shapes of all possible sizes, and huts and houses here and there among the tall, delicate trees and abundant, flowery bushes, built in very similar bee-hive fashion.
　　Then they flew north, surrounded by swarms of bees pleased to be flying with them, to other apicultural colonies living in the high hollows of white-limbed trees. These were the giant rainbow-bees, several of whom Eli had already encountered in

the gardens of Castle Davenia: they were gaily and crazily striped in every combination of colour imaginable! Living with them, under the smooth, pale-barked trees, were the rabbit-folk, for this was their principal community in the realm of Faërie. Eli had never seen so many rabbits in all her life: it was a riotous and gorgeous sight.

Aulfrin told her that it was here that Brocéliana had made her first Initiation, when only eleven. From the kind and wise rabbits she had received the light blue tourmalines that graced her ear-lobes, he said, and also a deep and calm philosophy of life. It would, he added, no doubt help her to navigate the difficult passage back into the human world, when Eli returned to her rightful place as the Princess Mélusine and her sister would be called to return to the place of her own birth.

Eli nodded, but her heart was filled with other layers of concern for her dear half-sibling; for not only was Brocéliana's happiness threatened by Eli's ultimate decision to re-inhabit her fairy-form, but now there was also the complication of the deep love she shared with Garo, son of Erreig and heir to the Sage-Hermit. Yes, Brocéliana would be needing the calm philosophy of all the enlightened teachers of this enchanted world --- or any other --- in order to sail the high seas that lay before her.

They had continued their peregrinations north and east, still and ever in the territory of the bees of Vivony, where the largest populations of this sacred creature had their various kingdoms --- or rather queendoms! In the centre of the province's wide peninsula were the Golden Honey Woods, home to trees that Eli had never met in the human world. They were akin to oaks in their growth, their girth, and even the shape of their leaves; but those leaves were huge --- sometimes eight or ten inches long --- and veined in rich gold. And often they seemed to be waving or rustling without the aid of any wind. Vines crowded with flowers, and also with bunches of pink berries which hung like clusters of grapes, twined around the boles of these trees and at their feet were numerous families of brown mushrooms spotted with round blue bobbles and often half-concealing gnome-like dozing faces on the stems beneath their caps.

Following the same trajectory, Eli and the King finally arrived, on the afternoon of the third day of their voyage and the sixth day since Eli's arrival at Dawn Rock, at the delta of the Bee Streams. These were some of the branching arms of the river which rose in the Honey Woods and flowed either east to the Coombes at the top of Sea-Horse Bay, or north to this windy land of slow streams and running rivulets, just beside the greater estuary that opened into the Coloured Cove a little further to the west. But the delta where they landed, after having circled on their flying-horses above the creeks and firths, had its own small bay as well. This inlet was like a wonderful, heather-clad, Scottish loch.

The King told Eli that this region of streams and gorges was the furthest point to the north in all of mainland Faërie; only the great cliffs of Scholar Owl Island and of course its far northern isles and skelligs, were equally as boreal. Eli listened to his words, but her own heart murmured a contradiction: "There is another place, and it is also part of Faërie, and yet it lies even further into the coldest currents. It is the Garnet Vortex and the Fourth Portal, and *we* have been there. Peronne and I have ...." But the strangely impassioned voice in her head was interrupted by her father's gentler one.

"Too Far Cove, that is the name we give to this marvellous place. And it is true, for it is *too far* for us to come without pausing for refreshment! Here is hidden the home of someone I would like you to meet again, and I wonder if it will stir memories for you, my dear Eli. For when you were twenty, you undertook your final Initiation not far from here, and the lovely being who guided you on that occasion still lives here in Vivony. We will sup with her tonight, and sleep in her mansion. Come!"

A small, squarish appendage of stony cliff protruded into the noisy, crashing waves of Too Far Cove. The two sides of the Cove continued out in widening arms of blue-grey rock and purple heathers, but on this promontory stood the only dwelling Eli could see anywhere on this wind-swept and dramatic coastline.

A 'mansion' her father had called it, but it looked to Eli more like an old-fashioned English cottage or modest country-house, rather like a vicarage! It seemed much too humble and refined for such a spectacular location, in fact. Eli would have expected a foreboding fortress, rather than this quaint and peaceful-looking abode.

There was a lynch-gate covered in climbing red roses, and the two-storied thatched house had many prettily curtained lattice windows with over-flowing flower-boxes of petunias and pansies. The garden pathways were lined with lobelia and campanula, and behind them plants, bushes and tall flowers jostled for place: delphiniums and hollyhocks, fuchsias and scented stocks, geraniums and tiger-lilies, and many roses of all colours and styles. A small, bubbling fountain and a frog-pond were just visible beyond a mass of honesty and black-eyed rudbeckia-daisies. Bees and butterflies were everywhere, as well as rabbits and cats, hedgehogs and weasels, mice and field-rats, songbirds and hens who all mingled and moved about, relaxed and contented.

But the greatest wonder and delight for Eli was to come. For the top half of the double door was open, and a white-haired woman as charming and gentle as her garden leaned over it, smiling at the visitors coming up her path. She opened the lower part of the door as they approached, and there beside her was Jizay! Eli knelt as she had at their first meeting in Demoran's Castle weeks before, and her hound of joy charged up to her, barking in giddy delight, and leapt into her open arms.

When the kissing and face-licking and barking and laughing had finally ceased, Eli rose and regarded the beautiful woman-fairy at the open door. Her father led her closer, and introduced her, though Eli could have said the words in unison with him.

"Banvowha, the fairy of the rainbow, the guide and protector for your final Initiation. She awarded you the precious gems that you, as Mélusine, wear in the lobes of your pointed ears."

Eli was overjoyed, and confused, and humbled and at peace --- all at once. She bowed to the fairy, greeted her politely, and then mumbled almost to herself, "I have *pointed* ears? Do I really? And what *are* the precious stones set into their lobes?"

Banvowha laughed, and it was the most musical laughter Eli had ever heard. "A blue and a red," she replied, tilting her head in tender appreciation of seeing Eli's joyful face once again, and now laying a warm hand on her former-student's cheek in a very maternal gesture. "A sapphire in the right ear-lobe, and a garnet in the left."

Eli's eyes opened wide as she heard the word 'garnet', but she did not ask any further questions. The rainbow-fairy's eyes flashed suddenly, but then returned just as quickly to their calm tenderness.

"Do come in, please," she said to them both, and to Jizay. The horses had remained beyond the enclosed garden, roaming happily over the heath. Inside the welcoming and well-appointed home, Eli was pleased to met Ferglas as well. The huge blue wolf-hound walked up to her, bowed his regal head to receive Eli's hand in a short caress, and then greeted her in his silent, but rich and chocolaty, voice: "It is a great pleasure to meet you once again, Your Highness. Welcome home for your second Visit."

Eli smiled and inclined her own head slightly to the regal dog, who seemed to smile back at her. The collar of white and pastel-green seashells around his neck jingled like tiny bells as he turned and took his place beside the chair of his master, the King.

The large, round tea-time table was beautifully laid, and Eli was not at all surprised to find delicacies resembling crumpets served with jam, and a rich cream of some kind as well to spread on them. She wondered if the 'cream' was really that, for she had seen no cows anywhere either on this or her previous Visit. Perhaps it was made from sheep's-milk, she thought, for she had eaten a sheep's-cheese at the *Inn of the Curly Crook*. In any case, milk or cheese seemed to be a great rarity, as far as she could tell, here in Faërie.

As they ate and sipped their floral tea, Eli studied the face of Banvowha. She felt that her eyes were playing tricks on her, or that the light refracted from the lattice-panes and the rows of tiny prisms hung from coloured threads against them had affected her ability to focus clearly on the fairy-woman's utterly ageless countenance and mounds of wavy snow-white hair. But everything else in the room, rather cluttered but with elegant taste --- like a Victorian home decorated in the Pre-Raphaelite style --- was clear and distinct.

What she *could* discern was that Banvowha was smiling rather knowingly at her. Eli wondered if she should address their lovely hostess directly with her questions, or if she should wait to be spoken to. But, with a somewhat full mouth, it was the King who spoke first.

"I am pleased to find the hounds here, my gentle Banvowha. I wondered that we did not see them, and the rest of the company, running beneath us as we flew north. They took another route, perhaps. And the riders, they are not still here?"

Eli looked at her father as he spoke, questioning him a little with her eyes. He added, replying to her unspoken queries before the fairy-woman answered his own.

"I knew that we would be rejoined by Ferglas and Jizay at some point, but I did not know exactly where! They have been travelling with certain *chevaliers* of Demoran's household, patrolling --- one could say --- the northern parts of the realm."

Banvowha answered and elaborated upon the King's explanations: "The company of moon-dappled horses and their joyous riders arrived late yesterday afternoon, Your Majesty. Many hounds were with them, and many deer following too. Several great stags were among the cavalcade, also. It was a pleasure to have them all here to dine and to dance, making merry music far into the night. They departed today at mid-morning, galloping off towards the Coombes, with Curious Cove as their destination for this evening. Only noble Ferglas and golden Jizay remained behind, to await your arrival with me."

"Excellent," nodded the King, taking another crumpet and smiling as Banvowha poured him more tea. "And as I have had no disquieting word from Corr Seylestar, I assume that they found nothing amiss in the lands they passed through to come here to you?"

"Nothing," she confirmed. "They were one and all in good spirits, and I heard no shadows of worry in their hundred bright voices. The great stags, always very vigilant, were in particularly gleeful mood and their set-dances with their friends the hounds were boisterous and carefree!"

Eli could not contain her perplexity longer. "A hundred voices?! But your home, though very lovely, is not immense, dear Lady Banvowha. Where did a *hundred* fairies and all their dogs and attendant deer find to dance and feast here?"

The rainbow-fairy's laughter was even more wonderful and warm than before. Hearing it, Eli had to laugh too.

Banvowha shook her head slightly, still with a broad smile, as she said, "You are Eli, and not my protégée Mélusine yet. You have forgotten my teachings, and my nature; but it will be restored to you, in the end.

"All that you see with your human vision is conjured in your own mind's eye, and you paint pretty, or fearsome, pictures on a white canvas with the brush of your limited perceptions and distorted expectations. That is quite normal, my dear. My home on this rocky outcrop of cliff and heather is, in its true nature, nothing like what you are seeing. You wear the playful glasses of your own projections springing up from all of your life's experiences. But not from the Truth. Not yet.

"This is not to say that you are not --- perhaps --- a little surprised by my quaint cottage --- or that you might not have prefered another style of dwelling. But you see with the state of your *heart* and *mind*, as they are now ... They colour the visions possible for you; they fill your eyes with fleeting clouds, as it were.

"The company of fairy-riders and their beautiful beasts, who feasted and danced here last evening, were received into another perception of my 'reality': a vast mead-hall, well-suited to their own needs and desires and personal images of themselves --- as this snug and picturesque cottage is to yours, my dear Eli. But I live in neither of those architectural fancies.

"My *demeure* is the expectant ivory-white of the canvas upon which anyone may paint. Mine is the sombre sky alive with glistening rain-drops or the pale one filled with balmy sun-light; mine is also the blue-grey of the cloud-page where the rainbow is drawn. Mine, too, the invisible stars of day-time, the infinity of unimaginable hue and tint, all the tones of the colours of creation. You came to me to learn this way of seeing and perceiving, and you loved the endless and ultimate Truth so deeply that you chose --- two-hundred-and-fifty years later --- to brave the sublime challenges and ordeals of the Great Charm. Your thirst for ultimate Truth, in fact, was so *passionate* that it drove other *passions* to the margins of your life.

"But you will turn your attention to them at last, my courageous Mélusine. Maybe now, maybe later. For those passions are still there, hidden in the hedgerows that border your path."

"What passions did I push aside?" asked Eli, the house and the tea-table and even her father and the dogs fading as she seemed to fall headlong into the multi-coloured eyes of the wondrous white fairy-woman.

Banvowha's voice was almost chanting now. "Love, Eli. Love. But of what kind? For there are many loves. There is the love of a small child, of a shining little Princess for her royal father. There is the love between siblings: the love of that same little girl for a brother, a half-brother, a half-sister.... or for a mother who is not a mother, but only the dream of a mother. And there is love for her true and mystical, enchanted mother. Or for a lover...

"Yes, there is the love of the heart of a high and regal woman. You knew well the flame of passion, and your heart was alight with it. But the passion for the Truth does not necessarily exclude the passion for a lover --- that passion which is the true and great love of your hesitant but romantic heart. The white flame is a lily, but the red flame is a rose. Which are you, truly and in Truth, Mélusine? For there are lilies and roses, magical queens and wild-eyed princesses, kings and princes, lords and lovers; there are male and female, husband and wife, brother and sister, father and mother, sun and moon, summer and winter, and dawn and dusk...."

Banvowha's voice became so soft and whispery that Eli could no longer discern the words. But words of her own were now floating into her mind, and she could not stop them from being formed on her lips. "Colm," she murmured. "I can't remember loving him, because I hurt him too much. I have lost the memory of our life together and all of our romance. And Yves? Surely that was not love --- *or was it*? What was I seeking? What was I learning? Was I in love, or in fear? Why that monstrous experience, and why others? And...." Eli's voice was choked with tears and her hand was covering her heart, which seemed to be ready to burst. "And...Reyse. Did I love him, long ago *here*, or did I in the world? Did I truly love Liam? Do I love him now?"

The chanting, humming voice was there again. "The Lord Reyse sought your love for the first time when you were only eighteen. You rode with him in your second Initiation, with the horses of the half-moon. You won a small, cloudy-white moonstone --- like those in Reyse's ears --- and it was set into the tender skin over your heart."

Eli clutched more desperately at her chest, for it was like the point of a tiny knife driving into her breast. But no, even as she covered her heart with her left hand, there was no longer any pain. None at all. It was not a knife, but the opening of a flower, or of an entire field of flowers. Starry white lilies and heady red roses were bursting into bloom, in her heart, as Banvowha spoke.

"You refused him then, Mélusine. And you refused him over a century later, in the year 1500 --- and his suit then was very ardent. You refused him as kindly as you could, but firmly. And his sorrow was so great that he pleaded with powers far, far away to host him in his own Great Charm. For three-hundred-and-thirty-three years he sought to escape his heart-break and to soar beyond the pain, as an eagle might. But you were both his sun and his moon. And he could not forsake you in his longing and his love."

The voice stopped. And Eli cried and her chest heaved with the sobs. No one spoke, but Jizay at last stepped up to her, and laid his great golden head on her lap.

Many minutes had passed when Banvowha spoke again, but now in a clear and bright voice, as if nothing had happened at all.

"Walk on the heath with Jizay, my dear, and the sea-wind will refresh you. Do not think overmuch. Love is always there; it never ends and never disappears. You cannot elude it. But it does not require thought, only peace. Be at peace, and walk by the sea. Ferglas and I must speak with the King."

Eli rose and dried her eyes with her pristine white serviette. She sighed and then she smiled. She felt that a tempestuous and sudden rain-shower had caught her unawares and drenched her to the skin, but that the sun had reappeared now and dried her in an instant. Jizay went with her to the door, and she took her long cloak from the peg where she had hung it.

Beyond the charming house and garden, a swaying rope bridge spanned the gorge of the dancing river that flowed into Too Far Cove on the right of the promontory. They crossed this, Eli and her hound of joy, and wandered wordlessly and in great peace indeed, with very few thoughts, along the cliff-walk.

Looking far off into the northern seas, Eli watched the distant swell becoming individual waves which galloped in slow-motion towards the shore. Some were small and cheeky, some towering and impressive. But in her imagination all were crested with white horses, moon-dappled horses; and all were sparkling in the sunbeams that slanted through the high-mounded clouds far off in the west.

In fact, the entire rippling and rolling carpet of the water's surface seemed to be sprinkled with white moonstones, like starry flowers, glistening and winking at her.

****

Chapter Seven:
Yellow Writing on a Red Page

Eli did not see Banvowha again that evening, nor the following morning.

She was glad, in a way, to be alone with her father and the two dogs. The rainbow-fairy seemed to know so much of her heart, of her fears and weaknesses, of what lay behind and before, and of what was hidden on either side of her path, that Eli felt thankful and somehow less exposed without her there. It was clear that she was no longer in the house, the moment that Eli had returned from her long stroll with Jizay. The energy was different: rather empty and less colourful, but also less scrutinising and all-seeing!

A fire burned in the decorative grate surrounded by small, painted tiles, and there was hot soup and fresh bread for their supper. Although high summer in Faërie, as in the world, this northern coast was wind-wracked and chilly at night. The sound of the waves feathering their spray up the high cliffs was like thunder.

But Eli's mood was peaceful as she retired to her upstairs bedroom decorated with busily-painted murals of pink dog-roses and interlaced convolvulus and a strange *trompe-l'oeil* window in the southern wall. This 'false' window presented an almost lovelier view than the opposite sea-ward gable one. It was small but very realistically painted, with a golden-flowered vine climbing in over the convincing perspective of the window-sill and a mass of silver leaves framing the landscape beyond. It was a simple scene, with a winding river and a distant wood. There seemed to be a castle half-hidden among the line of trees, but it was very far-off and shadowy.

Eli yawned as she undressed, slipped into a long nightdress and then under the fluffy quilted coverlet of the high bed. An oil-lamp with an opaque globe stood on the bedside table, and she decided to read a little of Lily's journal before she slept.

Sitting up in bed, propped against two over-stuffed pillows, she opened the notebook almost reverently.

With my Eli gone on a holiday to Ireland this summer, I feel more grateful than ever to have the visits of Sean. He has come to me twice already since Eli went to Cork in late June; he knows that I am a bit lonely without her. She has not travelled so far afield before, not out of the country like this. I suppose this is the first time she's really had the money to do so.

It's a pity that we could not have afforded holidays as she grew up: she's twenty-two now, so it's high time that she spreads her wings a little. In any case, she'll be back to me and our little Brentwood home in a fortnight or so now.

How glad I am that we could at last leave our shabby lodgings in the east of this swarming city of Los Angeles. Although that old converted garage-house was blessed, for me, by being the place where Sean first came back to me, it is much better to be in this modest but much more comfortable home. Eli's brilliance at school paid-off for us: with grades that won her a scholarship to a beautiful little private college just up the road from us here --- not far from the canyon where she was born, in fact. Well, no, not her. Of course, that was our daughter Brocéliana who was actually 'born' there. But my changeling fairy-daughter, my belovèd Eli, came to me that night --- and so, for me, it's her birth-date too.

This cottage is even smaller than the one Sean and I had for those first precious couple of years here in America, when we were together --- awaiting our child and then watching her grow and delighting in her first steps and first words! Yes, that was a charming little home, but this one is nice too; and how lucky I am that Eli, although really an adult now, has chosen to remain here with me rather than renting a place of her own. I know it won't last forever, that situation; I'm enjoying it while I may. With the publication last year of the little book of poems by dear Leo --- which I illustrated with Sean's help and suggestions --- I'm in greater demand as an artist, and now my income has improved to the point where I can afford this rent, so Eli can save what she is able to earn in order to travel and perhaps move, one day very soon most probably, back to the 'Old World' where she dreams of living.

It's been ten years now that my Sean has been back in my life. Ten years since that first miraculous visit heralded by sweet, brown-eyed Leo. Ten years that I have kept this a secret from my Eli. I wonder, does she guess that I entertain a mysterious visitor behind her back?! I think not... She is very forthright, and if she had an inkling that I was seeing anyone, I'm sure she would tickle the information out of me! And I'm quite certain that she does not guess her own true fairy-identity, nor imagine for an instant that her father is living.

I turned sixty this year, last January. Sean told me that I look as young as when we met, but he has not lost his beguiling Irish charm and his way with the ladies! Indeed, all his former allure is intact, including the irresistible attraction he holds for me as a man.

I found it strange, at first, that we did not make love, did not fly into each other's arms to taste, again, the passion and the complicity and the bliss we had known as husband and wife. I wondered if we would; I wondered for the first two or three or four visits.... But then, as we kissed one day --- I think it was easily a year after he had begun to come to me, probably his fifth or sixth visit (I must look back and see if I wrote about it then) --- as we kissed, long and tenderly, I simply knew. I knew we could not love again. I knew that it was me, in fact, who was holding back. And I was right to do so.

I believe it was what Sean had told me, oh only on his second visit I'm sure, of his true life as the King of Faërie. He has other children, not just Eli (who is called the Princess Mélusine there) and Leo (who is called Prince Leyano). There are two other sons as well. When I asked him if he had a wife in his kingdom too, he explained the situation to me. She had had an affair with a lesser chieftain of some kind --- many centuries ago --- and she was banished for her crime.

*I love Sean with all my heart, just as I did when he was my darling husband; but now that I know about his true life, I cannot **not** know. He is married to another woman, though she is living in exile in some other part of his fairy-land. But he is married nonetheless.*

*Now, it isn't a prudish question of sin, of infidelity, of adultery, or of scandal. It's more complicated and subtle than that in my heart. My Eli, my own dear Eli, well, she is **not** my daughter, not the daughter of my flesh and blood. She is the daughter of the Queen of Faërie. And my Eli is a glorious girl, and now a very wonderful young woman. I see a great deal of Sean in her, but I also see other traits, other gifts, other qualities. Do some of them come from her true mother? If so, then she must be very lovely, very splendid.*

And I wonder if this queen of fairy-land misses Sean, her husband, as I missed him when we were first sundered. I wonder if she still loves him, as I do. I wonder if her heart is aching, or broken.

*It is a blessing and a miracle for me, of course, that Sean can come to me here, come to visit me from his fairy-home and stay with me for an hour or an afternoon. But his real life is **there** in his kingdom. He is not just 'my Sean'; he is a King and the head of a family, and the husband of the Queen. He is not **my** lover any longer, grateful as I am to be with him sometimes.*

*This situation is very strange; but it is very, very beautiful too. I have Eli, and I have Sean sometimes, and my life is rich and full. I am very happy. We are not here on earth on some sort of merry holiday --- we are here to grow and to learn, to strive back towards God, because from here we can see Him and long for Him, and **choose** to strive. I don't ask for any superficial happiness out of life; I ask for <u>true</u> happiness: the joy of knowing --- in the end --- that I have journeyed well, and far, and courageously, not **accepting** what comes but **welcoming** it --- because all that comes, comes for a reason, and the source of that reason is always, always Love.*

And so I choose to <u>welcome</u> this fantastical story that is happening to me.

Love is a little word, but it contains a whole dictionary!
I'm happy to learn as many of its meanings as I can, while I'm here. And one of them seems to be akin to "releasing", something about letting loved ones go. I let Yann go when he died --- oh so young; and at his death I let Sean go too. Now I must let him go once more, in another sense, to be who and what he really is. As I must let Eli go, too, to voyage and to discover herself and her own path...without me clinging onto her.

*But, though it might be about **letting go**, love is never really about **loss**. That is <u>not</u> one of its definitions! So, my Eli, I will always be with you, although we are parted in space or in time. Love is endless, just as it is beginning-less.*

And it is noble and worthy of respect; and so our loves, and our romances, must be filled with <u>respect</u>. I'm respecting love itself in my realisation that I cannot, again, be Sean's lover. And he feels that too, I'm sure, and knows why. For the love we feel in our hearts isn't just for our lovers; I can also offer my love to the wife of Sean, as I offer it to her daughter: her princess and my Eli.

*Eli, always **respect** love, please. I'm not asking you to have old-fashioned ideals of proper conduct or to be stuffy or puritanical or full of that dreadful word 'no'! I'm asking that you be chaste in the purity of <u>pure respect</u>: to yourself, to your lover, to all who cross your path. Don't love only with your head, or your body. Love with your heart and soul, for with those you will never enter into dishonesty, to another or to yourself.*

Eli lifted Lily's journal, still open, to press it against her heart. She blinked a tear out of her eye, and tucked a wayward strand of her greying red hair behind her ear. She looked across the room in the milky light of the oil-lamp. And she smiled at the pleasant little scene in the painted, false window.

And as she looked, in a light that was --- it's true --- dim and uneven, she saw a new element in the woodland painting. She was sure it had <u>not</u> been there before.

A Delicate Balance

She rose, still hugging Lily's notebook, and walked almost on tip-toe to the southern wall. There was no question about it now.

At the eaves of the distant wood, peaking out from the line of dark trees beside the half-concealed castle, was a tiny unicorn. A lily-white unicorn. It was meticulously painted, for it was very small in the scene but every strand of its crinkly mane was finely indicated, and its eye was very bright. Its long, spiral horn was the same silver as the leaves around the window-frame. Only now it was shining, more and more.

Ah! there was the source of the new light: behind the single turret of the silhouetted castle was the moon. But that hadn't been there before either! It was a full moon, and Eli was sure that she would have noticed *that*. It was so real that its pearly beams were illuminating the horn of the unicorn --- quite impossibly...

More and more incredible. More and more wonderful. The moon was rising, inching almost imperceptibly (but more quickly than was realistic) up over the forest, moving from left to right in a graceful course across the sky of the *trompe l'oeil* landscape. And as it climbed into the sky, and Eli looked on in astounded silence and delight, the unicorn came out from the margins of the woods and cantered around in the foreground of the painting.

Eli watched the scene for many minutes, and at last the moon's trajectory took it out of view behind the silver leaves. She followed its final glint before it was altogether gone, and then looked back down to find that the unicorn was also departed from the scene.

A long sigh escaped her lips, and then a broad smile occupied them. Jizay's head was pressed against her thigh, and his tail was wagging as she stoked his golden coat and went with him back to the bed. He curled up on the rug as she slipped back under the quilt, placing Lily's journal on the bedside table and turning down the lamp before sleeping.

****

In the morning, when Eli arose early and descended the carpeted staircase to the ground floor of the house, she found everything already changing. Her father was, of course, still there, and so was Ferglas. And there was a mug of excellent tea and a large slice of seed-bread toasted over the fire and spread with a jam or marmalade of a bitter red fruit that Eli could not identify but found delicious. But the house itself had clearly begun to change.

Aulfrin chuckled at his daughter's confused expression, and then they laughed together.

"This is what Banvowha meant, I suppose," smirked Eli, shaking her head. "I project my expectations or my desires to create my reality. And now, half-awake and ready for the next step of our journey, I've already released the Victorian country-house mirage I had conjured up?!"

The King straightened-up from toasting another thick slice of bread over the tiny, crackling fire --- which immediately seemed to die down into barely glowing embers as he moved away from it and back to the table. He broke the toasted bread in half and they shared it and the remaining marmalade, the light increasing as the morning brightened outside, even with the fire now thoroughly extinguished.

"Not quite, but almost," retorted her father. "Appearances, Eli. Superficial appearances. Sometimes we create them entirely; sometimes we distort them or mask them or colour them as if we were looking at a painting through tinted glass. But beyond all the forms and mirages there remains the white canvas which Banvowha referred to. *That* is not a mirage --- but we rarely see it; or at least, we rarely see *just* that.

"I think I saw the house as you saw it yesterday, but perhaps not. Perhaps I saw what *I* wished to see, expected to see, <u>thought</u> that *you* were seeing...! While Banvowha spoke of the half-moon riders, I saw the mead-hall, but I was not sitting in it in the present with you. And when you and Jizay were walking along the cliffs, I did not see the house at all, one could say, for I was deep in silent conversation with the rainbow-fairy and with my wise blue wolf-hound. The canvas was simply white."

Ferglas rose from his place on the hearth-rug and came to his master, his tail swishing and his collar of shells jingling as he moved.

"Ah! you are right, my sensible dog," nodded the King. "Time to go now. We have much to see and visit today, and a long flight ahead of us to reach even our *first* destination."

"Well, I'm ready to go…anywhere!" affirmed Eli, finishing her tea and rising with the King to walk to the double-door, take down their cloaks, and walk out into the garden. Eli glanced back before they closed the door. The house behind them was simple and bare, uncluttered and very peaceful. It was not the well-appointed, rather busily-decorated interior of yesterday; it was even lovelier. Eli thought it looked a little like a church or a meditation-and-yoga room.

As she turned to cross the garden, she shook her head yet again: only grasses. A lovely, clean, dewy lawn stretching to an opening in a low, stone wall. No flower-beds, no lynch-gate, no scurrying animals, no roses. Kittiwakes called overhead and the ocean roared and carolled when its white, lacy waves peeped up over the cliff-edge, as each breaker arrived with immeasurable energy against the promontory.

Her little shoulder-bag, containing Lily's journal, was safely held against her back under her cloak, itself tied with a soft cord around her waist. Her father's long green cape billowed out behind him in the sea-wind. Pink morning clouds were rolling across the sky high over Too Far Cove as the two majestic winged-horses walked into view from behind a mass of great, grey rocks to the left. They stopped by the low wall, stretching their feathery wings in the strong breeze and pawing the sparse grass.

"What about the dogs?" asked Eli, looking first at Jizay and then at her father.

"*We* have over two hundred miles to fly this morning," replied Aulfrin. "But they will not arrive at our destination by the same circuitous sky-road that we take, for they go by a much more direct path across the land, and they travel with good speed. I don't doubt that they will catch us up this afternoon, unless they go off on their own adventures *en route*! In any case, they have expressed their intention to be with us no later than this evening, at the Sea Goose, the furthest of the White Willow Isles from here. That is where we are headed."

"Those are the Isles you mentioned on my last Visit, I remember. It's the place where I was educated as a child, and where my tutor, Reyse, lost me one day when I wandered off and saw a ....unicorn!"

"Quite so," Aulfrin assented. "We return today to the lands you knew as a very young fairy, the Isles carved out by the meandering course of the River Nazzy as it flows from Shooting Star Lake to the sea. The largest, and closest, is just at the tip of Blue Harpers' Bay, and that's already one hundred and fifty miles' flight. But merely a couple of hours, by wind-blown winged-horse. A short pause there, and then on to the Sea Goose, the Isle so named because it resembles the head of a goose at one end, and a curling fish's tail at the other. More a mer-goose, I suppose!

"Now, are you ready to take flight?"

"With pleasure!" laughed Eli, kissing Jizay's head and then using the stone wall to mount Peronne. Just to make her catch her breath, she imagined, her father trotted his mount to the very precipice of the cliffs and took off over the roaring and dramatic waves. Of course, she and Peronne followed, but Eli found she had to close her eyes tight as they left the ground and rose into the eye of the wind. Only when they had circled and flown back over the heath with its gorges and rushing streams could she breathe somewhat normally once again and open her eyes to look in wonder and gratitude at the unfolding landscape far beneath her.

Later that afternoon they arrived, as planned, at Sea Goose Isle, and the two great dogs were indeed already there to greet them.

Of course, Eli and the King had spent a long while on the other two White Willow Isles downstream and much further to the north, where they had landed at mid-morning. They had wandered for several hours there, enjoying the many different varieties of willow and the many birds living among their graceful branches. And the Isles were, truly, *white*, both in the colour of the trees' bark and also in the strange soil of all the terrain. Eli had never seen such a light shade of earth --- if earth it was. It looked more like the colour of fine and fired clay.

She had finally inquired from whence came its hue, and the King had explained that the Isles were filled with many thousands of years' accumulation of the white earth (not at all clay or sand, but truly soil) that was washed downstream from Shooting Star Lake. The fairy-tradition was that it was dyed, at the bottom of the deep Lake, by the light of stars, especially falling stars! Eli laughed, but she found the idea very lovely all the same.

There were dozens of types of willows growing here, if one counted all three of the Isles, according to the King. They saw a multitude of distinct sub-families on the greater of the two northern Isles, but on the smallest islet, lying just over a leaping stream at the north-west extremity of the major island, there were almost exclusively crazy curly-willows. These had twisted, almost spiralling leaves hanging down from equally convoluted twigs and branches, coiled like corkscrews.

More and more wonderful it was, for Eli, to see wood-sprites and peeping faces and quick-flitting miniature fairies here and there. This was the proof for her that she was surely much more 'fairy' herself on this second Visit, if --- in fact --- these creatures had been everywhere she had already visited and it was only now that she could begin to perceive them. Or, perhaps, they had been hiding from her, thinking her to be an intruder, and only now they had learned of, or accepted, her purpose in being among them and so were willing to show themselves.

When she and Aulfrin left these two most northerly isles to make the final flight of the day to the Sea Goose, they took the time to loop far out over the western countryside before veering back southwards. From about fifty yards up, the view was wide and filled with beauty. The fields below were coloured by flowers or laden berry bushes, and far in the west were patterns of soft hills draped in green mantles of trees or blowing grasses. Groups of deer or families of wild boar could also be seen, and great companies of birds would sometimes appear at a distance, making surging shapes like schools of tiny fishes. One such swarm of birds, a 'murmuration' like that of starlings, came very near the flying-horses at a given moment and Eli saw that they were brightly coloured in green and red. These were the small birds she had seen from the balcony of Demoran's Castle when she had first arrived in Faërie!

As they flew farther south, just before they turned back to the east and to the Sea Goose, the King pointed to a huge, dark forest to the west. Eli understood that he was indicating the home of these marvellous, parrot-painted birds.

"The Fire-Bird Forest," he called, his voice almost lost in the rush of the wind and the gentle, slow flapping of the horses' wings. Eli nodded and gazed over her shoulder at the pointed tips of the great blue spruces and deep emerald pines, mixed --- it seemed --- with immense clumps of swaying bamboo and even more exotic and tropical vegetation..

She had hoped that memories might come tumbling back into her mind when they arrived at the last isle, the Sea Goose; but unfortunately she had no immediate recollection of her days here as a child, with Reyse as her tutor. Evidently it was here that she had lived and studied between the ages of eleven and fourteen. Although the place was unfamiliar, still, to her, at least she was again with Jizay now; for the two dogs had seemingly arrived only shortly before she and her father landed.

The island was narrow and as curvy in form as the willows on the smallest isle to the north, and the soil was as white. But here, as well as willows, there were also many pear trees. Their crop was not yet ripe, so they could not sample the fruit, but under an enormous weeping willow the King and Eli found a table spread with delicious foods and cool drinks, both for them and for the two hounds. It was mid-afternoon, and they followed their meal with a short nap on the soft grass beneath the tree while the winged-horses wandered off to find a clearing carpeted with clover further off among the white salleys.

Lying on her back, with Jizay's head heavy across her hips, Eli sighed and slept soundly for an hour or so. Perhaps prompted by her disappointment that no images from her childhood had resurfaced for her here, in her dreams she saw Reyse, youthful and dashing, his kind brown eyes with their amber rings around dark pupils shining with --- perhaps --- tender love. She awoke with a warm, tingling sensation running down her arms, as though he had just embraced her.

"I think I *must* be falling in love," she said, silently and secretly to herself. Jizay rose and licked her face with such enthusiasm that she could only guess he had heard her thoughts.

"Father," she inquired as they walked out from beneath the mighty dome of the willow and continued, on foot now, along a winding pathway through the woods, "may I ask you about Reyse?"

Aulfrin raised a bushy, red eyebrow. "What do you need to ask, my dear Eli, that is not already in your heart? You wish to have more details of his love for you, which Banvowha told you of last night?" He placed a fatherly arm around her shoulders as they walked.

Eli was silent again for a moment, and then she said, "Perhaps, yes, I wanted to know more about his love for me, and his suit. But maybe that is a strange thing to ask about. You are right, all I need or want to know is probably somewhere in my heart --- but my heart is in two places! There are things in Eli's heart, and there must be much more in Mélusine's."

"When a changeling returns on their three Visits, before they have made their final decision to come back completely…or not," Aulfrin resumed, speaking rather thoughtfully and slowly, "it is quite a perplexing feat of judgement to know what should be revealed, and when, and how. Difficult for me and for the other fairies of my realm, and difficult for the changeling. You will have all the answers, or at least most of them, if and when you return. But your curiosity while here on your Visits is very important too, for it will re-awaken some knowledge and stir the longing to know more. It is a delicate situation, and Banvowha (as ever!) supplied you with tantalising information, just enough to urge you to embark on an inward search, daring you to go further into your own reflections.

"But as regards Reyse, and you as Mélusine, you are right. You are Eli at the moment, and not a fairy, so you cannot fully recall or know *her* heart. That said, you are still Mélusine in your deepest soul, even without access to all of her memories and emotions, and it was certainly to that very core of your spirit that the rainbow-fairy was speaking. Now, you are also a romantic human woman and so I don't doubt that you feel the stirrings of some strong sentiments for that great fairy-lord on that level too.

"He is a fine fairy, and a brave and noble one. He is very dear to me, as you have seen, and has been implicated --- directly or indirectly --- in the education of *three* of my children and often he has been of inestimable help in the governing of my kingdom. But I am not going to tell you that it would be a good and wise thing to fall in love with him. For that is, indeed, the business of your own heart, or should I say 'hearts'! I will say, though, *if* you fall in love with him while you are visiting as a human, then it is likely to be the human who does the falling, and not the fairy. And love affairs between the two worlds can be, well, *very* complicated to say the least."

He fell silent, and Eli knew that he was thinking of Lily.

After a moment, she surprised even herself by asking, "Father, were you very deeply in love with my mother?"

Aulfrin stopped, his arm still encircling his daughter's shoulders, and he breathed a long, slow breath. He did not look at Eli, but rather out ahead along the tree-lined path. "I loved Lily very deeply, yes, and I think I still do. Yes, I still do. That is perhaps why I cannot decide what to do about Rhynwanol, my Queen...."

Eli bit her lip hesitatingly, and then she spoke again. "But I *meant* the Queen. When I said 'my mother', I meant my *real* mother."

Aulfrin turned and looked into Eli's eyes, and a smile stole over his lips. "Of course," he nodded, "of course. Rhynwanol is your mother, and for a moment I was thinking that you meant Lily."

Eli smiled now too. "I could have meant her, also," she admitted. "I could have asked the same about both...my mothers!" Father and daughter laughed, but with a deep understanding in their laughter.

Yellow Writing on a Red Page

Now Eli judged that her father did not wish to pursue this line of questioning. And so she changed the subject as they began to walk again.

"You said that Reyse was the tutor of three of your children, so *two* of my brothers, as well as *my* tutor?"

Aulfrin stoked his short beard, and pursed his lips before he answered.

"He was yours and Leyano's, yes, but not Demoran's. He *could* have been Timair's --- they were very close, and I thought to ask him. But then Timair found another tutor, himself, for his work with oak trees. That was his final Initiation and soon thereafter he made his request to go into the world, like you. But, as I told you, he chose not to return."

The King's voice was very heavy as he said these words, but then he sighed and continued.

"Finnir, my half-fairy son, he worked very closely with Reyse, but I suppose I could not say that it was exactly a relationship of student and tutor. No, they are friends, very close friends, but even in his earliest Initiation, at the age of eleven, Finnir did not need or want a tutor of any kind. He worked with small eagles then, and many other birds, especially swallows, but if he sought any counsel from Reyse it was only ever as one friend to another, between equals, I would say."

Eli kept a respectful silence for another couple of minutes, and then she added another question. "And are they still very close, Reyse and Finnir, and Leyano too?"

Aulfrin squeezed her shoulders a little, and laughed. "Ah, yes indeed, the whole tribe of them --- and some among them are plotting and planning like mad! Reyse rather casually 'drops in' on Leyano, Finnir is as ever in contact with Reyse, and Demoran finds characteristically subtle ways to communicate with *all* of them. And there are even meetings with the White Dragon clan, as you know, my dear Eli. Erreig and his son, Garo, have been --- more than once, I'm sure --- to

Mermaid Island, though I think only Garo has been to Barrywood."

It was Eli who had stopped walking now. She turned in confusion and surprise to her father.

"You know about all this, and about Garo being involved?" she whispered, almost smiling, but not sure if she should. "You know about the, umm, the 'plotting and planning' as you call it, between your sons?"

Aulfrin dropped his arm from her shoulders and took both her hands, facing her with a consoling expression on his wise and loving face.

"Oh, please don't tell any of them that I know so much, my dear Eli; it would spoil their fun. For that is the very most delightful game for children, to be sure. They always love to think that they are doing things that are completely beyond the ken of their parents: that is the principle joy of children, to plot and plan behind their parents' backs. Oh no, we must not let them know that I know!

"And I will add, my dear daughter, that to *know* and not to let on *how much* one knows, is one of the great diplomatic tools and talents of a king, of any ruler. Don't forget that, Eli. Power is not in warfare or in aggression, it is in subtlety and comprehension and the graceful play of not showing your hand completely or revealing how much of the game you have comprehended. Not too soon, anyway. They are doing very valuable work for me, my busy youngsters, especially where Erreig is concerned. Work I could not do so well myself, for the Dragon-Lord would probably be very wary of my even trying."

They had reached a wide clearing beside the banks of the river now, and Eli sat down on the lawn of soft, short grass, with Aulfrin taking a seat on a large stone beside her.

"Is Erreig a great danger in your kingdom, father?"

"Erreig is not a great *anything*, at least not as great as he would like to be considered, and that is what troubles him so! He fervently desires to be 'great', and to demonstrate his *power* to change this realm, to divide it, to close it tight behind its doors. He would like to have Rhynwanol by his side. But I do not believe he will ultimately succeed, not in any of these projects.

"It is a rare malady for a fairy, but he suffers from exaggerated and crippling **pride**. And, as usual, that proceeds out of **fear**. He needs to be *someone*, and to do *something*, that will win him acclaim. He needs and wants to be remarkable. What a pity that he cannot see that he is already, just by being a fairy and a dynamic part of nature and of Life."

"You think him *remarkable*, father? But isn't his 'pride' a sort of sin, like that of the devil in the Christian religion, in the Bible? Isn't it somehow making him *evil*?"

"He is <u>not</u> evil and he is no devil, Eli. He is just a fairy, like me, and like you. If I understood them correctly, from my visits into the world, the tenets of your Christian religion --- which was so precious to our little moon, Lily --- hold that the devil in the Bible wanted, and still wants, to overthrown the reign of God, the Kingdom of goodness and of light, and to control all. No, Erreig does not fit that mould. He is not seeking to destroy or to pervert goodness into evil. And he does not seek to have *everything*, just a small part of my kingdom and a title, something to give him an 'identity'.

"He would be happy to be a petty king in the realm of a great king, I think. The problem is, he is not a king of any kind. I would be very pleased to have him hold a high and honourable place in my guard, as the superb dragon-rider that he is. My father sought to offer him such a role, truly a *princely* role, when he was very young. But his ego is, in fact, the only thing that is powerful and great in him: and like all egos, it desires to stand apart, not in unity with others.

"Now his son Garo, that is another story."

Eli pricked up her ears even more at this remark. Aulfrin was looking calmly at the dances of giant dragonflies over the surface of the stream. He continued his ruminations as the huge insects cavorted all around him, with one very lovely individual landing on his outstretched hand and regarding him, it seemed, eye to eye for a long time. At length, Aulfrin spoke again.

"I had never actually met Erreig's son until the day that Reyse and I flew to Mermaid Island, and found him and his father and the mighty Bawn conversing with Leyano. I was not pleased that Erreig was there without my leave or my invitation, and I do not think he had Leyano's either. But Garo clearly had. I think he and Leyano are on very good terms.

"And that is not displeasing to me. He is an amazing fairy, if my intuition of so brief a moment together is correct. He is gifted with profound insight, and profound kindness also, if I am not mistaken. He and Leyano are much alike."

Her father did not say more, but Eli's heart was beating fast, filled with a new and previously unimagined hope that the King would not *entirely* disapprove of the union between Garo and his half-fairy daughter, Brocéliana, if he learned of it. But that relationship, it seemed to her, was not yet among the things that he had guessed but was keeping to himself!

They both rose now, and the dogs jumped up too, to continue their wandering around the pretty river-island. They did not walk the entire length of the twisting Sea Goose, for they were still over ten miles from the tip of the goose's tail. But they strolled for a good distance and saw many small mink-like animals with wide eyes and wagging whiskers, many pure white birds and numerous red deer. Eli even nodded to some very timid pixies, not unlike Periwinkle, who were bold enough to step out from behind a willow-trunk or who could be glimpsed straddling gnarled branches high up in some of the old pear trees.

They returned, in the cool of the summer evening, to the place where they had come to land, and were rejoined by Peronne and the king's flying-horse, who Eli learned was a mare and named Cynnabar. Riding, though not flying, with the dogs trotting beside them, they went a bit further up towards the 'head' of the Sea-Goose, and there found a very agreeable lodging for the night.

It resembled a log-cabin, built in a cone-shaped circle, rather like a bee-hive, of ancient pear-branches and interlaced willow-wands. Its many windows were curtained or shuttered with material like the off-white and semi-opaque oval covering of honesty seed-pods --- but they were much bigger than those normally found on that plant. The pear-pixies, now once again in hiding, had prepared their meal and their beds, explained the King. They would sleep here tonight, and on the morn continue south-west to fly the whole length of Shooting Star Lake.

Eli was delighted. "And will we arrive at the pool of the Smiling Salmon, to meditate with him?" she inquired, washing her hands before dinner in a wide and beautifully-grained pear-wood bowl, expertly turned and polished till it nearly glowed.

"I think not, my dear Eli, or at least not on this journey taking us back to the Silver City. I must return to Fantasie tomorrow, so our path will be quite direct and will take us a little south of the Salmon Haven. We will not have time to stop there on this trip, but we will see if you might return, perhaps later in your Visit, or on the next..."

As they ate and drank, Aulfrin asked if Leyano had recounted the story of his two brothers' imprisonment by Erreig, and of their ultimate release from their respective places of arrest. Eli wondered if her father knew of the healing of Leyano's mortal wound by the song of the Dragon-Lord, and also what he knew or had guessed regarding the role of the Black Key, which Leyano had not used, but which he said had finally been requested by Reyse of the Lady Ecume, and used by him.

A Delicate Balance

She simply said 'no', that she did not know the tale of her brothers' incarceration --- which was quite true --- and so she prepared to learn the King's version of what had transpired while he was forced to remain with Lily and baby Eli in the human world.

The Red Bird Mountain and the White Cat Caves

The Heron-Fairy, Corr Seylestar, recounted much to me upon my return to my realm after I had traversed the paths of the underworld in the autumn of the year 1961. And Ferglas, also, gave his report, as did the chief of the Scholar Owls. I later asked details of Demoran, but it seemed a deeply dramatic and most distasteful chapter of his life to relive even in story; it was, for him, too soon after the actual events, and we have rarely broached the subject since. As for Finnir, he is ever a trifle elusive about speaking of himself. He is an inscrutable fairy.

Of course, it is understandable that Finnir is not quite like my other children. When he was an infant he was accepted, both by myself and the Queen, as our true --- though adopted --- son. Rhynwanol knew that he was not her babe, but she recognised that he was mine. I have told you, before, how gracious I thought it of her to love the boy as if he were her own; but it was not hard to do. Everyone loved Finnir. He was beautiful and filled with light: his bright yellow hair was like an aureole about his fair face, his piercing clear-blue eyes were always filled with laughter and stars! However, as in the case of Brocéliana, we did not expect him to remain with us, but to be required to become a human once again when our true son, Timair, returned to us. Thus I had never anticipated Finnir becoming a guardian of one the Portals, let alone the most frequented and by far the most magical.

When Timair made the decision to remain a human, in 1352, Finnir was eighteen. Though only half-fairy, he seemed more a true fairy-lord than any fairy I have ever met. Though both myself and the Queen were deeply saddened to lose our belovèd Timair, we felt privileged and grateful to have Finnir remain in Faërie. I thought it perhaps more 'correct', nonetheless, to give the guardianship of Barrywood to Demoran when he would come of age (he was only two at that time), but Reyse counselled me to reconsider. He had come to know and respect the noble young half-fairy Finnir, and he insisted that the Portal of the Heart Oak would be well-served by him. I delayed another two centuries, but I grew to concur with the opinion of my friend, and Finnir was made guardian in 1550 when he was twenty-six.

Ah, they are as mysterious as each other, the guardian and his fiefdom! Indeed, Finnir was the right fairy for the Portal of Barrywood, and I do not regret my decision; but the magic of the place has only deepened under his eyes and his care, and his own magical and mysterious mien has increased as well. To ask the Prince Finnir to give a clear account of what happened to him in the Caves of the White Cats would be like asking our belovèd moon to describe the dark side of her face!

Nonetheless, I think I can give you the bones of the story, but fifty years later I am still uncovering certain facts, so it is a tale that continues to grow in the telling.

When Erreig invaded the Silver City in my absence, at the Winter Solstice of 1959, I had thought that my kingdom was secure and could long be maintained by the protectors I had installed in Fantasie: Ferglas and many of his kin, and one hundred of the Scholar Owls --- among the wisest and most erudite administrators and seers in Faërie. But the greatest threat to any kingdom is always to be found within its own borders, not without.

The six lieutenant dragon-riders of Quillir, the elite of Erreig's household, descended on the City one frosty mid-winter morning and drove the blue wolf-hounds and the great black and silver Owls into retreat to the north. Most of the fairies and pixies residing in Fantasie at that season were also forced to leave, and only those remained who were sympathetic to Erreig's policies. For at that time there were Sun-Singers as well as Moon-Dancers in the Silver City, though it is true that I already gave greater hospitality to the latter.

Since the affair between Rhynwanol and the Dragon-Chieftain, centuries earlier, I had somewhat hardened my heart towards the

A Delicate Balance

people of the Sun. Many were hesitating in their loyalties, and some were out-rightly supporting the designs of the White Dragon tribe. They saw the Sun-Singers as rulers and law-givers, the Moon-Dancers as subservient and ineffectual, merely existing to reflect the glory of the Sun's brightness but having no role or influence of our own. And they saw this kingdom as an isolated and insulated entity with no need to communicate or interact with other shees or other worlds.

*So, as the Dragons and the Sun-Singers took control of Fantasie, Erreig made a solo flight --- very bravely, I must admit --- to the Dappled Woods. There he encountered the usually placid and gentle Demoran, enraged and astounded. But it is impossible, I believe, to make Demoran **fight**. He may have danced, and probably did, but the moon was dark at the turn of that year, and not even the new sliver of a waxing crescent would have been visible in the sky until the following day's sunset. Erreig's stratagem had been well-devised and he did not seek to aggress Demoran overmuch, for he knew how to instantly win his complicity. He sought out Vintig, and then allowed Bawn to hold him in the thrall of her gaze --- a trick of her own uncanny magic wherein she uses her piercing red eyes to arrest a fairy or other creature and hold it in a spell of utter stillness and silence. Erreig could easily have thus captured the aged groom and borne him away to imprison him...*

I do not imagine that Demoran thought that the dragon or her lord would actually harm Vintig, but the Prince took no risks. In any case, even the humiliation *of his dear groom would have torn his heart. He bowed to Erreig's demand that the Portal be locked, but --- strangely enough --- he secured the right to retain the great golden key himself, for it seems that Erreig did not insist on confiscating it, or perhaps did not know that such a key existed. Castle Davenia itself was locked and emptied of the Prince's fairy-attendants, but it was* not *occupied by Sun-Singers or dragons. Erreig seemed ignorant of the intelligence or resourcefulness of the animals living with the Prince, for he saw no reason to drive away all the animals or attendants of his household --- who therefore remained hidden in the woods about the closed Castle. It was his undoing to allow Ruilly to* remain; but Dragon-Lords do not necessarily understand much about rabbits!

Demoran was carried by Bawn (in her claws, but quite carefully and without harm) to the White Dragon Fortress in the pass of the Beldrum Mountains. While the first prisoner was thus safely put under arrest in a tower dungeon (evidently rather cold and bleak, but furnished with hammock and blankets, and even boasting a small window or two), Erreig and Bawn flew across Margouya and northern Karijan to Finnir's Castle on the banks of the Inward Sea.

But, to the Dragon-Lord's chagrin, the Prince was not in residence, and would have to be sought in the depths of the magical Glens. For it seems that Ruilly the rabbit had advised the shining raven-black winged-stallion of Demoran, Dinnagorm, to leave Castle Davenia moments after his master was taken prisoner, and to await further instructions on the Crescent Isle in the River Ere. The clever rabbit also sent his kin to bring word of the kidnapping to both Peronne and Cynnabar. Our two horses had been cast out of Fantasie, and were taking refuge among the roses near the basking-whale falls of the Swan's Joy River. A company of Ruilly's rabbit-runners met them there, and it was suggested that Cynnabar fly to Finnir in Barrywood, and then on to Leyano, to bring word of the rebellion and of the capture of Demoran. And Peronne was sent in all haste to Scholar-Owl Island, where you were engaged in the preparations for your transformation into a human babe, planned in three months' time.

Cynnabar had found Finnir at his castle, only a brief hour before Erreig's arrival, and she had carried him to the Heart Oak Portal, deep in the Unicorn Glens of Barrywood. Now this is where I have had scant help from your brother in comprehending what happened exactly that night! Cynnabar did not remain with Finnir, for the Prince felt it most important that Leyano be warned and aided, so he urged her to fly to Mermaid Island before dawn.

Did Finnir lock the Portal to Gougane Barra himself, knowing that Erreig was prepared to force this act from him? Did he have time to communicate with his servants and allies on the other side of the doorway, dwelling among the mossy-toed trees of that mystical wood in the south-west of Ireland? Did he warn the unicorns of the Glens *or any other of his subjects living near the Portal? Did he perhaps even have prior knowledge of the 'coup' planned by Erreig, before Cynnabar arrived at his castle?*

All that my winged-horse could offer me as a hazy clue --- which I have, as yet, not been able to fully decipher --- was the fact that, when they met at the Castle on the low promontory jutting out from the Inward Sea's northern banks, Finnir was carrying huge sprays of yellow flowers on long branches. She did not know what they were.

But I think I may know. As she described them, they were not flowers from a small bush or soft-stemmed plant; they were truly the blossoms of a tree. She said they were not petalled but rather resembled soft, fluffy balls, very tiny and very deep yellow. It sounds to me like a tree called mimosa, but it does not grow in Faërie --- well, not in this shee, at any rate. But there are other shees, Eli, in the greater realm of Faërie. One, very distant and of a very different culture to ours, is called the White Kangaroo Shee. Its seven Portals all open into the human lands in the southern hemisphere, in Australia or New Zealand or New Caledonia. And there, in that Shee, there are many varieties of such trees, which they name 'wattles'.

Many hundreds of years ago, the father of my father, the mighty Aulf, adventured there; and he brought a wattle tree back to our shee, and he planted it in a protected and secretive spot, in a chapel on the Island of Windy Hill, in the midst of the Inward Sea. Well and good, if Finnir had been to Windy Hill, and had gathered a bunch of mimosa to decorate the rooms of his sombre winter-tide Castle; but *I believe that the wattle-tree does not bloom in winter. In that case there would have been no yellow blossom on it at the turn of the year...*

Whatever may be the explanation, and whatever Finnir knew beforehand, the result was that Erreig found him, not at his Castle, but at the Portal, and alone. *Quite alone, or so Finnir assured me. And that is very odd, for Finnir is* always *accompanied by an animal, be it squirrel or swallow or unicorn; but he was adamant that he was solitary at the Portal when Erreig appeared. I have no further details of their meeting or the ensuing voyage, but clearly Bawn bore the*

Prince to join Demoran in the dungeon of the White Dragon Fortress, arriving there in the early morning hours of the following day.

Erreig did not wish to leave the two brothers together, in case they might conceive of some plot to escape, but he likely wished to close the third Portal, that of Leyano, also. Or perhaps, just perhaps, he did not wish to close the Dawn Rock doorway immediately. Perhaps he hoped to lure me through it sooner than I then thought to come --- though at that time I was still far from America, living with Lily in Brittany, in France --- or perhaps he realised that he would need a channel of communication with me in the human world, in his negotiations regarding ransom and treaties. In any case, he turned his attention to finding more suitable prisons for the two older Princes before venturing further into the east, and his choices were very telling: Demoran he placed in a large, lantern-like cage high on the snowy slopes of the tallest peak of the Beldrum Mountains, the Red Hoopoe, and Finnir he sent to the Caves of the White Cats.

In all, the Prince Demoran would spend more than a year-and-a-half in his mountain prison, only to be released after I returned from the human world. I will tell you a little more of that story in a moment, for I was implicated in his release, working with Reyse while Ferglas was occupied with the initial recapture of Fantasie, and when I had finally returned to my kingdom, from my human death, I challenged Erreig to a sort of single combat of song and dance, sun and moon, ebb and flow --- with the rip-tides of our opposing wills doing battle in place of our spears.

But Finnir's escape from the White Cats, _there_ is a curious mystery!

The giant white cats are, like the great white dragons, ferocious and almost indomitable. They are easily twice the size of lions or tigers in the human world, closer in muscular mass to polar bears than to felines, in fact. And they have magical powers, granted them by one of the Sage-Hermits of a bygone era, who raised the first litter of the giant kits under the concealing and mystical fog of the Stone Circle. They do not, as far as I have ever heard, kill or eat fairies; but they are reputed to be the predators of some of our larger animals and legends survive which hint at their being quite blood-thirsty at times. Under

Erreig's orders, it is possible that they had permission to kill Finnir, should he attempt escape.

This is what I heard from Demoran's cats, his small cats in Davenia, upon my return in September of 1961, when I --- as Sean Penrohan --- had died in the arms of my little moon and had left my human family, my wife and changeling-babe, to return to my beleaguered kingdom. I arrived in Faërie by the Portal of Dawn Rock, but I lost no time in taking flight aboard Cynnabar, who was awaiting me there, and hastening to Davenia. Hearing these reports upon arrival at the Castle, I was ready to turn my first and most urgent efforts to the cause of Finnir's rescue, rather than that of Demoran, for his predicament seemed to me the most dangerous. But Ruilly --- intuitive rabbit that he is --- and the ancient Vintig as well, told me, when I found them under the autumnal and richly coloured branches of the Wood, that Finnir was beyond my help, and that I should go with all speed to my second son in his frozen, mountainous cage: a desperate plight, indeed, for a fairy. And Erreig was bargaining fiercely with me now, using Demoran as the wedge driven between my Moon-Dancers and his Sun-Singers.

My fears were aroused for both my boys. Demoran was threatened with a still more secret and secure incarceration than his present one on the high slopes of the Red Hoopoe Mountain, and for many years or even centuries, if I did not comply with Erreig's demands. The Sage-Hermit was in alliance with the Dragon-Lord, and not only as regarded the parallel flow of time in both human and fairy worlds. It seemed that Demoran was to be transferred to the Star of the White Seal, the tiny island that lies to the west of Star Island where the Sage-Hermit dwells. Two of the arms of the greater Star throw out rings of rippling force which encircle this smaller 'skellig' and render it not only inaccessible, but usually invisible and even, so legend has it, able to be displaced much farther out to sea, or even under it!

And as for Finnir: what did the rabbit and the ancient fairy mean to imply? How was he 'beyond my help'?! This was truly alarming, if it meant that he had already been imprisoned in some impenetrable grotto guarded by the massive White Cats, to be retained in his secret hiding-place for many ages to come. Even more fearsome was the *possibility that their dark words referred to his death. Had Erreig, or the Cats, already killed my belovèd and brave Finnir?*

If I had thought it possible to delay even an hour more, I would have called for a harp to seek insight and advice --- but I could not spare the time. I decided to go immediately to Demoran, and I issued a challenge to Erreig by messenger-bats to meet me on the slopes of the Red Hoopoe Mountain. Reyse joined me, unexpectedly but as if in answer to my prayers, in mid-air as he flew to the high lantern-cage of Demoran amid the snows at the ever-frozen peak of that range, a mighty and haunted mountain named for its sacred race of red birds.

But it would be the blood-red sunset of that exhausting day when I would finally turn my attention to Finnir.

As we approached the snowy slopes, Reyse, mounted on the pure black flying-steed of Demoran, soared higher to find the Prince's crystal-ice prison, as I descried Bawn alighting on a narrow ledge of powdery snow and jutting rock half-way up the mountain-side. With a gust of fire like yellow diamond-shards, Bawn melted the snow at her red-clawed feet and ribbons of water flowed in many fingers down from the precipice, only to freeze again instantly into icicles of several yards' length. Erreig, astride her, was singing: red songs, dragon and hoopoe songs, sun-songs. I was unable to moon-dance, mounted on my winged-horse, and so he had a certain advantage, or so he surely believed.

Snowflakes were filling the air with a paradoxical softness as the huge dragon took to the skies and swirled about me. Erreig brandished his pearl-white spear but it was the searing light from his forehead, from the white diamond **Kalvi-Tivi***, which menaced me most blatantly, as well as Bawn's fiery breath. He then faced me, hovering in mid-flight as I also paused on Cynnabar and turned to him. Spitting more and more dangerous and eerie sparks of hot-light was the gem embedded in Errieg's chest, the blood-red fire-opal* **Gurtha***. This was ever his most efficient weapon, for in it is concealed an ancestral fire of strange potency. It blinded me even as I raised my hand to counter him with the brilliance of the cluster of minuscule diamonds and sapphires which were shining from my outstretched palm.*

The Dragon-Lord sang on, his powerful baritone notes making the snowflakes sizzle and flee between us. But I had other weapons, and I was confident in their greater strength.

Encircled by shrilly-singing flocks of bright red hoopoes, I and Cynnabar assailed Erreig and Bawn, as we had over the silver turrets of Fantasie six centuries earlier. And though I clasped my own spear in my right hand, I had no intention of using it to wound either dragon or dragon-rider this time. Mine was another tactic altogether.

I closed my left hand and the blue and white light subsided as Bawn circled and now climbed above me in our aerial dancing. And then I closed my eyes as well, and willed my thoughts to open the streaming light and power of my tracery silver crown studded with green stones. These were the gifts awarded me in my final Initiation, nearly twelve-hundred years earlier, when I was taken into the midst of the Circle of the Great Trees to lay the foundations of my coming kingship. Dark green emeralds and paler, but no less potent, peridots: these were bestowed upon me by the Trees themselves, and woven into a diadem by my own mother, the Queen Morilande, interlacing the coils of silver cord as she slowly danced around the source of waters at the centre of the Stone Circle.

These precious jewels blazed up suddenly and intently now, in intertwining strands of many hues of green, like the lights that frequently aureole the Trees themselves; and they played in vortices and in branching fire-works of rich green imagery over my head. Erreig and Bawn were caught in them as they flew over me, and my will --- unified with that of the Great Trees of Fantasie --- clashed with the Dragon-Lord's egoic desires and his prideful fears. His song faltered and died away, and the luminosity of both **Kalvi-Tivi** *and* **Gurtha** *was swallowed-up, falling back into the hearts of both of the beautiful gems.*

As in my battle with him over the Silver City, when my Queen was banished, so in this encounter: I vanquished Erreig --- for my powers of sovereignty are given me by the hearts of the Trees and the dancing soul of the Stones, and my will and theirs are far, far stronger than his. He and his matriarch dragon fell from the skies and nearly came to disaster, careening fast and low along the sides of the mountain and only at the last moment pulling up again into exhausted and slow flight over the foothills. They withdrew in sullen disgrace, chastised and silent, back to their Fortress; and the red hoopoes dispersed.

I landed on the charred and tempest-blown slope where Bawn had commenced her attack, just to draw breath. After several moments, I and Cynnabar climbed through the now lessening snowfall of the icy skies to the peak where I expected to rejoin Reyse, but he had already left. As I approached, the seven tall sections of the crystal lantern-gaol were falling ever-so-slowly open in heavy, glistening segments and Demoran could be seen, standing proud though wearied by his long ordeal, on the plateau at the centre of his now sundered prison. I searched the skies for Reyse, but instead I saw only the noble black flying-horse: Dinnagorm, Demoran's own mount whom Reyse had been riding earlier. I presumed that Reyse had departed using his own wings. When Dinnagorm descended onto the plateau created by the opening segments of her master's prison, my son climbed wearily onto his back and they flew the little way to where I waited. They arrived and alighted in the deep snows on a ledge of the high peak; the marvellous horse's blue-black coat was covered with snow-flakes and his wide wings were lacy-white with wonderful ice formations.

I embraced Demoran long, but with few words --- save to say that I would be with him in Davenia as soon as possible. I saw him safely off and watched for a moment as Dinnagorm bore his dear master away, and home at last. And then I myself flew towards the last crimson stains of sunset on the horizon.

As I arrived within sight of the western coasts of Quillir, flying high to avoid the incoming sea-winds, I looked out over Sun Slumber Bay to the southern-most islands of the Sea-Serpent Archipelago. Sinuous monsters were cavorting in the autumn swells of those capricious seas, and beneath me, now, the lands of the cat-caves were shadowy; however, their mounded dens were outlined with a sinister red glow. The sun had set, so the gleam of red was not from him. It is the colour of the Sun-Singer's ensign, and so I believe it is painted by magical arts on all the dwellings of the Cats since the rise to petty-power of the Dragon-Chieftain.

A Delicate Balance

But it was not the only sign to welcome me to those bleak coasts and foreboding caves. From my high vantage point, riding on Cynnabar in the cloudless early evening sky, I could see the crescent moon just setting in the sun's wake, chasing him over the indigo islands and the rim of the darkening horizon-line.

I circled down to the cat-caves, and three or four of the immense beasts sprang towards me as my horse landed. But my wrath and urgency were evidently as fierce as their desire, or their orders, to prevent me! I may have brandished my spear, but I believe it was the fire kindled in my eyes which met their own huge yellow-green ones and drove them back before me. My orders over-ruled those of their dragon-lordling, as I commanded them to show me the whereabouts of Finnir.

They did not growl or roar, but exchanged glances almost furtively. I wondered, my breast burning with anxiety, if this belied their crime of murder. Their leader, a tall and towering Cat with patches of grey tabby-fur decorating his otherwise gleaming white coat, came forward. He spoke wordlessly to me, and rather reverently.

"I am Isck, sovereign of cats, and I salute you royally, Aulfrin son of Aulfrelas son of Aulf. I will take you to the mouth of the red cave where the Prince Finnir dwelt with us. Follow me, but fly if you will, for the ground is trembling with rumours of earth-quake and rumblings of death and life interwoven. You and your horse would be wise to fly at least a foot or two above it."

Unsure what to make, as yet, of his strange words, I and Cynnabar obediently flew behind him, gingerly manoeuvring only a few inches above the ground, which was indeed constantly shaking and shuddering with earth-quake tremors. I wondered if I would be shown Finnir's lifeless body, and his lonely tomb, but my heart told me that he was not there at all, the moment that we arrived at the dark, gaping mouth of the red cave.

Red the stone, red the earth around the rock, red as the banners of the Sun-Singers. But I felt no vibration of my son's presence.

"Is he gone?" I asked Isck, still conversing in silence. The cat-king did not answer, but his pale khaki eyes sparkled as he nodded once, and then he turned his regard to the narrow pathway descending *under the red rock and into the black cave-mouth. I followed his gaze, and had to smile.*

A winding stream of softness, a delicate serpentine of colour, ran all along the dark red path, down into the shadowy cave perhaps--- or out from it. Now I could see the trail, slightly luminous and on the verge of blowing away in the rising breeze. Tiny balls of yellow fluff, tiny foreign flowers as yellow as the banners of the Moon-Dancers, a meandering trail of mimosa that continued from the mouth of the silent cave-door and disappeared among the trembling pebbles far off among the other caves.

"Wattle flowers!" I cried in amusement and relief. "The yellow path cutting gently through the red lands! It is the yellow writing upon a red parchment page. That is a fine premonition of many good tidings, for the trail of the Moon's yellow glow is sweetly traced over the face of the red Sun.

But more joyful even than that message of hope is the cry ringing in my heart: Finnir lives, and he is free!"

****

A Delicate Balance

Chapter Eight:
The Lake of Lily-White Stars

ithout another word, Aulfrin kissed Eli's forehead and retired to his bed.

Breathing deeply, and smiling with the strange mixture of emotions and images twirling in many-coloured patterns in her head, Eli also went to bed. But she could not sleep, not yet.

Indeed, the many bright hues and questions continued to swirl and tickle, until, in the small hours of the morning, the sickle moon appeared at the window, its contour softened by the creamy white of the honesty-seed-pod shutters. Eli rose, as silently as she could, and gently pushed open two of the large oval discs, and gazed into the night sky over the lands of the Singing Hives.

The arm of the River Nazzy which wound about the belly of the Sea Goose was singing to itself in the darkness between the cabin and the plains of the Hives, and its watery song was mingled with the voices of many placid, nocturnal spiders spinning their webs or contentedly reposing in the centres of them, their beautiful lullabies and tender voices still a wonder to Eli's ears. The land was not very hilly between this curly isle and the distant coast of Sea Horse Bay and Curious Cove, and so Eli could watch the moonrise almost from its beginning. The silver crescent was very large as it commenced its climb up into the tapestry of constellations.

A Delicate Balance

Acting entirely on instinct and sudden impulse, Eli looked behind her to where Jizay had been sleeping beside her bed. He was sitting up now, alert and wakeful like her, and beside him, on the ground, was Eli's shoulder-bag. It contained little more than Lily's notebook and it was in shadow, and what's more it was of a woven fabric that was thick and dark blue.

But, nonetheless, it was glowing in the faint moon-light.

Understanding her unspoken curiosity, and perhaps even outright request, Jizay turned and took the satchel in his mouth, and brought it to his mistress. Eli caressed his golden head as she received it, and drew out the stained, ivory-white journal of her own little moon, to read by the light of this one.

It fell open in her hands and she remarked inwardly, with amusement, "Chance does not exist!"

There were few words on the two pages she beheld, which were predominantly filled with sketches: two sleeping cats and a rabbit sitting beside a large open book, a squirrel scampering over a leafy branch and three swooping swallows --- their long, divided tails splayed behind them, their joyful movement captured perfectly even in the still moment of grace drawn in fine pencil-lines. The caption on the left-hand page, over the cats and rabbit, read "Demoran's companions". And on the facing page, where the other illustrations were, were the words "Finnir's *totem* animals - which share his life."

Suddenly Eli saw another animal drawn quite clearly at the bottom of this page. How and why had she not noticed it at once? It was a tiny unicorn, and over it was placed a crescent-moon. How had she missed that element of her Lily's designs? In any case, there was no other caption to explain the unicorn; it simply completed the cast of Finnir's beloved creatures, evidently.

Strange to call them 'totem' animals, thought Eli; but, quite true, they were the three beasts that her father had said were always to be found with Finnir. And he had been greatly surprised that his son had insisted that *none* of them were with him when Erreig arrived at his Portal. Eli remembered that detail clearly; it had impressed her, and puzzled her, for some reason.

She continued to look long at the word *totem*, for it attracted her eye. And she also stared at the phrase the animals which *share his life*. She studied her Lily's pretty handwriting, rereading the words a couple of times.

"Well," she thought, "she simply means they share his life like any other pets..." But she knew she was missing the full importance of the words that were staring up at her from the page. A *totem* animal *sharing his life*, a spirit guide, an animal guardian --- rather like she believed she had a guardian angel, perhaps. "No," she concluded, again recognising immediately her error, "closer, somehow, than an angel...if that were possible!"

Anyway, these were probably the animals that had been the guides or mentors of Finnir's Initiations, though she knew little about those challenges in the case of her eldest brother. She hadn't completely understood what exactly "Initiations" even were.

She turned the page, hoping that her little moon had written more explanations after having made the sketches. But before she could begin to read, in the growing clarity of the moonlight, she was taken aback by the book-mark tucked into the join of the next two pages. It was a large, bright silver leaf.

It was just like the painted leaves on the *trompe-l'oeil* in the bedroom at the house of Banvowha. But this was surely a real leaf, not a painted one. It was dry and brittle, but obviously real. Or was it? Suddenly it seemed to be made of true silver and then, almost at the same time, it was very clearly a specimen from a real tree. And the text that Lily had written was as odd and marvellous as the leaf itself.

Sean has told me the tale of his sons' imprisonment, when you came to us as a babe, my Eli. Very exciting, and very dramatic, and a time of hardship and immense testing of their characters for both boys, it seems to me. And I wonder if I have also gleaned some insight into how the animals close to these two princes may have helped them...

Now, Demoran, Sean's second son, lives in a Castle in the woods far in the north-west of the kingdom. There he has many feline friends, but two especially are very dear to him, a tortoise-shell and a pure black cat. But his most devoted 'pet' --- maybe not the right word for such an <u>intellectual</u> creature --- is a grey rabbit. And I say 'intellectual' and not merely 'intelligent', because this rabbit evidently spends long hours in the royal library, reading (Sean actually said 'listening to'!) the books there.

While Demoran was held captive, these two philosopher-cats and this incredible rabbit remained nearby in the woods which encircle Demoran's Castle, with the old gardener-cum-groom, a very aged fairy whom Sean respects profoundly. They had been unable, even with the strength and courage of the Prince Demoran, to keep the great Dragon-Lord from finding and sealing the doorway into the human world that is hidden among the trees not far from this Castle. But the Prince had kept the key to the locked door, and they had been able to hide close-by in the forest, even when he (and the key) had been carried off to be imprisoned.

*Sean told me that the cats were successful in protecting the instruments of music and also the splendid books housed in the Prince's dwelling-place. It seems that it was vital that the Dragon-Lord and his allies did **not** find such things, for they would have gained great insight and information from them. The grey rabbit, with the help of the fairy-gardener, watched-over the gardens and woods --- insuring that they continued to blossom and thrive, unlike many of the plants and trees in the King's great City, which 'fell asleep' during those months of 'occupation'.*

Now, about Demoran's prison: I haven't drawn it, because I can hardly imagine what it really looked like --- even with Sean's descriptions to help me. He tells me it was made of crystal and hung high up a snowy mountain peak! It was the size of a small cottage, and Demoran lived in it for a year and nine months. It was, quite obviously, a magical cage without door or lock, but fashioned of seven pieces, like tall wedges of clear glass, which closed together to form the walls. It must have been a very lonely and very cold time for the Prince...

But it is Finnir's animals that intrigue me the most. Very tame beige or blond squirrels, exuberant swallows, and pearly-white unicorns. Yes, unicorns! Sean tells me that these are the three species that guard and guide his eldest son, but more than that. They are not merely his companions, but it seems that they somehow 'carry' a part of his life-force. Sean says that he does not understand it completely himself, and that this one of his sons is very much more magical and mysterious than the other two and has not explained it very clearly to him either. From what he can piece together, these animals bear a part of the energy that animates Finnir --- that's how he put it. It's not that he cannot live without them, but rather --- Sean thinks --- that the force of his life-light is so strong that it can spill out into any, or all, of these beasts and be mingled with their own living energy. And one or more of them are always with him. Now, I don't really understand it --- but it somehow thrills me. Especially to share one's 'life-force' with a unicorn!

It's only a guess, but when Sean said that he has wondered for years why Finnir told him that none of these important creatures were with him when he was captured, a faint idea took shape in my own heart. I believe that Finnir allowed his animals to go into hiding with some of the essence of his own life-force, his being, concealed within them. In that way, it would be impossible for the Dragon-Lord to actually kill him. I don't know why this came to me; and it seems a very mystical and strange explanation, but there you are! That's what I feel, intuitively.

Sean could tell me nothing much of Finnir's many months of imprisonment. He was held in a cave in the west of Faërie, in an inhospitable part of the land where giant cats roam. And when Sean arrived to rescue him, he was already gone. When he told me that, I almost expected him to say that his three animals, or perhaps great tribes of them, had come to free him --- but of course he did not. Given *how he described the Great Cats, it would be very dangerous for squirrels or small birds and even for unicorns to try to do battle with such beasts, I'm sure!*

He did learn, years after the event, that Finnir had not been harmed or tortured, but rather that <u>he</u> had tormented, in a way, his captor! For it seems that the Dragon-Lord, who had placed him under the watchful eyes of the great white cats, came often to speak with him; but these interviews were a subtle battle of wills and wits, or perhaps of magic, and the rebel-chieftain was confused and troubled and greatly weakened by the exchanges with the captive Prince. But Sean has learned very little of what these mind-battles or spirit-duels were really like, for Finnir is reluctant to talk much of them, maybe because he is very modest about these victories.

Eli, you must have known this amazing fairy-prince when you were a fairy yourself. He is much older than you, but he is part of your own family. And you will one day meet him again. I envy you that! And I am grateful that you have such a mystical and powerful brother to protect and defend you, should you need it, in your life as the Princess.

I would have loved to have had a brother for you here in your human life with me. I wish that Sean and I could have made another child together, to be a loving and protecting brother for you. But, it is true, I had great difficulty to raise you in any semblance of comfort even on your own. Two children would have been impossible for me.

You see, it was all as it should have been, and it was not by <u>chance</u> that I had only one darling youngster to raise. But, as you know well, there is certainly no such thing as chance!

Eli stopped reading, and turned the page back just once more to look again at the lovely sketches. Then she closed the notebook and sighed, fingering the cover and gently stroking the little booklet.

It was very late now --- or rather very early morning. The moon had passed high into the sky, and clouds were gathering, no doubt, for she had become invisible now. Oddly enough, a moonish glow still filled the cabin, though there were no lamps.

"Starlight, probably," thought Eli. "The stars over Faërie are probably much brighter than they are in the human world."

She returned the journal to its bag, with the silver leaf still marking the page she had just read. Had Banvowha slipped it into the book? Had it magically fallen from the painted vine trailing over the *trompe-l'oeil* window-sill?! Or had it been Lily's bookmark from long ago?

Eli curled up in her bed and drifted off to sleep, with the questions unanswered and her head still happily tingling with colourful images of magical beasts and the fantastical tales of her two brothers.

****

The second week of Eli's second Visit dawned just as fairies like best: washed with rain and musical with the constant staccato notes of its drops on the roof and the white earth all around the circular cabin. As soon as she was dressed, she went to the open door to watch her father, the King, pirouetting and waltzing, with Ferglas and Jizay barking whenever he leapt and clicked his heels!

Even the two winged-horses could be seen among the boles of the white trees, cantering and weaving, executing flying-changes and cabrioles, and occasionally lifting their great wings to flap vigorously in the wet air like happy ducks.

The pear-tree pixies, as ever nowhere to be seen, had obviously come earlier, for there were small bowls of sweet tea and hot candied-pear-muffins smelling of spices and honey on a low, round table mid-way between the two beds. Eli did not join the rain-dancing this time, but continued to stand in the doorway, her wooden tea-bowl cupped in her hands, and a beaming smile on her face.

When the happy downpour had abated, Aulfrin joined his daughter for breakfast.

"Ah, Eli, you could have had your morning shower with us!" he chortled, but then added, "oh ho! I know: you hope to bathe in the Shooting Star Lake. Also a very nice way to wash --- you're quite right!"

"Is it a long flight, over the Lake and home to Fantasie?"

"About two hundred miles --- not too long, no," answered her father, biting into a muffin and then swinging his green cloak around his shoulders. "But we'll take our time this morning, stopping soon for a swim and to enjoy some of the wonders of the long lake with its delightful inhabitants and beautiful shore-line. Let's start by flying high, so that you can get a good view of the shape of this well-named body of water: you have to be high to see the shooting star form."

"It really looks like a falling star, then?!"

"Come and see!" And passing Eli her own cloak from an ornately carved hook near the door, he ushered her out into the white willow-wood where every branch and leaf and web was hung with rainbow-light droplets.

Ferglas and Jizay, Aulfrin explained, would cross the River Nazzy on the other side of the Isle where the current was swifter but shallower, and then they would take the long way back to the Silver City, through the forest of the tiny fire-birds and then across the grain-fields of Aumelas-Pen, to arrive by the north.

"They have messages to deliver for me, as well as other duties. They will rejoin us in the City tomorrow or the day after, I should think," he concluded.

Eli nodded, and knelt to embrace and kiss her hound of joy. With silent, loving words they bid one another good-bye, and the two dogs trotted off through the woods. Father and daughter mounted their wondrous horses, then they walked out from the cover of the dripping trees to the southern shore of the Isle before taking to the air.

Flying in lazy circles over the first part of Shooting Star Lake was already, for Eli, like a dream of paradise. This was the 'star' itself, with the rest of the huge body of water trailing out to the south-west like a broad 'tail'. Beneath the slowly paddling hooves of their flying mounts, Eli and the King looked down on the seven-pointed star-form of turquoise blue, forty miles long and about half as wide.

Except for the stony tips of the six broad and thinly tree-covered points reaching out into the lapping water, its banks were almost entirely covered in dense woods, with only a few grey boulders peeping through at the very margins of the shore. In between the 'fingers' of the star-form, just where the pointed peninsulas met, there were little rounded areas of sand, shingle and pale pebbles. At the farthest end of the star, where its tail-form began, were numerous gentle cascades; the threads of falling water glistening gold in the sunlight which now shone through the departing clouds.

They continued to circle and to admire the view beneath them for about a quarter-of-an-hour, it seemed to Eli, but then Aulfrin gestured that they would begin their descent. He indicated that Peronne follow Cynnabar to the sandy outcropping at the angle between two of the southern star-points. It was, in fact, a quite generous triangular beach of whitish-grey sand, jutting out from the rocks and woods beyond.

The horses landed one after another, splashing in the pebbly shallows and then walking up onto the strand. Eli had no time to take in the beauty of the landscape, for she was instantly absorbed in the scene before them: the beach of silvery sand was almost entirely occupied by several families of muskrats, otters and beavers, all busy playing together and --- it appeared --- talking and possibly telling ridiculous jokes to one another, for they all seemed to be drunk with joy!

She and her father dismounted, but no one among the crazy mustelids and water-rodents took the slightest notice of them. Young and old, they were all carrying on with gay abandon, rolling and tumbling, clicking and squeaking and chirruping, sitting up to rub whiskers or dashing after one another in circles or in figures of eight and then diving into the water to continue their dancing there, or to lounge on their backs or swim along with twigs or bunches of leaves or flowering water-mint in their mouths. Eli laughed till she cried!

Finally the entire mad crowd had all moved on, either into the shadows far away under the trees or farther out into the wide water.

Aulfrin told Eli that the waters in the small bays between the 'fingers' of the Shooting Star's points were comparatively shallow, while the centre of the Lake itself was of unguessable depth. She would, he advised, be happiest and safest bathing in the sandy shallows, and anyway the water would be many degrees warmer there. Eli went one side of the beach and her father the other, and both enjoyed a long swim and a refreshing occasion to wash and to delight in the silky currents of the water.

Eli noted with interest that, except for such recreation shared with Brocéliana and Muscari near Leyano's castle, it seemed the fairy-custom to bathe in solitude, or perhaps it was a tradition that men and women fairies did not swim naked together. She wondered if this were done for her, or if this was part of the true culture of this land.

She continued to paddle and play, rather like a happy otter herself, until her arms and legs felt relaxed and limber, and her breathing deep and peaceful. She walked up the slope of the short bank and put on her clothes, which she had left laid-out on an isolated rock near the shore.

As she finished dressing, and began tidying her hair with the red coral-comb that Leyano had offered her, she looked out along the shingle-sand to the water at the other end of the beach, where her father was still contentedly swimming. He, also, resembled an otter! For he was floating on his back, his arms slowly pushing his outstretched body through the water.

But near him was another swimmer, more *beaverish* in style, with his head just out of the water and a deep wake of shining wavelets streaming out behind him. And on the shore, not very far from the two swimmers, were three other male fairies; these were fully dressed, of course, and very regally at that. And they were talking softly amongst themselves.

Surprised to see all four of these newcomers, Eli hoped that none had overseen her bathing; but she thought not. As well as the stone where she had left her clothes, which had screened her a little from view when she had emerged from her bath, Peronne was standing not far off. She felt rather sure that he would have alerted her to any visitors or on-lookers. In any case, even here on the far side of this miniature 'cove', she was easily about fifty yards from where her father was swimming, now joined by a friend it seemed. And the three beautifully clad fairies were even further up the shoreline and closer to the trees.

She hesitated a moment more, but as she began to walk a little closer, she noted that both Aulfrin and the other rather more dynamic swimmer had left the water and were already dressing. And in a few more steps, her heart was beating faster and she was registering a thrill of delight. The tall, brown-haired fairy beside the King was none other than Reyse!

He had seen Eli now, too, and his smile was brilliant. He moved a few steps in her direction, while her father remained still; but the King was clearly smiling also. Eli walked quickly, but the sun had just risen over the hillside of dense trees far behind him, and Reyse's face was now in shadow. Still, it seemed to her that she could *feel* his sparkling brown and amber eyes looking into her sun-blinded ones even if she were only blinking at his silhouette.

She checked herself before embracing him, or even throwing herself into his arms! Whatever caution she had been warned to exercise about falling in love with a fairy-lord while still a human-being, Eli had to admit that her heart was now speaking much more loudly than her head, or her common sense.

Nonetheless, she was --- at least as a human-woman --- fifty years old. That is to say, relatively mature and not utterly capricious. She mastered her emotions to the point of simply reaching out both of her hands so that Reyse could take them in his, and then wordlessly and very softly lift one of them to his lips to kiss it. They both remained silent for a few seconds. Indeed, there was nothing more to say.

Eli basked in the warm moment of contact with Reyse, until the King strode up beside him.

"A good place to choose for our morning dip," he laughed, "or so it seems! I counted on seeing Reyse some day soon, and Finnir, Brea and Aytel this evening in the City; but it is much nicer to cross all of our paths here between the woods and water."

Eli stopped short in her reverie of new or rekindled infatuation for Reyse. "My brother is here?!" she whispered, turning wide-eyed to her father. "*Finnir* is here?"

Aulfrin nodded. "We spoke of him last evening, and so it is only natural that he turn up! In any case, I would have presented him to you tonight. I realise that, although he is your eldest brother, he is not very well known to you, even as the Princess Mélusine. Except that in your fairy life, you would have heard more tales of him, or at least rumours of his adventures, especially those with Reyse."

The three gentlemen-fairies were still at a good distance from Eli, Aulfrin and Reyse as they began to walk over the sand and low stones and shoreline grasses to join them. They were standing in calm silence now, though there were many birds singing their morning symphonies from the eaves of the woods, and many swallows darting and tumbling though the air and swooping close over the surface of the turquoise lake and then darting up the shore again, to fly about the trio.

Amid the birdsong and the lapping water, and the background drone of the short waterfalls, Eli could also hear the rustling of leaves behind the fairies and the whistling of the breeze. Her sense of hearing seemed to be sharpened, and as she looked up the sandy shore, her vision too seemed to become more precise and lucid. Brea and Aytel she could now see as though in 'close-up'; they were tall and fair, richly clad in tunics and trousers of greens and pale oranges, golden ochre and bright white threads interwoven. Their long hair was blowing about their shoulders and glistening with stranded gemstones. Both were standing at ease yet very proudly and very straight, like solid oak trees.

But it was easy to recognise which of the three was Finnir, for he far outshone the two other noble fairies in beauty and in hidden power as well. He was dressed in mottled green and blue: he wore a tunic longer than the others and loose trousers tucked into short tan-coloured boots. Many of the swallows were crying aloud as they circled close to his short-cropped, curly blond hair, and in his arms he held a little light-brown squirrel --- very like the creature on his lap in the dream vision Eli had been shown before her first Visit.

But what stood out more clearly than all the rest, even at this distance, were his eyes. For they were turned to her, and even more visible than all the other details of her brother's features. They were piercing but very gentle, and of a clear blue that seemed to reach out into infinity, like the morning sky. Eli was looking into them, and they into hers. And she could not turn away.

After what seemed an age, she was able to look not only at his eyes, but a little higher. Set into his forehead was a jewel, the pearl awarded him in one of his Initiations, which shone almost as brilliantly as his eyes. She recalled the white light she had discerned when she had seen him in the Silver City, riding with his handsome company and playing on a pretty lap harp.

"*That's* my brother?!" she heard herself say, though the voice did not seem to be hers. "That's my eldest brother Finnir?"

Her father was striding forward to rejoin the trio, saying "Well met, well met! But are you not bathing, too?" He called the two companions of Finnir by their names as he touched his heart --- though with no sign of bowing, of course. They both inclined their heads low and reverently, and with gracious smiles.

"Aytel, it has been many seasons since last we met! I am delighted you could make the journey. And Brea, my brave one, are none of your hounds with you today?"

"They are playing under the acacias and oaks, my Sovereign," laughed Brea, and at the sound of his voice, two lanky and amazingly tall wolf-hounds emerged from the woods behind him, barking as they bounded towards their master. They were very pale in colour, a warm and creamy white. One had eyes which were gleaming olive green, rather like his master's, but the other's were a soft brown, similar to Reyse's.

Reyse. Where was he? Eli looked around suddenly; but he had not moved from his place beside her, though he had released her hands and was standing motionless and rather serious, still gazing at her. She smiled warmly at him now.

"It is many, many years since you have beheld your brother, Finnir," he remarked. "There is a strong energy between you. One can feel it rushing back and forth between your eyes. I have voyaged long and far with Finnir, and have known him and worked closely with him for many centuries. He is, indeed, a most impressive fairy. He has that in common with you, my Lady."

Now Reyse wore the hint of a smile once again. It somehow reassured Eli and brought her back to *terra firma*. She exhaled, and turned to look once more at Finnir and his two companions; but the King was blocking her view of her brother, whom he had obviously just embraced and was continuing to address in a low voice, his hand on the Prince's shoulder. The little beige squirrel was running about on the ground now, playing with the dogs.

Another echo of the 'strong energy' which Reyse had noticed tingled through her body as she began to walk closer to the group, but Reyse placed his own hand on her back as if to guide her forward, and at his touch the tingling subsided.

It returned, only for a split-second, as they arrived at Aulfrin's side and Eli was formally introduced to the fairies she did not know, and then presented to her brother. Finnir's eyes were truly incredible, a sunny and twinkling blue. In his ear-points were set chunks of amber but they were partially hidden by strands of golden hair. Eli suddenly recalled that she had seen another fairy, also very striking and with whom she felt an intense bond, who had amber in his ear-points --- but also, in his case, beside his eyes. That had been Aindel.

But from looking briefly at his ear-gems, Eli was drawn quickly back to the pleasure of looking into her brother's eyes. They were, indeed, laughing and very starry eyes. But at the moment Finnir himself was not laughing. He wore an expression of wonder and even of curious interrogation. When he spoke his voice was like the singing of the spiders or the fall of dancing rain.

"You are like Mélusine, and yet you are not her: you are Eli." He seemed to be seeing both of her identities at once, and balancing or interchanging them in his mind. Then he finally smiled and added, "I am so happy to meet with you, once again or for the first time! It will be a great joy to speak with you, this evening I hope, in the Silver City."

Eli was trying, really quite desperately, to reply with some sort of gracious greeting, but no words would come to her lips. She just nodded, and smiled back at her shining sibling. He and Reyse now entered into a brief conversation; indeed, their long and close friendship was very evident even in the exchange of a few intimate words. Eli studied them together, fascinated by the glowing energy of many years --- or centuries --- shared, by their beautiful ease and the bond between them as they spoke.

"You travel by foot, and not by wing, I see," said Aulfrin, not noticing in the least --- it seemed --- the impression made upon his daughter by Finnir, for Eli was still simply looking on, very silent and thoughtful. "But then, you have the hounds with you, of course."

"Yes," concurred Finnir, "we ride by the shore-paths of the Shooting Star. Look, even as we speak our impatient steeds come forth to hasten us along!"

Laughing, the Prince turned to the sound of branches rustling several yards behind them. Half a dozen other great, milk-white wolf-hounds were gathered there, and three horses were now visible, just coming out from the forest's closest trees.

"Farewell, until this evening then," waved the King.

The three handsome riders turned to their steeds, mounted in light-footed leaps onto their bare backs and took up the dark blue ribbon-reins that hung over their long manes. Two of the horses were very pale dapple-grey, like a mottled sky of fleecy clouds, but Finnir's steed was pure white. Over his withers hung a sort of saddle-bag (though there was no saddle!), which he now took up and slung over his shoulder.

Eli would, normally, have made some delighted comment, for protruding from the open bag was his beautiful little grey-wood lap harp. But something else had taken her attention right away from the musical instrument carried by her brother.

As the horses bore their riders back into the forest, Eli griped Reyse's arm. At last she found her voice, but it was trembling.

"Was that what I think? Did I really see what I just saw?!" she gasped. "Finnir is riding a *unicorn*?!"

She looked inquiringly from Reyse's furrowed brows to her father's bemused face.

A slightly uncomfortable silence followed, and then the King softly remarked, "You are perturbed and your vision confused by the light of Finnir's pearl, perhaps. It casts a strong glow and can trick the eye. No, dear Eli, his is a white *horse* --- a very elegant and perfectly formed horse --- but a horse nonetheless. No, that was *not* a unicorn."

Eli gave him a very startled look, and turned to Reyse for support and confirmation. He said nothing, but only continued to look sceptically at her.

"But I saw a horn on its head: a long spiral horn of silver, on the horse's forehead," she insisted, speaking slowly and almost to herself.

Aulfrin stroked his short beard, and then he smiled once again. "Did you now? Well, that's the effect of Finnir, I'll warrant, at least on some of the more sensitive souls who behold him and his lovely mount, Neya-Voun. Or perhaps it is quite simply the magic of his pearl, for he won it in his second Initiation and that was passed in company with the unicorns of Barrywood's Glens. You are very perceptive to the vibrations of unicorns, my dearest Eli, or were as the Princess Mélusine, and so you may have been granted a mystical vision, for a moment, of an animal dear to you both.

"But there are no unicorns outside of Barrywood, even though the marvellous Prince Finnir be present!

"Now, let us continue our own voyage. Do you fly with us, my dear Reyse?"

Reyse seemed serious once again, but in only a second he had found his composure and was kissing Eli's hand and bidding farewell, in a very normal tone of voice, to the King.

"No, your Majesty, I am on my way to Davenia to see your second son. My own horse awaits me together with the pixie Piv on the other side of the Falls. I will hastily fly to them there and then pursue my course at a gentle land-gallop, for I have tidings to deliver to Demoran from Leyano, and Piv wishes to make a stop in the woods of the Fire-Birds at mid-day. We were met, early this morning, by Jizay and Ferglas, passing along the northern banks of the Star, who told me that you and Eli were probably bathing here. It was a happy chance that we also found Finnir and his companions at the same moment. A happy chance, but that is an *absurd* word to use," he added, looking quite seriously at Eli, once again.

"I will hope to rejoin you all in Fantasie, if the gift of absurd and happy chances continues to haunt me --- as soon as I may. Until then, my half-moon blessings upon you, Sire….and upon my Lady *Licorne*."

He turned immediately and walked proudly back across the sand to where Eli has taken her swim. From there he rose directly into the air, his broad wings appearing instantaneously from his shoulder-blades. They were white and brown, finely veined and decorated with small golden spots and various other glistening motifs, it seemed. He flew swiftly out of view across the wide Lake.

Aulfrin was thoughtful for a moment, and then he lifted his hand and beckoned to the two winged-horses. He gave Eli a foot up, as she seemed a little shaken by her meetings with both Reyse and Finnir, and then he mounted Cynnabar.

With a warm nod, now, to his daughter, he led the way to the same point where Reyse had taken flight, and as if climbing up the steps of an invisible staircase, both horses took to the air and circled up over the Star, and then continued to sail slowly far above the glorious Falls and over the first few miles of the Lake's 'tail'.

****

From the skies, the current in the centre of the wide Lake was clearly visible. In fact, the Shooting Star's tail, flowing from the Salmon Haven to the falls which cascaded into the Star itself, seemed to Eli like a blue and green rainbow: she had never seen so many different hues of the same family of colours! The central ribbon of faster flowing water was brilliant turquoise; the swirling arms of ripples and waves to either side were mixtures of greenish-blue so dark they were emerald in places, contrasted with a bright cobalt blue threaded with streaks of ultramarine. Near the shores were lighter shades of cornflower blue and wavelets with starry white points of light flashing on their lavender-blue crests.

Eli's gaze was held for many minutes by these twinkling and dancing stars. Her eyes, she surmised, were most probably watering with the sharp breeze of the flight and the bright sunlight. Even so, her vision seemed lucid and crystal-clear as regarded all else; but the crests of those little waves were playing her tricks. Or was she seeing with her heart, more and more? On every rising and tumbling arc of sparkling water the white stars were turning into a garden. Lilies, tiny white lilies, lilies-of-the-valley. All the long shore as far as she could see was host to these flowers, appearing and disappearing, almost teasingly.

Her breath was caught in her throat, and her eyes were now losing their focus, because they were brimming with tears. Lily, her little moon, her own Lily was filling her heart so that she thought it would break. She did not know what to do with her emotions, what to think of this strange vision, what to believe was real or imagined or hallucinated. And her father was flying ahead, out of earshot of any remark or question.

She tucked the beautiful and very strange image, and the burning memories of her human 'mother', deeply into her swelling heart, and bid them remain there until she could understand them fully. Immediately she felt relieved and relaxed once more. She looked back at the pageant of blues and greens nearer to the centre of the Lake, and she stroked Peronne's flowing mane and then twined long, thick strands of soft hairs around her fingers as he gracefully nodded his head in his flight.

About halfway up the Lake, Aulfrin turned Cynnabar towards the northern shore, and Peronne followed. Both horses landed delicately on the broad shoreline of white sand skirting the edge of the forest. There were many chestnut trees, already in bloom, with tapering masses of white or pink flowers like coloured candles on their outstretched arms. Oaks were visible too, as were proud beeches and mottled sycamores. Eli noticed two or three handsome rowan trees, reminding her of the ancient, gnarled tree on the heights above the City of Fantasie, where she had first met Garo. These rowans were younger, certainly, than that solitary tree, for they seemed to have a youthful glow and exuberance about them --- but they were very tall. They were decorated with flowers, too, snowy white clusters that made Eli think of hundreds of small wedding bouquets.

It was probably mid-day now, and the sun was warm and shining down vigorously on the south-facing beach. The riders dismounted and strolled along the shore-line, splashing their lightly-booted feet in the lapping water.

Eli was about to comment to her father that the white of the sand recalled the Willow Isles' soil, when she stopped short, her eyes suddenly drawn to look into the shadows under the nearest trees. Dozens of faces were smiling out at her, their eyes bright and curious and glinting with the play of the light beneath the leaves and blossoms.

"An invitation to luncheon with some of my subjects," the King reassured her, "as I thought you would now be well able to see more of the true fairy-folk of the realm, and that it would be pleasant for you to be re-introduced to families and clans who have missed you these past fifty years."

"I knew these fairies, when I was the Princess Mélusine?"

"But of course! There are pathways to and from the White Willow Isles on both sides of the Lake. The banks are forested, and some roads wind through them; but beyond the woods there are open fields which are delightful to travel across as well. You became acquainted with the populations of all this region during your childhood, and you retained the contact and strengthened the friendship you had established for centuries thereafter."

Eli shook her head. "It is *continuing* to make my head spin to imagine how long my life has already lasted!" she laughed. "My brain is still a human brain, as yet, I'm afraid. It can't get around the idea that I'm centuries old. I will have to come back into my fairy-form before I can really digest it, I suppose."

Aulfrin paused before turning to approach the forest-eaves, and placed a strong hand on his daughter's shoulder. "I am happy to hear you make such a comment, for it encourages my belief that will choose to do so. Yes, when you re-inhabit your sleeping body, you will be entirely at ease with being a *young* fairy-woman of about six-hundred-and-sixty!"

Eli laughed with him. And then she asked, "Does everyone in Faërie know that I have been away in the human world, that I became a changeling?"

Aulfrin continued to remain facing her, and his eyes seemed to shine.

"Many know," he said, "but not all. Your family, of course, is well-aware of your story and we have all been missing you since you left us. Many of my animal subjects learned of your decision or perhaps 'felt' your departure from Faërie, and some of the greater fairies of the kingdom, such as the rainbow fairy Banvowha as well as the Lady Ecume and many of the mer-people, offered their support and their blessings upon both your human-infant form and also --- continuously --- upon your cocooned and hidden body awaiting you on Scholar-Owl Island.

"But it was only when you had re-entered Fantasie for the first time that I agreed to allow knowledge of your tale and of your three Visits to be shared with those in the Silver City. And though it was me that gave the permission, the sharing of that information came not from me, but from the Great Trees. I do not know if all the inhabitants of Fantasie are aware of your adventures now, or if the Trees have been selective in their enlightening of certain fairies only. However, news tends to circulate quickly in the City!

"But beyond it, no, I do not think that too many others have heard the tale of your leaving, or of your returning as a human now. The fairies we have already met in our travels, on your first Visit for instance, have understood who you are, naturally. And I have told *these* fair-folk, with whom we shall dine now, by the means of the faithful messengers who left us this morning: Ferglas and Jizay."

The King hesitated, and then continued in a whisper, "But I think that I would be right in saying that Erreig knows *nothing* of your transformation into a changeling child, nor does he know that your absence from this land is now drawing to its close.

"I will add a word more, Eli, before we enter the woods and delight in the welcome of my people here. *Beware of the dragon-chieftain Erreig*, and be warned that --- for some reason --- it is clear to me that he fears you greatly. I have my own ideas why this may be, but I am not absolutely certain. In any case, his apprehension and avoidance of you, ever since you were a child I believe, are tangible in my perceptions of him --- dim as those often are at the distance usually maintained between us. He fears my bold Finnir, also, after his encounters with him in the White Cat Caves; but his fear of you is even greater.

"I have told you already of certain skills and certain kinds of knowledge which are vital in the role of kingship. But what I will tell you now is perhaps the greatest lesson to learn as a ruler: it is only **fear** which incites any and all acts of violence, of dishonesty, of treachery, of hatred. Without fear, there is only peace. Beware Erreig's fear."

****

Fairies of all ages, tall adults and laughing children, plus dogs and deer and badgers and birds, welcomed Eli and even danced merrily and skilfully for her. There must have been close to a hundred of Aulfrin's subjects at their festive luncheon, but curiously it felt a very intimate and informal affair. Many fairies, even the very young, Eli surmised, could move and talk and eat and drink with such grace and with such elegant reserve that it seemed like the choreography of a ballet or the perfectly tempered notes of a great symphony.

Few of the adult fairies actually spoke to Eli directly, except to offer her their greetings and blessings, and the fairy-children seemed rather too shy to do more than look at her with wide, sparkling eyes --- of all colours imaginable. Eli wondered if some were pixies, like Piv, rather than youngsters, but Aulfrin assured her that these were families of the greater fairy-folk, and not members of the smaller races, such as pixies and leprechauns, sprites and imps, brownies and the like.

"If you wish to catch a glimpse of the hidden Little People, you must be very sharp-eyed and very patient," he laughed. "As the Princess Mélusine, you had the skill to see them everywhere, and were even befriended closely by some --- such as your belovèd Periwinkle. But they are, even with us of the larger races, very secretive and rather elusive. Try looking at the tall grasses there, in that beam of sunlight falling through the branches. If you relax your eyes and open your heart, you may perceive more than green and golden vegetation!"

Eli turned to look at the clumps of high, wild grasses and aromatic herbs in the rays of light between the trees which her father had indicated. The sunlight was falling in bold, dusty columns of warm yellow, illuminating the gently swaying dark green blades and the pastel flowers. She tried to stare into the depths of the undergrowth, but could see nothing unusual.

Finally she relaxed her vision and slowed her breathing, almost as if she were meditating. From far away it seemed (though it was only a few yards behind her, where the long tables were laid with fruits and nuts, leaf-platters of breads and chalices of mead), came the notes of a fiddle, mingling with the songs of blackbirds, robins and sky-larks.

As she continued to look at the sea of grasses, now with a gentle smile on her lips, Eli raised her eyebrows. She did not dare to say anything or to make any abrupt change in her breathing or in the soft focus of her gazing eyes. But there, quite certainly, among the tall blades of grass and almost a part of the pattern of the stems and blossoms, were faces. A pair of almond-shaped eyes here, a crooked smile there, a long nose or a pointed chin, flowing hair the colour of corn or a fringe or curls falling over one eye as green as the grass around it…

When she tried to strain her eyes, even just a little more, to see in greater detail, all was gone. Only grasses remained, with the tune of the fiddler now beckoning her to turn back to the colourful company of taller and completely visible fairies.

Aulfrin introduced some of the beautiful folk to her, explaining their skills or arts in many domains. These were fairy-families associated with certain flowers or animals, or with various crafts. Some were devoted to particular kinds of trees or stones, butterflies or beetles. There were tender and lovely individuals who looked after birds' nests or rabbit warrens, caterpillar-cocoons or blind baby hedgehogs in their twiggy burrows. Others were artists working to create strange and wonderful patterns of moss or lichen, fungus or criss-crossed branches and roots. Some were introduced to her simply as 'painters', and Eli wondered if they were skilled at adding delicate dots to birds-eggs or stripes on the legs of very fashionable frogs! And a few --- held in very high regard, it seemed --- were engaged in collaborations with the marvellous interlace snails of this region where the borders of Vivony met those of Aumelas-Pen.

Eli and the King spent a wonderful two hours or so lunching and sometimes chatting, sipping sweet mead and listening to the airs of the fiddlers and whistle-players, accompanied by the birds and spiders. At last, it was time to rejoin their flying mounts and take to the skies on the last leg of their journey home to the City of Fantasie.

As they rose into the air, Eli could see the misty white spray of the great waterfalls that fed the Shooting Star Lake from the River of the Grey Man as it passed out from the secret recesses of the Salmon Haven.

Suddenly, a thrilling thought came into her mind and made her catch her breath. "I'll see him in the City, this evening! He will be there!"

But before she could understand why her own heart had uttered such a joyful exclamation, she heard another voice, also springing from the depths of her mind, which asked, "Who will you see? Reyse? Will Reyse be there tonight?"

She shook her head. No, Reyse had not promised to be in Fantasie so soon. He was going to Davenia to see her brother Demoran. She looked down at the multitude of blues and greens, silvers and whites, in the waters far below, and she could see, once again, the myriad lily-of-the-valleys sparkling on the crests of the shore-line wavelets.

"It's not Reyse I'm excited to be seeing," she heard herself admit --- though which of her interior voices was speaking, she was not sure. "It's my brother Finnir who will be there. My brother with eyes so blue and clear that they contain the whole universe. My brother with a silver-grey harp in his hand and a glowing pearl set into his forehead. My mysterious and beautiful brother who I am *sure* was riding a unicorn…"

The noise of the majestic falls, very near now, was deafening. But despite their roaring tumult, Eli thought that she could clearly hear the tiny bells of the lilies --- singing to her from the sparkling crests of the waves.

****

A Delicate Balance

Chapter Nine:
Sapphires and Potpourri

Flying up close beside her, the King spoke to Eli as both horses soared over the hamlet of Shepherds' Lodge.

"The Silver City is coming into view, my dear Eli," he called. "Let us circle above it once, all around the oval of its walls, for you will thus have a perspective of the fountains and woods, the Moon and Star towers, and of the Great Trees, that is truly breath-taking!"

Delighted, Eli and Peronne followed close behind Aulfrin on Cynnabar, arriving at the limits of the City where the eastern, or Fifth Gate stood midway between two of the Star Towers and was itself situated at the base of one of the seven great Moon Towers. These lunar towers were very imposing and as beautiful as graceful young trees, albeit giant trees: each was over four hundred feet high, with the Great Tower of the King twice that height. Eli and her father passed close beside this most easterly Tower and then turned swiftly to the south to follow the sweep of the curved confines of the oval City.

From the back of Peronne, Eli indeed had an astounding view of all the wonders contained within this incredible metropolis. The silver-turreted towers and the luxuriant bushes and lesser trees, the lawns and flower beds, workshops and houses, were all glorious to behold, but it was true that the scene was utterly dominated by the sacred Garden at its centre. Taller than any trees Eli had ever seen in the human world, even including the majestic redwoods and sequoias she had recently visited in northern California, the Great Trees of Fantasie not only claimed all the attention of the eye, but that of the heart as well. Their energy was tangible and vibrating, a constant tidal-wave of pure and powerful *joie de vivre*!

As father and daughter sailed slowly above the Southern Gate --- just beyond the ellipsis of Fantasie --- Eli's view of the Great Tower of the King on the opposite and northern side of the City was obscured by the coloured mists and flickering light that swirled about the heads of the Trees and all along the ring of their inter-connected branches. And just before that greatest of the Towers passed behind the veil of mauve and blue and rosy light emanating from the magical Trees, it changed into a tall tree itself. It was no longer even quite solid, but simply a wavering vision of a huge tree, silver-grey and immense, but insubstantial. And then it was hidden.

Unable to keep her eyes on the Great Trees for too long at a time, Eli turned to another force that drew her attention now. Far below and to her left, outside of the limits of the City but somehow very much a part of it, was the Stone Circle. She turned her head and gazed into the vapours of white and grey fog that she could see languidly dancing around the three closest megaliths of the Circle, though they were still far off.

She recalled her visit to the edge of the Circle with Aindel, and meeting Garo and the twins coming out of the enchanted mist. But now, for some reason, the Stones seemed to exude a far greater, even threatening, power --- almost a roaring voice calling out to her. Unsure if the force she felt was truly 'awful' or simply awe-inspiring, Eli felt --- nonetheless --- completely overwhelmed; and then she panicked.

Suddenly she screamed, and leaned far, much too far, to one side of Peronne's withers. Her hands grasped for the long, flowing strands of his white mane, but she was out of reach of them. She felt herself slipping from his back!

Simultaneously, three things happened.

Peronne lurched to the right, feeling his mistress losing her balance, in an attempt to centre himself once again beneath her and to keep her astride him. Cynnabar, just ahead of them, pivoted abruptly in mid-flight, folded her great russet wings close into her body and she and the King swooped back to approach Peronne --- but just a little lower, in case Eli should indeed fall and they might be capable of catching her in mid-air. And thirdly, from the pathway below her, leading out of the great southern Gates of the City and down to the Stone Circle --- the road that Eli herself had taken with Aindel when she had surreptitiously gone to this enchanted place near the end of her first Visit --- a flash of brilliant blue light shot up into the sky.

Eli continued to teeter dangerously to the right --- trying to hug Peronne's generous body with her legs, but slipping further with each passing split-second away from the force of the Stone Circle's incense-like fog and the shock of energy radiating from the three standing stones closest to her. But in the very midst of her fall, she felt the piercing counter-charge of the ray of blue light.

It seemed to be touching her head, or more precisely her right ear; and though she felt herself on the verge of losing consciousness, the sensation of this cool, clear, reinvigorating blue light sent a rolling shiver into her head and throughout her body.

Time seemed to utterly stop and Eli found that she could turn her head towards the almost burning coldness of the blue light where it had touched the lobe of her right ear --- and where there was still the sensation of a whispering, echoing chill. She wanted to lift her hand to touch the strange, icy prickling of her ear-lobe, but she reached out instead to the ray of blue that she could see, for it was streaming upwards towards her, fine and slender, like a twisted cord of cloudless sky-light. The palm of her right hand touched it, and it was solid --- or at least forceful, like a strong jet of water. She held her hand open, and the blue beam pushed against it until she was sitting solidly once again on Peronne's back, where he was hovering almost stationary in mid-air. Her left hand grasped a clump of his mane, and her legs tightened around his flanks.

She was safe again.

Cynnabar was leading the way, now, down to earth within the City walls: a steady and gradual descent, but urgent and swift nonetheless.

Eli was beginning to breathe normally again, and she laid her head on her mount's arched neck. Through the billowing strands of his mane she looked back to the pathway beneath her, just passing out of view as the southern walls and high hedges obscured it from sight. A man was there, a tall figure in blues and greens. His left hand was raised as if he were nonchalantly picking stars from the heavens, and from the back of his hand a final wink of piercing blue light could be seen. It was quickly swallowed back into the hand, and disappeared. As the man was lost to view behind the walls of Fantasie, Eli touched her fingers to the lobe of her right ear. She was not wearing any ear-rings, but for a split-second she felt a hard, multi-faceted stone there. Then only her own soft skin.

Peronne turned gently and came to land not far from the fountain of Lysandel. Aulfrin was already dismounted and his arms were immediately there to receive Eli and help her to glide down off her horse's back. He embraced her and the rushing, warm wave of energy which enveloped her was like slipping into a hot bath. She sighed, and smiled.

"You and I will have special thanks to offer to your brother this evening!" declared her father, beaming and continuing to hold her close in his arms.

When he at last released her and looked into her face with concern still clouding his deep green eyes, Eli questioned him with her own. He nodded, and sighed with relief.

"Yes, yes. It was Finnir who was there to hear your cry and witness you falling, or fainting, over-come by the force of the standing stones of the Circle. All the blessings of the Moon-Dancers on him, dear boy! He may be a very calm and aloof fairy, but he reacts quickly in a tight place."

"Finnir saved me? The blue light, that was from Finnir?"

"In his final Initiation, my bold Finnir won the great sapphire called the *Eye of the Innumerable Falls*. It is set into the golden tanned skin at the back of his left hand. It is one of the most powerful gems in all of Faërie.

"And, by strange coincidence, Banvowha awarded you a sapphire also, at the completion of your last Initiation. It is smaller than the great stone of those waterfalls in the east of Faërie which pour their cold draughts into the Inward Sea of Finnir's princedom, but it is of the same family. It is set into your right ear-lobe, my sweet Mélusine. It seems that Finnir commanded his own stone to join with yours: though yours is invisible in your human form, I could see a spark of your modest sapphire's colour that joined itself to the thread of intense blue light which gently but firmly forbade your fall and redressed you onto Peronne's sturdy back. I do not think that your winged-horse, or even your alarmed father, could have saved you from that fall, for you are not yet Mélusine but still the changeling Eli, and you have no wings of your own again yet. Thanks be to Finnir, a hundred thanks, for coming to your rescue!"

Eli could find no words, but softly touched again her right ear, and saw in her mind's eye the tall fairy-lord, his arm reaching up so calmly and gracefully, and the sparkle of blue light as it disappeared, recalled into the back of his hand.

But no, there was nothing to say to her father just now, for she had no words, no language, for what she was feeling at this moment.

****

Finnir had gone to the Stone Circle, and his two companions were visiting the City; they would not arrive at the King's Tower before late in the evening. This was explained to Aulfrin and Eli when they arrived --- mounted but riding on the ground at a gentle trot --- in the Entrance Court of the palace. The King then decided to go to his Music Room and Council Chamber before their supper, and bid Eli relax in her own bedroom and calm her shaken nerves for a while.

She happily climbed the wide staircase with her father, and then continued up another few flights of broad, inlaid steps after he had turned down the long corridor to his private rooms.

Trying to restrain her tendency for drama, she tried to breathe deeply and think in a detached and calm way of her near-fall, and to send up a prayer of gratitude for the tall fairy and the thin strand of blue light. It was over, and she was safe. And she wished Finnir well, imagining that he and his companions would soon be, most probably, enjoying the *Swooping Swallow Inn* near the southern Gate, or some other place of camaraderie and perhaps good ales. In any case, she felt slightly relieved to be on her own, especially since a restorative tea had already been delivered to her own bedroom high in the western wing of the palace.

Leaning out over the balcony of the generously proportioned turret, she could see down into one of the courtyards, still high up in the complex architecture of the royal dwelling, which connected the central Tower to some of its adjacent arms. She was just about to turn back to her airy room and her half-finished tea, when the rays of sunset threw a crimson glow onto two creatures hurrying across the courtyard towards the staircase leading up to her bower.

A gleeful "Aha!" escaped her lips. It was Piv and Jizay!

She hadn't the patience to await them, so left her turret and arrived on a landing one flight below just as they were reaching it too. Piv was flying in whizzing little circles around Jizay, himself jogging happily and bright-eyed up the stairs, and when the pixie saw Eli he darted ahead in a blur of bright green wings to wrap his chubby arms around her neck and kiss her cheek. She only had time to return a hasty kiss on his own rosy cheek before Jizay was barking and inviting her to incline her face for him to greet her with a joyous kiss as well, in the form of several enthusiastic licks.

Although the pixie and the two hounds had been travelling all day, and at a good pace, neither Piv nor Jizay seemed unduly tired. Ferglas had already gone off to rejoin his master. Periwinkle was bursting with tales of his visit to the Fire-Bird Forest, where he had joined the dogs in their journey to Fantasie; but he also had heard from Reyse that Finnir, Aytel and Brea would be meeting with the King this evening. He told Eli that he imagined they would be closeted away in clandestine councils of some kind, and that he and she --- with Jizay of course --- could perhaps take a starlit walk after dinner to exchange all their news. He reminded Eli that the moon would not rise until the wee hours of the next morning, and in any case she was as thin as a weaver's curved needle, for she was nearly dark now, or 'sleeping with her eyes tight closed', as he put it. But, he assured her, there is always a compensation for the absence of our dear ones, such as the moon, and also the Lord Reyse, and so there would be brilliant stars to illuminate their walk!

Eli agreed that such a plan would suit her well, and they decided to go down to the Council Chamber to see if the King was there, and to ask if they might have his permission for such an outing after dinner.

But Aulfrin was a step ahead of them, for he met them at the foot of the stairs, and bid them follow him to the dining room, where a light meal awaited them before the other fairies would arrive. Always pleased by an invitation to a meal, Piv flew excitedly on ahead, and Eli --- her hand resting on Jizay's head as they walked --- accompanied her father in the same direction.

Eli asked if she and Piv and her hound of joy would be free to go for their starry walk while the meeting took place with Finnir, but Aulfrin seemed surprised by such a request.

"You don't wish to be with us? It may be a *private* meeting, my dear girl, but our conversation will not necessarily include subjects to be kept secret from *you*! In fact, I think your presence would be most welcome. Are you in any way reticent to be in the company of your brother…and now your rescuer?"

"Oh, I had certainly planned to thank Finnir and that with all my heart," exclaimed Eli. "I just thought that, following my words of gratitude, you would probably have important things to discuss." But she had to admit that the thought of being with him did make her feel a little timid, somehow. How odd, she conceded, inwardly. I'm hardly shy with men!

But *that* thought was even more perturbing. Referring to her brother as a 'man' gave her a very strange feeling indeed. She shook her head, as if a fly were buzzing annoyingly around it. The King stopped for a moment, and turned to her.

"Do you shake your head to say 'no', you do *not* wish to be party to our discourse? Or do you refuse some other thought?"

Eli looked up into her father's eyes. As ever, they were merry and wise, concerned and knowing, all at once. How much, she wondered, smiling rather self-consciously now, does he know or guess of my most private feelings and thoughts!?

"I'd be happy to stay, of course," she assented. "And happy to know Finnir better. He seems in every way a most remarkable, powerful, magical being."

"That's a good girl! And yes, quite true that all of those qualities are found in your sibling. But please remember that he is also simply your brother, at least your half-brother, and so you need not be *quite* so impressed by him, certainly not to the point of being ill-at-ease in his presence. He is a part of your true family, my Eli."

Piv was disappointed, but only for an instant. His cheery nature would not allow more than that. Their starlight stroll would be postponed until another night, and he would be happy, instead, to go dancing with several of his cousins this evening among the toadstools and flowers of the blue circle of the Garden of the Great Trees. A favourite occupation of his when in the Silver City, so it seemed. He was not even annoyed *not* to be invited to the council; he said he much preferred dancing to discussions!

They all dined together however --- Eli and Aulfrin, the pixie and hounds --- before Piv flew off through the wide windows to his starry dancing-appointment. Eli now felt much calmer and more relaxed, even *before* her father offered her a small blown-glass goblet, like a crystal acorn on a delicate stem of moonlight, filled with a *liqueur* made from violet plums and wild strawberries and also a curious spice that Eli felt she should be able to identify. She was sure she had encountered the perfume before, but could not remember where. But in any case, the *liqueur* was delicious, and quite strong.

"It was made by your mother, by the Queen Rhynwanol," remarked Aulfrin, as he poured some for himself. "She had a little 'concocting cell' here in the Tower, not far from the Music Room that you visited. She particularly liked this recipe, and made quite a store of it --- before she left us." He paused thoughtfully, and then sipped his drink.

"I did not touch any of the bottles for many centuries, but when I returned home after your first Visit, my dear Eli, I had the strange and irrepressible urge to taste this nectar once again. She used to call it her *love potion*, but it is no such thing! It is simply a mixture that suggests, in the mind and heart of the imbiber, the face of the loved one. I thought you would be interested to hear that I expected to see the lovely face of Lily in my mind's eye when I tasted it again, but in fact I did not. I saw the exquisite face of Rhynwanol, with her blue-black hair framing her fine features and her lavender-mauve eyes filled with tenderness, and even affection.

"A dream-vision, I imagine, and a memory of long-ago. For my Queen's heart is now given to the Dragon-Chieftain, as I well know. But it is nice to remember, with the aroma of her cherished spices filling the nose and caressing the palette, that she was once upon a time, most certainly, my 'loved one', and that my heart has not forgotten that deep love.

"Ah," he broke off suddenly from his musings, "here is your brother, and his two brave companions!"

Eli's mind was confused by several thoughts at once. She had been somewhat shocked by her father's confession of love for her mother the Queen, and curious to know why this desire to taste her 'concoction' had come just after her own first Visit home to Faërie. She was also recalling the heady odours she had noticed coming from the room along the same corridor as the Queen's Music Room; so *that* was where she had smelt this perfume before! And now it brought back memories of that day she had come across the harp of her mother and seen the phantom-like image of the incredibly beautiful Rhynwanol, who had looked upon her for an instant with her piecing and yet very loving violet-blue eyes. Eli shuddered with the rising emotions in her chest, and had to close her own eyes tightly for a second to stave off the tears.

And as she did so, in the darkness of her momentary blindness and with her throat hot with the sensations of the fruity-spicy *liqueur*, she saw the face of a man. Or rather of several men. For even in the spilt-second it took to swallow her sip of 'love potion', the face before her changed four or five times!

First she saw the gentle and rather wistful eyes of her Irish husband Colm, and then the cold but very intense regard of Yves. Then the face became ruddy and tanned, and the chestnut hair was short and curly around Liam's pleasant face, and then it was long and wavy as the image altered ever-so-slightly to become Reyse as a true fairy-lord. She opened her eyes, or thought she had. And there was the radiant face of her noble, fair, blond and blue-eyed brother Finnir. And he was greeting her.

It was unusual for Eli to be lost for words, but she found no courteous phrase or salutation in reply to Finnir. She couldn't even summon the gratitude or courage to thank him for saving her life! She simply smiled, and that rather timidly.

That seemed enough for him, however, for he returned a very sincere smile for hers, and as he did so he tilted his head and his clear blue eyes flashed like stars. A lock of golden hair moved across his forehead as he did so, and the pearl set into the skin just above and between his thin eyebrows glowed like a tiny full moon. Eli had the overwhelming desire to continue to gaze into his eyes by the light of that moon forever. It made her smile even more timidly and tenderly, and rather amusedly too.

But as she murmured her 'hello's to Brea and Aytel, and all five of them took their seats around the wide, circular table, she felt suddenly very uncomfortable. She found it impossible to stop imaging the joy of being lost in her brother's eyes ...endlessly. And *that* felt too much like falling in love! She couldn't be falling in love with her own brother!

"I am still Eli, and not Mélusine," she reasoned with herself, lowering her eyes and idly scratching Jizay's soft head and velvety ears, "and so I am not fully conscious of having brothers at all. When I return to my true body and role here, I won't entertain such daft infatuations for my own kin."

She looked up again, meaning to glance around the table at everyone; but her eye fell immediately on Finnir once more, and remained there for a long moment. He was looking at her also, and his regard was ambiguous and a little questioning. Eli wondered if his magical powers had allowed him to read her thoughts and hear her unspoken words. No one else seemed to notice their exchange of looks, however, for Aulfrin was proposing a serving platter of various fruits and seed-sprinkled crackers covered with nut-butter, as well as small chalices of a sweet yellow wine, to the two other fairies. There were no attendants in the little dining-and-meeting room that evening, but the King seemed very relaxed serving his guests and talking informally with them at the same time.

"I am happy to have my returning daughter here with us," began Aulfrin. "She may not yet be the Princess Mélusine once again, but I see no reason to exclude her from our conversation, for she will appreciate the knowledge this will give her of her home and its present dilemmas and diplomatic developments, and we may be enriched by her insights and advice as well, during tonight's exchanges and perhaps also in the future. Though Eli, still, she is of royal lineage and bears ---- deeply hidden in the depths of her spirit --- the wisdom gained from the Great Charm and from her earlier Initiations." He smiled with respect at his daughter, and Eli felt the surge of tingling pride rise to her cheeks and make them redden.

"It is well to have a human representative here, if Eli will permit me to call her that," added the Prince. "For the current challenges facing your realm, my Sovereign and father, are intertwined with that world, and concern our relationship with humans."

"To some extent, yes, Finnir of my heart," agreed Aulfrin. "But what I chiefly wish to discuss with you this evening is the state of affairs within my own family, and among certain fairies closely allied to my children. Eli knows that I am aware of the communications, and perhaps negotiations, going on between certain Moon-Dancers and one or two of the Sun-Singers…"

He looked pointedly and pridefully at Eli once more, and then he turned towards Finnir again.

"As you also know, my son. You are well aware of these confederacies and arbitrations. And you are sole among my three sons to know how much *I know* or guess. Though I find it difficult to believe that Demoran and Leyano, with their subtlety and wisdom, do not imagine that I know much of what has been going on. However, it would appear that they do not --- for they continue to pursue their scheming and their furtive meetings behind my back.

"It is like a tree," Aulfrin laughed. "I came to that image earlier today, as I was cogitating on this rather amusing situation. My rule and my comprehension of my realm are the thick trunk of the great tree, with roots of my many centuries of kingship stretching deep and wide into the foundations laid by my forefathers, Aulfrelas and Aulf the Mighty. My branches are far-reaching and there are many birds that alight upon them with melodies of harmonising news or discordant rumours.

"And then there are the leaves --- for what is a tree without leaves? And my leaves are the lively and living and dancing power-plays and plans and plots of my children! Those desires and goals and difficulties and connivances would not, could not exist without the structure of my roots, trunk and branches. They take their life and their unique style from me. But they are not me. They sprout from my kingship, but they will flourish and fade and fall. However, I well understand that they are a living part of who I am and of what Faërie is, while they are there. Truly, they nourish my realm: these attempts at alliances and these clandestine conspiracies, these dreams and desires, they feed me and serve me and are a part of my life and of the force of my kingship. I therefore respect my children's activities, and I do not belittle them. Yet neither do I fear them!

"Many many years ago, my father, the King Aulfrelas, explained it to me thus, in similar images: *Your ancestors are alive and growing still, through you, every day of your reign, Aulfrin. They course through your veins, their voices echo in your thoughts, their deeds --- both great and ill --- colour your present rule. And likewise your progeny play their part: they will adorn your reign with buds and blossoms, leaves and fruit. The energy of their contribution, season after season, will flow down with great and natural beauty into the story of your kingdom and into your governing of it.*

Remain ever open and curious about their ideas and their life-force, even their discontent or their hunger for change. For there lies great richness for you in your children, just as in your forebears. Some of your offspring will leave you, others will cling to you. Some will bless you, others will bring you tears or trouble.

But your true wisdom is never, never to accept *what they bring to you --- do not accept any of it:* welcome *it and* embrace *it! Honour it all, with gratitude and fluidity. Liken your attitude to the nature of water, for water opens to receive what falls into it, it turns gracefully around what obstructs it, it quenches the thirst of what is dry, it swells the seed, and it cleanses, refreshes, and revives. And* **nothing**, *not even the hardest rock, is stronger than water! It is our beginning and our birth-place, the element and the symbol of our unending cycle of life, our cradle and our tomb and our new birth.*

Keep growing and flowing, Aulfrin, and you and your realm will know the truth of the trees and the wisdom of water.

"And therefore, my dear children and my trusted Moon-Dancers, I welcome the news of these schemes, and even what could appear to be the disloyalty or sedition of contacts with Erreig and his son Garo. I fear neither of those dragon-lords, nor do I discount their nobility and their courage.

"But I will not remain inactive either, nor allow my children to play *all* the parts in this epic-tale! For I share your desire for a better future for Faërie, and for the alliance of our race and that of humankind. But as for that latter goal, I am warier than your generation, I think. I can claim to know much about the human world; but much that I know is not encouraging. I remain optimistic, but posed and patient, guarded and careful. I will not be rash, and I will not tolerate any rashness in the acts of my subjects or my children or their comrades."

Finnir's face was utterly mysterious to Eli. As he listened to his father, his eyes shone and the corners of his generous lips rose ever so slightly. But Eli could not guess if he were amused or impressed.

Aytel and Brea both nodded their concurrence with Aulfrin's speech. Eli looked from one to the other, seated at a short distance on either side of her at the large round table.

Aytel's profile was angular and chiselled, very noble and beautifully proportioned. Like Finnir, he was fair-haired, though his locks were longer that her brother's, falling just below his shoulders. When she had first met these three fairies beside Shooting Star Lake, the hair of both Aytel and Brea had blown loose and free, stranded with gemstones, as she recalled. Those coloured jewels were still glistening here and there, reflecting the light of the candles held in the wall-brackets all about the intimate dining hall where they were seated, but they were less obvious, for both fairies now wore their hair in several thick, shortish braids.

Brea, seated on Eli's other side, had hair that was slightly redder, the colour of pale peach-skin, Eli thought. He was less classically handsome, but almost more 'human'-looking, with a warmth and roundness in his tanned cheeks and chin, the dimples of a little boy and very merry eyes, sage-green and bright.

After a moment or two, Finnir spoke. His voice was deep and gentle.

"Father, would you be willing to meet with my brothers, and speak openly of these negotiations, to allow them to understand your position more fully?"

Aulfrin shook his head with a smile. "As I have said to Eli, it would spoil their game and their enjoyment of it, their 'fun', I believe I said. But I will recast that comment in more suitably serious words now. It is not 'fun' that would be hindered by my revealing all I know, it is *progress*. While they are secretive and careful --- of me --- they are nonetheless working like bees who build a glorious honeycomb-edifice for the betterment of Faërie. I think they will continue to weave contacts and soften barriers, smooth rough edges of obstinacy and polish or sharpen the reflections of similarities between our two clans. I will wait, watch and wait, a little longer. The Moon-Dancers are moving gracefully and their choreography advances my causes and those of all Faërie. And the Sun-Singers are less aggressive or impetuous, now that they begin to feel tides moving and a sea of mutual respect shining with new light. Sun *and* moon light! I sense that their tension and fear is less, even though their policy and position have not really changed. That is a good terrain for new growth and advancement.

"While the Alliance of young fairies is creating such an atmosphere, I shall not intervene, therefore. I do not wish that any of you here this evening reveal to them what I have told you, not yet. In my own time, at the *right* time, I will step out of my sideline shadows.

"But before that time arrives, it seems prudent to me to gain a little more information than I have thus far collected. And for that reason, I have invited you three brave fairies here to discuss a small adventure I have in mind."

Aulfrin's eye swept gently over the faces of Finnir, Brea and Aytel, and he also glanced at his daughter. Eli felt a warm tingle: it was the pleasure of utter recognition in her father's profound (and at the same time almost mischievous) regard. She knew she was remembering it, somehow, from her human infancy --- before Sean left her and Lily --- but she thought, as well, that his expression was probably resonating much further and deeper within her and touching even older memories.

His was a wonderful face! Eli smiled at the allusion he had made to being like a tree: so true! Seeing his merry forest-green eyes, with the delicate laughter-lines branching out from their corners, was like looking at a stately old oak tree with such a wise and ancient character that you felt you could see a face smiling back at you from the marvellous patterns in its bark! Yes, her father, the King of the Fairies, was just like that to look upon. She felt a great surge of joy at being his daughter, mingled with waves of respect and devotion, a good measure of curiosity …. and also sublime and secure peace.

Finnir and the two other fairies were alert and attentive to what Aulfrin might ask of them. There seemed to be a veil of hushed stillness and anticipation draped over the room now, and Eli felt privileged to be allowed to be present and to overhear their discussions, though she did not have much to add to them. At least not yet.

Aulfrin spoke slowly:

"Eleven days ago, on the night of the full moon almost at the end of the month of May, I suddenly perceived an unusual energy emanating from the Stone Circle. I descended late in the evening, with the moon high above me but half-hidden by the drifting cloud-forms, to take a closer look. The high-sailing cirrus was less obstructive, however, than the low fog surrounding the Stones. I have rarely seen the Circle clothed in so dense a shroud; but what was more alarming was that I could not enter! Indeed, it is the first time I have ever felt such a barrier, either during my reign or before it. I was clearly forbidden to pass and was denied entry.

"I heard voices, unintelligible to me, murmuring or chanting beyond the Stones closest to me --- almost like the buzzing of bees. Ferglas was beside me, and when I looked down at him, I saw that he was trembling. He said no word to me, and he has not spoken of it since."

At this, the King looked with love and deference at the huge blue wolf-hound lying beside him. Eli could not see Ferglas from where she sat, for the crystal-light dais of the King was on the opposite side of the table. She knew the dais was there, for it glowed almost imperceptibly and it accounted for the fact that Aulfrin was seated higher than the others by about a foot-and-a-half. The King continued.

"At mid-day, the following day, I was able to enter the Circle at last, for the moon was now underfoot and the sun himself was watery and weak, like a pewter disc in the heavy single-clouded heavens. I crossed the ring of the circular stream, which was sleeping and snoring in its bed, and I then walked all around the central Source --- very slowly, going from north to west to south to east, keeping a distance of several yards from the powerful and pulsating vibration of the Source-Well itself. But I could hear it and feel it nonetheless. And blended with its voice were other voices. Fairy voices. Their words were still impossible to distinguish clearly, but I could recognise some of the speakers.

"Now, as I have revealed to you all, I know that my sons are deeply involved in these conspiracies with the Sun-Singers, and have even met with Erreig and his son Garo. I know that other great fairies are implicated too. And, though the voices were intertwined and somewhat confused, it seemed to me that I could identify those of my two younger sons. But no one was there: it was a ghost-play of past voices, full-moon meetings, secrets shared many hours before and now replayed in the lingering ripples of their accents and the cadences of their fading voices.

"I do not think that Reyse is involved in any communications with the Dragon-Chieftain or his son, though he is surely in constant contact with all of my sons --- but if he is directly involved with any of the Sun-Singers, he has chosen to remain *incognito* as far as I am concerned, and to divulge nothing to me as yet. And I am quite certain that I could <u>not</u> hear his deep, warm voice among the moon-phantom ones. That said, if he *is* implicated in these exchanges, I will tolerate it and *not* be angered; but I doubt it to be so. Reyse is my right arm and has for so many centuries been joined to me, heart to heart, that I do not believe he could keep a secret from me for long!

"But there in the Stone Circle, I felt other presences among the foggy voices, or at least I continued to perceive their echoes. I believe that Alégondine, Errieg's daughter by my own wife, had been there. I have not heard her adult voice in person, but I imagine it to be feminine and yet rather deep, like the sombre shade of her skin. I think it was echoing there. And I wonder if Garo himself was not with her, for I believe that I could recognise his accents too. There was another male voice, very familiar to me, but I cannot place it. I am struggling to unearth in my memory the bearer of that lovely voice; but so far I have not succeeded. I'm sure it will come to me. The silent twins, who sometimes visit the City, I sensed too: Belfina and Begneta, for their soundless speech is very sweet, and their two voices are ever overlaid like harmonious chords of complementary notes. After several minutes, strangely enough, there was clearly another 'double' voice, taking the place of the duet of the fair twins. I don't know why, but I am tempted to wonder if it was not that of a pair of ancient female-fairies whom I know of but have never met: the daughters of my Queen, before she became my Queen --- Mowena and Malmaza. They came to my mind intuitively and insistently. But now I am even questioning if I truly heard their tandem accents, of it if was not a distorted echo of Belfina and Begneta.

"It would be news indeed if the daughters of Rhynwanol and Grey-Uan were here. They elected to go into the human world over eight hundred years ago. They are half-fairies, as are you my darling Finnir, but even in the world they have (so I believe) retained the blessing of their fairy-aging, so they would be roughly your age now, my dear Eli. But I have not heard of them ever returning to greater-Faërie, not even to their own birth-shee of the Little Skellig, let alone to my kingdom. As far as I ever knew, they had remained long in the land of their human father, the shepherd Grey Uan, in the county of Donegal in Ireland. But many, many years of life may have given them the opportunity for far-flung travels and even the gifts of great magical learning and enchantment. I cannot deny that I felt a keen intuition that they were there in the Stone Circle, under the full moon of the preceding night."

Aulfrin breathed deeply, and Eli could see the intense look in the eyes of her brother as he fixed his regard on their father.

She now noticed, for the first time, that the little beige squirrel she had seen in his arms at the Lake-side was still with him. It was curled-up, fast asleep, on his lap; it was dreaming, for its long, bushy tail was twitching over its back, which was only just visible behind the rim of the table.

"It would be quite amazing, as you say Your Majesty," commented Brea in a low voice, "if the daughters of Grey Uan were here in Fantasie. I have had some dealings, these past few decades, with the fairies of the Sheep's Head and those of the Little Skellig, for as you know I often venture forth from the Heart Oak of Barrywood to visit the corresponding human lands, in Cork and Kerry, of those two shees --- for I have kin in both of them. But I have heard no rumours of Mowena and Malmaza in all my travels; though the other twins, Belfina and Begneta, I have once or twice encountered or heard tell of in the Sheep's Head Shee. I have not been to Donegal, it is true, for in that land there is only one Portal of the Little Skellig Shee, and it is used almost exclusively by leprechauns and bird-sprites, rarely by the greater fairies now."

Aytel now remarked, "I have had news of those slow-aging twins, my Liege, the daughters of our Queen. I was, not a half-century ago, in the far north of Scotland, near to the Portal of the shee of Lord Reyse, and there I met fairies who knew of those half-fairy ladies. They were, it was said at that time, working in company with the long-ago lover of Reyse, the fair Ceoleen --- whom he came here to your kingdom to court about the time that Grey Uan's children were born, I think. I did not meet Mowena or Malmaza, but I saw Ceoleen, though only from a distance."

A tickling sensation irritated Eli, all up her back and neck, at the name of Reyse's ex-lover. She smirked at herself, and at her possessiveness of the handsome fairy-lord who was now, and evidently for many ages, courting *her* in place of Ceoleen. For a second, she recognised that she felt proud and rather haughty, knowing the great Reyse to be *in love* with her! But in the next instant, she felt ashamed of herself and her childish airs, and of the twinge of jealously and of arrogance she registered when Ceoleen's name was mentioned. She noted, however, the curious detachment she felt from all of those emotions the moment she turned her eyes toward Finnir. Now, looking at her beautiful brother once again, she drifted off for an instant into the longing to simply look deeply into his face, as if plunged into profound prayer, in silence and in joy --- and possibly for all eternity!

Inwardly she rebuked herself. "This is likely less about 'prayer' and more about your romantic inclinations. Stop yourself, you silly girl! You know that your infatuation is coming from your human-woman heart, and you know that the attraction you may be feeling for him is --- in truth --- *sisterly*, and not sensual or amorous. Stop it, before you embarrass yourself!"

As she steadied herself anew, Finnir's musical voice broke the short silence.

"What do you wish us to do, father? How may we help you to unravel the mystery of these voices, and of your full-moon hindrance from entering the Circle?"

Aulfrin reached over to his son, so radiant he was practically glowing --- seeming even *more* golden, Eli thought, in the flickering candle-light --- and he laid a hand on Finnir's shoulder.

"There was another voice, my lad, which I recognised clearly. A very old and very beautiful voice. It was much, much clearer to me than the others, and I am convinced that it was leading or guiding the discussions; perhaps it was even the voice of the *instigator* of the meeting the night before. I have not heard it for many long years, not since my father, the wise and dear Aulfrelas, died; it was only a week after that event --- in the year 1300 --- that I heard that voice for the last time. It was the voice of my mother, Morliande."

A rushing wave of surprise broke over the listeners, and even Jizay, at Eli's heels, sat up and cocked his head sideways with an inquiring light in his dark eyes. The three creamy-white hounds of Brea, who had been lying at a respectful distance behind the chair of their master, rose to their feet and began wagging their tails.

"Your mother, the Queen Morliande, is still alive then?" exclaimed Brea in delight. "I thought it was no more than a happy legend of the south! Does she then truly dwell in the farthest reaches of Quillir, as the tale tells?"

Aulfrin sighed deeply, and then he, too, smiled a little.

"Finnir's --- and Eli's --- grandmother does indeed still live. Where the Black Boar River flows across the hidden beach of tiny, dark shells looking out over Silkie-Seal Bay, she is reputed to dwell in peace and privacy. She was, and ever is, a silkie herself, and so she probably passes much of her time on one of the small islands far out to the south of Star Island where the hundred clans of the seal-folk have their havens. I have not spoken with her nor seen her since her departure close-following the death of my father, her husband. I think no one else ever has, either.

"At least not until the night of the full-moon of May. For I am sure that it was *her* voice that I heard."

He paused, and took a deep breath once again. And then he continued, "I cannot go to her, for the delicate situation which exists between myself and Erreig would make such a voyage imprudent and probably easily misconstrued as some sort of aggression or challenge. But I would like to send royal messengers to her, to ask her to confide in me through them. And that is the mission I wish to charge you with, my beloved trio of brave fairies."

There was no answer from any of the three, but it was not a shocked or anxious silence. It was a resounding compliance and acceptance, immediate and obedient, trusting and resolute.

Even to Eli, it was tangible. The air was full of a unanimous and silent 'at your service', coupled with a 'when do we start?'!

In a moment, all the dogs lay down again comfortably, and even the squirrel clucked in his sleep and rolled over on his back, so that all four of his tiny paws were visible, gently curled in the air over Finnir's lap. The atmosphere relaxed, and the candles seemed to glow a little more brightly.

"So," said Aulfrin, as brightly as the flames of the tall tapers, "then that is agreed, and we will discuss the details tomorrow! Now, a little glass to seal our contract and to toast your marvellous mission, stealthily travelling into the farthest south-west corner of the realm, where legends walk abroad --- or at least swim and splash! Let us celebrate your voyage and your quest, and the precious contact with the great Queen Morliande that it offers, and her insight and help --- so I hope."

Finnir rose, and as he did so the little squirrel scampered up and draped himself over his shoulder. He then went to the side-board where a tall carafe of green and gold enamel stood amid twining leaves. He brought it to the table, along with five pottery goblets on a golden tray.

Was it heady hydromel or well-aged red wine, champagne or fiery brandy? Eli had no idea. Her eyes met Finnir's as he filled her goblet, and though she sipped it slowly and tried to appreciate all its aromas and subtle tastes, she simply remained lost in the endless blue of those eyes.

"Avoid him. You must avoid him," she heard herself chastising her irresponsible self, the giddy human girl that she still was, the schoolgirl with an overly-romantic streak. "Wait to see him again until you have come home to *live* here, and you can be at ease with him as the glorious brother he surely is. Avoid him until you're a fairy again, because *this* is utterly ridiculous!"

There and then, she firmly decided that she would *not* be coming to the meeting tomorrow, even were she invited.

****

To Eli's surprise, her father graciously accepted her wish to go walking with Jizay and Periwinkle the following morning, instead of taking part in the planned meeting. He seemed to feel that this would be a practical planning-session for the trio of adventurers, and that Eli would find it of little real interest.

"Quite sensible of you," he assured her. "We will possibly have a more sociable and relaxed moment together later today, before Finnir and his companions depart.

"They leave this evening, then?"

"I expect so. That will be decided this morning, between us. But I sense that Finnir is keen to undertake this voyage, and to make the acquaintance of his grand-mother. He will not wish to delay, I imagine."

Eli was contented and relieved. She would find another excuse for her absence that afternoon or evening; at least for this morning, she was free to wander with her dog and her dear pixie, and try to put the heavenly blue of Finnir's eyes out of her mind.

Piv was all excitement, recounting for Eli the *dancing and prancing*, as he called it, enjoyed with his cousins in the starlit gardens encircling the Great Trees. He tried to lure Eli there for their walk, but she declined, saying she simply wanted to visit the fountain of Lyathel, and perhaps the excellent bakery. But it did not require much time for her dear friend to become aware that her attention was elsewhere --- or nowhere.

They all three lingered beside the beautiful fountain filled with its schools of tiny, starry-white fishes, all leaping and cavorting and somersaulting, adding the sounds of their constant splashing to the music of Lyathel's tall columns of singing water. Piv could see that Eli's mind was filled with questions and imaginings.

"You are miles away, my Mélusine," he chided. "You don't look worried, but you are preoccupied. I think you are thinking of the Lord Reyse! Do not despair; he will be arriving this evening, I expect."

Eli was startled out of her reverie. "Will he? Will there be meetings with Finnir and his companions *and* Reyse?"

Piv furrowed his brows, and then hunched his shoulders once. "I don't know that, my sweet friend. Perhaps."

Jizay remarked, in his silent voice, "If the hounds of brave Brea are well-informed, the three fairies of Barrywood will likely leave this afternoon. I think they will miss the Lord Reyse. But they are good friends, and will surely meet again soon…"

Piv then continued, "Now, are you going to come back to this bright morning moment with me and tell me more about last night's secret meeting, or would you be happier to be on your own? Well, not alone, it seems, for you are in company with some very mysterious thoughts! But I understand completely, if you'd prefer to day-dream in private for a while."

Eli smiled lovingly at her little friend. "You are so good, my dearest Piv. You know, I think I would like that. I thought, at first, that our walk this morning would take my mind right off the strange thoughts that are filling it; but it's not the case. I think it would be good for me to just retreat to my bedroom for this morning, and relax a little perhaps. You really wouldn't mind? We can meet at lunchtime, if you like."

"Only if you'll loan me Jizay," laughed the pixie, his bright little voice as fluty and gay as ever. "For then he can tell me more about his own adventure coming here, running over the summery lands with the beautiful blue Ferglas!"

Jizay seemed happy with this plan, too, and so Eli returned to the King's Tower on her own while her hound and her little green-winged friend went off together to share their stories, promising to be back in time for a meal together at midday.

She passed the place where she and Jizay had rested on the grassy slope and she had first seen Finnir --- unknown to her then --- leaving the City by the north-eastern Gate with his shining company of riders. Her heart felt pulled in many directions at once. Reyse was indeed on her mind, and the thought of seeing him that evening was very pleasant, and a little exciting. But Finnir's face was predominant in her thoughts, as was his amazing and yet utterly composed act of rescuing her from a mortal fall. Their father had reminded her to keep her elder brother's impressive character and skills in proportion, and not to be in awe of him. Was it *awe* which she was feeling? Was she infatuated? Was she star-struck by his beauty, or his enchanting and enigmatic gifts and princely prowess?

Perhaps what she really needed was to know him better: not to avoid him entirely, but to come to feel naturally more at ease with him. It wasn't possible in *diplomatic* meetings with the King; she needed to have a few moments in private with her brother, to be able to thank him and speak normally with him. But he was in the Council Chamber now, deep in deliberations about the mission that Aulfrin was sending the three fairies on.

It would probably be impossible to find the time to be together with Finnir before he left, and such a voyage would most likely last longer than this second Visit of hers. Ah well, if it was meant to be, it would happen in its own good time. Maybe she would not see him before her third and final Visit. Or perhaps not until she was indeed home again for good. And maybe that would be for the best, after all…

Eli mounted the wide, central staircase with the intention of continuing on to her bedroom in its western turret. But as she reached the landing encircled by honeysuckle, pale pink wild roses and exotic-looking passiflora, she turned down the left-hand corridor instead of continuing up the next flight of spiralling stairs.

Thus she found herself faced with the fork in the hallway that had, on her first visit, led her instinctively to the Music Room of Queen Rhynwanol. There on the right was the narrow sweep of the corridor that led to the magical harp and perhaps even to the ghostly form of her mother playing. The geometric tiles in shining black and powder-blue beckoned her --- but another notion came to her now.

To her left was the room exuding spicy odours, surely her mother's Concocting Cell, as Aulfrin had called it. She hesitated for an instant, breathing-in the heady perfumes and studying the shadowy doorway. It was a rounded arch of carved stone or wood, so shiny a grey that it was impossible to tell which. Engraved all around it were faces sprouting leaves and flowers, some very beautiful, some almost frightening. But the aromas were too inviting to resist. Eli found herself tiptoeing under the arch, and feeling with her fingers along the walls as she advanced into the darkness.

As with the geometric passageway, but in the opposite direction, this narrow hall bent around its half of the tower in a gentle curve. Soon the light grew, and Eli could see that the close walls now opened out into a small, circular, dimly-lit room --- presumably near to the tower's centre. There were thus no windows, but a warm light came from a squat vase like a flower-pot, about seven inches in diameter, sitting on a low table in the middle of the room. An orangey glow rose from the depths of the vase, which bathed the entire room in a light which was perfectly suited to the tangy, sweet, smoky and savoury smells escaping the bottles and jars, bowls and boxes on the shelves all about the walls.

As Eli drew closer to the curious container she could now see that it was carved in the likeness of a stylised head, with a serene face subtly traced in low-relief: delicately half-closed eyes, a peaceful suggestion of a smile, a rather wide and almost aboriginal nose, strange ears with long and pointed lobes, and a lovely crown which formed the rim of the vase.

She stared at it entranced. She could almost feel it speaking to her, or at least luring her forward to be caught in the gentle rays of light welling-up from its depths.

"*It is called the Queen's Head Vase,*" said a voice as sweet and intoxicating as the perfumes hanging in the shadowy air. Eli jumped and almost cried out in alarm. But the voice, which was <u>not</u> coming from the primitive vase, simply continued in gentle and measured tones.

"Her Majesty Queen Rhynwanol, and before her, the Queen Morliande, and before them both a long line of beautiful fairy-women wedded to the Kings of this realm, all have contributed to the rich and feminine light which rises from the Queen's Head. They have all warmed their hands over its unwavering glow; they have all sprinkled into it the pungent kernels and crystals of incense, the dried leaves and petals which feed its fire; they have all listened to its voice and its wisdom.

"Perhaps you have come to listen, like them, Eli? Or is it the soul of Mélusine longing to reawaken in you that comes here, to warm her sleeping embers to life once again, and to perhaps learn what decision she should make: to be human, to be fairy, or to be both, if that is possible?!"

As he spoke, Finnir had come forward from the shadows to Eli's left, and moved close beside her. She had felt alarmed, yes, but quickly her surprise had melted into the music of his voice and now she was smiling and looking back and forth from the glowing vase to the glowing face, richly coloured by the yellow and orange light.

He smiled too, and after a moment Eli felt enough at ease to pose a question, or two or three.

"Why are you not in counsel with our father, Finnir? Is your meeting already concluded then? And why are you come here; are you yourself seeking answers or advice from this marvellous and magical vase?"

Now he laughed, and shook his head. "No, indeed not! For only a woman may hear the wisdom of the Queen's Head Vase.

I had a much less elevated errand to fulfil: I was sent to seek a jar of spicy potpourri for the wondrous silkie Morliande, a gift from her son the King, and a sign of his gratitude --- should she be willing to enlighten us as to what transpired in the Stone Circle nearly a fortnight ago."

As she had anticipated, or at least hoped, Eli felt strangely and completely at ease with her brother now that they were alone together. Perhaps it was the darkness or the sweet fragrances, or perhaps the enchanted Vase was whispering its reassurance to her.

She regarded him closely for a moment, and breathed deeply. It was invigorating to inhale the scented air of this room, and soothing to bask in Finnir's presence and his closeness. She wondered if her silly 'infatuation' was now naturally transforming into *sisterly* love for this fairy-prince; if it was, then this was a deeper fraternal love than she had felt with either Demoran or Leyano. She felt *connected* to this mysterious fairy, as though she had known him very well all her fairy-life and human-life combined --- although she had been told that, in fact, they had not spent much time at all together in the past. No matter, she was at ease now, and she felt the bond between them and it made her profoundly happy.

"But perhaps you know already! Even before you go on this secret mission, do you already understand about the voices in the Stone Circle?" she asked.

Finnir's sparkling eyes grew wider, as did his smile. "Your keen insight and your depth of seeing are intact, even in your changeling form, Mélusine. Yes, I know much about what has been happening in the Circle, and elsewhere. As does, most probably, the Lord Reyse. As does Aindel, certainly. But the King does not think that Reyse is involved in our Alliance, and he does not know that dear Aindel, of the Sheep's Head Shee, has become such a frequent visitor to these shores. And he does not seem to know that I play any role in all of these 'conspiracies', as he calls them.

"But beware, Eli, when surmising what Aulfrin knows or does not know! He is very subtle and very masterful in all games of state, of diplomacy, even of espionage and perhaps also the interwoven strands of linked friendships and feuds. He may know much more than he says; he may know that I am already a part of the Alliance, and one of its principle players --- and sending me to speak to Morliande, under the very nose of Erreig and within sight of the Sage-Hermit's island home, may be a very daring move on the chess-board of his strategies. It would not surprise me."

"But you will go, nonetheless?"

"Of course. I am the Prince Finnir, and the obedient servant of my King and my father. And, what is more, I relish the idea of paying a visit to Morliande. She is a legend in herself."

Eli admitted, "I'm sorry you are leaving Fantasie so soon, Finnir. I would have liked to talk more together. At least, I should take this opportunity to offer my thanks --- for saving my life."

Finnir bowed his head slightly in reverence to her, which made Eli cough once or twice with nervousness. "It was a pleasure and a privilege, my dearest Mélusine. For Mélusine you were at that moment, or I could have done nothing. It was the resonating vibration between our gem-stones which came into play, almost without any formal intention on my part. The sapphire in my hand felt the call of that which is set into your ear-lobe, and they acted spontaneously to keep you from harm. At least, that is how I felt it. Our jewels are powerful beings, dear Eli; they protect us and guide us, reveal truths and illuminate our paths. In fact, you should thank, not me, but the stones themselves --- and those who gave them into our keeping at the time of our respective Initiations."

Eli nodded, and fingered her ear-lobe for an instant, but she could not feel the sensation of the angular stone there now.

"That is very lovely, that we have the blessings of such precious stones" she remarked. As he had inclined his head,

Finnir's other gems had glistened in the light of the Vase: the ambers in his own ears, and the perfect pearl in his forehead. The amber made Eli think, once again, of Aindel.

"You know Aindel well, then, I suppose? I wonder if I knew him too, when I was the Princess Mélusine, but he says it is not likely. I feel some sort of affinity between us, but I can't interpret what it is. There are so many secret threads of connections linking the personages of this land, and so many in my own story --- or stories. I wish it could all become clear and that no more *secrecy* was needed or imposed."

Finnir's lovely face took on a very profound stillness for a moment. Eli thought that she could detect a sigh in the deep breath he drew.

"One day, one day soon I hope, all that is hidden will come out into the light, and be revealed, Eli. The secrecy is there for a reason, and it is a good and worthy reason; it is not there out of dishonesty or to cause deception or trickery. It is there to work wonders, and it will, in the end. I hope it will be soon, for I myself am part of many secrets, as is Aindel and several others among our families and allies. It will be a great relief when *all* can be told."

A very intense look came into Finnir's eyes now, an unusual deep blue in the dim light of this room, and they met Eli's. Both held the other's gaze for many seconds. Eli could feel the aromas and the gentle heat that rose from the Queen's Head Vase like a spiral of invisible vapours swirling around her entire body.

At last Finnir spoke, breaking the momentary but very deep cord of energy that united them, and he turned to the doorway. His voice seemed rather sadder, and this brought tears to Eli's eyes for some reason.

"I must take my leave, Eli --- of you and of Fantasie; for Silkie Seal Bay lies many long and cautious miles from here, and Brea and Aytel await me in the courtyard below. I hope to see you again, before your Visit is concluded. If I am delayed, it will have to be on your next, your final, Visit. Or later... when you are once again the Princess."

Eli did not want Finnir to hear the tearful tremble in her voice, and so she simply nodded. As her brother walked to the doorway, where the curved corridor wound its narrow way back to the landing, she felt something rush past her head. Now she saw it in the slightly brighter light of the hallway's arch: a tiny, swift swallow circling Finnir's blond head and then flying off before him.

In only a moment he was out of view. Eli looked back at the glowing Vase, whose steady light had turned from orange to deep red flecked with violet. She banished the idea of approaching the warmth to ask her questions or to listen to any premonitions or revelations. She simply inhaled deeply, filling her lungs with the piquant perfumes of the room before she, too, walked slowly back along the winding hallway, and then up to her bedroom to meditate and wonder...alone.

****

Chapter Ten:
The Key of the Ghostly Chapel

Piv awakened Eli with a gentle tapping on her bedroom door; she must have dozed off.

Her dreams had been very odd, deep and fragrant with spicy incense-odours. In them she felt her way along shadowy corridors which twisted and turned but never seemed to arrive where they were going. She was seeking someone or something, but she was unsure whether it was the Queen's Head Vase or the violet-eyed Rhynwanol playing sweetly on a cobweb-shrouded harp. But there were many more pathways than just the choice of right and left --- the corridors leading to the Concocting Cell or the Music Room.

The hallways in her dream were like a labyrinth, tricking her with false turns and dead-ends, and locked doors behind which she was sure there waited a strange series of people wanting to see or speak with her. At last she knew that she had chosen the correct direction and she felt reassured, though still rather lost. But the doors to either side continued.

Reyse, she knew, was in one of these locked rooms and she could see the door-knob moving as if he were trying to turn it from the other side; his keen eagle-like eyes were looking at her right through the door! She hurried past, as if for some reason intent on avoiding him.

Behind the next was an even more alarming presence, with an energy so strong that it repelled Eli bodily and forced her to walk on tip-toe, cowering against the far wall: it was Yves, and she could hear chanted mantras and far-away resonating Tibetan meditation-bowls being made to hum and vibrate. Sounds normally imbued with sublime beauty --- but in his presence fraught with some hidden terror.

The smell of a wet garden under soft rain came from the following door, a blackbird was singing and a cuckoo was calling from woods far away. Eli knew that her Irish husband was there, Colm, and she imagined him cycling along a winding pathway beyond a low stone wall. She tried the door-handle but it came off in her hand, and then crumbled into moist mulch or peat and fell to the floor.

Another door presented itself, radiating warmth and glowing deep red, as though the door itself was hot to the touch. "Dragons," Eli thought, "There are dragons within!" And suddenly she could see in her mind's eye the huge head of Bawn, with yellow-white flame escaping between her bared teeth; but the eyes were closed and the head was resting calmly on huge paws of white leathery hide, red-talonned and crossed comfortably under her chin. "Is Leyano there with her, or Garo?" she wondered, but she didn't dare to try the knob, in case it would crumble at her touch as well.

She walked a long way with no doors at all appearing for a long way, until --- just as the corridor was clearly coming to an end --- two final ones faced each other across the hallway, which was now growing slightly brighter. Ah! the light came from a silvery glow, like moonlight, peeping out into the dark corridor from the narrow space between one of the doors and the dim blue-and-black tile floor. But Eli turned from that door, for facing it was another very alluring one though with no handle, only a large and intricate lock fashioned of black tracery designs. She stopped before this door, and all her remaining fear was transformed. She felt peaceful, and yet still confused --- a bewildering peace.

Finnir was there, undoubtedly, facing her on the other side of the door. She could feel him, almost see him, as though it were her own reflection in a tall mirror --- and yet not her. Her turquoise eyes grew wider, aching to see *through* the door and behold his clear blue ones. She lifted one hand and laid her palm on the smooth golden oak of the high, pointed door. As she did so, she knew that Finnir had done likewise, in unison and just as slowly. Now their hands were opposite one another, as if laid palm to palm --- but they were separated by the oaken door. "*My King,*" she heard herself say, in a low and very tender whisper. "*My Queen,*" came the reply, audible and warm and resonating with incredible love.

Piv knocked again, and now his piccolo voice was in Eli's dream too, insistent and cheerful: "Are you there, my Eli-een?! It's long past lunch-time, and Jizay and I are hungry. Are you coming to join us?"

"Yes, yes, my darling Piv," called Eli, fully awake now and sitting up to swing herself out of her hammock. "Here I am, here I come."

****

Eli's dream hovered in the back of her mind for a moment or two, but then it wafted away and left her feeling very serene... strangely serene.

Indeed, she was bright and happy at lunch, and Piv and Jizay also. Her pixie-friend and her hound of joy had already seen the three riders leaving the City, for they had been to the little coppice of trees around a small and sheltered pond, fed by the waters of Lysandel, just to the south of the huge lake where Eli had watched the beginning of the fascinating rituals on Beltaine morn. Looking out between the lithe and graceful trunks of the coppice, they had watched Finnir, Aytel and Brea cantering across the fields between them and the single Star Tower to the south-east, the only tower which stood far from the walls of the oval.

"They wore their dark blue cloaks and their hoods were up and concealing their fair faces, but it was clearly them. Brea's hounds were running at their heels and swallows were tumbling though the skies overhead. They left by the Seventh Gate," explained Periwinkle. "And very right and proper to do so, for the Prince Finnir is as magical as the Sage-Hermit, in his own way of course. *Seven* is the Hermit's special number and it is, indeed, a merry and cunning number of great magic, and Wineberry is the seventh and so to all intents and purposes the *last* gate of Fantasie. I wonder if they were going to the Salley Woods, for that is a wondrous forest and Reyse once explained to me that the Prince, when young, went there to learn to make harps."

At these remarks Eli felt herself at a loss, for she now had several questions to ask and didn't know where to begin.

"Oh dear, my darling Piv, you do make my head spin!" she laughed, as the pixie flew around the table with a chunk of bread and a dollop of some delicious sort of hazel-nut curd poised on top of it, to finally hover beside Jizay's head and offer it to him.

"Because I buzz about you at table? Yes, it is rude of me I suppose," apologised Piv with a chastised air as he returned to sit on the high stool at Eli's side.

"No, no! Not because of that," returned Eli, patting his green-capped head affectionately. "It's all this about harp-making and magical numbers and 'last' gates. I want to know about it all!"

Piv chuckled with relief, and took another morsel of nut-curd-topped-bread for himself. When he had swallowed his mouthful, he resumed with twinkling eyes:

"Ah, I see! Well, it's very simple really! There are *seven* gates in the walls of the Silver City, and they go like this: south (the Great Gates), north-west, north-east, due west, due east, south-west, south-east. The first six ones are named in a kind of rhyme: *Ioyeas, Dwitherum, Treytherum, peep! Quatherum, Setherum, Rhex to sleep!*

"The Seventh Gate, the one to the south-east, has a very different-sounding name, from another ancient language: the closest I can come to it for you, my Eli, is to say it as I did, that she is called *Wineberry*, and she has a rhyme all to herself:

> *Here am I on threshold bright,*
> *On one side the cup of light,*
> *On the other berries black,*
> *Hesitating I look back,*
> *Night and light and moon and sun,*
> *Sip my wine and all is one!*

"But, to be perfectly truthful... there are also *three* other gates, which are called *Wigtail, Tarrydiddle* and *Den*," he rattled on. "However, they are kept tight closed, for they are very mischievous and wily and will lead unwary or unwanted visitors directly into the waters of the three great fountains --- splash! --- or high up onto the pointed pinnacles of a Star or Moon Tower. So we don't count those doors, because fairies don't use them. Some legends speak of an eleventh gate, but it has no name --- or it has been forgotten.

"Now, about magical numbers I can only tell you that it's all quite obvious, my precious little Mélusine! In fact, *all* numbers are magical, but some are stronger and some are softer, some are sour and some are sweet. Three is the stoutest, seven is wise and beyond our ken, and eleven is shining with starlight. Two is the rose in a lover's hand, five is watery and winsome, six the wind of a galloping horse, and nine is the number of the lily: the queen of the flowers."

At this, Eli stopped mid-bite in the juicy abricot she was eating, but she didn't wish to interrupt Piv, so she said nothing.

"And as for harp-making," continued the pixie, pausing only for a handful of fat blueberries to finish off his luncheon, "the

Salley Woods are a wide and withy land where grows the most excellent wood for the most beautiful of harps. In that land the willows are greater than anywhere else in all Faërie, even greater than those of the White Willow Isles; and other trees grow there too which make harps with voices as sweet as a nightingale's or a spotted spider's. And when you come home to your own self, my Princess my love, you will at last recall our own tree, yours and mine! For it is at the very northern eave of the Salley Wood that the Red Coral Tree grows, and he was our special and good and kind friend. And you have a harp, laid very near your bier on Scholar Owl Island, made from one of his great branches and two of his hoary roots. Jizay has told me not to trouble you with too many tales of that tree or your special harp, for you will meet the Red Coral again when you come back, and you will know him as well as you know me. So there is no rush, and your clever hound is right to say so…

"But in regard to the Prince Finnir, Reyse told me that he went there when he was very young to learn the art of harp-making from the Lustrous Willows --- those that are so silvery that they seem to shine like moonbeams. His own little harp he made there, and it can sing like the breeze that whistles past the high head of the Yellow Wren Mountain, smiling down on the Salley Woods and on the foothills where the flying horses are foaled. Ah, they say that the bonny Finnir is a fine harp-maker, and also a wondrous harper who can charm and sooth and make you dance or weep or dream."

Periwinkle stopped, and looked lovingly at Eli for several minutes. Her eyes were closed, and there was a gentle smile playing around her lips, but there were also tears running down her cheeks. Jizay had risen from where he had been lying, and now had laid his golden head on his mistress's lap; her hand was idly stroking it and fingering his soft, short ears.

"You are overcome by sentiment, dear Lady Eli, when one speaks of ….harps, I suppose," said a rich and masculine voice at the door of the dining room. It was not the King, for he had sent word that he was spending the early afternoon in one of the quiet prayer-rooms along the southern wall of the City. Eli opened her eyes and turned towards the voice, and smiled as she dried her tears.

"Reyse! I thought you were arriving only this evening."

At the warmth of her welcome Reyse smiled broadly too, and the slight tension that had seemed to colour his voice disappeared as he replied.

"Your pleasure at seeing me is reassuring, for I would like to think that you have such strong sentiments for me as you demonstrate for the tales of your brother's skills at music and harp-craft."

Unsure quite how to take this remark, Eli nonetheless recognised much genuine pleasure in his welcome, so she simply rose and faced the tall fairy with an outstretched hand. She wasn't sure if she was inviting him to shake it or kiss it, but he did neither. For from under his long green cloak he produced a white rose. He passed the lovely flower into Eli's open hand.

"Of course," he said, as she accepted it with a very unintentional blush stealing over her cheeks, "a fairy never *picks* a flower. But I passed the Rose-Beds along the Swan's Joy River as I came here, and I think the flowers read my thoughts --- which were predominantly for you. This rose was offered me, to give to you. It is not a lily, the *queen* of flowers as Periwinkle reminds us; it is a rose and the emblem of the number two, and like you it is a *princess* --- as you are not a queen, but a beautiful Princess, my Lady."

Suddenly Eli recalled her dream, and the title Finnir had spoken to her, through the golden oak door: 'my Queen'.

Her eyes went wide and glassy for a second, but Reyse did not see this, as he was moving to the arched window beyond the table, to look out at the Great Trees and the coiling, streaming lights flowing about their interlaced ring of branches.

"Rare to see those colours, deep blues and coppery reds, and those tiny sparks of purple among the mists," he murmured. "Very strange. Is it to do with my dear friend's presence here, or has he left? I cannot feel him within the bounds of Fantasie."

Speaking more audibly now, Reyse smiled and turned back to where Piv and Eli sat. He inquired, "So, this harper Finnir --- who once made a harp for me, also I might add --- has he already gone forth from the City?"

"Yes, yes, he is gone; but none knows where!" chirruped Piv. "I have my ideas, though maybe my dear Mélusine has heard more than my guesses, for she was permitted to join their council last evening."

"Ah, but not this morning," added Eli hastily, feeling sure that it was not her place to discuss the mission proposed by Aulfrin, even if it were to her father's close friend and ally Reyse. "I listened to some of their polite conversation yesterday, it is true, but I was not at their meeting today before they departed. Piv and Jizay saw them leave."

"I'm sorry to miss them," conceded Reyse, "but happy to see you, Eli. And perhaps to have the opportunity to talk with you, hmm, in private --- if I may?"

Periwinkle grinned at this request, and flew up to circle his friend Reyse's head once before flying to the window. "Yes," he agreed, "very strange colours the Trees are wearing today. Have a lovely talk, and perhaps a walk, and I hope we will be together later, all of us, my darlings." And with that, the pixie whizzed out happily into the sunshine.

****

Whatever nervousness or trepidation Eli had felt in her dream when confronted by the door she knew Reyse to be behind, in his actual company she felt only ease and happiness. Together with Jizay, they left the King's Great Tower and turned to the west. Eli thought that Reyse was probably heading for *The Tipsy Star*, but he led her instead close beside the stream flowing from the fountain of Lymeril and eventually they crossed a small bridge and found themselves in a wonderful flower garden.

Eli still held the white rose in her hand, and suddenly she asked if she should not have left it behind, in a little vase of water perhaps. Reyse laughed, and offered her his arm as they walked amid the flower beds, some of which also boasted beautiful roses.

"She will not wilt," he assured her. "Or if she does feel thirsty, she will tell you. You are in Faërie, and you begin to hear and see with a fairy's heart again, I think. Can you see the little sprites among the plants here, Eli?"

"Indeed I can! There are dozens of delicate and tiny beings half-hidden among the stems and leaves! Oh how amazing all of this is," she sighed, and Reyse placed his free hand on hers, which was lightly laid over his arm. She could feel the gemstone in his palm where it touched the back of her hand.

"What is the precious stone set into your hand, Reyse?" she asked. "Does it have a name, as I think many of the jewels from our Initiations have?"

"All jewels have names," he replied, "but they don't *all* tell their true names to everyone! But some do, yes. Mine is a ruby, called the *Blarua Criha-Uval*, awarded me almost twelve centuries ago, by the wise apple trees and their generous blossoms, in my own shee. It was my second Initiation, and I was not yet eighteen. It is a powerful gem, rare and wonderful."

"Yes, I begin to understand that some jewels are indeed very powerful." Eli wondered if she should speak of her life being saved by Finnir's sapphire, and her jewel too, working together it seems. But before she could say more, Reyse continued.

"You have impressive gems also, my dear Princess. Very august and potent stones. You carry the white rose I offered you in your right hand, but if you take it in your left I should not be surprised if you felt at least a tingling or a slight burning there."

Eli looked questioningly at her escort for a moment, and they stopped walking. Without taking her left hand from where it lay on Reyse's arm, she transferred the rose to it. A soft cry of "ah!" escaped her lips, and she smiled up into Reyse's tanned face, framed beautifully by his wavy brown hair. His eyes were sparkling.

"What stone is making that feeling in my palm?"

"An amethyst, my lovely Eli. You were sixteen, studying with the rose-folk, when you won it. I do not know its name, for when you undertook your first Initiation, I was already travelling far and wide with Finnir. And that close friend and companion, your eldest brother, has been gifted with quite amazing jewels himself."

Unable to retain her question, Eli asked, "Can you tell me more about his sapphire? I think my father said that it is called the *Eye of the Innumerable Falls*. What do you know of it?"

There was an uncomfortable silence. Eli could feel Reyse considering something: was it his knowledge of the sapphire's properties? She thought not. Was it the enthusiasm or affection for Finnir belied by her tone of voice? And perhaps his weighing of his own deep and long friendship with her brother, and his reticence to allow a petty sting of jealousy to cloud it.

But if it was that, Reyse rose to the occasion and dispelled that thought as unworthy of himself, it would seem. He simply said, "I know it to be, yes, an extremely powerful and renowned stone, and that he won it at the age of seventeen, as I did mine. And curiously enough," he added quite quietly, almost as if musing inwardly, "he is not the only fairy of this realm to have worked closely with waterfalls. Finnir's third

Initiation, in 1338, was hosted by the myriad, indeed truly *innumerable*, falls that feed the Inward Sea. But when I went to his aid and rescue in September of 1961 --- with the clarion calls of the dragons and the whistling of the bats of the Sun-Singers still filling this fair City of Fantasie --- Finnir told me that two hundred years earlier the Dragon-Chieftain Erreig (soon, he said, to be on the very point of battling with your father, the King, in order to free Demoran) had also won a jewel from a waterfall. It was a fire-opal, the *Jewel of the Ancestral Fire*, he called it, though he gave its true name as *Gurtha*. It was the great cascade in the Beldrum Mountains that awarded him that mighty stone, and the dragons whose eyries overlook it complemented its powers with a golden torc and armband. When Finnir told me these things, as he walked free from the caves of the Great Cats, he winked and added: *Thus we are, in a way, brothers, Erreig and myself: for we are both foster-sons of the water-falls --- but he has found my cascade-jewel cooler and its blue more penetrating than the red fire of **his** stone, and he was doomed to writhe beneath its peaceful rays of gentle light, when we came to face one another in….our encounters, and in our wordless conversations."*

Eli had listened to Reyse's words, spoken so softly that it was truly as if he were merely thinking aloud but very privately, and she found herself imagining the ordeal of Finnir in the Caves of the White Cats. Or was it Erreig's ordeal, and not her brother's?! In a whisper like Reyse's she asked, "Was it, then, Finnir's sapphire that overthrew Erreig, and allowed my brother to escape from Quillir? Did it triumph over the Dragon-Lord, and did it save its bearer's life and allow him to walk free from his prison guarded by the giant Cats?" Eli was shivering as she spoke, and the white rose was trembling in her hand.

And then, another question coming to her mind suddenly, she looked up into Reyse's hazel-brown and amber eyes. *"You were with Finnir before our father arrived to find and free him?"*

Realising that she was speaking in a rather excited voice, Eli calmed herself. She continued to look into Reyse's eyes, but his expression was very difficult to interpret.

"I'm sorry, Reyse. This is probably not at all what you wanted to talk with me about."

Later, Eli would admit to herself that the wave of tenderness which she could see sweeping over Reyse's face was evidence of his great love for her; for he could have easily been thrown off-balance by her questions and remarks. However, instead of faltering in any way, he simply smiled down into her wide green-blue eyes with his ancient and very kind ones.

"I had no particular subject which I wished to discuss with you, my Lady Eli. I just wanted to be with you, walking and talking in a glorious flower-garden, your arm in mine."

He began strolling with her once again, and now he led Eli into the shade of the trees to their right. Under a canopy of flowering vines and gently waving branches (appropriately enough) of a crab-apple tree, he found a low bench of carved, cool stone and they sat side by side, Jizay lying at their feet.

"I'm happy enough to tell you the story, my dear Eli. I think no one else, besides Finnir and myself, knows it. Though quite probably Demoran has heard most of it, but from another source. In any case, I *like* to tell you of my adventures, and especially of my victories and my daring deeds. I'm a *very* courageous fairy, you know!" At that, he laughed merrily, and Eli joined him.

And so, shaded by the subtly perfumed boughs of the crab-apple tree, Reyse told Eli his tale.

The Black Key and the Chapel of Windy Hill

In the crisp autumn sea-breeze of that day, almost forty-nine years ago, your brother Leyano stood with his noble guard at the threshold of his Portal, ready to welcome the King when he arrived at Dawn Rock. Aulfrin, following his amazing voyage through the underworld

--- which he has in part recounted to you already --- stepped out from the crevice in Dawn Rock and into the peace of Mermaid Island and what seemed to him an inexplicable calm. All the rest of his realm was held in the grips of anxiety, occupied or threatened by Erreig and his Sun-Singers. Nonetheless, in all the nine islands of Sea-Horse Bay, a year-and-a-half of non-aggression had blessed this eastern and maritime region of Faërie.

He questioned his son, the Prince Leyano, only very briefly regarding his defence of his Portal, and his own well-being during the turmoil of Erreig's taking of Fantasie. But then he turned his attention to the whereabouts of that brazen fairy.

"The insolent Dragon-Rider is not here to challenge me as I return to my kingdom? I imagined that he would be well-informed of my movements, for he is not without spies whose ears and eyes have no doubt been finely-tuned and turned to my death in the human world and my passage by the deep-places of root and fungus to reclaim my throne and my authority. Or have I been concealed by the arts of the Mushroom Lord and thus granted a margin of brief time to surprise my rival?! Aha! I will seize it! I see that Cynnabar is ready and waiting for me: I will fly to Davenia and have news from Ruilly and the felines of Demoran, and from Corr-Seylestar too if he is alerted to my return. From there I can reach my imprisoned sons --- though in what order, I do not yet know.

"Farewell, my brave and blessed Leyano; you have obviously rendered Erreig fearful and wary of trespassing on your hospitality here. I praise your bravery and the strength of your defence. We will enjoy a family reunion and celebration in the days to come, in company with your older brothers, and you will recount your campaign and your victory to me. I will send you word swiftly!"

And the King took to the skies on his winged-horse.

It would seem that, re-assured that Dawn Rock was still free and open at least to his royal re-entry, your father did not seek news of the Black Key or require of Leyano the amber-token that the Prince, clearly, had not needed to use. But, as ever, it is difficult to surmise what Aulfrin knows, or does not know, or guesses.

In any case, the King flew to Davenia. But I had been in that province before him.

*I had arrived in Faërie a day or two before in fact, by way of Leyano's Portal also. I knew that Sean, in the human world, had died. That had been on the 7th of September 1961, when only the merest sliver of the **waning** crescent moon was visible. She had then been 'new' and invisible on the 9th, and from then until the 12th, Sean had experienced the days of his burial and his strange travels underground. On the evening of the 12th of September he had begun to climb up to the light once more, and had arrived at Eagle Abbey, and it was then in his true role as King Aulfrin of Faërie that he had seen the crescent of the young **waxing** moon in the sunset skies over the Pacific. From Dawn Rock he would fly through the darkest hours of that night to arrive at Demoran's Castle in the wee hours of the morning of the 13th. Before its gates he was indeed met by the Heron-Fairy and also by the ancient blue hound Ferglas and by the leader of the Scholar-Owls. He rested only until the light of day, before flying --- according to their counselling --- to the Red Hoopoe Mountain. The King there met Erreig, now aware of his return, and they battled in the snowy skies. And Demoran was freed.*

As I say, I was in this shee before Aulfrin's arrival; and I had been given the amber-token by your brother Leyano, for it was my mission to free Finnir --- or at least, to fulfil the eerie ritual that would affect his release.

Not long before Aulfrin's arrival in the Dappled Woods, I had achieved my own mysterious quest in accordance with the instructions which I had received by Demoran's cats: instructions that they, in turn, had been sent by Finnir himself, via another king in the realm, other than your father. This was Isck, King of the White Cats, who had graciously allowed a young cat, a half-grown 'kit' as they are named, to leave Quillir and cross the River Dragonfly under the eaves of the Hazel Woods, and thereby put all the long miles of the King's Rise under his swift paws in order to reach the Castle of Demoran two weeks before. This had allowed time for Ruilly to send stealthy rabbit-runners to the borders of Barrywood --- a dangerous

The Key of the Ghostly Chapel

journey through Aumelas-Pen and across Mazilun, both occupied by dragons and patrolled by the great bats from beyond the Yellow Wren Mountain. (But they are marvellously clever, the rabbits of Ruilly's ranks, and can often travel underground also.) These good rabbits had relayed their message through the wolves and other woodland animals of the Unicorn Glens, and so word had finally come to the closed Portal of the Heart Oak.

Now, the Heart Oak is a curious place and even I do not know all of its mysterious characteristics. I have stepped and ridden and flown through that Portal a hundred times, but it is never the same. Even before your mystical and overtly magical brother Finnir took up its guardianship, the door of the Heart Oak had been an enigmatic frontier between the worlds. It opens in the forest of Gougane Barra, in Ireland. But I have never stepped out in exactly the same place twice, for the Portal of that more-than-alive wood displaces itself constantly! And at that time, though 'sealed' by Erreig, and locked by Finnir himself, it still retained the quality of being vaguely transparent and could also allow sound to pass through.

Before it had been locked, shortly after the Winter Solstice of 1959, many fairy-creatures had passed into Ireland, to dwell in hiding and in safety among the mossy-toed trees of Gougane Barra or among the grey boulders, golden gorse and crimson fuchsia of the hillsides around its calm lake. The small animals who helped to carry Finnir's message, brought to them by the kit of Quillir and then the rabbit-runners, whispered and murmured though the veil of the Heart Oak; and they were heard by the leprechauns and woodland fairies on the far-side. Thanks to them, hawks were found in the high trees and up the mountain-sides, and they flew from county Cork to county Tipperary, where --- not far from the Rock of Cashel --- they could pass into my own shee, the Shee of the Dove, and bring word to me that I was needed. Harkening, with great joy, to their news and to the hope of seeing Finnir released at last, I sped into Scotland via another of my shee's Portals, and from there I flew to Wales. In Wales there is a Portal into the Shee of the Red Lizard, a small but doughty shee, governed by a race of dragons, but quite non-beligerent ones --- at least in regard to fairies! They granted me passage to another Portal *of theirs, concealed by a waterfall (a motif which seems to repeat itself often in tales of your eldest brother!) and which opens into the west of America, but further north than Leyano's. By this doorway, I arrived in Oregon and could easily and quickly make my way to Eagle Abbey, and thus to Dawn Rock.*

And so it was, on the early morning of the 10th of September, with Aulfrin negotiating the passages of the underworld, I entered this realm and met with Leyano and told him that I had been summoned because his brother Finnir needed to be brought back to life --- for I had learned that his form in the Caves of the Cats was but a phantom. Accepting, as I did, the urgency and force of this macabre news, Leyano ceded to me the amber-token, and bid me to go to the Lady Ecume in Moon-Mad Bay, and there to ask her to exchange the amber pendant for the Black Key. According to Finnir's message, this was what I would need in order to liberate him.

Drenched by a particularly exuberant storm which slowed my flight during many hours --- as I was using my own great wings --- I at last found the fairest and most ancient of mer-harpers on the rocks of the northern-most isle off the coast of the Kitty Cliffs, where the Bay meets the open sea. The storm had exhausted itself into gentle breezes and clear skies again, and her Ladyship seemed to be expecting me.

There was, encased in the amber droplet, a minuscule black form, like the fossil of an insect perhaps. As I passed the token into her webbed hand, I could see the creature moving and growing, filling all the jewel. To my utter amazement and distress, she straightway and very nonchalantly tossed the droplet far out into the water. I knelt beside her on the pink granite rock, silent and shocked, as she strummed her lovely little sea-horse harp, almost idly it seemed. But no more than three minutes had passed when, from the spot where the amber-token had disappeared into the rippling wavelets, a large and intricately wrought key appeared, floating slowly towards us on the surface of the water. The lovely mermaid bent forward and took the Key from the water, and then handed it to me.

"Go to the Crescent Isle, in the great loop of the River Ere, and there you will find Dinnagorm, the winged-horse of Demoran. You

will need him with you in order to be capable of seeing from the Point of Vision, in order to perceive the place where you must go. Be of good courage, worthy Reyse, and do what you must."

I spread my own wide wings now once again, and was borne away into the west, carrying the Black Key with me.

In Davenia, flying low over the many miles of the Crescent Isle, I spied Dinnagorm grazing on star-flowers, his black coat shining with blue highlights in the now brilliant afternoon sun. I alighted, and recalled my own wings into my body for I knew I would not need them with the swift Dinnagorm to ride. I showed him the Key, and explained what I knew of Finnir's plight and his request to me. He nodded once with a sharp whinny, and the locks of his blue-black mane danced about his proud head.

It was not far to fly, going up to the northern cliffs beyond the Sweet-Faced Flower-Beds, but in the short time it took, huge clouds grew up from the horizon before us, and the sun was darkened. It seemed to be black midnight rather than high afternoon!

I sat upon Dinnagorm's muscular back, the great sombre-feathered wings arched around me, and we gazed out from the Point of Vision. It is only with a wise and willing animal companion that a fairy can be granted the powers to see what the Point may show. Below us, loud waves were crashing onto the narrow beach of pebbles and silver sand, but it was too dark to see the shoreline. Only the mer-horses, white and tinged with phosphorescent spray, were visible on the crests of the breakers. But in an instant, my eye was drawn away from their beauty to the wide, dark waters of the Sound, and to the terrible and yet glorious vision I was permitted --- in the presence of the winged-horse --- to see.

The head of an island now appeared in the black water, rising slowly like the rounded back of a huge whale or giant sea-tortoise. It was bright white, but not simply the white of sand or stone. There were trees and grasses covering the island, and all were white. It was as if the island and all of its vegetation were made of dense fog or static mist. It did not waver or tremble; it was solid and appeared very real: so real that I felt it demanding, insisting, that I look upon it. And now, as if fashioned from the white trees and white flowering *grasses, a building took form. It was a chapel. And I heard the waves crying with voices, like wailing sea-birds. And then it seemed that it was the island, or the holy little 'kirk' itself, which cried out.*

"Windy Hill! The Chapel of Windy Hill! Beware, beware, for I am both house of prayer and sepulchre, a tomb of men's dreams and also a shrill white flute made of the bone of a wild creature who has long ago ceased to run on earth. I am the white of the force of many waters, or of a congregation of myriad stars. I am the blinding glare of lightning. I am the shimmering edges of grey clouds. I am the spiral of a unicorn's horn caught in the kiss of a moon-beam. I am the white hairs of the oldest of she-wolves and the royal and pristine petals of the sacred lily…"

The voices, for there seemed to be many overlapping lines of this incantation of chanted names, subsided. I suddenly realised that I was tightly grasping the thick mane of my silent horse, and my hands too were white: white with fear or even terror. For I had not felt us move, but the Chapel had drawn closer. And we were no longer on the cliff, but hovering over the dark, churning waters of the Sound, and the Chapel of Windy Hill was before us, and the island was gone. The white 'kirk' stood squarely on the waves, and it was a ghost-chapel, and as cold as death.

I glanced away from the vision for only a spilt-second, for I could feel the Black Key in my breast pocket where I had hidden it, colder even than the icy breath of the winds whirling around the ghostly ediface. I closed my eyes as I reached into the pocket and drew forth the Key, and as I did so Dinnagorm seemed to evaporate and I found myself standing on the stony white threshold of the Chapel of Windy Hill. I looked around, my hair blowing across my eyes, and I could just see the silhouette of the winged-horse on the cliffs far behind me, where we had been standing together. The skies beyond him were pale with rain-washed blues and mauves, but everywhere else it was deepest night. I turned back to the dimly glowing doorway before me.

The seas were roaring, and the winds too. I took a deep breath, wondering if it would be my last, and walked up the three steps climbing into the Chapel, into silence and utter darkness.

Indeed, the chapel was a tomb. And the corpse that awaited me, lying on a bier of white marble or perhaps a huge white tree-trunk, cut and carven, was none other than Finnir.

I sank to my knees and my body was wracked with tears and sobs.

"Is this the vision I have been granted?!" I wailed. "Is this what my journeying and courage have won me: to behold my friend, closer than brother, **dead**? Is this the vision of what has befallen him, and of how I must find him in the Caves of the Great Cats?!"

I cried and shuddered for many minutes. But, at last, I wiped my eyes and looked with love and desperation at my beloved Finnir on his deathly bier. And then, with a start, I realised that right before me, amid the intricate carvings in the wood or marble of his resting place, there was a lock.

It was the voice of my dead friend, of my darling Finnir, which now spoke. A ghostly, phantom-voice, but it was his.

"My long work in the Cat-Caves is ended, and I must come forth and be restored to life. I could not abandon Barrywood, for the destinies that are intertwined in its quivering branches are not for the Dragon-Chieftain to discover! I remained there in body, concealed in animal-form; I went with Erreig in spirit. Now I must return to my Glens and their wonder-filled woods and waters in both body and soul united.

"You must help Neya-Voun to come to me, for I have confided my life to her, concealed in her heart. She has come here with this phantom-chapel and even now she is concealed in its crypt; and with her is the yellow blossom that will permit her to gallop to my ghost, lingering in the Caves these past months. The blossom will pave the pathway to our freedom, both hers and mine. Unlock the passageway to the vault, my dear friend. Fly before Neya-Voun to make a carpet of blossom, and thus she can come to me. United with her, I will live once again."

I turned the Black Key in the white lock, and the body of my dear Finnir simultaneously burst into flame! I recoiled from the brilliance and the searing heat of his pyre, but it was extinguished as quickly as it had been ignited. And there, standing proud and glistening white amid the soft grey ashes, was Neya-Voun, Finnir's horse. Only now, she was not a horse, for at the top of her high, concave head, there shone the spiral silver horn of a unicorn of Barrywood.

The Black Key was gone, as was any trace of Finnir's funeral-pyre or his body. As Neya-Voun pawed the ground with delicate silver hooves, cloven like a goat's, the ash seemed to glow golden with renewed heat. But no! It was not fire, but simply a change of colour, and of matter. For where the ashes had been, there was now a heap of branches all bearing tiny, soft balls of yellow blossom.

"Mimosa!" I murmured. "I have never seen this flowering tree in the Shee-Mor! It grows in the White Kangaroo Shee, and near that shee's Portals on the other side of the human-world's globe."

I gathered up armfuls of branches, and Neya-Voun stood to one side to await me. How I was to create a 'carpet of blossom' for the unicorn to rejoin her master, I had no idea.

But when all the mimosa was gathered and cradled in my left arm, I took one long spray in my right hand and, suddenly knowing exactly what I must do, I turned to the door of the Chapel where it opened onto the wild waters of the Sound. I gingerly shook the branch I held, and one or two of its tiny, bulbous blossoms drifted down towards the lapping water's edge.

But as they floated towards the ground, instantly there was no longer any of the Sound to cross. The Chapel's three steps led me down onto the cliff where Dinnagorm stood. As I, and the unicorn, stepped onto the grassy ground of the Point of Vision, the sun smiled out from behind the departing clouds, the sky became rose-petal pink, and the ghostly Chapel blew away like a breath of sea-haze.

I mounted Dinnagorm, and flew very low over the Dog-Delight Hills, across the Swan's Joy River, the Rose-Beds and the River Navid, the King's Rise and the River Dragonfly. All along my route I shook blossoms from the branches of mimosa, and a yellow pathway was created along which the enchanted Neya-Voun, now in unicorn-form, could run. As she ran, the soft round balls of the flowers carpeted her light step, but as soon as she had passed they were --- whiff! --- blown away by the wind.

The moon, a tiny and almost invisible crescent as she undoubtedly was, had obviously long ago set when we arrived in Quillir, for it was deep night and the sky was crowded with dancing, twinkling, gyrating stars. It was the night of the 11th of September by my reckoning, but not by that of the bay-brown squirrels who came to greet us as we passed under the eaves of the Hazel-Nut Woods on Quillir's northern borders. They urged us to take rest with them, and refreshment, but not one among the three of us felt hunger or thirst or weariness --- only the burning desire to see Finnir alive. It was the squirrels, however, that told us it was not the 11th, but the dark pre-dawn of the 12th of September.

Had we not noticed that an entire day had passed? Had we been lost in time as well as in space? Where had the dawn and the morning gone, and where the afternoon and twilit evening of the day before?! As we turned from the overhanging branches of the high hazels and I shook, again, a long branch of mimosa to make my yellow rain of blossom and lay the magical carpet for the silver-horned unicorn, we looked out to the west. There, just beyond the last slopes of the arid plains between ourselves and the coast, was the majestic pinnacle of Kingfishers' Temple, deep purple against a sky streaked with magenta and fiery orange. It was not pre-dawn after all, but only twilight! And there, in the midst of the sunset palette, was the fragile arc of the waxing crescent. But what was even more beautiful was that the entire moon was visible, for even the unlit regions of her roundness were clearly painted for us to see: deep grey, almost violet-blue. She was lovely!

"There, you see," squeaked the squirrels joyfully, there is the setting moon-lash, so slim, so shy, in the western tapestry of the sunset. This is the 12th of September, and the Prince Finnir's freedom day! We knew it would be today, tonight, at sunset! Hasten to him, hasten!"

Not able to solve the riddle of the date, I was nonetheless delighted for Finnir, knowing how he loved the 12th of September: a day that he had always celebrated, for as long as I have known him, as an anniversary of some great deed or event that he was bound by solemn promise to guard as a secret, so he said. Indeed we hastened on, and at a speed that made the wind whistle in my ears and brought salty sea-tears to my eyes.

As we flew into the imposing lands of the Cats, and Neya-Voun ran on over the yellow blossoms, we saw that the ground was trembling, and sometimes fissures would open in the dry earth and oblige the silvery unicorn to leap skilfully and lightly over them. On the mounds of the stark cave-hills stood or lay many forms of giant white felines, but none hindered us. One was particularly impressive, and not entirely white --- as the Great Cats usually are. He had patches of tabby-tiger fur and a long grey-striped tail, which twitched and coiled around him where he sat, proud and silent, on the highest of the sombre red hills. At the foot of this mound was the mouth of a dark cave; and standing in the shadows of the doorway, a near-transparent figure, wavering and trembling like the earth itself. It was Finnir!

Dinnagorm landed several paces from the cave-opening, but Neya-Voun cantered on without stopping, grasping the last of the mimosa branches in her mouth as she passed me and sped on towards her master. She quickly reached the Prince, and tossed the emptied branch high in the air before walking close to Finnir and laying her finely-sculpted profile against his breast, her horn resting lightly on his shoulder. As he touched it, caressing its luminous spiral with his long fingers, his white and ghost-like body took on greater colour and substance, and his smile illuminated his fair face.

"A thousand thanks, Reyse of my heart," he said, coming close and then embracing me. "I have the leave of Isck to bid farewell to my prison now, and I will go with Neya-Voun, who has brought me the blessing of my re-invigorated body, to the Hazel-Nut Woods and rest there this night with the squirrel-folk. Tomorrow evening there will be a sweet reunion with Demoran and with the King, in Davenia, and then we must rout the remaining dragons from the Silver City. But the worst will be past by then, for Erreig is to be chastised and vanquished tomorrow morn. But I think that the King has need of you, and Demoran too, for they are yet on the brink of great danger and Demoran will not be able to leave his mountain cell without the wings of his dear Dinnagorm, for his own wings are as weak as his body, after his long ordeal. Fly to them, my darling Reyse, and we shall meet again tomorrow. But fly by the loop of the northern sky-paths, for there are hot dragons in ambush in the shallows of the River

Silverfire, and they will be filled with wrath at the humiliation of their overlord, Erreig."

"We will do as you say, my wondrous Finnir! How my heart is overflowing with joy and gratitude to see you alive! But I will have questions for you when we meet again, for these have been the most mysterious hours and days of my long life."

"It is good that there be mysteries between even the greatest of friends," he laughed. "We must never learn all there is to know about one another, for that would quench the curious fire of our love!"

It was then that he added his words concerning waterfalls and their jewels, and the unlikely kinship he felt with Erreig, as I have already told you. And with that, Finnir mounted his graceful unicorn and they returned along the path of mimosa, for since we had entered Quillir, the blossoms had not blown away but had remained as a yellow carpet of softness winding through that hardest of red lands.

Dinnagorm and myself stood together, breathing deeply shoulder to shoulder, gazing out across the desert-lands. We would fly to the north and take our night's repose among the great roses on the banks of the River Dragonfly, and in the morning we would go to the prison of Demoran on the heights of the Red Hoopoe Mountain, arriving just when the King appeared also.

The silver sliver of the moon now set into the rich alizarin of the west, where coloured clouds and dark islands jostled for place along the rim of the horizon. When the moon had gone, we turned to look back to the north-east but the forms of Finnir and his mount were already departed towards the distant and whispering trees of the Hazel-Nut Woods.

Only Isck remained, high above us on the rounded head of the hill, filling all the quaking plains of the Great Cats with the sound of his thunderous purring.

****

A cool evening breeze, coupled with a soft lavender light, filled the glade where Eli and Reyse were seated side by side under the crab-apple tree. Jizay had sat up, attentively, during the tale of the ghostly Chapel of Windy Hill. As for Eli, her bare arms were covered with goose-bumps and her faced was flushed, after having grown quite pale during several tense moments in Reyse's story.

She couldn't find any words to say to the story-teller, but she lifted her eyes from where they had been lowered, staring at the red campion and exuberant dandelions among the grass, and she turned to took up into Reyse's face.

Still no words to speak to him came to her; but she thought to herself:

"I feel that I have been *with* this brave and devoted man, this fairy I mean, on the quest he achieved in order to free my brother. I have felt in my own heart and body the anguish and fear, the wonder and terror, of his experience. And I am, yes, impressed by him and his deeds. But what I know now, beyond any shadow of a doubt, is that I love Finnir. I am bound to his life, his death, his secrets and mysteries, his adventures and his destiny. My life is inextricably mingled with his. I am *profoundly* in love with him.

"I am *not* in love with Reyse, wonderful as I recognise that he is. I admire him and love his company, as if he has been my dearest friend for centuries. **He** feels more like a brother to me! But Finnir is the great, perhaps the only, love of my life --- fairy or human. I know it as surely as I know that I live; I know it as I know that God exists, that the sun and moon exist, and all of creation. It is as natural and as evident to me as breathing or thinking or dreaming or playing music. It is who and what I am.

"I am in love with Finnir. And Finnir is my half-brother. And I think, I somehow know, that in Faërie as in the human world, that poses a serious problem, that it makes my love for him somehow *impossible*, or at least forbidden…"

Eli's silent monologue was swallowed-up by her welling tears. But she was suddenly brought back to the present.

"Come," said the warm, deep voice of Reyse. "We should be getting back to the Great Tower. Your father and your cheeky pixie-friend will both be wondering where we are!"

He smiled, exhaling deeply. And so did Eli. But her heart was beating fast, and the white rose was still trembling in her hand.

****

A Delicate Balance

Chapter Eleven:
Magical Beings

t had been wise of Eli not to divulge the errand of Finnir, Aytel and Brea to Reyse. At dinner that evening, her father concealed their mission to find the ancient Queen Morliande, saying simply that the trio of fairies had been sent into Quillir to reconnoitre and to gain what information they could of Erreig's strategies and manoeuvres from the birds and squirrels. So much was true, as far as it went, Eli conceded inwardly, pleased that Aulfrin was not actually lying to his dear friend. Indeed, in order to cross the province of the Dragon-Lord, the riders would need to learn as much as possible from the animals they encountered. But, of course, there was more to their journey than that.

Aulfrin spoke in only limited detail, also, of what had occurred at the Stone Circle. He said, both to Reyse and to Piv, that he had felt movements and heard voices in and around the sacred megaliths, and that this was why he wished to know more of Erreig, and to learn if the mysterious gathering he had perceived in the Circle was somehow linked to him.

Eli looked sidelong at the King, from under her lashes, and caught the slightest hint of a grin playing about the corners of his lips. Was he teasing or luring Reyse into revealing how much he knew? Was he hoping to be vindicated in his opinion that his heart-friend was not implicated in an alliance with any of the Sun-Singers?

But it was not only in regard to Reyse that Aulfrin seemed to be fingering pieces on a chess-board and weighing his words as if he were contemplating what move to make next. His eye was also on Piv. It was clear, as the conversation turned about Erreig's potential plots and how best to discover them, that the King entertained great respect for the pixie and his insights or intuition about the situation.

Periwinkle was the image of a child's fairy-tale character: no bigger than a doll, dressed in bright colours with a cheeky expression and a rosy face, as well as fluttering vibrant-green wings and bright little cornflower-blue eyes. But it was very evident that, to the experienced King and the well-travelled fairy-lord, he was a venerable being and to be taken with all seriousness. Sitting cross-legged on the corner of the table, which was a long and thick wooden plank cut from a great tree-trunk with intricate and swirling grains running all over its highly-polished surface, Piv listened to the words of his sovereign and then shook his head. The little golden curls that had escaped his jolly green cap waggled and danced. But his expression was not jolly at all.

"You think he is possibly planning another attack, Periwinkle? You believe that Erreig is on the point of open aggression once again?" Aulfrin's questions were tinged with concern as he regarded the pixie and awaited his opinions to be voiced.

Piv ceased to shake his head, regarded his King solemnly for a moment, and then said, "In my humble opinion, Sire, he is *looking* for someone. I think it is Erreig who has begun to gather information, before you, my royal and belovèd Liege-Lord. But he isn't wondering what *you* will do next, or if *you* plan to attack him or what *your* policies are as regards your rule of Faërie. He knows all that."

Aulfrin continued to look intently at the pixie, with deep interest and attention. It was evident to Eli that her Father was prioritising which line of Piv's comments to follow first. He was surely curious as to how the pixie knew how much Erreig knew! But in only a fraction of a second, the King had made his choice of which subject was of the greatest importance, for the moment.

"You think he is <u>looking</u> for someone, you say. Whom does he seek, and why does he seek them in the Stone Circle, dear Periwinkle?"

"He doesn't seek them *there*; he perhaps thinks that the Stones will tell him more. He can't get into the Silver City itself, to ask the Trees or feel what they know. I don't even know if Erreig himself was in the Circle at all, and I don't know if the voices you heard are anything, really, to do with the Dragon-Lord's search. Maybe it was him, maybe it was his agents or spies or allies; and maybe it wasn't directly linked to his *hunting*. But it doesn't change my conviction that he is looking, looking with more and more urgency all the time. He is hunting, and you should be aware of his hunt and protect his prey.

"For he is looking for Mélusine," he intoned solemnly.

There was a breathless hush around the table.

"Yes, my Eli, my darling little human-still-Eli, must be careful, and must be protected," Piv concluded.

The King wore an expression of dumbfounded alarm. As did Reyse. But it was Eli herself who spoke first.

"Erreig is hunting....*me*?!"

"Why do you think this, Periwinkle?" whispered Aulfrin.

And Reyse's deep voice echoed the King's: "Why Mélusine, or rather Eli? What makes you say this, Piv?"

"And why haven't you said anything before this?" added Eli, rather nervously.

Piv flew up and circled the table once, alighting to stand beside Eli, his two little soft-booted feet squarely planted on the edge of the table. He laid a tiny hand on his friend's shoulder, and smiled resignedly. "Don't worry, my Eli. I'm saying this now, because I have only just learned it, and I want us *all* to be more careful. You're only *visiting* us at the moment, and so you're not the Princess. She, the true 'you', is very strong and very aware and very able to protect herself! But you're not her again yet, and so you're a bit --- well --- vulnerable.

"My Eli-een has been keeping to herself rather a lot lately, lost in her own thoughts," Piv continued, looking now to both Aulfrin and Reyse in turn. "And so, as I've had more time on my own; it's given me the space for reflection and a bit of *research*. I've had the time to visit some of my special friends here in the City; for there are mushrooms in the Inner Garden that are very wise indeed, because they have singing threads of filament that go right to the toes of the Great Ones, the mighty Trees themselves. And they have told me things.

"Now some of the things that I know, I keep to myself," announced the pixie, with a tiny finger raised as if in admonition, "and some I share with one friend and some with another. But this news I learned this evening before twilight, and it's rather important, so I have decided to tell you, all three of you, oh I mean *five* of you --- excuse me Ferglas and joyful Jizay. But because of what I've learned, we should all of us take some precautions, I think."

Both Aulfrin and Reyse were very quiet and their eyes were unblinking. Eli's silence was much more anxious, and she found herself twisting her serviette in her lap. But Piv sat once more on the table, with crossed legs, and he told them what he had learned from the mushrooms and the Great Trees.

"Bram is the name that the fungi-folk of the circular flower-gardens give to the Western Tree. It's surely not his true name, or at least not his full title, for that would be very long indeed. But they know him as Bram, so I will call him that too. And Bram is one of the two Trees who knew the Princess Mélusine very well. The other that was a special friend to her, to the north-east, we name Rhadeg; but this information about Erreig comes from Bram.

"Now let me begin at the beginning. It seems that you, my King, sent Eli messages this past springtime --- as is quite usual and correct --- to ease her back into remembering who she really was. You probably sent her visions, or even dreams, did you not?"

Aulfrin smiled slightly, and nodded. "Both, indeed, and others: a meditation-vision in a chapel, yes, and another vision in the clouds, a few words linked to a piece of harp-music and a dream of how I had met Maelys, our little moon."

"And I sent her a message myself," interjected Reyse, "in the form of a little love poem." Aulfrin raised his eyebrows slightly, glancing at his friend. He had not known the form of the message before now, and was agreeably amused, it seemed.

"But there was another dream-message, was there not, my Eli darling?" asked Piv, turning to look up into the rather confused turquoise eyes of his friend. Eli nodded slowly.

"A very terrifying dream, yes. Or at least, part of it was frightening," said Eli softly.

"Another dream?" interrupted her father. "A dream besides the one of my going to the Abbey of Timadeuc to meet Lily, and our falling in love and marrying, and choosing our child's name?"

Eli looked enquiringly at her father, as she nodded slowly. "Yes, there were two dreams that same night, one fading into the other. Didn't you send me the dream about the dragon-fight?"

"Dragon-fight?!" Aulfrin's hands had become rather tense on the rim of the table now. "You were shown a dragon-fight? The battle I fought with Erreig to free Demoran?"

"Ah no, not that one," clarified Eli. "This battle was when I was a fairy-child, for I was in the scene that I saw afterwards, in a great round room here in this very Tower-palace, with my brothers there too. It was a dream about the day that my mother the Queen was banished. I saw Mélusine --- as if I were watching a film of myself as a little girl of only about nine or ten --- just after I had been shown a part of a battle between you and Erreig, over the silver turrets of Fantasie. You were on Cynnabar, and he was riding Bawn and…"

"Why were you shown that? And by whom?!" exclaimed the King. He suddenly turned to his noble friend. "Reyse, my heart, did *you* send Eli that image?"

But Reyse was as baffled as the King. His forehead was furrowed with confusion and concern. He shook his head slowly. "Not I," he said. "I was not in Fantasie when the Queen Rhynwanol was banished, and was not aware of the details pertaining to that day nor of any importance it could hold for Eli as a changeling. I have heard of that battle from other sources since: the brief, aerial combat when Erreig came to challenge you because he had been found to be your wife's lover, and their child Alégondine was stolen away by the Sage-Hermit."

Aulfrin, nodding his assent, was clearly about to say something, but Piv recommenced his own tale instead.

"Exactly," he began. "*That* was the dream sent by Bram. And it was my clever Mélusine herself who had asked for it to be sent by her dear Tree-friend. She wanted to be reminded of the risk and menace of Erreig when she came back on her three Visits. And no one knew but Bram, and one other. But what is strange is that, in the opinion of the magical and mighty Tree, the dream was too short and left somehow incomplete that night, and Eli didn't receive all that she had planned to be reminded of. She was awakened too soon.

"So now, Bram wants you both to know, your Majesty and my dear Reyse, all that it *should* have shown her, in order that you might better protect her.

"But I must point out something else, and right away, for you have one thing quite wrong, my sweet Reyse. Erreig did *not* come that day to challenge the King, the husband of his clandestine lover. Their affair had been discovered, and now the Queen would certainly be banished. There was nothing more to do about that. He would have *wished* that she could come with him to live in Quillir, but of course that was impossible. He wouldn't have really dared to imagine it. No, no, he came here for another reason, not to fight with the King."

Both Reyse and Aulfrin remained silent, their expressions perplexed, pale and stern.

"The Sage-Hermit, who was already showing his allegiance to the Dragon-Clan at that time, had come to abscond with the little Alégondine, then only five. Demoran was with her in the high courtyard when a battle began overhead between you, my Liege, and Erreig --- who had arrived in Fantasie only just before the Sage-Hermit, and almost as stealthily. Demoran has recounted that tale to me, and how he was rendered powerless by a strong charm of the Sage-Hermit, and the child was whisked away while the skies were filled with flame and tumult. But even the great magician of Star Island did not know what Mélusine would later come to know. Only Bram knew, Bram and the Queen herself."

"The Queen?!" Aulfrin's voice was as tense as his hands now. "The Queen was not in Fantasie, she was in hiding and in disgrace, having retreated to Kingfishers' Temple that very morning."

"Not before warning her daughter," remarked Piv, calmly and with satisfaction at unravelling his tale with such suspense. "But she did not know all, nor tell all to the Princess. But Bram knew, at least he learned the full story in the seasons and years that followed, as he and the Princess became close. Now, I will explain."

If possible, the amazed silence of his listeners became even more intense.

"In great distress at having been discovered in her infidelity, the Queen Rhynwanol had gone, at dawn, to the Great Trees, to bid them farewell and to beg them to watch over her daughter Mélusine. She then went to her Music Room, to play one last time on her magical harp Gaëtanne. And she took the child Mélusine with her there, and played for her. And in her music was woven much love and sorrow, and all the pain of her being parted from her children in the wake of her illicit romance with Erreig, and also what she had learned of her lover's plans. For though she did not understand them fully, she was aware that not only would Alégondine be kidnapped that day, but that Mélusine was also to be seized."

No recollection of these things was coming to Eli as she listened to the pixie's tale. But her tears were hot and falling in rivulets onto her twisted serviette. She could feel the Queen's anguish at leaving her family, and she could somehow also feel --- deeply buried in her own heart --- the pain of separation from her own true mother.

Piv, continuing with his story, turned to comment to Eli, "You heard much as she played, I imagine, whispered in the notes sung by the tall and sweet-voiced harp Gaëtanne, and you harkened to the advice of both the Queen and the instrument to remain at the side of your two brothers, Finnir and Leyano, *within* the King's Tower. By nature, you would surely have been outside to witness the clash of the two opponents, as were Alégondine and Demoran. For Erreig had been perceived in the skies over Fantasie, perceived by the King and by the Trees; and it was evident that your father would challenge him. Probably, you would have chosen to be outside and to witness the encounter. But now you knew that you must bid your remaining brothers to stay with you, where Erreig and his servants would be unable to enter, in the high room with the seven windows: for each window of that great central Chamber is linked to a Tree and to a Stone, so the place is enchanted with potent and perilous charms of protection.

"The Dragon-Lord had not come to Fantasie to openly challenge the King. He had come to distract him, so that the two Princesses could be taken by the Sage-Hermit and by the great black bats. But these lesser servants, whirring about all the silver towers and turrets while the battle raged, were now at a loss to find and grasp Mélusine, for they had anticipated that she would be outside with her half-sister. They had been ordered to lift her in their many claws and to carry her as prisoner back to the White Dragon Fortress, or more likely to bear her to an even more remote and secure corner of his province, until…"

"Until *what*?" The voice that cut into Periwinkle's discourse like a flaming sword was Reyse's. "What were his designs on Mélusine?" The eagle-lord's eyes were flashing with amber darts and his usually kind voice had a ring of effrontery and defiance in it.

"Until she would be of an age to marry," said Piv, very slowly and very softly. "This is what my little Mélusine had learned from the rippling voice of Gaëtanne --- something even the Queen had probably not comprehended in the music. And this is what she had asked to be reminded of in the dragon-dream that would be sent to her, as Eli, by her friend the Great Tree. Erreig's intention was to keep the Princess for his own."

Reyse was breathing fast, and his eyes continued to glow with fury. Piv took up his tale once again, after a pause of only a moment.

"At first, indeed, he was in love with your Queen, my dear Majesty Aulfrin; but later he was even more desirous of her daughter, your daughter. At that time, already, he had learned --- shall we say --- of her *potential*. She was only a young child, but the Sage-Hermit probably had seen or felt much of what she would become, and of the character and destiny that would show themselves in her. And Erreig had learned of it, and wanted all of that for himself.

A Delicate Balance

"It was in 1359 that Queen Rhynwanol met and fell in love with Erreig, and their child Alégondine was born --- presumed by all to be the child of the King Aulfrin --- in 1362, after the normal three years of pregnancy. In 1367 you, my Sovereign, had learned of the treachery of this affair and that the dark-skinned little dragon-fairy-girl was <u>not</u> yours at all; and so the banishment of your unfaithful wife was decreed. But, previously, in the years of Alégondine's infancy in Fantasie, Erreig had found means to see his daughter from time to time. And often she was in company with her older sister, older by only about four-and-a-half years, but already radiating her regal stature to come, her beauty as it would unfold, her magical and mysterious allure, her queenliness. And Erreig's heart cooled a little in regard to the wondrous Queen Rhynwanol, and turned --- rather perversely --- towards the young child Mélusine, and the high royal personage she would grow into.

"But it seems that our brave and brilliant Princess here was told of this situation by the wise harp and in her music sang the voice of the Great Tree Bram too. She became more and more aware of his designs, quite early in her youth and soon after her mother's exile; yes just before her first Initiation. Yet even in her adolescence, she did not communicate what she learned of Erreig's disappointed plans and his on-going infatuation for her to her banished mother, or to her father the King. For the Queen had not heard all that her harp, Gaëtanne, had spoken to little Mélusine on the morning of the battle; she had only understood that the Dragon-Lord wished to kidnap *both* of her daughters. The Queen did not know why. But her daughter did.

"Mélusine had comprehended *all* the message of the harp, and so had learned of Erreig's desires --- though at first she perhaps did not understand them fully. But as she grew, well-disguised messages would sometimes reach her, and she repudiated the advances hinted at and the declared affection which was so distasteful to her. As she grew to young adulthood and of an age to undertake her Initiations, the Princess spoke often to Bram, and to Rhadeg also no doubt, of her growing anger and her constant rejection of the Dragon-Lord's secret suit. Then, when the Princess was in her twenties, between the years 1400 and 1600 in fact according to Bram, Erreig more actively tried various means of subtle seduction upon her, though still warily and secretly.

"Disgusted and indignant, Mélusine refused him again and again. Though his attentions were very wily and discreet, and could not really be interpreted as out-right proposals of a romantic nature, Mélusine perfectly understood what was his heart's desire. During the centuries that followed, she would send ever more icy replies and rebuttals to the leader of the Sun-Singers.

"Until finally, as she grew to her full adult nobility and strength, she would make him understand that she would not only reject his attentions and his suit, but --- rather than divulging all to her mother the Queen, and to the King himself --- she would find the means, herself, to topple his plans for petty lordship, and his dominion of the realm of Quillir would be taken from him, *by her*.

"Erreig has been, thus, for many long years, wracked with fear and tortured by desire. He loves and longs for Mélusine, but he now fears what she is capable of doing to not only reject him personally but to destroy his growing power and his ambitious dreams."

Both Reyse and the King were struck dumb, and for a long moment neither said a word. Eli was pale and trembling, and she too was utterly silent. Jizay's head was now under her shaking hand, and his dark, seal-like eyes were gazing lovingly up at her. Piv sighed deeply, and resumed his tale.

"During the fifty years of Mélusine's changeling adventure, Bram and all of the Great Trees have woven a veil of confusion over the far-reaching network of the fungus and throughout all the channels of knowledge and news among the creatures that bring information to Erreig, especially via the Mushroom Lord. They have done this so that Erreig would *not* know that Mélusine was absent for those years, and it has doubtless given the Dragon-Cheiftain many sleepless nights of worry, wondering what she may have been up to! But now, very likely, he is becoming aware of what has transpired, and he knows that she is in Faërie and in Fantasie. For news is circulating these past weeks regarding the visits of a changeling --- a royal changeling --- and the *'return'* of the Princess Mélusine to the Silver City, and Erreig will surely put the pieces together for himself.

"And as Eli is not really Mélusine, not yet, so her powers are not yet restored to her. She cannot protect herself, and she cannot overthrow the Dragon-Lord, and Erreig may take his chance to try to destroy her, or --- much more likely --- to seize her and attempt to force her into a union with him, or at least to use her as a means to bargain with you, dear Majesty.

"Thus, for many long years, he is seeking her and hunting her. But he is also tormented in his search and he is pulled in two directions at once. For his fear of her is very great, but his love and desire are even greater.

"I'm sorry if I have frightened you, my sweet and beautiful Eli-een. But I tell you these things here and now, before your father and your most loyal champion Lord Reyse, as Bram has urged me to do, so that we can, all together, devise our plans to keep you safe and sound, until you come home in all your strength and shining Moon-Dancer light!"

While Piv had recounted his long tale, the candles had burned low and now the dining-room was dim and filled with quavering and ominous shadows. Eli was trembling violently, and Reyse rose and went to her, kneeling beside her chair, on the opposite side from Jizay, and placing both his strong,

Magical Beings

brown hands on her: one on her shoulder and one on her thigh. He looked into her shining, blinking, teary eyes with his determined and confident ones.

"I will remain in this shee, and never far-distant from you, Eli, throughout your Visit, if you and the King give me leave. No agent of Erreig's will approach you, none will harm you, nothing will threaten your peace or safety here."

Eli's tears were flowing unchecked now. She could not answer him. It was her father who spoke.

"I thank you, my good and loyal Reyse. And I think Eli will join me in giving you leave to protect her, with gratitude from both of our hearts. I will remain near, much of the time --- though I may make a brief visit to the Stone Circle, in urgency, tomorrow. Jizay will obviously not leave his mistress's side. As for Periwinkle, I may ask him to return to the Inner Garden, and pose one or two more questions for me, if he is willing to interrogate the fungi-folk, and the Great Trees, further on Eli's behalf. Piv nodded once, with solemnity.

"For tonight, I will arrange that Eli's sleeping-quarters be changed, and she will be housed in the great Council-Room. It was that circular chamber that Periwinkle mentioned, my dear girl, and that you saw in the dream sent by Bram. Yes, I know his name as that also, among other titles and in other tongues. And as Piv remarked, the seven open windows of the Council-Chamber are each one aligned in energy and magical charms of great power to the seven Trees and the seven Stones. There you will be safe, for no one may enter unbidden there. It is a large room, and there is ample space for a hammock-bed for your champion Reyse in one of the alcoves too. Will you agree to that?"

Still unable to summon words to her lips, Eli slowly nodded her assent.

"I will add one further remark," said Aulfrin now, as he rose and descended the glowing dais of his throne, with Ferglas at his heels, to come to his daughter. Jizay and Reyse both stood, as did Eli now.

The King took both her moist, trembly hands in his, and he smiled and said, "My dear one, you have been home for three weeks on your first Visit, and over a week on this, your second one. Erreig has not perturbed you, not so far! Perhaps he has not yet fully comprehended that you are here and that the changeling-come-home is indeed the Princess Mélusine. Or perhaps he realises that to interfere with you while not yet re-inhabiting her form would be vain and useless, and also extremely dangerous with me here in the realm, as well as all of your brothers and the noble Reyse too.

"He is not an idiot, this dragon-boy --- though now I see him in a light less flattering than ever I did before. But, that said, he has had the good taste to fall madly in love --- and truly in madness and folly --- with the two most beautiful and glorious women-fairies who have ever graced the lands of the Faërie. I can't fault his choices!"

Despite all of her agitation and anxiety, Eli had to smile. Her dear Father was amazingly good-humoured and calm, even amid all of this horrifying news. Her tears subsided, and her cheeks recovered a little of their colour. She turned to look very lovingly at Reyse, and even more tenderly at Piv, who was standing near the rim of the table and discreetly nibbling a last little square of an oat-and-almond cake left-over from dinner.

"I wish to propose a glass of apple brandy, just to relax us all, and to seal our bargain of greater precaution and heightened protection for Eli. But before I call for that, I'd like Eli to accompany me to another room, for only a few moments, as I would like to have a moment, in private, with my lovely daughter. You'll excuse us Reyse, and Periwinkle?"

"Of course," agreed Reyse, adding that he would organise his improvised sleeping-quarters in the meantime. As for Piv, he offered to go to the circle of blue flowers in the Inner Garden right away.

"The waning crescent always makes the mushrooms there more talkative," the pixie explained. "It should still be a good moment to ask if they have had any more news of Erreig."

"That's perfect," concluded the King. "We will be back shortly, then." And with a warm smile to Reyse, Aulfrin ushered Eli, with Jizay following, out of the dining-room and up the nearest spiral staircase.

****

To Eli's surprise, her father led her quite directly, though by this smaller and more modest staircase, to the level of the Great Tower where both the Music Room and the Concocting Cell of Queen Rhynwanol were situated.

As they approached the flowery landing, coming down another short corridor nearby, Eli recognised the choice of passageways: one with its black and powder-blue pattern of small floor-tiles and the other with its rich and spicy fragrance.

"Many elements of Piv's tale jolted me, I must admit," said Aulfrin, and he and Eli halted at the branching of the hallways. "I am rarely so taken off my guard by news in my own realm! Usually I know at least a little of what is transpiring. But the dream you requested to be shown, by the Great Trees, and all its content and characters, has humbled me, for I had never guessed any of it.

"Of course, I knew that your mother the Queen was in the habit of bringing you to listen to her highly enchanted harp Gaëtanne. I should have guessed that she would do so, one last time, before she left in such disgrace and dismay. But that Rhynwanol knew of her lover's plot to take *you* as well as Alégondine, I had no idea; and the fact that she did not share this information with me, mystifies me. I could have protected you, more surely than your brothers. My Queen was, and is still of course, the wisest woman-fairy I have ever met, save only for my own mother Morliande, whom I would deem to be even richer in wisdom and magical powers than Rhynwanol. So I am inclined to accept that she must have had her reasons.

"Well, perhaps the players in the drama were already in motion, or maybe she was unable to speak with me in my anger and under the imposition of her exile --- for she went very early that day to the Kingfishers' Temple, and from thence to the Sheep's Head Shee. Perhaps she had not known before that very morning; for it seems that she had learned of Erreig's plot from the Great Trees when she had visited at sunrise of that fateful day. In any case, that is not the only bolt of lightning that has startled me this evening.

"So, Erreig has --- long ago --- experienced a change of heart: from his audacity in desiring and seducing my own wife, he fell yet further into folly and insolence in becoming enamoured of our young daughter! Though, as I said, I cannot fault his good taste...," here Aulfrin winked at Eli, "still I am profoundly enraged and alarmed.

"But, I will add yet another confession of my ignorance, though I am not so much surprised by the news as proud and delighted, and somewhat vindicated in my own premonitions: that you, my daring Mélusine, pronounced such threats to the rebel Erreig, vowing that you would throw him down yourself. Ha! That is excellent, and very worthy of your proud and independent character! I have long known that one of my daughters would be at the heart of the matter in resolving the tensions between myself and the Sun-Singers. And I have always expected that it would, most likely, be you."

The King's arm was around Eli's shoulder now, and he pressed her to him as he laughed. "Well done, my brave and bonny lass! You have impressed me, and reassured me. It is destined, I believe, that my little Princess should be intrinsically intertwined in the defence and dignity of the Moon-Dancers, and in the resolution of all conflict concerning them. I saw it all coming true, in my mind's eye, as your darling pixie-friend spoke. And I think it not unlikely that you *will* have the ultimate victory over Erreig, in some as yet unimaginable way."

There at the branching of the two corridors, father and daughter regarded one another for a long moment. Eli began to breathe more deeply, and perhaps the rich aromas of her mother's Concocting Cell encouraged this and also brought other blessings or boldness to her as well. At last she found the courage to murmur her own thoughts to her father, as she leaned her head onto his shoulder.

"Two things are also surprising *me*, my father, or maybe three. But they are not really linked to the news from Piv, or not directly. Though they have to do with … love."

"Ah?" muttered Aulfrin. "And what are these surprising, but lovely things?"

"I'm as shocked as you are about Erreig's suit, that's true," began Eli, straightening up and looking into the green depths of her father's eyes. "I'm shocked and a little frightened, but less than I thought I should be just now. It seems, as Mélusine, I've always known my own mind where men were concerned, and have been able to refuse them with some authority when I saw fit, and with a good measure of self-confidence; I wish I'd always been so strong in my human life! But that isn't what's surprising me at this moment, for I think it's part of who I must truly be.

"A *real* revelation and amazement for me is --- firstly --- the memory, not of the *insight* I was granted by my mother and her harp, but by the love that she and I shared. I can't remember, not really, that morning in her Music Room; but I can feel the love I had for her, and still have for her, burning in my heart.

"For there's another love, and I feel it there too, hidden and yet swelling in my breast. It was kindled by Reyse's words tonight. As he reacted so defensively, so gallantly to the news of Erreig's interest in me, and when he came and offered me his protection, I felt myself soaring like an eagle. I suppose that's love, and I think I've never felt it, not truly, ever before."

There was a gentle and very contented smile stealing over her father's lips. Perhaps it was that which gave Eli the courage to continue --- for she had not been sure that she should actually say what she wanted so desperately to confide in him.

"But there is a *third* wave of something, surprising me and overwhelming me, and I think it must also be very great love. I think so… It was when Piv spoke of my menacing Erreig with his own downfall, at my hands, that I saw a vision, and not for the first time. I was on an island, and my hair was blowing in the wind and my arms were stretched out and my head was held high. I could see a great dragon, a white dragon I think, wheeling away --- chased away, I suppose, by me. But I was not alone. There was another fairy on the island, near to me. A man-fairy. When I saw the vision before, I could not recognise him. But when Piv was speaking, and I saw it all again so clearly, I could. This time, I could. It was my brother."

Very softly, as he nodded in growing understanding and great contentment, Aulfrin whispered, "Leyano. Of course. He is in league with Garo, and he has become acquainted with Bawn. With these links forged, he will fill the role, with you, of bringing Erreig's plans to naught, and your victory will be interwoven with his. My daughter and my son…."

"No, my dear father," interrupted Eli, startling Aulfrin out of his reverie. "No, it was not Leyano --- I had thought of him, too, before this. But it was not him, I feel sure now, at least not as I perceived this vision again tonight. It was a great fairy-lord, a royal, kingly, magical being. And the love I felt leaping into my heart as Reyse knelt beside me, I knew that it belonged in truth to this mighty and yet so gentle fairy-knight who was with me, beside me, in that scene on the island.

"Great Trees and standing Stones, dragons and harps, eagle-eyes and champions' hearts, my royal mother and my human mother, you and Reyse and Piv and mermaids and white cats and unicorns, they all flew and spun together and they all amounted to the same thing. A love more fierce and more peaceful than anything I have ever felt is growing, like dawn, in my very soul."

Aulfrin's brow was furrowed, but he held Eli's gaze and there was infinite tenderness and patience, a limitless regard and respect for her in that gaze.

"Whom do you love, Eli? For whom is this all-encompassing love that is dawning in your heart?"

Eli exhaled, and tears welled up, once again, in her own blue-green eyes.

"It's impossible, I imagine. I *should* be in love with Reyse. But I'm not. I'm in love with my brother, my eldest brother. I am in love with Finnir."

There was a long silence between father and daughter, but it was not at all tense or stressed. Eli felt a tidal wave of relief and honesty washing over her, just to have said aloud, to her dear father, what was in her heart.

As for Aulfrin, he seemed reflective but a little sad. At last he spoke.

"I had thought we would go to the Queen's Music Room, to see Rhynwanol there perhaps, in phantom-beauty, and to listen to the dream-notes of Gaëtanne. But now I think it would be wisest to take the other direction, and go to her Concocting Cell, her room of spices and scents. Come with me, Eli, to that wondrous room."

Eli took his hand, and they walked under the carved and ominous archway. She did not mention that she had been there that morning, and had met Finnir there as well.

As they came into the heart of the rounded room, and approached the table with the Queen's Head Vase glowing softly with lemony light, Aulfrin continued.

"I wonder how much you begin to recall, my gentle Eli, of magical beings and of the sometimes very curious laws that govern them. In fact, we, all of us here in Faërie --- you included as the Princess --- are magical, enchanted creatures. But there is a certain... hierarchy among us.

"I am not a king only because of my genealogy or because I have fought and won great battles of will or wisdom, though both contribute to that status. It is not as in the human world, not here. In this land there are highly honoured and enchanted families who possess extreme and extraordinary powers, even for fairies: just such strengths and characteristics as Erreig perceived in you, and in your mother, and which incited his passion and his desire. He does not have them, and no amount of intermarriages or victories in combat can change that, to his great dismay.

"As I say, your mother and you her daughter are heirs to this gift of greatness and of heightened enchantment. All the women who have held the right to enter into this cell have been graced with this distinction: my own mother among them, and the Queens before her. For in this room dwells the Queen's Head Vase, as you see. It is not a magical being itself; it is not alive, save with a current of energy which permits a communication of sorts, a very feminine channel of communication. No male fairy can hear its voices, but all the *royal* females can; and they have come here for many thousands of years, one after the other, to listen and to learn and to share with the women before them.

"One day, oh perhaps in three or four thousand years, I will cede this kingdom of mine to my eldest son, to Finnir. He will become the King of Faërie, of the Shee-Mor, in his turn. And he will take a wife, a great Queen of the Fairies, and she will be of the same magical mien as he is, without a doubt. She will come here, then, and hear the voices of the Queens before her. For to be counted among the royalty of Faërie is not a social or political honour, nor is it akin to being born among a wealthy or particularly cultured or cultivated aristocracy. It is often like that in the human world, I'm afraid; though sometimes it may be that it is, as it is here, the recognition of something innate and ineffable, like a talent for music or art or science. In any case, it is a blessing and a birthright --- much like the hidden destiny of a great and infinitely wise tree is always there, from its very nut or acorn.

"Now, there is another difference in our realm from that of men. We do *not* have regulations, legal or religious, relating to consanguinity, rules which protect our race from physical or mental weaknesses by forbidding us to intermarry within the same family. We do not forbid such unions between cousins, or even between half-brothers and sisters --- as would be the case with you and Finnir, for he is my son but not related to Rhynwanol, your mother. And some fairies in my realm *do* marry with their own kin, just as may happen among the animals or the plants which reproduce along certain branches of the same family at times, with no great harm taken. It should not be the case too often, not with fairies or with plants or with other creatures, for it is best to broaden the influences and traits within a family, and not turn them in on themselves; that is common sense. But love is inexplicable, and so such unions do, at times, occur.

"But in the case of your love for your half-brother Finnir, and not even knowing if he shares this sentiment and deep stirring of the heart, I will say no more just yet; but rather, I will ask you to step close to the Vase and to listen. You are a Princess of Faërie, a royal and magical being, in your deepest soul. I think you may hear for yourself the explanations you need at this time."

Eli was mesmerised by her father's words, and more so by his invitation for her to approach the Queen's Head. She did so, and just as Aulfrin had known that she would, after a short and humming silence, she heard its voice.

Sister and brother, of royal race,
Share innocent love with no disgrace,

But to bind in marriage or lovers' embrace
Will call forth the charm that will debase
The powers sown in both their lives;
For the force uniting such husbands and wives
Weakens the magic that in them thrives
And naught in their intimacy survives
Of their enchanted destiny.

Thus royal kin are far from free,
For should they wed their powers shall flee
And weaker both lord and land shall be;
Such love shall wither the strongest tree.
This seems a curse, and a source of woe,
To deny true love which strives to grow,
But if they be wed it is surely so:
Their loving will lessen the magic's flow.
Ever it was and ever will be.

Heed the wisdom the wise ordain,
For the might of that mix one could not restrain;
Their powers cannot be blended in twain:
So rich a blend it would prove their bane,
Too wild to tame, too bright to see...

Just as Eli thought that the whispering chant, evidently sung for her ears only, had faded and come to its close, an even softer refrain swelled up from the Queen's Head, and tiny white sparks of light mingled with the lemony yellow glow:

But hearken, my child, to your own heart.
Can you and your love be torn apart?
Magical beings have truth to impart:
And to drink of love is the highest art.
It may be that secrets shall come to light
And you shall be aided in your plight.
Believe, believe without respite,

And seek for the sun in the moonlit night;
Therein will lie your victory.

While these last words had risen to Eli's ears, the light of the Vase had changed colour: from a pastel yellow, through ochre and woody brown, and finally to a clear, pale blue. Now it glowed orangey red, but less intensely. Soon it died down, almost completely swallowed up into the open crown of the Queen's Head. The room became quite dim, and very silent.

Eli turned to her father, her eyes wide and round. But Aulfrin's expression was calm and rather expectant.

"Did you hear any voices?" he asked, simply.

"You did not?" asked Eli.

"I am not of your sacred sex, dear daughter of mine! Only a royal and *female* fairy may hear what the ancestral voices say or sing. However, I must admit that I had a strong sensation of a presence in the room, and so I have my ideas as to which of your forebears spoke to you."

"Was it my mother? Was that the voice of Rhynwanol? It was like the music of the backwash of the tide, as it strokes the sand and pebbles and tiny shells of a white beach. It was beautiful, and musical, and as timeless as the ocean --- just as I would have imagined my mother's voice to be."

Aulfrin shook his head slightly, but with a winsome smile. "Ah no, not Rhynwanol that watery word-music, if that is how you can so poetically describe its sound. Your mother's voice is like leaf-play and birdsong and the harmonising strings of a joyful harp or the mysterious whistling of the breeze in a starlit forest. But the presence I felt here while you listened would coincide with your description perfectly, and I feel convinced that it was surely she whom I heard lately in the Circle. It was your grandmother, the Queen Morliande. Her voice, especially when singing or declaiming poetry, was always to be likened to the music of the sea, for she is a daughter of the ocean and herself an enchanted half-seal.

"And, so, did the Silkie-Queen explain to you why it is forbidden for a royal brother and sister to be united in our world?"

Eli was staring at the sleepy orange glow which was now playing around the crown of the Vase.

"My grandmother? The legendary lady that Finnir has gone to seek? Yes. Yes, she did tell me: it is too strong a blend, the two powers of the royal lovers. It lessens both, or even removes their magical strength altogether. She was here, then, in this room?! Will Finnir not find her, then? Will he return here swiftly?"

Aulfrin could hear the emotion in Eli's voice, even as she pronounced her brother's name. He sighed.

"Morliande was not here. She is undoubtedly far off in Silkie-Seal Bay, where --- indeed --- Finnir has gone on his secret quest. He will meet her there, I am sure. But my kind mother's heart has responded to your questions and to your dilemma. And I hope she was gentle and yet firm in her reply to you."

Eli looked at her father, whose face was quite shadowy even though he stood close beside her. The smells of the spices and blended potpourris were very heady, and Eli felt extremely tired, or even a little drunk. The King turned to go, and gestured for Eli to precede him out of the dark and perfumed room.

As they passed under the arch with its leafy heads and other strange carvings, he spoke with finality and authority, although still with kindness and love.

"Finnir will require all of his magical powers as the future King, and you, I deem, shall also need every drop of yours, when you come to fulfil your destiny as the Princess Mélusine --- or perhaps as the wife of Reyse one day, and the first Queen of the Shee of the Dove. As yet, that shee has never known a royal family, and your children created with that noble fairy-lord would form the first dynasty to bear such power and enchantment. I'm certain he hopes for that, our dear and brave Reyse.

"In any case, as the venerable Morliande has clarified for you my darling daughter, Finnir and you may **not** wed; it would be folly, and it is forbidden by our very natures as royal fairies. Love him with all your heart, as your brother. But not more.

"Not more."

****

A Delicate Balance

Chapter Twelve:
The Seven Arches and the Seventh Gate

For the next three days and nights, Eli would be guarded and protected (she would have said, by the end of that time, 'kept under house arrest') in the great Council-Chamber with its seven soaring arches.

The diminishing sickle of the waning crescent peaked around the edge of the window to the east in the very early hours of the morning of the first two of those nights. Eli could rarely sleep more than a couple of hours at a time, as her thoughts and emotions were troubling her constantly. She was therefore awake to catch sight of the 'moon-lash', as the squirrels had called it, when it rose. But on the third night, there was no moon at all, for she was 'new', and thus the skies were given over entirely to the hosts of stars and several strange, pulsating, shining planets.

Reyse slept in one of the alcoves across the room from where her own bed had been placed. His hammock was behind a tapestry curtain, and hers was hung with lacy drapes of fabric veined like leaves or the wings of dragonflies. They were, therefore, discreetly separated; but this did not prevent Reyse calling out his tender words of "good night and starry dreams" and then playing music for her, to lull her to sleep. Although she knew that he could play the harp, he did not choose that instrument for these lullabies. It seemed that he played on a small violin or more probably his *vielle*. Eli could not see it, but the sound was very sweet and poignant, peaceful and rather angelic, she thought.

During the day, except for their dinners together, both Reyse and the King were absent, leaving Eli to be guarded by Jizay and often visited by Piv. Quite obviously, within this circular Hall, there was no danger. The high, open windows, overlooking all the various and contrasting landscapes of Fantasie, were actually protection enough. Eli wondered why Reyse was there at night! It seemed, quite clearly, that he simply wanted to be chivalrous and gallant. And also that he wanted to be near her, no doubt.

But both he and Aulfrin spent their days occupied with their errands and investigations, perhaps conversing with the mighty Trees or even the lesser ones, or the birds and beasts of the City, or perhaps even with the megaliths of the Stone Circle. Maybe they were patrolling even further afield to gain news of Erreig's whereabouts or insights into his plans.

Periwinkle had visited the blue flower beds of the Inner Garden on the very first night, under the diminishing moon which encouraged the mushrooms to be 'more talkative', as he had said. He had returned once or twice since, but no more ample information seemed to be forthcoming from Bram or Rhadeg or any of the other Great Trees.

"They hum sweetly to themselves, the mushrooms say, even with the voices of their many roots underground. And high in the air, also, they chant and sway and sing and pray, as ever," Piv reported. "That's all. No more news, no more warnings, no worry or wisdom to share. The fungus-folk are all whispering too, but it's not about Erreig. They speak of breezes blowing in Margouya, east of the Dragons' Drink and down to Leaping Bay and the ponds of the Wise Frogs."

These were his 'official' words, told to Aulfrin and Reyse at dinner on the first evening. But the following morning, Piv lingered after their breakfast-time together to chat with Eli, and he said that the mushrooms' words were many and 'more filled with music' than he had said to the others.

"I think their sing-song gossiping was actually alluding to the passage of Finnir and his two companions, my little Eli. They were chuckling and almost dancing when they spoke, as if the music of your brother's silver harp was ringing in their wide-brimmed heads! I think they've gone that way, the riders. But why? Are they headed to Laughing Bay, or even further to the Bay of Nod?"

"I don't know what their route is, my dear Piv," Eli replied, safely but honestly. "I couldn't say..."

Piv seemed contented with this reply, and simply chewed thoughtfully on a huge walnut. "Perhaps they will turn towards the Sun-Song Cliffs and the long, warm beaches of the south. Ah! I would like to see the three swift steeds and the pale hounds of Brea racing along those sands, in and out of the tide-foam, and hear Finnir playing his pretty harp to the coiling blue waves glistening with sun-stars!"

Eli sighed. "So would I, my little friend. So would I."

Following their meal together on the evening of the third night, the 12th of June, the King and Eli and Reyse were all brought sturdy pottery mugs, and they sipped a minty-peppery-tangy infusion --- more like a mulled wine than a tea, though it surely was the latter --- as they walked together past several of the great, open arches.

"How is it," asked Eli, "that each window is *aligned*, as you said, with one of the Great Trees and one of the Standing Stones? They are in the same order and orientation, I suppose you mean? And the Trees and Stones guarantee a protection to this room from their respective windows?"

"You are not too far off," smiled her father. "Though it's a little more, hmm, *clever and interesting* than that! I will try to explain.

"As we may sometimes play with <u>time</u> in Faërie, so too there are games which juggle or distort <u>space</u>. And the Great Trees and the Stone Circle are skilled in that art. Yes, the windows of this room could be said to be in the same order or a similar one, as you surmise, as their corresponding Trees or Stones. But more than that, those beings are *actually* here as well, in a way. It is as though the individual creatures of those two great centres of energy and sources of enchantment for this realm, use this circular Chamber as if it were a clear, glass-like pool. They come here to look into it, and they see their own reflections, and they see their brother-and-sister beings at the same time. When Bram comes to his window here, he is mirrored and magnified, and he also perceives the pillar of living stone from the Circle beyond this City which has come into alignment with him at that moment. But it is not always the same Stone and Tree which regard one another at these windows. They move like the constellations in the sky: not their material selves --- those stay where they are! --- but these, their 'beholding presences', they spin around in their rings. In that way, they can come together here in any combination of Stone and Tree, and look both in and out, and see the minds of one another and speak in timeless tongues that none, not even the most ancient and wisest of the fairies, not even the Smiling Salmon himself, could possibly understand and interpret.

"Because of this powerful and silent and invisible exchange, going on outside of time and space, but also here and now, between all the possible combinations of the seven Trees and the seven Stones, these windows are charged with energy stronger than dense crystal panes or the mightiest bulwarks of a great *château-fort*! They are as impenetrable as the thoughts and conversations of the Trees and Stones themselves. That is why you are very very safe here, indeed. And that is why neither you nor I nor any other visitor to this room can generally have free access to its very centre."

Eli looked into the middle of the room, which she had --- of course --- seen clearly all along. But now she regarded it anew. The great central pillar of the Council-Chamber, from whence sprung the rounded vaults of the high ceiling, was completely covered by heavy, overlapping curtains. Eli realised then, if the *windows* were the places of the energies of the combined Trees and Stones themselves, then, of course, the centre of the room would be like the sacred, central space of both circles. Jizay had explained a little to her about the centre-points of those places, on her first day alone with him in this great Hall, standing at the window looking directly southwards and therefore in line with the Great Trees. She had difficulty, still, to endure the clear sight of them for more than a moment or two.

Her knowledgeable hound of joy had told her that at the very centre of the Great Trees, the stream flowing from the Fountain of Lymeril at last arrived at its destination and tumbled into the tiny pool of bright water at the heart of Fantasie. But it was not Lymeril which nourished the Trees, oh no! There, deep down in the core of the Garden, were the waters of Fantasie herself: the food and drink of the Trees, their own bubbling cauldron of light and of joy and of knowing. And in the centre of the Stone Circle was the volcanic point of power around which turned the bizarre ring of the rivers --- at times going one way, at times another --- from which were born both the Dragonfly and the Grey Man, flowing away in opposite directions and filling all the Shee-Mor with their uncanny vibrancy.

Aulfrin led Eli to the central column now. And, asking her to stand back a few paces, he gently parted two of the curtains, just a couple of inches. Eli was not directly facing the place which the King manipulated, and she was grateful for that! For from that tiny opening shot out a brilliant harpoon of light: white and yellow, flecked with green stars and hissing with vortices of pure gold and deep red and blinding blue. Her father closed the gap in the curtains in only a second, and the beam of coloured fireworks flew out the opposite archway into the night. Following it with her eye, Eli could have sworn that where it disappeared from view, the stars themselves exploded into a riotous dance of colour and delight.

"I'm very glad I haven't explored the pillar without you!" she admitted, stunned and trembling, but with a smile on her lips.

"You could not have come within two feet of it, or raised your hand to it with such an intention in mind. Especially as you are still more human than fairy, you would have been forbidden on the spot, and turned away," replied her father.

He wrapped one arm about her waist, smiling again now also, and led her back to their table to sit beside Reyse and himself, and take another mug of their mulled-mint beverage.

"But," he added, as Eli regained the control of her breathing once more, "you were not too timid to do so, when you were the child Mélusine! Both your mother and myself found you, on several occasions, seeking to draw back a chink of these heavy curtains, to look within."

"How could I do that?!" cried the astounded Eli. "Can young fairies withstand those darts of light?"

"Not usually, no," said Reyse, winking at the King, and now taking up the tale. "And normally it is given only to the King or the Queen of Faërie to even lay a hand upon those drapes. I have certainly never done so. But you were ever an untameable child, dearest Eli; as your erstwhile tutor, I can attest to that!

"However," he continued, "sometimes a child is, indeed, permitted to come into contact with the light of the sources, and you probably held cherished memories, from your infancy, of such a moment. You see, when one of their Majesties wishes to confer a very special blessing, or power, or gift upon a child-fairy, they will 'anoint' them, as we say, with an exposure --- a very brief exposure --- to the lights of the double centre, the radiance of the Pillar of the King's Tower."

Aulfrin now added, "When my father, the King Aulfrelas, wished to bestow a royal blessing upon the child of Erreig and his foreign mother Vanzelle, he anointed him with those playful lights and colours, and so he was touched by the grace of one of the Great Trees."

"That was Garo," nodded Eli. "That was the special gift of King Aulfrelas to the new-born Garo."

"Ah, you know of that story?!" exclaimed Aulfrin, and Reyse raised an eyebrow also.

"I told it to my Eli," interposed the pixie, to Eli's relief. "I told her the tale of Erreig and of the golden-skinned Nordic fairy Vanzelle, and of the secret blessing of King Aulfrelas upon their babe."

Aulfrin smiled indulgently, and genuinely. "It is a good tale," he admitted. "A very good tale, indeed. And my father, Aulfrelas, was gifted with great and clear perception, and so I do not doubt that his anointing of Garo has surely had some effect, and it will prove not without importance in the unfolding destiny of that young fairy."

As he flew up, ready to take a late night flight to the Inner Gardens, Piv winked at Eli quite privately. She smiled and lowered her eyes discreetly as he buzzed off.

She looked rather baffled immediately after he was gone, however, and asked, "How is it that *Piv* can fly out of one of these potent, protected windows --- just like that?!"

Both the King and Reyse grinned, but it was Ferglas who replied this time.

"Because *he* is Periwinkle!" Eli heard clearly, though not spoken aloud, and the great blue wolf-hound placed his noble head back on his crossed paws, with a delicate shake of his seashell necklace, and a wise smile wiggling his grey whiskers. Jizay was smiling broadly too.

****

Aulfrin had said nothing to his confined daughter of what he had, or had not, discovered during his days with Reyse. Torn between curiosity on that subject and her great desire to travel further afield herself, Eli finally decided to speak, as the King was preparing to go to his own bed-chamber for the night.

"Half of this, my second Visit, has now passed," she ventured, as her father bent slightly to kiss her forehead. "Will I have to remain here, in your beautiful Tower, for the rest of it?"

Aulfrin stepped back and tilted his head to one side. "Beautiful, but becoming boring, if I read between those lines," he smirked.

"A little," Eli admitted. "Have you and Reyse discovered any reason for concern? Do you still think it likely, or possible, that I'm in danger from Erreig while I'm here?"

Reyse was already playing softly, hidden from their view in his curtained alcove across the wide room. Aulfrin motioned for Eli to sit on the side of her bed, and as he bent his knees where he stood a charming little stool, fashioned like a sea-horse and made of white driftwood, it seemed, took form to receive him. He spoke in a whisper.

"I can well understand your impatience to continue your rediscovery of Faërie and its beauties. I, we, simply needed to be certain that it would only be beauties, and not terrors, that you would find. But I think we have almost, now, reached the point of being able to allow you your freedom, to some extent, my little caged birdling!

"It is true, we do not tolerate cages in my kingdom, nor in any corner of Faërie. It was perhaps the most loathsome crime of Erreig's, to place Demoran in a 'cage' of sorts in the Red Hoopoe Mountain. No other form of torture was needed to weaken that bold Prince, or to bring him close to deathly sickness. He was less wounded by the cold and the hunger imposed upon him, than by the simple fact of being caged.

"Of course, your cage is rather a lovely one, here. And you have endured it three days rather than a year-and-three-quarters! Still, I can comprehend that you are anxious to find your wings once again, or at least the wings of Peronne to bear you."

Eli nodded in agreement, and asked, "You can *almost* see clear to liberating me, you say? Have you still fears for my safety?"

"Only one more messenger to hear from, tomorrow shortly after dawn, I expect. And then I will know if Erreig is indeed occupied with other matters, and not likely to interfere with you. The Heron-Fairy is coming to me from Margouya, where he has had news of the progress of Finnir and his two friends. From other sources I have gleaned information --- which Corr-Seylestar will confirm, I hope --- and which both puts my mind at a certain ease and also makes me extremely proud to be the father of such a resourceful and clever Prince as Finnir."

Eli's eyes shone, but she checked herself as she caught the shadow of a reprimand in her father's own eyes, reminding her to curb her affections for her brother.

Aulfrin continued, even more softly --- though the caress of Reyse's fine bow on the strings of his *vielle* was wafting gentle melodies throughout the room, enough to cloak the King's words.

"It would seem that Finnir took into account my words to him, the day he left, that Erriég might not remain quiet in his White Dragon Fortress, but would probably often resort to his various lookouts in the Beldrum Mountains, from whence he has a good view of Star Island and also of Silkie-Seal Bay. And, of course, he and Bawn are often airborne in Quillir, and so the piercing eyes of that dragon matriarch --- even keener than those of her very observant master --- would be an even greater threat to secrecy.

"Now, if anything could hinder Erreig and make him think twice before asserting himself or making any threatening gestures to you, it would be the possibility of meeting Finnir face to face. He has, shall we say, very uncomfortable memories of his encounters with your brother in the Caves of the Great Cats. However, the last thing Finnir desires is to be perceived by Erreig while seeking to make contact with the Queen Morliande. So though it would strike fear into the Dragon-Lord, he cannot reveal himself or drawn his eye to the extreme tip of the province.

"But --- and here is his brilliance and good fortune shown --- Finnir took a rather circuitous route through the mountains beyond the Salley Woods, called the Turquoise Sisters, and then skirted the foothills just to the east of the Dragons' Drink to arrive at the branching of two Rivers flowing south: one is called the Woodpecker and the other the Lizard. And just downstream in the first great bend of the Lizard River, there is an islet known as Mauve Dragon Halt. And to Finnir's great delight, so my sources have told me, he found the colourful worm at home!

"Finnir is quite friendly with this particular dragon, who occasionally crosses the wide lands of the Flute-Reed Marshes between her Halt and the western shores of the Inward Sea, because she is fond of swimming in the magical waters which are part of the domain of the Prince. An excellent ally to have at such a time, it was clear to dear Finnir. He sent me word that this charming pale purple reptile --- who is, I might add, only a little less impressive in size than Bawn herself --- was willing to create a 'diversion' for him. This would take the form, I understand, of a rare and surprising visit of this dragon to her cousins residing along the shores of the Dragons' Drink, just to the north. These, I should add, are dragons under the sway of Erreig and his Sun-Singers --- unlike our mauve comrade. And there a *rumour* would be sown by the mauve-worm-dame, of the imminent arrival of Finnir's own servants and even the Prince himself, to eavesdrop on the dragon-talk of Erreig's hosts and to hearken to the chattering of the massive black bats in the overhanging trees, who know all that goes on in the ranks of the Sun-Singers.

"Any other spy would doubtless cause only the merest ruffle of concern to the Dragon-Lord, for he is quite confident in his dragons and his six worthy under-lords to deal with intruders; but Finnir himself daring to cross into Quillir, would alarm him greatly. Especially if he has had word that you, the Princess Mélusine in the guise of a returning changeling, are in the Silver City! He would surely imagine that the Prince was also placing himself between him and you.

"Of course, while Erreig's eye is turned to an imagined and covert visit of Finnir, and possibly some of his unicorns (Erreig would probably not know that it is quite impossible that the phantom unicorns could be perceived outside of Barrywood), Finnir will actually be descending with all speed to the Bay in the far south-west, where dwells his grandmother."

Eli breathed deeply, and many scenes paraded before her eyes: visions of the wide rivers and the lakes where the great dragons drink and gather and spawn, and the courageous passage of her blue-eyed brother through the passes of the mountains of the same hue and down to enlist the aid of this remarkable, giant purple reptile! She sighed.

"And now you are waiting to know if Erreig has taken the bait?" she asked her father.

"Just so. If he is hunting for a hidden Finnir or a ghostly troop of unicorns on the southern side of the Yellow Wren Mountain, he will not only ignore the south-western limits of Quillir, he will also have little vision or subtle perception of what goes on here in Fantasie, for his investigations on that side of the mountain and his own fears will prevent him! With the Dragon-Lord thus occupied, we may be able to leave, unobserved and momentarily overlooked, to make a visit to Demoran, for example. Or even to go for a moment of much needed calm and meditation to the Salmon Haven."

"Oh, that would be lovely!" smiled Eli, trying to keep her voice down even though rather over-excited by all of this.

"I should have news for you at breakfast, dearest girl." Her father rose from his sea-horse stool, which promptly evaporated, and kissed his daughter once again, before retiring to bed and leaving her to her own thoughts.

****

Eli tried to sleep, even though she was wishing the night away so that she could learn if the new day would bring her the liberation so longed for. Finally she drifted off. But only nightmares came to her, rather than the starlit dreams that Reyse had wished her.

It was certainly because of what she had learned of Erreig, that he was cast as some sort of villain in her dreams: and the fact that he had 'fallen in love with her' in her childhood possibly suggested to her sleeping mind the images which now took dreadful form.

In this very room, in another dream-vision, Eli had been shown *herself* as a little girl of nine or ten. The same ability to look upon herself, from outside as it were, was now also given her, but it was not quite the same little girl that she saw.

In her restless dreaming, she saw the child Eli, not the Princess Mélusine. She was slightly younger than in that former scene --- perhaps only seven or eight --- and she was in the garden of the converted garage that Lily had rented in Los Angeles.

Where was her little moon? Here in Faërie, the moon was dark, or 'new'; and in this eerie, misty dream her own dear mother, her moon, was missing too. Where was she? Eli, the little girl suddenly ill-at-ease in the midst of her solitary play in the unkempt garden and overgrown shrubbery, was looking very worried and anxious.

Maman? She heard herself call, softly but in some panic. *Maman?!* And then, as there was no response, she froze, and going down on all fours she crept under one of the bushes and into the tall grasses between it and the garden wall. And now her calls changed. *Laurien! Laurien, come to me now!* It was the name she had given to her invisible playmate, a large golden dog.

Her imagination had been very vibrant as a child, Eli confessed to herself in her own detached mind, as she watched this scene unfold in her dream. But had she *really* been able to see movements in the grasses and bushes when she invoked her make-believe dog? For the bushes she had just crawled through were moving and the child Eli looked up, expecting --- it was certain --- to see her dear pretend-dog come to life.

But it was not Laurien, nor her mother. A man was there, a stranger. Or was he?

As Eli dreampt, her witnessing-self, watching the dream, looked up beyond the form of the man who was gingerly parting the bushes where the little girl had now crawled farther in. And in the sky, far up and almost out of sight, were forms that Eli had seen here in Faërie --- but not in Los Angeles --- ever! They were dragons.

Just as she had seen in the skies over the jacaranda trees around the courtyard of *The Inn of the Curly Crook*, the dragon-riders of Erreig were there. There were seven dragons, but even from so far away Eli could see that there were only six riders. The great white Bawn, foremost in their formation, was alone. Where was the Dragon-Lord?

Eli looked back down at the man fumbling with the dense, leafy growth of the bushes, searching for the little girl. She had never seen Erreig, except in the vision of the dragon-battle. There, he had been a fairy-warrior: bare-chested and adorned with gleaming jewels, golden torc and twisted arm-band, wielding a pearl-bright spear --- and flying too swiftly to be very clearly seen, in any case. Was this man, dressed in modern jeans and red-checked cotton shirt, *Erreig*?

If so, what was he doing here? He had never been into this part of the human world, surely. He had not known that she was a changeling child. He could not have come to Los Angeles to find her out! What nonsense was this?!

But this was not nonsense, this terrible dream. This was a horror-story.

Eli watched in panic and disgust and utter helplessness. She wanted desperately to cover her eyes with her hands, but she could not. The only blessing was that, as the man climbed into the high bushes to where the child Eli was hiding, she could no longer actually *see* either of them. But she could hear them.

The muffled screams of the little girl joined with her own, both as the dream-watcher and as the dreamer fast asleep. And thankfully they awakened her. But not soon enough.

She knew what had happened. She had no more true memory of the event than the witnessing 'Eli' had while watching this dream-scene. She had no memory from the perspective of the little girl. But the surroundings and the sounds, the fear and the vulnerability, the confusion and the shame and the intense pain: those she recalled now. Yes, those she had known, and now remembered clearly.

Reyse was beside her bed, pulling open the filigree draperies and taking her in his strong arms. She had stopped screaming, and was only crying now.

"Why? Why was I shown *that*?!" she wailed, over and over, but more and more softly. And finally Reyse, caressing her long red hair in disarray and wiping her wet cheeks with his gentle hands, spoke very softly.

"Don't speak of it yet, my Lady Eli. Don't fight with the questions or the ghosts. Let them go, and come back to the present. You will tell me later, if you wish, what you saw. We will try to understand, together. But for now, just let it go. Let it go."

Eli breathed deeply, and allowed her tears to roll down her cheeks until she could feel her shoulders relaxing. She bent her head onto Reyse's breast. Brushing a strand of her hair off her own face, she opened her eyes as her tears abated. Reyse's were closed, his head resting on hers. She glanced past his chest and out into the calm, wide room beyond the curtains of her bed, and the whole of the circular Chamber seemed to be bathed in silvery light. It was beautiful, and worlds away from the drama of her dream, from the brutality and the violence of her nightmare and of the awful reality of those traumatic memories as a little girl in the world.

Suddenly she cried out. "What's that? Reyse, how can that be?!"

He lifted his head and turned, still cradling Eli in his arms. "What, my dear Eli? Did you see someone?"

Eli sat up, though she did not release her arms from around Reyse. The room was very shadowy, dim, regal and silent. Jizay was standing by one of the arches, gazing up into the starry sky.

"What or whom did you see?" repeated Reyse.

Eli shook her head, her brows wrinkled with doubt, but her eyes becoming brighter and rounder by the second. "I saw the moon, for just a second I saw it, I'm sure: I saw the full moon," she whispered. "But there's no moon tonight. Am I still dreaming?"

Reyse looked to where Jizay was standing, and then he lowered his eyes to meet Eli's. He smiled.

"There is always a moon, Eli. Always. She is always somewhere, and always where she should be. And some of us see her always, and ever-full."

As he spoke, Eli had the strangest sensation of falling upwards into his eyes. They were dark walnut-brown in this midnight moment, but the rings of gold around their pupils were glowing very slightly.

She wondered if eagles felt like this, flying into the sun…

****

Though she had planned to be up early to greet her father, Eli overslept, missing even a delicious breakfast. *That* was behaviour which bewildered Piv beyond words. Still, Reyse insisted that the pixie allow his friend to have a long, late, dreamless sleep this morning.

"How do you know it will be dreamless, my darling Iolar-MacRey?"

"Because I charmed her with my music, my dear Periwinkle, after a bad dream this midnight, and she will have the rest she needs now."

"That is very kind of you, Reyse of my heart," said the King, overhearing their conversation as he strode into the Council-Chamber and took his place on his oaken throne, appearing on the shining dais of warm light behind the long table. An attendant poured him a bowl of streaming barley-and-acorn milk and he reached for a wedge of fruit-cake. "I will have pleasant news for her, when she does awake."

"Then the diversion you told me of, my dear Aulfrin, has succeeded in confusing Erreig, and his eye is turned from Eli and from Fantasie?"

The attendants had withdrawn, and the King nodded to Reyse, but now addressed all the company: Piv and Jizay, Ferglas and even the slippered form of Eli, emerging from her canopied bed and yawning as she took her place at the table. Reyse served her a cup of milky tea, and she smiled at him.

"Yes, as I told you, certain Moon-Dancers have worked well and masterfully to draw the attention of the Dragon-Clan's leader to another remote corner of Quillir." Aulfrin spoke in few and measured words, Eli recognised. It seemed that Reyse was *not* informed of Finnir's mission in any great detail, and neither was Piv. She still wondered why this would be kept a secret from them, of all fairies. But she imagined that her father must have his reasons, so she simply sipped her tea thoughtfully.

"And so," continued the King, turning with bright eyes to his daughter, "your wish shall be granted, and your winged-horse returned to you. We fly, this morning, to the Haven of the Smiling Salmon, and then we'll take our lunch at the Inn further upstream before deciding what the next leg of our journey will be. Certainly, that journey will eventually lead us to Castle Davenia, but I do not know by what circuitous route! Does that meet with your approval, your Highness?!"

Eli was relieved and delighted. If anything would help her to chase the evil images and haunting sounds of her nightmare from her head, it would be this visit to the wisest and oldest of all the creatures, save the Great Trees, in this glorious land.

"I will think of it as a pilgrimage," she found herself saying, though she was not sure why she spoke these thoughts aloud. "I wish to let go of certain thoughts and images, and so to meditate beside the sacred Salmon Pool will be just the thing! Thank you, my dear father."

Aulfrin, clearly believing it to be Finnir she had decided to chase from her heart, smiled with deep pleasure. "That is excellent, obedient and wise, and I am proud of you," he affirmed. "I'm sure such a time of soul-cleansing and heart-brightening will be a perfect *pilgrimage*, as you say."

Eli understood, immediately, the direction his thoughts had taken. But she did not offer any further clarification, nor mention her horrible nightmare. Strangely enough, she wondered if her father might be right. Maybe she *should* bare her heart to the wise fish, and seek to empty it of the impossible love she felt for her brother. And maybe she should breathe on the glowing, orange embers that were warming that same heart this morning: the pretty little sparks of fire and sun-soaring, the white roses and full moons, and the strong arms and midnight brown eyes that she could still recall from last night.

"Will we all go together, then?" she asked the King, as they rose from the table and she turned to the young fairy-girl who had arrived with her clothes for the day.

Aulfrin had approached Reyse as they moved towards the door, and now turned back to Eli, his hand on his friend's shoulder.

"I'm afraid not, my dear girl. Corr-Seylestar has messages to bear to Demoran, and I must ask my loyal Reyse to take similar news to Leyano, if he will. But Jizay and Ferglas will make their own way to *The Smiling Salmon Inn*, and so rejoin us there later. And as for Periwinkle, I do not know. My dear pixie, do you fly with us, or find us again later?"

Eli had turned to look at Reyse, with evident disappointment in her eyes. Her regard did not displease the tall fairy lord at all. He would have spoken to her, saying that he would come back to find her, wherever she might be, as soon as possible after his journey to Mermaid Island, but it was Piv who spoke.

"Dearest Eli, I would love to come to the deep church of the fish with you, but I have business here in Fantasie, and in that way I may be of use to my King, too," he added, flying like a wild bee about the room in the warm sunlight which streamed in from all three of the eastern arches. "I will keep an eye on your Silver City, Your dear Majesty, if you will permit me the honour. And then, if anything curious or worrying arrives, I will be the hero to deal with it! Or at least to send you word, if you prefer," he added in a softer and more modest tone.

All the others laughed, but Aulfrin was quickly composed once again, and very politely thanked Piv, adding that his offer was accepted with deep gratitude and humble thanks. The pixie beamed, and flew back to the table, to sit cross-legged on its corner and take another piece of fruit-cake.

"I'm only waiting for my pretty Eli-een to dress, and splash her rosy face, and then I'll say my farewells," he explained, his mouth full.

Smiling, Aulfrin added, "And Reyse will say his in the courtyard below, before we take flight. We will await you there, dear Eli. But take your time --- we have several things to discuss, and there is no great hurry this morning."

As they left, Eli took her clothes to the alcove where Reyse had slept, and there she dressed and washed her face in a bowl of warm, petal-strewn water. She looked with wonder at the beautifully carved and inlaid *vielle*, laid under Reyse's hammock. She sighed, and combed her hair slowly, feeling his hands caressing it as he had done when he had come to her during the night.

****

Piv was awaiting Eli at the table when she reappeared a few minutes later. He explained that the two hounds had already started on their journey, and that Reyse and the King had gone down to the courtyard at the next level below this wide room, to speak for a few moments together, and to meet with Peronne and Cynnabar. Reyse would be riding a normal horse to the east coast, though extraordinary in her way: Eli's own mount from her first Visit, Rapture. The palomino mare had been in Fantasie these past days, but was now ready to make a visit to Curious Cove, and from there Reyse would use his own wings or even travel by boat.

"She is a marvellous horse, Rapture," agreed Eli. "Of course, now that I have the even more incredible Peronne to ride, I have not seen her on this Visit. I should have been happy to say a 'hello' to her, now that I hear she's in the City."

"It seems likely," Piv commented, "that she'll be going to Castle Davenia after her travels with Reyse, for she said that she is missing Vintig's clover-beds! If you go to see your brother the Prince Demoran, as Aulfrin said you would, you can greet her there. I'm meeting a dear friend of mine here in Fantasie today, and I think we shall both be making our way to Demoran's province soon; for a rather interesting meeting is planned there, and you might be lucky enough to be invited too."

"You're always putting questions and mysteries in my path these days, my dearest Periwinkle. What now?! With whom do you have an important appointment today, and what is the subject of this curious meeting in the Dappled Woods?!"

"Aha!" chirruped the pixie, clearly very pleased to be presenting Eli with a guessing-game; but he quickly decided to give her the answers. "I will tell you and not keep you flummoxed, my beloved Princess! It is the adventurer Garo meeting me today, and he is hoping to be granted an audience with Aulfrin in four days' time, on the 17th of June, the sacred day of fair Ævnad when we like to recount --- in mid-summertime ---a tale of winter: the legend of her babe born in the snows and warmed by the wings of doves. Well, it's not all organised yet, but I have a strong hunch that he will succeed, my leaping-hart Garo-lad."

Eli was twisting up her hair as she listened, and now fastened it with the pretty broach of coral. She hesitated and looked intently at Piv.

"Well, that *is* news! And I'd like to hear that legend. So, is the Alliance of the Spiralling Stars on the verge of making their programme known to the King, then? Are others of the Alliance to be present? Will Aindel, and even Alégondine be there?!"

Piv slapped his hands on his tiny knees and raised his eyes to the ceiling in mock-exasperation. "Oh, my merry Mélusine, how you do rush ahead --- as ever! One step at a time, one note after another in the making of music. And time for many silences between those notes! We will go slowly, but nonetheless we advance."

Eli had to laugh. It was true, in her human life at least, she had always been wont to jump to conclusions and to take decisions at full speed, rather than going gently and cautiously. It was really only when she left Colm, in Ireland, and went to England and then finally to her Uncle Mor's in Brittany, that she had --- for the first time in her life, most probably --- tried to *pace* herself and find her way more slowly, thanks to the sage advice of her dear Lily. And now, thinking of the delicacy of the situation in her father's kingdom and of all the moving pieces on the board at once, it was true, she should not expect everything to come into the light in a flash.

She rose and went to her curtained bed, and from the little side-table she gathered up Lily's journal and the white rose that Reyse had offered her four days ago. She took her small travelling-bag and went to put the two items into it. But she stopped to finger the rose for a moment.

"How strange, and how wonderful," she whispered. "It hasn't wilted at all. There's even a drop of dew on one of the soft petals. And its perfume is richer even than it was when he gave it to me."

She tucked the thin stem into the notebook of her little moon, and with the rose's pristine white head protruding from the centre of the booklet, she carefully slid both into her shoulder-bag.

As she came back to the table, and Piv broke in half a bunch of dark berry-like fruits to share with her, the pixie winked at his friend.

"Love is like that," he giggled. "Never wilts, always smells sweet, goes with you everywhere, and keeps your place in the story."

Eli cocked her head on one side, and smiled back at him.

"You are a wise and rare pixie," she laughed.

"Thank you my *red*-haired, *white*-rose Princess!" he laughed. "You are very wise, too. So wise that I think you will recall the rhyme I taught you about the seventh gate. Do you?"

Eli bit her lip. "Hmm, something about thresholds and black berries and wine?"

"Oh, your head is in the clouds, or in love," Piv chided her. "I will tell it you once again. Now pay close attention:

> *Here am I on threshold bright,*
> *On one side the cup of light,*
> *On the other berries black,*

Hesitating I look back,
Night and light and moon and sun,
Sip my wine and all is one!

"There now, do you have it? But don't fret," he added, seeing her worried expression, as though trying to solve the riddle. "I shan't ask you to unravel all of Wineberry's twists and turns, meanings and prophecies. No one has ever been able to do that, I think! But we keep the little poem preciously in our heads and hearts, to be solved one day.

"But maybe I've solved a tiny loopy twist in the riddle, and I wanted to tell you about it."

Eli was still standing, rather impatient to go down to her father and the flying-horses, at least before Reyse left. But she slung her bag over her head and 'round her shoulder, placed her hands on the back of the chair nearest her, and studied Piv's sparkling, cheeky, very bright eyes.

She smiled lovingly, and playfully, with her little friend.

"Alright, go on, tell me then! What part of the riddle did you unravel, my sweet little Piv?"

The pixie agitated his green wings, glowing almost florescent in the sunlight streaming into the room now, and he buzzed once around the table and then came to stand squarely on the seat of the chair, facing Eli and looking up into her face.

"Did you see it too?" he whispered, as though sharing a very private secret with her. "You did, didn't you? She was only there for an instant, just at the darkest moment of the middle-night. But she was there, full and bright and wide awake --- not sleeping on the other side, sleeping sound with her eyes tight closed, as she should have been!"

Eli's own eyes were wide and filled with utter amazement.

"You saw the moon too, Piv? I didn't just imagine it? The full moon was *really* there last night, just for a moment?!"

"Yes, yes, yes," squeaked Piv, almost too excited to contain his voice. He clapped his hands once or twice. "Of course she was! She came for you. I was coming out of *The Swooping Swallow*, with a friend --- oh, I must tell you and can't give you any more mysteries to puzzle-over, my darling Eli-een! --- I was with Aindel, for we had been sipping and talking, talking and sipping together. And we had walked past the sixth Star-Tower, so we were within view of Wineberry, and Aindel said to me, oh so softly like the velvety gliding of a swan over a misty lake, he said to me: *Let us go to the threshold of the Gate, and see the Cup of Light!*

"And we did go, and we did see! There, rising up over the rim of the world, was the full moon. She was like a 'cup of light', just as he had said! We stood together, and I hovered by his straw-coloured head of hair, blowing around his proud face in the breeze from the stars, and we watched her sail up and over the City --- oh much too quickly, as if she were in a great hurry to dance across the sky and off its stage once more.

"And so it was, for in only a minute, she had tip-toed behind a cloud come up from nowhere at all, and she was gone. She never came back, though the cloud was only a wisp."

Eli had not even the slightest desire to ask if such crazy events occurred regularly in this enchanted land. She knew they did not. She knew this was uncommon and extraordinary, even for Faërie. And she knew that she had been meant to see it, as had Piv and Aindel. Though she could not imagine why.

It didn't matter why, not yet, not now. The rhyme floated in and out of her memory and she felt peaceful and comforted as the words repeated themselves deep inside her. She recited, reverently and calmly, the line that came to her most insistently:

> *Night and light and moon and sun,*
> *Sip my wine and all is one!*

"All is one," she said, in a voice very low and soft. And then, to the pixie, she said more clearly, "I think it was the moon *and* the sun, Piv. I think they were both there." Though, hearing herself saying this, she was a little surprised.

But Periwinkle did not seem shocked by her odd remark. In fact, he added one of his own, very matter-of-factly.

"The sun is always there, somehow, somewhere, when we see the moon full. Otherwise we couldn't."

****

Chapter Thirteen:
The Deepest Dell in Aumelas-Pen

ot wishing to expose Eli to the dangers of the Stone Circle once again, Aulfrin nonetheless permitted a little aerial meander above the large lake in the east of the City, where the opening ceremonies of Beltaine morn had taken place.

Delighted to be astride Peronne once again and enjoying the astounding sensation of his languid, graceful flight, Eli exhaled deeply as her fingers played with the long white strands of his mane. His wings were beating very slowly, and sometimes held outstretched and quite motionless, as they looped and glided above the lake and even took a turn around the Star Tower which stood on its own amid the high grasses and meadows of ripe grains, red poppies, blue cornflowers and tall white daisies.

Eli felt as though the breeze itself were massaging her shoulders and caressing her face, inviting her to relax fully and to sink deeply into the glories of the present moment. She felt such a contrast in her emotions since last's night terrible dream, thanks to the fairies who loved her so deeply and faithfully here.

First, there had been Reyse's tender attentions when she had awoken him with her screams; how reassuring and strong were his arms, and his deep, delicious eyes. Then the extraordinary exposé of Piv this morning, claiming that the full moon had come into the starry night just for her (perhaps), or at least as a very miraculous explanation of the riddling-rhyme of

Wineberry --- disappearing again as quickly and mysteriously as she had arrived. And then, Reyse once again, just before this morning's flight from the high courtyard, standing at Peronne's near flank once Eli had mounted. He had looked very enigmatically up at her, his left hand laid gently, but firmly, on her leg; she had felt the ruby in his palm where it touched her thigh, even through her trousers and long tunic. Reyse's right hand was on his heart as he inclined his head and bid her farewell.

"May the blessings of the eagles and of the Half-Moon herself be with you, as we say in the Shee of the Dove, my Lady Eli. And, as we are here in Fantasie, I add the benediction of the Moon-Dancers, just for good measure!

"And to both of those," he concluded in a whisper much too soft to be overheard by the King, already mounted on Cynnabar and trotting off in the direction of the courtyard's far balustrade, "I add the well-wishes of a heart devoted and pledged to you."

Eli must have registered some surprise, or perhaps thrill, in her eyes, for Reyse at once lowered his own, stepped back, and breathed deeply before looking back up at her with a shining smile. Without another word, he pulled the hood of his long green cloak up over his wavy brown hair and his pointed ears studded top and bottom with moon-stones, and he turned to walk back into the King's Tower and down the great staircase to the stables at ground-level, where Rapture awaited him.

Now, father and daughter invited their flying mounts to cross the wall and high hedges and leave Fantasie, rising higher into the bright morning skies to the east in the direction of the hamlet of Shepherds' Lodge. The altitude of their sky-road did not allow Eli to see much detail below her now, though she tried to pick out *The Inn of the Curly Crook* and even the hut of old Kirik. Many of the jacaranda trees were still in bloom, and the purple hue of their blossoms made Eli think of the obliging dragon that Finnir had collaborated with in Margouya. A mauve dragon! Eli had to laugh to herself, or --- in fact --- out loud.

Hearing his daughter's mirth in mid-flight, Aulfrin turned to look back at her, joining in her contagious laughter and then pointing below and slightly to the left. Eli followed with her eyes, and saw how beautiful the bridge was, over the River of the Grey Man. Its high trellised gateway was covered with woven vines of trailing flowers, and the broad waters of the river were streaming under its sturdy planks in joyous patterns of white froth and myriad wavelets studded with diamonds of sunlight.

Slowing his own flying horse so that Eli and Peronne could catch him up, Aulfrin called to her through the whistling breezes. "Let's go down for a little bathe, where we stopped before, in the pools on this side of the next bridge, shall we?"

Eli nodded enthusiastically, and thus about half-an-hour later their journey was broken in mid-morning to allow for a relaxing moment in the 'bath-tubs' among the stones and bog-cotton.

"You seem much less troubled in your thoughts," her father remarked, after their bathing. "Your doubts and worries are behind you now, are they, my Eli?" he inquired, as they went to mount again, for the last leg of their flight. "Or do you bear them just a little further, to be cleansed and utterly forgotten in the Salmon Haven, where our theme of washing and renewal will be continued, I hope?! Perhaps the Smiling Salmon will bless you with forgetfulness and new perspectives."

It was a pointed and quite parental comment, Eli thought, surely referring to her confession of a romantic love for Finnir. But it was also made with the unwavering good humour and compassion that seemed to be the two pillars of Aulfrin's character. Eli could not feel offended or annoyed.

She answered in a warm tone of voice, but her words were serious.

"I am still haunted by images and sounds from a dreadful nightmare of my human childhood, I think they will stay with me all of my life; but I hope they will do less harm in my conscious mind than they have done in my subconscious. For I think they've dwelt *there* for many years, festering and turning toxic. I believe they have been a dangerous pollution to my soul and my heart's equilibrium --- at least in my human life, despite being for so long utterly forgotten. So I'm glad, in a way, that they have come to the surface; and yes, now I hope that they might be somehow 'cleansed' and made less contaminating and noisome, even if they can't be done away with completely."

Aulfrin turned where he stood beside Cynnabar, and walked back to Eli, though without taking her hands or touching her. He looked deeply into her eyes before he spoke again, still remaining at a distance.

"Although you have not described your dream to me, I see in my own heart now what *you* saw, or at least some of it, for it is floating in the far-reaches of your lovely blue-green eyes, my daughter. Have you then discovered that part of your past in the journal of our little moon? She had told me that she would not write the story there, but of course I have never read her notebook, for it was written for you and not me. Did she decide to recount that sad event, then?"

Amazed and somehow comforted by her father's profound powers of perception, Eli shook her head. "No, no, it was not there; or at least, yes, I *did* come across some ... *allusion* to it, a good while ago now, but that was not exactly what gave me the nightmare, I think. Last night, I seemed to have been shown the details of the scene without really re-living it all as the little girl I was then. Like a vision of that buried memory, but from outside. Very strange. I was a *witness*, not exactly the *victim*. Very strange that."

Eli's words had stopped her own thoughts where they were, and she considered what she had just said.

"Father, is that the key? Is *that* what will help me now?"

Aulfrin smiled and coming closer he placed his right hand on her face. Then he stepped back again, and surveyed her with pride and admiration.

"You are a wise fairy, my Mélusine; but you are also a very wise human woman as Eli. You may not be Lily's daughter by blood, but you remind me of her intelligence and her enlightened philosophies of life. Yes, you are indeed right: in every dark and threatening scene of horror or suffering, anger or fear that we might experience in our journey, the key is to be the *witness*, and not the *victim*. Yes, that is the key."

There was a brief silence between them, brief but beautiful, like the pause in a musical composition which allows a modulation or cadence well-resolved to be digested and savoured by the ears.

Aulfrin supported Eli, just lightly under her arm, as she swung herself up onto Peronne's back. He then leapt lightly onto his own horse and as they trotted a few paces before becoming airborne he said, "Well, now on to pay a visit to another wise and wonderful creature! We'll fly along the River on this side for a while, and cross at the Falls, then turn back to the west and to the dell of the Salmon Haven. Here we go!"

Both horses continued at a trot, though straightway rising into the thin air, up and up their invisible stairways with their long manes rippling out and their whinnies ringing in Eli's head and heart.

****

For some reason, she had visualised the Salmon Haven as being a very modest little grotto of stone and ferns, with a dark pool in its centre, completely in shadow. That had been the image, in any case, created by her own imagination. Her father had called it a 'dell', and that word had conjured up the picture of a tiny pilgrim's-chapel in a cleft of the gentle hills beside a sacred source, or a holy-well shrine half-hidden by fuchsia and brambles in the landscape of Connemara.

But what she was about to see was no chapel; it was the most breath-taking cathedral she could have ever imagined. Rather than a dell or dingle, the Salmon Haven was like a mythic glen, a veritable vale of a hundred 'dells'.

The King had led them in a low flight over the Falls, which Eli had already seen when they had flown home to Fantasie over Shooting Star Lake. On that occasion, she had been several hundred yards from them, and very preoccupied by the vision of the lily-of-the-valley sparkling on the crests of the waves along the shoreline. But this time, they were flying right over the great Falls, and their thunder was in her ears and their high white spray, filled with rainbow refractions, was moistening her face and bare forearms.

Circling slowly and elegantly to fly above the north bank of the River, they left the Falls behind them by perhaps seven or eight miles. The woods were very dense beneath them, and the River majestic and wide, bright cobalt or deep sea blue and dotted with swans and geese, with families of ducks and moorhens closer to its banks. At some places, there were stretches of beach along the shoreline, dark grey or purply-blue sand flecked with bright white pebbles. She could see otters and even a few raccoons playing or washing or scuttling about, in and out of the lazy current. Closer to the Falls, there had been white-water and hissing rapids that flowed around high, pointed stones; but here, further upstream, the River was placid and thoughtful. Probably, she thought, because it has just passed the Haven, and feels contemplative and calm thanks to the Salmon!

They landed in a clearing only just big enough for their two horses, encircled by tall pines and elms, about a quarter of a mile from the river-bank, Eli guessed. Walking just before or beside their steeds, who had crossed and lowered their feathery wings over their backs, they entered a gently curving avenue that ran between the trees. It was only a couple of yards wide, and the trees on either side were all hazels or walnuts, though beyond them the wood seemed to be mostly oaks, sycamores and wonderfully knobbly old plane-trees. Many were alive with squirrels, most had large and complicated spider-webs in them (with accomplished singers, of course, in their centres), and all were filled with birds of more varieties than Eli could name, though a great percentage of them seemed to be soft grey or pure white doves, cooing in harmony with the spider-songs.

The avenue between the trees was quite possibly cushioned with many years of fallen leaves, but these could not be seen. Underfoot, all along the pathway, were petals, as though the blossoms of the nut trees had just recently blown down. It was high summer, and Eli wondered how it was possible that these petals could still be here, and so fresh and soft. But of course, she only had to recall her white rose from Reyse. Flowers in Faërie had their own ideas on time and aging, on remaining springtime-new or fading into a perfumed death!

But even as the thought of Reyse and his dew-flecked rose crossed her mind, another thought ran up behind it. This road of blossoms was not the first she had heard of. Reyse's story of the ghostly Chapel of Windy Hill had contained a similar wonder, that of the mimosa flowers and the yellow carpet they had created for the passage of Neya-Voun in her unicorn-form…

Just as she stepped out from the shadows of the last tall trees to behold the glorious Salmon Haven, Eli's mind was filled once again with thoughts of Finnir. Reyse, and Finnir --- but mostly the latter. Suddenly, she could hardly breathe, for her heart was beating fast with the scenes of the phantom chapel on the waves of the Whale Race Sound, and the pyre of her brother's body bursting into flame, and the flight of Dinnagorm with Reyse scattering the tiny, fluffy yellow balls before the delicate hooves of the running unicorn, and Finnir waiting at the opening of his cave with the King of the Giant Cats perched above him...

Finnir, his blue eyes sparkling, his voice soft and as musical as a harp's, filled her and delighted her; she could even hear him speaking with her in their mother's Concocting Cell illuminated by the Queen's Head Vase.

But no, she was wrong. Queen Rhynwanol was *not* his mother. Finnir was a half-fairy, the son of Aulfrin, but not of Rhynwanol. Who *was* Finnir's mother, she wondered. What was she like, and in what ways did he resemble her? For it seemed he did not bear a great likeness to their father.

Not her true brother, not her *full* brother, she thought to herself. But still, it is forbidden that we love...

Why these thoughts, so persistent, so invasive? She had not *meant* to think of Finnir! She shook her head, closing her eyes as she stopped beside her father, both of them now standing in the sunlight and facing the dwelling of the wisest animal in Faërie. She had not even seen what was before her yet, with her head so filled with images of her brother, or rather half-brother...

She came back to the present once again as she opened her eyes. And she gasped with the breath-taking beauty of the vision before her.

The Haven of the Smiling Salmon was not a single pool, but many interconnected ones. The River was flowing here, wide and divided by many islands and fingers of rock and grass and woods reaching into it from the banks on either side. In some places it fell over short ledges in hundreds of threads of silver water, creating circular basins --- some the size of a whirling dervish's billowing robes, some as big as a Roman amphitheatre. The Salmon Haven was an entire *metropolis* of round, deep-blue fish-mansions!

The further bank of the River of the Grey Man was far, far away and obscured by wreaths of coiling mist like those that settle in fields on an autumn morning. The late-morning sun was already very high, and the waters of all the circular pools were blazing with jewel-light and sun-stars.

Aulfrin took Eli's hand and led her out onto the nearest peninsula of grass and dark, flat stones. The point of rock and earth rose slightly at its tip, and afforded a view over the Haven. At her feet, Eli could see dozens of fishes of myriad sizes swimming just under the surface of the water. Trout and salmon, catfish and pike, perch and bream, bass and bluefish, bright goldfish and lithe little minnow. All beautiful, all colourful, all contented. Dragonflies whizzed over the surface, and frogs disturbed it now and then by their sudden leaps into it.

"Is he here?" whispered Eli, awestruck, to her father. "Is the Smiling Salmon here in this pool, among all these fishes?"

"Very rarely. He prefers to keep to himself in the deepest waters, like those of the great lake of ultramarine just there; do you see it?" Aulfrin pointed a little to their right and further into the middle of the wandering, loitering River. "There are several fairies sitting in the bulrushes around that particular pool, as you can perhaps just make out from here. That would probably indicate that he is there today. They have almost certainly come to meditate with him, and it is not difficult to feel where he is: the air above him is always vibrating like the notes of a flute or rising and falling in energy like the resonating chords of a great organ."

Eli wondered how, without a fairy's wings, she could approach the huge lake-pool near the centre of the River where the other fairies were silently sitting all but concealed by the tall semi-aquatic plants around its edge. However, Aulfrin seemed unconcerned by this, and simply led her off their small promontory and back along the narrow strip of beach skirting the northern shore until a series of small stones, flat and dark like those on the little jutting finger of land they had just left, appeared and made a stepping-stone walkway out into the complex pattern of large and small pools. Eli could not decide if they had been there all along, or if her magical father had summoned them into being just for her!

Many of the fairies sitting among the bulrushes, quivering reeds and clumps of water-mint --- their eyes not yet closed in deep meditation --- stood up as the King arrived. Each one bowed with his or her hand over the heart, and to Eli they also made a similar reverence, though with simply a slightly inclined head. Aulfrin smiled warmly at his subjects, but said nothing; instead he found a place a little removed from the other meditators, and he and Eli sat comfortably on the thick grass of a small mound beside the dark blue lake.

Frogs were croaking, birds calling, wind rustling in the tall trees to either side of the River of the Grey Man. How, thought Eli, was one to *meditate* here? In the first instance, she had no desire to close her eyes, for the place was too beautiful to believe and she wanted to look and enjoy, and listen and continue to tell herself that she was really, truly here!

She watched as a couple of fairies arrived to join the others, further back around the sweep of the slim semi-circular lawns that bordered the pool on this western side. The southern side was mostly high, grey rocks, and to the east the waters overflowed the brim of this ample and glorious lake to feed another. The new-comers to this hallowed place did not seem to notice that the King of Faërie was among them. Aulfrin did not notice them either, seemingly, for his eyes were already closed and his expression very peaceful.

But Eli watched them in fascination, for they were carrying large acanthus-like leaves, almost as they would trays or platters. And before finding places to sit and contemplate the musical vibrations in the air and to harken inwardly to the wisdom of the ancient Salmon, the two fairies took him their offerings.

On the large, gracefully curled leaves were hazelnuts. They placed these, one by one, at the very margin of the pool, so that they were lapped by the tiny currents and moistened. Almost imperceptibly at first, the music in the air --- itself so soft and subtle that it was difficult to distinguish it from the birdsong and leaf-rustling --- grew stronger and louder. Soon Eli could hear it clearly.

Indeed, there were flutes playing! And behind their melodies was woven a many-layered counterpoint of organs, hurdy-gurdies, euphoniums and deeply keening or hymning 'cellos with the addition of strange harmonics chanted by unseen singers high, high above all the perfectly blended instrumental sounds. The music's crescendo rose like a fiery sunrise or a mounting tidal wave.

And then it was gone, and only the gentle breeze and birdsong remained. Moreover, all of the hazelnuts were gone too. Rolled, Eli supposed, into the blue water, there to be ceremoniously ingested by the sacred Salmon, like the shewbread offered on the holy table in the sanctuary of the Tabernacle, with the wise fish as the consecrated priest or oracle!

The two fairies had found places to sit, cross-legged and serene, adjacent to the fronds of some graceful papyrus. Eli smiled at them, but they, too, had already closed their eyes. She breathed very deeply and glanced once more all around her at the incredible beauty of the place: the intensity of the greens and blues, the brilliance of the water's surface where the sunlight blazed and sparkled on it, the sweetness and purity of the few vagrant cloud-forms that floated along idly in the summer sky.

She summoned up all the resolve she could, and finally she closed her eyes as well.

The silence now was complete. Everything was suddenly so still and quiet that Eli had the odd feeling that all save her had disappeared completely: her father and the other fairies, the frogs and birds, even the wind itself. She could not even hear the running water and myriad waterfalls. She could not hear her own breath.

But she kept her eyes closed. For though all sound was utterly gone --- so she thought --- all sight was not. Her eyes were closed, but the summery light was warm on her face and all about her. She was not in absolute darkness. And, even with her eyes tight shut, her mind presented her with clear images. She had the impression that she was underwater, in a blue-green universe of current-caressed undulating forms in soft-focus, filled with half-perceived plants and fishes and rocks. It was like looking through the colour of her own eyes...

And then she realised that the silence was not so complete as she had thought; for there was more than silence here in this green world. The music which she had heard a moment ago, when the hazel-nuts had disappeared into the pool, was within her now. It was certainly no longer *outside* of her. She had swallowed the symphony, just as the Salmon had perhaps swallowed the nuts! Not a single note came to her *ears*, for they were exterior and turned outwards, and this music was only within. But she could hear it there, very clearly.

Eli had practiced the art of meditation for many years, but she had never experienced such a strange sensation or such altered perception as this. As in normal meditation, she released any control over her thoughts in order to let them come as they would, and pass away again. At least, such was her instinctive plan. But now *no* thoughts came. She could hear the interior music, but her mind made no comment on it. She could see, very vaguely, forms and movements and a little light; but likewise she had no mental dimension of commentary or even appreciation of these facts. They were; it was. That was all.

She was. That was all.

All *was*...

How long she remained in this state, she did not know. It was not like being asleep, nor anesthetized, for she had never been so aware and awake in all her life. She was in the Presence of something or someone, and everything else was drenched in the liquid greenish light of that Truth.

At last, something changed. There was a change of colour, or the music had altered its key, or the morning had changed to afternoon. She resisted the change, ever so slightly, for she did not want to lose the beauty of being simply in the presence of this Presence. But as soon as that ripple of resistance ran through her, she heard a voice in the inner music: *allow it, receive it, welcome it*. And so she relaxed again, and the change took form.

The world about her was no longer green or turquoise. It had changed to yellow and then to pure white light. And a strange, very human, very incongruous and fearful idea came up through her body, from far down in her pelvis and up into her stomach and finally into her lungs --- and it made them feel pinched and tight. *I don't wish to die, and this white light is probably just that!* She felt the idea like a tiny soap-bubble, rising through the vast, clear skies within her. To her great relief, it immediately popped and dispersed, leaving her in peace once again.

Death?! Not at all ! Surely this is coming fully to life... Her own voice or another, unspoken but unmistakable, was chuckling as the words echoed and danced, repeated and chanted themselves in a thousand languages... and in none.

As if she were swimming underwater, Eli stopped breathing. Of that she was sure. Her eyes were closed, but wide open at the same time. The white light had opened to either side like curtains at the theatre, and her vague vision became crystal-clear. In the centre of her seeing was water, turbulent and yet majestic: as terrifying as God in the midst of creation and at the moment of the birth of the universe must have been terrible and awesome. A raging water that was at once a sapphire blue and also a deep jewel-red, and it was swirling like a tornado. Was it a whirlpool going inwards and downwards, or indeed a tornado lifting her upwards into its extending and racing vortex?

The Garnet Vortex. Eli had said the words, or another voice had done so. Was it the Smiling Salmon saying them, showing her this, telling her...telling her *what*?

Up or down, drawn into a drowning oblivion or flung high into the crimson skies roaring with wild winds: she had no idea which. Where *was* this vigorous funnel or explosion of blood-red water, and where was she?

But she felt no fear. Incredible motion and noise all about her, but no fear within her. No fear at all.

And then many images, drawn from many tales and meetings it seemed, rushed into the vortex with her. Ah no, it had gone. Eli was standing on an island, and the Garnet Vortex was not to be seen or heard any longer. The images were there, however, and all jumbled like the pieces of coloured glass in a kaleidoscope. She could not make them come clear, and so she released all desire to do so. She allowed it, received it, welcomed it. And it became clear on its own.

Jizay was there, that was the first thing to come into focus. Peronne was in the distance, and another horse. No, not a horse. A unicorn was there, with a silver horn, like the tiny painted one in the *trompe l'oeil* window of Banvowha's home. There were beautiful trees, with yellow blossoms and silver leaves, and the full moon was rising, although it was broad daylight. And there was a man, or a fairy. A king.

Eli recognised him, and was with him, and was quite certainly not dead, but *more* than alive. Much more alive than she had ever felt before...

Aulfrin was bending over her, and his long-fingered, gentle, strong hand was laid on her thick, red hair. He caressed it very slowly, so as not to startle her.

"The Smiling Salmon has swum away to his private pool of profound waters, further upstream. And we must go too. Come back to the day and the sunlight, my darling Eli. Our meditation has ended."

Eli opened her eyes slowly.

"I was in the light all along," she said softly, and very contentedly. "I was absolutely and undoubtedly in the light."

****

At lunch, at *The Inn of the Smiling Salmon*, Aulfrin told his daughter that her eyes were sparkling like the sunshine on the hundred pools of the Haven.

"It is the most remarkable place I have ever visited, here or in the world, or in my dreams --- good and beautiful dreams, I mean!" she replied, with a very warm tone in her voice, and no trace of the tension or distressing emotions of these past days or of her troubled night. "And though you call it a 'haven', which is quite true in every sense of the word, you have also referred to it as a 'dell'. I thought that very odd and not at all apt when I first beheld the great expanse of water and the majestic kingdom of the Salmon. But now I think you're right."

"Do you? Well, I'm pleased you grant me that!" laughed her father.

"Yes, I do so indeed!" she chuckled in her turn. "It is the deepest dell in creation, I suppose. It is the little, private vale that leads into all of us, that each one of us carries concealed in our hearts."

"You are waxed very poetic, my dear Eli, following your meditation! But I must say that I agree with you entirely. It's just that, the Salmon Haven. That is why we go there; that is why we reverence the place and the great, wise fish. Did you see him, by the way?"

"See the Salmon?!" exclaimed Eli. "Did he show himself? When?"

"As we left, when we were walking back across the stepping stones. He leapt into the air from the lake-waters to our left, as he was making his way to his private chambers higher up the Haven."

Eli looked a little disappointed, but only for a moment. "No, no. I didn't notice that. I would have loved to catch a glimpse of him, though."

"I didn't think you had," said the King, his eyes twinkling. "You were dancing, and so I thought you probably hadn't seen anything but stars --- the ones you were looking through, the ones in your eyes!"

"I was *dancing*? Well, well. I'm not surprised to hear it!"

Eli ate her flowery and many-leafed salad in happy silence for a minute or two. And then she asked, "Are we going to Demoran's Castle now? Or do we linger with the Salmon a few more days?"

"I will give you a choice. We can go to the Dappled Woods, yes, or we can make a detour to the Fire-Bird Forest, or to the Bay of Knotty Roots and the Thousand-Toed Trees. We have two or three days' grace, before we are actually required to be at Castle Davenia."

Eli thought of what Piv had said to her, and imagined he referred to the meeting that was planned with Garo on the 17th of June. That was four days away still; but she decided not to ask for any details from her father, but to leave things to unfold as they would. She had another idea for their journey.

"Where I would truly like to go, if possible, dear father, is to the Salley Woods. Periwinkle told me that it is where the best trees for making harps grow. I would love to see those trees, the Lustrous Willows, I think he called them."

Aulfrin hesitated, and Eli realised why.

"Ah, of course," she admitted, "the Salley Woods are to the south of us here, and so they are closer to Quillir, and to Erreig and his dragons. It would be unwise to go nearer rather than farther, I suppose."

Aulfrin fingered his beard, and then he sipped his chalice of some sort of pale-green bitter-fruit wine. He was considering, and not refusing immediately, Eli noted.

"It would be very much nearer to where I believe him to be at the moment, yes. The Salley Woods climb right up to the feet of the Turquoise Sisters with the Yellow Wren Mountain dominating that range to the west. On its far side lies the Dragons' Drink, where I believe Erreig's eye will be turned, searching for your brother Finnir or his servants among the trees of the black bats.

"That said," he continued, breaking off a piece of nutty brown bread from the long loaf on the table before them, "the more we draw his eye thither, the better for Finnir. We could visit the Woods this afternoon, and then come back here for the night. Yes, to go briefly to the Salley Woods, and to see those shimmering trees, would be --- perhaps --- a very good strategy for creating yet another diversion to confuse the Sun-Singers.

"It would be likely that the bats would feel our presence or sense our passage, so near to the mountains. And other of Erreig's spies and co-conspirators are mingled with the animals living in that forest and also the Hazel-Nut Woods on the other side of the Yellow Wren. We would not linger long enough for you to be in any danger; and I will be with you all the time. Yes, it might very well prove an excellent move to safe-guard, even further, your brother's mission; and it will, no doubt delight you to see the harp-trees. You have a harp, as the Princess Mélusine, made from a tree of those Woods."

"I believe Piv mentioned that to me too, but I think Jizay told him that it was too soon to say much about it, not while I'm still a human." Eli looked down at her dear hound, snoozing at her feet.

A strange thought flashed across her mind in that moment. Why had Jizay, in the form of her beloved, imagined playmate, *not* come to her when she cried out for him in the overgrown garden where had experienced such a tragedy? Surely he should have, *would* have come at her call.

Had her nightmare been an **accurate** account, shown to her, of what had really happened? She felt convinced that it had happened as she had seen it, for she had <u>real</u> memories of the fear and the pain of that attack now. But she had not actually re-lived it in the *first person*. If it were true, why was Jizay not there, or rather Laurien, as she had called him?

The thought blew away in the same moment it had come to her, and her mind felt at ease and calm again. She would ask him, perhaps, one day. She came back in her thoughts to the proposed trip to see the silver trees, and maybe even to catch sight of the Red Coral Tree that Piv had said stood at the very eaves of the Salley Woods, and which had given branches and roots to her to make a harp. The harp that lay near her, he had said, on Scholar Owl Island.

"Probably very wise of him to say that," Aulfrin remarked, as he drained his chalice and stood up. "You do not need to go *gathering information* on things you will recall naturally when you come home, such as your own lovely harp and your friendship with that unique tree. This will be a short voyage to a very magical and beautiful place, and then we will return here for a restful evening together, and perhaps some music."

"Do you intend to play the harp that you played for insight and advice on our last stay here?"

"Very perspicacious you are, my daughter --- as is to be expected! Yes, I will possibly play this evening, to have news on Finnir's progress. But, in fact, I was thinking of listening to other players here. There are several fairies staying at the Inn --- I saw them at some of the other tables, dining with us in this and the adjacent room --- who are very skilled musicians. If they are staying on here this evening, we may have a lovely concert upon our return.

"Now, are you ready? Shall we fly or ride? It's less than an hour, either way."

"Oh, I love both. But I'm still in the throes of sheer wonder at being carried by a winged-horse, so I suppose I would vote for flying!"

"Flying it is! Let us go by air then, and leave our loyal hounds to their napping."

They found Peronne and Cynnabar near the doors of the Inn, and both were interested to learn of their destination, though Peronne wore an inscrutable expression when the King explained that they would not be opposed to some rumours of their visit coming to the Sun-Singers' ears.

Eli looked into her steed's eyes. They were amazingly deep and at their indigo-blue centres were the suggestions of tiny white forms. She remembered noticing them when she had first been reunited with him, on Mermaid Island. At that time she had thought them to resemble stars, or perhaps flowers. But now they were much clearer. They were flowers, indeed: *lilies*. Not the shape of lily-of-the-valley; instead the forms were like that of the single, spiralling petal of an arum-lily. It was much more evident, this beautiful white shape, than it had been to Eli before. She stroked his velvety grey-and-crescent-moon neck. And then she mounted and they took flight, just behind Aulfrin and Cynnabar.

But Eli felt her dear horse to be much less enthusiastic than the King and his own mount about their direction, and she wondered if she had made a wise request of her father, after all.

****

A Delicate Balance

Chapter Fourteen:
Straying in the Salley Woods

t was only a short flight to reach the eaves of the Salley Woods, but Aulfrin continued on a little further, over the first ranks of the trees --- low and slow, allowing Eli to appreciate the sea of rippling willow leaves in the vast congregation of great green domes. They flew back to the threshold of the forest to land in a semi-circular clearing like a 'bay' of short grass situated between the arms of a wide, sweeping arc of dense trees. All the trees along the margins of the Woods were willows, of one kind or another. Though she looked, Eli saw nothing resembling a Red Coral Tree (a species known to her from her youth in Santa Monica and Brentwood where they lined several of the boulevards).

As they entered under the canopy of branches, Eli was astounded by the diversity of the willows; there were undeniably dozens of varieties. Some were osiers, some sallows, some had long narrow leaves, or curled and twisted leaves, or round ones or oval. Some were dark green, some pale, and there were even willows with white or pink leaves. Obviously, all willows enjoy water, and Eli and her father followed the well-defined paths which wound around the beautiful trees in order to avoid the omnipresent bogs and tiny brooks. There seemed to be water everywhere!

Cynnabar had appeared to be very contented with the idea of remaining in the green bay of tasty grass, but Peronne refused. He was clearly adamant in his decision to follow Eli into the Woods, much to Aulfrin's surprise.

"Well," he remarked, "the Flying Horse Hills are found at the southern reaches of this magical place, were the foothills of the Turquoise Sisters begin to rise up from the last lines of the trees and shrubs, between the two sentinel peaks of the Yellow Wren Mountain and the Feather Mountain. Peronne was foaled here over four-hundred years ago, and then raised by Reyse to be a gift for you --- from me --- to celebrate your twenty-ninth year. An important number for you, that, as you were always partial to the number eleven for some reason."

"Reyse raised Peronne?" questioned Eli, startled by this news.

"Indeed, yes. And it was a generous offering to make to you, and to me also who desired that your winged-horse be blessed by his expertise and skilful equine-schooling. Reyse was ninety-nine years into his Great Charm when Peronne was born, in 1599, and he came back from his distant adventures, to these Woods, to be present at the foal's birth and to spend the springtime and the dawn of the summer with him and his mother-mare. Thereafter, he took the colt with him to share the next year of his Charm and to continue his period of education and flight-perfection in close company with the great horse-lord. As a result, few know Reyse as well as does Peronne, save perhaps Finnir."

Eli stopped walking and turned to look over her shoulder at her wonderful horse, following close behind her now. He was mighty and delicate all at once, filled with hidden power and yet as graceful and tender as a new moon. His eyes were a darker blue than midnight, but the white-lily forms at their centres were glowing like tiny candles in a cold chapel.

She smiled at him, but he seemed to be anxious and ill-at-ease in these Woods, despite having been born only perhaps twenty or thirty miles further south. Why was he uncomfortable here now? The King did not seem to be aware of Peronne's misgivings or nervousness; it seemed that only Eli was perceiving her horse's mood and mind. But she heard no words, silent or otherwise, from him.

The Woods were not dark, but they were close and crowded with thousands of trailing and waving branches, richly hung with fluttering leaves. The path was winding and often criss-crossed by slender or sturdy roots, tangled and interlaced. One's eyes were more often directed to one's feet, in order to avoid stumbling, than given to looking farther ahead. In any case, what with bends in the path and curtains of foliage, the view was at best limited to about two or three yards before one's face!

Aulfrin had gone on rather more quickly than Eli, as he was sure-footed and at ease among roots and trees. Eli followed more cautiously and slowly, enjoying the fragrance of the willows and their ceaseless whispering music and the pale green light which was the 'shade' which they cast. But amid her pleasure at the discovery of this willow-wonderland, Eli's mind was torn between appreciation and anxiety. She could feel Peronne's uneasiness growing as they advanced. And her father was far ahead now, and out of both her sight and hearing.

"In a moment," she thought, "he will realise that I'm not keeping up. He'll turn back and find me; there's only one main path, I think. I should hurry on a bit, though…"

As she said these words to herself, she turned back to Peronne, to indicate a change in her pace and her desire to rejoin her father. But as she turned, her horse stopped short, frozen in a listening attitude with his ears turned backwards as if in annoyance or alarm.

"What is it?" Eli asked, in a hushed voice.

At last, Peronne spoke, noiselessly but with deep, rich, rolling words ringing in Eli's ears.

"We are watched and our steps marked," he said, still not moving but with his great indigo eyes now glancing beside and behind him, and then again at Eli. "There are bats in the trees, and salamanders on the stones in the streams. They are watching *us*, perhaps. Or they are simply sentries put on permanent guard here, watching *all* that passes. But there is another presence besides these, further ahead..."

Even as he spoke, Aulfrin's voice came clear through the dancing branches hanging over the path ahead; but he was still out of sight, around the next bend in the path.

"Eli! Can you hear me? Stop where you are; I'm coming back. The path is blocked --- by a dragon."

Eli stopped, but her heart was now pounding hard and she felt a shiver of terror running up her back. She was not normally given to fear, but the tone of her father's voice was none too reassuring. And a dragon is a dragon!

But just as she could see the movement of her father's form disturbing --- so it seemed --- the branches ahead, at the limit of her view where the path bent sharply to the left several feet ahead, two things happened simultaneously.

An enormous black bat suddenly swooped down through the trees to her right, trees which were towering over her by perhaps twenty or twenty-five feet, trees which were agitating their slim branches this way and that as though heedless of the wind's direction or even existence. And at the same moment, Peronne whinnied loudly and bolted, leaping off to the right of the path from whence had come the bat.

Eli ducked in fright as the bat whirred past her head, and in the very midst of that movement she turned to see Peronne disappearing through the columns of white tree-trunks, brushing aside the trailing branches with his tossing head as he ran. She thought she could hear a shout and footsteps, as of someone being chased by the horse.

Straying in the Salley Woods

As quickly as the two events had occurred, silence descended. Utter silence. Her father did not arrive, the bat had flown swiftly away, and Peronne was nowhere to be seen.

"Father?" she hissed into the green shadowland further up the path. "Father?!"

Eli considered it wiser to stay on the path and seek Aulfrin than to try to follow Peronne into the boggy and unmarked terrain between the trees. She took a few steps along the narrow roadway and pushed through a soft veil of corkscrew-willow fronds and their wildly twisted, long, pale leaves.

"*Father?*" she called again, a little more loudly, but somehow hesitant to make too much noise until she knew what had happened to disturb Peronne, and whom he had chased, and what had become of the King...and the dragon.

Beyond the living drapery of the branches, the path wound on to right and then left, deeper and deeper into the Woods. But Eli could see no sign of her father. She wondered if she should stay where she was, or continue, or go back to the bay of grass at the threshold of the Forest and await him there with the other winged-horse.

And then, right in the middle of her growing concern and confusion, a thought came into her mind. *Allow it, receive it, welcome it.* Eli was back in her meditation beside the deep dell of the Salmon Haven: she could feel herself stepping, *confidently*, out of the thunderous vortex of crimson water and finding there the king. Not Aulfrin, the King of Faërie, but the fairy, the king, of her vision. She was not alone, and she was no longer afraid. Not of anything.

"This is," she said to herself, in her heart and in her deepest being. "That's all. This *is*. I welcome it, for it simply is. I do not resist it in any way."

For a moment, the green shade of the Salley Woods changed to the dimmer hues of a truly shadowy room, a room where there was a slight orange or ochre-yellow colour in the air and a perfume richer even than the willows. She could distinctly see, ahead of her beyond the next flimsy screen of intertwining branches, a mellow orange glow. She smiled, thinking that she would find, in the middle of her path, the Queen's Head Vase from her mother's Concocting Cell!

She pushed the branches aside, and turned the next gently curving bend in the path. But the pulsating orange colour was not coming from the Vase.

She had found the dragon.

****

It is a well-known fact that our greatest fears are those of things <u>imagined</u> but not yet arrived: fear of what *might* happen, fear of what we *might* encounter, fear of what *might* befall us. Eli found that this was very true --- as regards dragons.

The thought of coming face to face with a great dragon --- not in a vision or a dream, but in waking and real life --- is certainly something which could and should inspire fear. But Eli discovered that, when she was actually about five yards from such a beast, in the flesh, with his jaws parted and a ruddy flame flickering about the hot-white centre of his furnace-like gaping mouth, she was not actually afraid of him at all. For it served no purpose to be so.

She could not fight him and she could not flee: the massive creature in the clearing just before her was three times the size of her great horse and he had leathery wings poised above his back in arches that reached nearly to the tops of the nearest trees. Battling or fleeing from this animal would be folly. And what was more, he was very beautiful.

Eli had seen visions of Bawn, the white dragon-mount of Erreig. And she had seen Bawn and other dragons in flight and at a distance. Those visions and sightings had been impressive, but she had not truly noticed how gloriously beautiful a dragon could be. Not until now.

Rather than choose fear, Eli chose wonder. It seemed more useful to her; for even if she were to be killed, here and now, by this beast, she wanted to have this moment to appreciate him rather than have her perceptions completely clouded by terror.

But she was not granted much time to do so.

Even as she was taking-in the shining ridges of green and blue on the tips of the dragon's smooth white scales, the sienna-red of his crest of pointed dorsal triangles, the gracefully twisted ivory horns protruding from just over his snake-like yellow eyes, the scene changed dramatically.

Aulfrin had returned. He was sending a blazing stream of light, like a long white and blue spear or a gushing projection of fire-works, from the uplifted palm of his left hand as he ran up from between the large but spaciously planted trees among the rivulets off to the side of this small clearing. A dragon-rider was running before him, and now leapt with practiced agility onto the back of the crouching beast, just between his shoulders from whence the wings grew; and now those wings were beating once or twice to lift the creature almost directly upwards and clear of the Woods.

Aulfrin's ray of white and blue light smote the cheek of the winged-worm as he rose, and thus he lifted his head higher and the spray of fire he was belching was deflected over the tops of the trees, rather than towards Eli --- who had been directly in its path.

The King approached his daughter, and the throbbing ray of light disappeared back into his hand. He embraced Eli, and both breathed deeply for a moment or two.

"Erreig's outriders and his black bats are patrolling these Woods," he said at last, straightening up and regarding Eli quite calmly now. "Exceptional, that, and surely significant. I do not think the Dragon-Chieftain himself is here, but at least *three* of his riders are near to us. I suspect that they saw us flying over the northern borders of the forest, and then they watched where we landed. I was coming back to warn you, as soon as I had noticed the bats to either side of the path, when I saw this rider landing further ahead. At that moment, he dismounted and offered a challenge to me, and so I decided to deal with him where he was, rather than leading him to you! And I knew you were with Peronne, who would protect you.

"But where is he now, your faithful steed?" he added.

"He rushed off the track, back where we were just now, and into the trees. I thought I heard someone running before him through the undergrowth," explained Eli, speaking as calmly as her father.

Aulfrin's eyes were alight with this news. "Well, let us go back then. I hope we will find him swiftly, and learn what he was chasing. Perhaps it was another dragon-rider, but I thought they were all further on, not to the *side* of the winding path which we were following. Come, let us look. Perhaps there are more than three!"

They retraced their steps, but arriving at the point where Peronne had dashed off, they saw no sign of the great winged-horse nor did they hear anything but the muttering leaves and the gurgling brooks. And then, Aulfrin pricked his ears and gazed intently into the misty ranks of white trees and green boughs.

"Yes, I hear something. It is no doubt another of the dragons or at least one of Erreig's Sun-Singers seeking to discover us and to mark *your* passage, especially, through these lands so near to Quillir. But what to do? I do not really wish to leave you alone, and I do not wish to lead you closer to any threat. And yet, I would like to see what is there, and why Peronne is delayed." Aulfrin was clearly hesitating, and Eli realised that she, herself, no longer felt any anxiety --- strangely enough.

"I think you could leave me for a moment, here, or I could make my own way back to Cynnabar perhaps. I imagine that your encounter with the dragon-rider who has just flown off will have convinced any others nearby to be on their guard, and that I am not alone."

Her father looked with great respect and pleasure into Eli's eyes. He found them bright and brave, and he realised that he was very very happy to have his changeling daughter coming back to take up her fairy-life once more.

"I think you are right, my dear Eli," he nodded. "You will not be in danger here for the few minutes I will be gone. May the blessings of the Moon-Dancers protect you, and the spirits of the salleys shield you from all danger. You were ever very devoted to this race of trees, since your youth in the White Willow Isles, and I sense that they hold you dear. Be of good courage, and I will return swiftly!"

With that, the King jogged off between the trees in the direction that Peronne had taken, and Eli was again plunged into cautious waiting surrounded by the green light and the whispering of leaf and water.

For several minutes, she heard nothing. The Woods grew quieter and were dreamily --- rather than eerily --- still now; they somehow seemed very calm and sleepy. She could hear no birds singing here, and that surprised her a bit; but she likewise could not see or hear any bats, which relieved her in a way. As she continued to listen to the pianissimo music of tree and stream, another soft sound became audible. It was an insect sound, or song.

There was a gentle buzzing, but not that of bees. It was very subtle, almost secretive. But it was persistent, and quite clear now. She peered around on every side, but could see nothing flying and could not pinpoint the source of the singing. Then she moved slowly around the trunk of the nearest willow, to look behind it into a glade of smallish, grey-barked pussy-willow trees. All about one clump of these trees Eli could see swarms of wasps coming and going, singing sweetly as they flew. She smiled at the sight, and the sound. But as she looked, another sight made her catch her breath.

Partially obscured by the thick growth of the pussy-willow stems and branches, and easily ten yards from her vantage point, was a figure in a cloak. The colour of the long cape blended beautifully with the greens and greys, but it was of another hue in fact. It was a deep plumy-purple.

The figure had its back to Eli, but there was no doubt in Eli's mind who it was. She could imagine the long black hair and the sombre-skinned face and the large, tranquil eyes concealed under the draped hood of the violet cloak. She was sure. Even just by the posture and regal stance of the person, or rather fairy. It was Alégondine.

Eli thought of the mysterious fairy-woman singing in the Castle of Leyano, intoning her lay of the spiralling stars, her voice so magical and so filled with the sighing waves of strange seas and the far-off calls of tempest-blown gulls that Eli had fallen into dreams and found herself lulled to sleep where she sat --- thereafter carried, no doubt, to her bed without stirring a lash! And now she could see that the wasps were swarming around the cloaked figure, encircling her as if they wished to honour her, to sing for her, to hear her wisdom and her own melancholic mezzo-soprano chanting.

With no clear thought other than that of joining her desire to that of the insects --- her wish to listen, with them, to the songs or the words of Alégondine, or simply to be near to her --- Eli stepped around the tree and off the path, gingerly making her way over the trickling stream at her feet and into the grove of pussy-willows.

But before she could reach the place where Alégondine stood, the figure moved away. She seemed to glide between the pussy-willows, with the wasps following her like a rippling scarf blowing out behind her form. Eli followed, as noiselessly as she could.

She did not go far. Pausing beside and partly behind a large pussy-willow with many thin trunks making a spray of grey arms and dusky-green oval leaves, Eli watched as Alégondine turned slightly and walked very slowly out of the grove of trees and across the stony brook. Her profile was just visible, as were the waves of dark hair falling over her dress's embroidered bodice where her cape blew open for a moment.

On the point of calling out, softly, to her half-sister, Eli stopped short. Another fairy was on the far bank of the brook, standing in profile to Eli also and no more aware of her presence than Alégondine was. As the purple-cloaked figure came to him, he turned --- in recognition and greeting.

The couple was far from Eli, and certainly neither had seen her. The man-fairy spoke, and his voice --- though distant --- came clearly to Eli's ears. His voice was not deep, rather it was almost feminine, but it was melodious and rich: tinged with authority though also with sorrow, Eli sensed. He wore a long cloak as well, so dark a shade of grey that it was almost black. All around the hem were patterns in yellow and red, like Celtic knotwork painted by the snails; though these patterns seemed rather to be stitched or woven into the heavy fabric.

"How did you know I was here, my daughter? I come stealthily and in secret to the far side of the Turquoise Sisters, sure that none can detect my presence, and you walk up to me as though we had convened a meeting here among the grey pussy-willows!"

Alégondine laughed discreetly and pulled her hood back as she stopped just in front of her father. "I knew you were here, for the insect-folk of many tribes are speaking of your worry and that you are haunting these Woods in search of the Prince Finnir. But he is not here; I can feel that. Neither is he nor any of his servants lurking about the shores of the Dragons' Drink. He does not seek to trouble you, father. You should not fear him so."

"He possesses a mystical but rogue power that haunts and hounds me, as the insects tell you I haunt the Salley Woods! I have wrestled with his mind and his spirit, in the Caves of the Great Cats, decades ago, and I do not wish to wage such battles ever again. He is too strong and too subtle. He is like his phantom unicorns, that Prince. I hope he will not too soon come to the throne of his father, Aulfrin. He would drive me from Quillir more swiftly than even others of his family seek to do."

Alégondine shook her head sadly, and her tresses glistened blue-black in the golden afternoon sunlight falling into this clearing beside the stream. "You live too much in fear, father of mine. Too much. Look for solutions and serenity, not for unborn problems! You imagine so many fairies to be against you, that you do not allow for the possibility of unity and compliance among the children of both Sun and Moon. What if *that* were possible?"

The figure robed in dark and heavy cloth now pushed back his hood also, and Eli could see him sighing exaggeratedly. He shook his head.

"Compliance? I do not see it," he admitted, his voice even sadder than before, but no less lovely for that. "I do not even entertain such a hope in my heart. No, my heart is troubled, not hopeful. Perhaps my son, your courageous half-brother, will find ways to help me when he holds the position of wisdom and power that is ordained and destined to be his."

"That position is not his by *destiny*, father. You know that. His fate, looming close now in his future, is there by your own 'ordaining' and by treaties negotiated by you and others, but not by him, and not by his design or destiny. And I hope that healing and help will come *before* he must take up his lonely role on Star Island, and that it be a *true* healing for Faërie --- and also for your troubled and hopeless heart."

There was a brief silence, and then Alégondine concluded by saying, "As I say, Finnir is not here in these Woods, nor is he on the southern side of the Sisters near the Dragons' Drink. But his father, the King, is. I can feel that Aulfrin is not far. If you would listen to my advice, my dear father, I would counsel that you return to your Fortress, and *not* draw King Aulfrin into any aggressive encounter today."

The man drew his hood up over his face once more, as if seeking to conceal himself from the eyes of the King. "You are right. You are wise and far-seeing, my daughter, and I should heed your words. I will recall my riders, and return to the pass of the Beldrum Mountains. You will come to me there?"

"Yes, my father. Garo and I will come, soon. We will talk more calmly and at greater length then. We will come in about a week's time."

"Farewell then, Alégondine, little dragon-flower of the Sun-Singers!"

The violet-cloaked fairy lifted a dark hand and the man-fairy did likewise. Their hands touched and then both turned. Alégondine walked further away and across the brook. Then, lifting her hood back over her stately head, she withdrew, passing between the dense and twiggy trunks of the last of the pussy-willows, where she was lost to sight.

The dark-robed man-fairy faced into the warm wind from the south and walked very quickly away in that direction. Eli followed him with staring eyes, until his form was obscured by a great bank of high-domed weeping-willows not too far off. Still gazing after him, she at last saw his figure, now without its cloak (which seemed to be held in a bundle in one arm) --- torso bare and hips covered by a sort of half-tunic --- rising into the skies. Erreig's large yellow and black wings were beating rhythmically, bearing him away into Quillir.

****

"Erreig!" Eli gasped in a hissed whisper to herself, as all her fears and forebodings regarding him simply dissolved. "So, *that* was Erreig! I do not wonder that my mother the Queen fell in love with him. He is utterly charismatic and very beautiful. Pathetic, tormented, and scarred in his heart of hearts. But he is as beautiful as the most plaintive music or the softest rain."

Knowing she should return immediately to the place where Aulfrin had left her, or at least find her way back to Cynnabar, Eli remained were she was nonetheless. Two or three minutes passed, but she was rooted to the spot, the image of Erreig still burning before her.

She had noted that his skin was dark, though less so than Alégondine's. It was not simply tanned or weathered, but was a natural and very lovely milk-chocolate brown, like the bark of a youthful tree in the spring sunlight. His hair was so short-shorn that she could not really guess what colour it was. Perhaps a deep blond, for it had seemed to shine like the golden torc about his muscular neck. In his forehead there had glistened, rather weakly on this occasion, the diamond named *Kalvi-Tivi*. The name she had recalled with no effort, as if it had come back to her the instant she had seen the gem. It was a powerful stone, Leyano had told her, as was the fire-opal that Erreig had won in his second Initiation, with the waterfalls. That stone she had not seen; it was embedded in his chest, and so it had been obscured by his dark cloak.

But his voice: that was the most remarkable thing about Erreig. It was a poem, just to hear him speak. Indeed, it was the voice of ancient Irish or Nordic poetry or heart-rending song, the high and distant honking of the great cranes passing along the long sky-ways of their migrations to and from the bleak northern lands, the weeping of winds caught among the crags of a rain-drenched mountain looking out onto steel-silver seas, the tears of a widow, the heart-break of a young maiden overwrought by unrequited love, the despair of a mother watching her only son leave her --- called to fight and die in the wars of a strange land... His voice was the plaintive poetry of all the ages, as pitiful as the wringing and imploring hands of unanswered and unanswerable prayers: the begging and impossible prayers which always ask that life be *other* than it is.

Eli found that tears were streaming down her face.

She shook herself free of the spell of Erreig's voice and the picture that was engraved in her inward vision of his grey-shrouded, strong, pitiful and poignant form. And she went with as much haste as possible back to the path she had left.

As chance would have it (if it existed, which it does not, she smiled!), her father was only just appearing in the distance, stepping over the miniature water-courses and between the slender boles of the trees, with Peronne following close behind him.

Eli was delighted to see them, but distressed as soon as she could see Peronne's forelegs, which were scorched and blackened. As her horse reached the pathway, she knelt down to examine his wounds.

Aulfrin spoke, rather than Peronne. "Not too serious, dear Eli. A brush with dragon-fire, but only enough to singe the hairs of his legs and fetlocks. I came up just in the nick of time, though, for Peronne had hunted the dragon and his rider into a quite generous clearing, and the great beast had thus the room to turn and confront his pursuer.

"Dragons are ill-at-ease in close woods, and there is so much water here, and so much magic, that burning the trees to clear a space for serious battle is not an option. In any case, this was not one of the six elite captains of Erreig's company, but only a lesser worm-cadet, sent to gather information and scout about the northern glades, no doubt. As soon as he saw I had arrived to second Peronne, he used the clearing to take flight, rather than to engage us in futile combat!"

Notwithstanding the minor importance of her mount's injury, Eli was concerned and asked if they should leave the Woods and return to *The Inn of the Smiling Salmon*, where perhaps the wounds could be treated.

"The best remedy lies closer at hand," came the reply, but it was now Peronne himself who answered her, quite cheerfully. "We are surrounded by healing trees here, for the willow has properties not only magical but also medicinal. A little deeper into the Woods, and to the west, and *you* will see the Lustrous Willows used for harp-making, and *I* will find a balm of willow-bark to sooth my blackened legs!"

As the trio walked further into the Woods, Eli's arm around Peronne's arched neck, Aulfrin called to a huge woodpecker drumming high up the trunk of a particularly large willow, easily fifty feet tall. The bird descended gracefully and alighted on the King's shoulder.

Eli was enchanted by its size and dramatic colouring. She had never seen a woodpecker so imposing: it was as large as a huge crow. Its wings were mostly grey-black, with touches of white where they curved along his body. When he had flown down, white patches on their undersides had been brilliantly visible. His longish neck was striped in the same deep grey and white, and his head was crowned by a flame-red, pointed cap of feathers. At the corner of his elegant beak was a little red moustache of the same hue, running along his cheek just under his bright eye.

The bird cocked its head to one side as it listened to the King's words, which were muttered --- to Eli's amusement --- in a language of *kuk-kuk-kuk* sounds, very throaty and staccato, varying in pitch and volume like the notes of a Vivaldi allegro! When the woodpecker had flown off, she smiled at her father.

"He seemed to understand your speech very clearly!"

Aulfrin raised an eyebrow in mock indignation. "I should hope so! I speak fluent *pileatus-dryocopish*, and with the accent of the local dialect!" Both chuckled merrily.

"In fact," resumed the King, "I asked my loyal subject to hasten to *The Smiling Salmon* and tell Ferglas and Jizay where we are and what has transpired, and ask them to come to us here --- just in case any further dangers present themselves. If myself or Peronne rush off again, you will have the hounds with you, and that would comfort me."

"That's rather a long way to run, even for those great dogs, is it not?" inquired Eli.

"For ordinary dogs, that might well be true. For fairy-hounds of enchanted lineage, as are both yours and mine, they will cross the thirty miles or so in a matter of less than an hour, I should think, and without fatigue. And the wood-pecker will fly to them in an even shorter time. What is more, both dogs will be nicely camouflaged, for --- as you noticed perhaps --- the plains between the River and the Woods are, at this time of the year, filled with tall sun-flowers and deep blue cornflowers. A golden and a blue dog will pass unnoticed!"

Eli continued to grin, and then she sighed with contentment and wonder at this world which was, it seemed, hers by enchanted lineage too. She felt a wave of benediction and gratitude wash over her.

"Ah, here we are." Aulfrin's voice interrupted her dreamy thoughts. "Look, there across the next brook: a purple willow for Peronne, and a little group of silver willows for you! The mulberry-coloured bark of the former will provide a salve for your dear horse's scorched legs, and the latter --- part of the race of willows which we call 'lustrous' --- will exhibit for you their patina of glowing skin and harp-befitting wood."

They left Peronne, who approached the purple willow to be tended by a small company of wood-sprites who had spontaneously appeared to daub his wounds with flakes of curling bark dipped in finely-turned little bowls filled with cool water from the stream. And now Eli and the King turned to examine the shining silver trees a little further on.

Though Aulfrin had called this a 'little group', the coppice of Lustrous Willows seemed, to Eli, to merit a more grandiose title. There were a dozen upright and slim-bodied saplings, and among them five much larger and more ancient adult trees, each with three or more trunks branching out from the great bunches of meadow-sweet plants at their feet. Their skins were pearly-grey, deeply ridged and furrowed, and host to many little moths and other winged insects dancing about them in the buttery sunshine.

But what stood them apart from any other willows that Eli had ever seen, here or in the human world, was assuredly their *luminosity*. Their trunks did not have a 'matt' finish to them, but rather an intensely satiny one. The afternoon light shone on many of the angles of the wrinkled and woven lines of their deep-fissured bark, and made them gleam like polished pewter or silverware. Higher up in the thick cover of twigs and withies, branches and long arms --- whose leaves were like garlands of tiny pale-green flags flapping in the breeze --- were small song-birds, chirruping and chiming as they hopped about or flew in and out of the trembling array of leaves.

"Are most harps here in Faërie made from these willows? May I touch the bark?" asked Eli, reaching her hand to reverently caress one of the larger tree's boles. Aulfrin did not prevent her, and so she allowed her fingers to wander over several of the ridges of silky bark. It was like skating on a frozen lake!

"Many, but not most, perhaps," answered her father. "The mer-harpers use other materials, and my own harp is not made of wood at all. There are musicians in various parts of the kingdom that have their own idiosyncratic preferences, also. Just as you were invited, by the Red Coral Tree, to use some of its limbs for your harp, other trees make similar offers to fairies whom they love and admire. Your brother Finnir has a little lap-harp fashioned from the willows of these woods, but he also plays a larger instrument, kept in his castle in Barrywood, made of whitebeam from a very ancient tree he met on the Irish side of his Portal when he took up his guardianship in 1550."

Aulfrin, like all fairies, was easily carried away with the talk of harps and their beauty and even their genealogies! He continued enthusiastically.

"He discovered that this particular tree had been protected by many generations of leprechauns in the area, for it had a fascinating history going back a thousand years or more. The tree was called Finnhol-Og, and it was near its death-day when they met. It offered its body to Finnir, to be transformed into a harp with a voice that is quite remarkable. Finnir named the harp Ban-Cocoilleen --- in the language of his enchanted Glens this could be translated as 'The Little White Hazelnut', for it is very white and its sound is particularly appreciated by the squirrels that keep him close company. At least that is how he explained her name to me when I first heard him play her.

"And your mother's harp, Gaëtanne, is even more extraordinary, for she is carved from a *single* piece of wood: the branching trunk of an equally ancient tree, but this one a pine. That tree grew on a stony plateau facing into the wildest of the sea-winds, in the kingdom of her grandfather, the Sheep's Head Shee; it had twin trunks sprouting from the same roots. They rose to the height of a young maiden and then they rejoined and grew together again, in a curious but very naturally harp-like form indeed! At the time of Rhynwanol's birth, in the year 1038, a brutal winter storm swept through the very exposed and rocky lands of the Sheep's Head Shee, and the strange pine was uprooted. Your great-grandfather found the elongated triangle of its fused trunks laid on a bed of moon-flowers nearby. These are a lovely and rare flower, small but very hardy, native to that shee. He had the wood slightly refined and smoothed into the frame of the unusual and extremely light-weight harp that you have seen. It was sent to his grand-daughter on the occasion of her seventh birthday, in January of 1045 --- in the Little Skellig Shee where she was born and educated; all very long before she became my wife and Queen in 1260.

"She was never parted from Gaëtanne, until her banishment. At that time, she herself chose to leave the harp in Fantasie, for she said that it had sung a hundred-year-long love song to me already, and might very well continue to do so after her departure in exile. She vowed that her music would never be sundered from the Silver City and its King."

Aulfrin's voice had grown soft and thoughtful as he spoke, and now his last words trailed-off on the breeze like the swirling butterflies. Eli looked up at him, with tears welling in her own eyes; but his were closed and the expression on his regal face was difficult to read.

****

They returned, now, to where Peronne stood beside the purple willows. The sprites had finished their soothing treatment of his forelegs, and the blackened hairs already seemed to be giving way to a new growth of fluffy-grey ones. As the King and Eli arrived beside the great horse, the last of the wood-fairies disappeared into the mass of long, bi-coloured leaves --- a dark green above and a pastel green on their undersides. Eli thought how beautifully the two tones complemented the ruddy-burgundy of the stems. She stroked Peronne's broad neck and continued her caress over his withers and then into the soft blue and yellow feathers of his wings, slightly arched over him.

"Father," she began, a little shyly but not doubting that her words would be acceptable to the King, even if very personal, "as it was in the mid-fourteenth-century that my mother left this shee, then she has been living in exile a very long time indeed. Well over six hundred years."

Aulfrin took a deep breath, but Eli felt assured that it was owing to his own emotions and not to any reticence on his part to answer her.

At last he said, "It was in 1367, to be exact. She departed in the early morning of a particularly bright and sunny late autumn day, only a month or so before the Winter Solstice. All the leaves on the lesser trees of Fantasie were ablaze with the reds and yellows of the Sun-Singers and the Moon-Dancers. Though Faërie was on the threshold of her winter, nature seemed loath to bid farewell to the sweet season preceding it.

"I remember thinking, as I stood looking out upon the City later that day, at sunset --- alone on the balcony where my Queen had always loved to take the evening air with me --- how lovely those two colours were together. I never wished or dreamt with greater desire to see the unity of the two clans, the marriage of Sun and Moon. But that evening they seemed farther apart than in all the long millennia of their existence.

"The red of the Sun-Singers was that of passion and possession, the reptilian eyes of the matriarch Bawn and the fire-opal in the chest of the Dragon-Lord. The yellow of our lunar dancers was that of the dying leaves: it was a brittle and fragile yellow, falling like tears from the branches that were preparing for their long, hibernal sleep. As I mused so sorrowfully, I turned to the streaked stains of painted clouds in the west, just on the horizon where lay the Sea-Serpent Archipelago. There was the tiny paring of the new moon.

"A sudden pang of unreasonable hope flashed into my heart as I beheld her. She seemed not to be sinking or setting, but to be sailing --- like the lovely little crescent-craft of Brocéliana, pulled by dolphins and lit with a magical lantern. That sliver of moon was bearing my Queen from me, far into the western seas, to her ancestor's shee of the Sheep's Head. A sorrowful journey; but not a disappearance.

"My dearest Eli, my Mélusine, we must never forget this: *the Moon returns*. She always returns. Her lantern is the Sun which illuminates her with pure light as white as virgin-snow, and her dolphins are the urging force of the globe itself. But her dance is a *rondeau*, a great and stately circle.

"I have often remembered that new moon of the month of November in 1367. She bore my Rhynwanol into the west, her heart still filled with her red passion for Erreig, I imagine. But Erreig's heart was not sure of its own course, and lately we have learned that it was inconstant and deeply perverse. But the Moon, Eli, is neither inconstant nor *lunatic*: she is as faithful and wise as the returning seasons and the rhythm of the flowing tides and the new life rising in the branches that seem to die and creak like ghosts in the chill tempests of *Imbolc*, in the dark days of winter's weariness.

"I had my own share of passion as regards the affair of my Queen, but it was cold and arrogant, not hot and fiery. It was the passionate effrontery of the cuckold's bitterness. Red as a dragon's eye, but a cold red, a stubborn and compacted and heavy red, the dry red stain on the point of a notched sword or spear. That is <u>not</u> the red of our banners, the blazing red of the regal Sun. Mine was not a king's royal red; it was not worthy of a king. And even the golden-yellow of our sweet Moon-Dancers, though defended and upheld by me, was thin and milky in those days: too pale and pallid, anaemic, devoid of the rich and flowing blood of its throbbing heart, robbed of the brilliant yellow glow of the summer sun."

Aulfrin stroked Eli's long red hair as she had caressed Peronne's grey-dappled coat. He smiled.

"I will have <u>two</u> subjects of interrogation for the sweet-voiced harp at the Inn tonight! I will request information on Finnir's progress, of course; but I will also ask news of your mother, in her exile, in her isolated castle on the northern shores of the Sheep's Head Shee.

"I believe that I have, with your return to us for these Visits, my Eli, at last found the humility to listen to the words of the Mushroom Lord. *Rhynwanol is still your wife*, he reminded me. He then asked me, outright, if she was banished for her crime of infidelity <u>only</u>; at which I confessed that my edict had been driven by burning sentiments of wounded pride. And he added, *Beware, Aulfrin, of where you step, for there are earthquake faults here...* At that time, I thought he was warning me to exercise care in those treacherous, subterranean tunnels. But as if often true, our life is all a poem of symbols and metaphors.

The real cracks and fissures he referred to are still threatening my realm and my dreams of unity for it. And they are within my very heart."

Eli looked with admiration and boundless love at her father. The small jewels in the points of his ears caught her eye: they were red and yellow, both colours set into each point like two halves of a circle, like a warmly radiant 'yin-yang'.

"What are the gem-stones in your ears, father?" she asked very softly. "They are so beautiful, and seem to be outshining the emeralds in your crown just now."

"They are common but very precious stones, my sweet Eli. They are jaspers. The red jasper is one of the most powerful and protective of all gems, for it is the blood of true courage pulsing in the veins of the warrior, the life-force of the earth itself, the red of passion but of a passion tamed and elevated to soaring prayer and exploding creativity. The yellow jasper is the path, the fullness of confidence in walking it, the blessing of peace laid upon the traveller, the healing of wounds, the thirst of the scholar for learning and understanding, driving him onwards and upwards and over all obstacles.

"I was given them at the completion of my first Initiation, when I was a princeling of barely eleven in the year 732; but alas, I could not decide upon my choice of hosts for that challenge! I loved all horses, and so I first asked to be guided by the wild herds of Mazilun or Karijan. But I also loved the mer-horses, and so I wanted to work with the sea-steeds of the northern ocean. And then there were the flying horses, and I begged to be apprenticed to the steeds of this land of the Salleys and the Flying Horse Hills at the feet of the Turquoise Sisters. Ah my poor parents, the King Aulfrelas and the Queen Morliande! In the end, they sent me to all three, and even allowed me to spend several weeks in the company of the unicorns of Barrywood. You see, I am a lover of unicorns too.

Perhaps you, and your brother Finnir, have inherited that from me!"

Eli laughed with her wonderful father.

Finding a comfortable and accommodating root, they rested a good while longer in silence, until their repose was interrupted by the arrival of Ferglas and Jizay. They could hear the sea-shell collar of the blue hound jingling as he ran up, and then Jizay barked his greetings to his mistress also.

Without any further words between them, they all walked leisurely back to the bay at the eaves of the Woods, where Cynnabar awaited them.

They had encountered no further hostility from dragons when leaving the Salley Woods, but there had been many bats to be seen, hanging rather nonchalantly in the higher willows and fanning themselves with an occasional outstretched and upside-down wing. In evidence, also, were many salamanders --- reminiscent, Eli noted privately, of the colours of Erreig's wings: yellow and black --- sidling about the brooks and bogs, but not crossing the path. She somehow felt sure that they, like the large black bats, were associated with the Dragon-Chieftain, and though they seemed unconcerned by the walk through the Woods of the King and his daughter, she suspected that they were in fact watching them closely.

Eli felt relieved to be reunited with Jizay, and to be riding (at ground level now) back across the flowery fields, concealed by high sun-flowers and wading through a cornflower sea. But even more than that reassurance, she felt most deeply happy at the change that steadily seemed to be blossoming in her father's heart in regard to her mother the Queen Rhynwanol.

****

Chapter Fifteen:
The Sunder-Stone of Kitty-Kyle

Although she would have been delighted to do so, Eli could not hear the rapturous instrument of *The Smiling Salmon Inn* upon their return, for Aulfrin played in private with only Ferglas near him. But she imagined that at least some of the insights and news spoken to him by the harp would find their way to her ears, sooner or later.

Nonetheless, her evening was relaxed and deeply enjoyable, for Jizay sat beside her at a comfy corner-table in the larger of the two dining rooms, and they listened to a glorious though informal concert given by the fairy-musicians whom her father had noticed earlier. There were three harpists (or *harpers*, as Reyse would have corrected her!), a lively fiddler, two fairies with instruments akin to uillean-pipes but even smaller and with voices like purring kittens, two others with dulcimers (*un*-painted but very lovely in their simplicity) and a gifted flutist whose high, wavering, liquid notes seemed to fly around the dark beams and in and out of the open windows, borne on warm June breezes and accompanied by a nightingale nearby in the black alder trees.

It had been a very, very full day --- to say the least! --- what with flying-horse voyages, Salmon Haven meditations, willows and dragons and dragon-chieftains too. Eli was filled with her emotions and visions, but also exhausted by them. She was soon nodding, despite her desire to stay and listen to sweet music.

Jizay accompanied her to her upstairs bed-chamber, and lay on the rush-mat beside her soft, over-stuffed mattress with its curtains of mist-white gauze. She hadn't even the energy to read a few lines of Lily's journal, but simply cuddled into bed and allowed the distant strains of the music from downstairs to lull her into a dreamless slumber. Or at least *almost* dreamless: for it was true that the notes of the impromptu chamber-orchestra of players seemed to conjure images in her drowsy mind of green, aquatic halls wavering in hazy focus. As she dropped off, Eli saw swaying leaves of water-celery and many-fingered fronds of egeria-weed dancing in the turquoise twilight of the Salmon Haven's pools. Rainbow-tinted sea-horses cavorted among them, contrasting with the slow-motion ballet of the underwater garden. Flute and harp music became transformed into 'cello and organ, and horns braying sonorously like the autumn bellowing of a many-antlered stag.

But after these images and sounds had receded into the shamrock-coloured watery haze, Eli fell into deep sleep, not to be awakened until the sun of mid-morning shone bright into her window and the nudging of Jizay on her lightly-blanketed form invited her to hasten downstairs to meet her father.

Despite the fact that she and the King seemed to be the only guests in either of the dining-rooms at his late morning hour, it somehow did not seem the time or place for discussions of what Aulfrin had learned from his harp-playing, either about Finnir or his Queen. He was cheerful, Eli noted, but thoughtful; and she did not disturb the silence as they ate their bread, nuts and sour-fruit jams with bowls of red-gold tea. Smiling warmly at his daughter as they shared the last of the rotund tea-pot's contents, Aulfrin finally spoke, proposing a plan for that day's travelling.

"It has occurred to me that there is a *very* remarkable place for you to visit, or re-visit, if you wish, my dear girl. And I think it would be a perfect, summer-sunny day on which to see it again. You used to love it greatly, ever since the first 'educational trip' you made there in the company of your devoted tutor when you were a little girl, for it lies not too far from the White Willow Isles. Thereafter, you returned on other occasions too, and you even went back later as an 'apprentice' to learn certain artistic skills. What's more, it was a spot beloved of your mother the Queen. I wonder if she may even have taken you there as a tiny infant, once or twice, though you would have been too young to have appreciated it as you did in later years."

Eli's eyes were bright with curiosity, but also a little sad.

"I wish I could remember my childhood here, my mother, my studies with Reyse, and all the things that touched me and taught me when I was a fairy. It still seems like a dream. It's not easy even trying to *imagine* that it was my *own* life, here in this glorious place."

Aulfrin rose and placed a hand on her head, and then he stepped back and offered it to her as an invitation to go with him to find the horses. As they crossed the room and then donned their capes for the flight to come, he spoke gently to her.

"It is an important chapter of your fairy-life, also, this strange threshold-time wherein you are balancing between the two worlds; and you knew that it lay ahead when you chose to pursue your changeling experience. Ah yes, you well-knew that it would be the most difficult challenge of all, especially for you who were ever so aware and perceptive and *in control*, enjoying a keen and full understanding of all that transpired around you!

"But for *any* changeling it is hard. On one hand, you are living a wild and delightful fantasy, informed that you are not human but fairy and that this magical land is your home. But on the other, you have not regained your memories, your full-fairy wisdom and comprehension, and so you feel half like an intruder, or at best a wayfarer in an alien culture. More and more insight gradually comes back to you, but it is almost teasing and taunting you --- for you cannot cross the frontiers fully until your final decision is taken and you return to Faërie to re-claim your body, your wisdom, your true heart and soul, completely and joyfully.

"But it *will* come, and soon now. You are more than half-way home, my Mélusine! A little over a week of this second Visit remains to you, and then your third. And from that Visit, I hope, you will never go back to the world of humankind --- not as Eli Penrohan, in any case."

Eli looked lovingly and gratefully into her father's sparkling green eyes. She bent over to kiss Jizay's forehead, and asked if and when they would be re-united with the dogs, following this adventure to come. Aulfrin explained that their flight would lead them north and east, many miles, and that from there they would most probably make a loop around Davenia to finally arrive at Demoran's Castle. Ferglas and Jizay were invited to make their way to the Dappled Woods directly from the Inn --- or as 'directly' as their inclinations ordained! --- and they would see them there in a day or two.

To this Eli agreed happily, and she and her father mounted Peronne and Cynnabar, and trotted through the woods of alder and walnut on the far side of the stable-yard.

Before climbing into the azure skies, rising on a warm current of the fragrant breeze --- while they were still trotting along side by side --- Aulfrin told Eli that their destination was a great inlet of the swift-running sound between the coasts to the north of the Fire-Bird Forest and the long, thin island where the kittiwakes and gulls had their colonies. This strip of water was called by many names: the 'Antler-Bight' --- owing to its form resembling the antlers of a stag; the 'Strait of the Sea-Horns' ---

for many of the Mer-men lived along these shores, and they were ever a race very fond of the music of a local type of exotic conch-horn; and also the 'Kitty-Kyle' --- its favoured name among the clans of the kittiwakes, for their homes were mostly found on the south-facing cliffs of the long island, overlooking this fabulous coastline.

"For fabulous it undeniably is," he continued, "with its view of the Sunder-Stone, the wonder we are going to look upon. The inlet I spoke of is almost mid-way along the Kyle, and it is very wide and grand. It opens out from the point where the Scarlet Ribbon, a sinuous river flowing from the feet of the last great Falls of the Shooting Star Lake and meandering through the Fire-Bird Forest on its course to join the waters of Moon-Mad Bay, tumbles into this strait. Its tumbling takes the form of a high, thread-like waterfall, issuing from a vertical crevice splitting in two a towering point of bright white rock, a little over seven hundred feet high. It is a breath-taking sight, both from the two sides of the inlet and from the Kitty Cliffs facing it across the Kyle. The majestic point of pearl-white-stone, standing quite alone and distinct from the lower cliffs of the cove, is neatly divided by the fissure and its silver strand of falling water, and so it bears the name of the Sunder-Stone or the Sundered Peak of Kitty-Kyle."

"How marvellous!" Eli enthused, and added, "Do we fly directly there, or do we visit the Fire-Bird Forest *en route*?"

"Ah, undoubtedly we must make a little pause among the tiny red and green birds, and several of my other subjects residing there. We could not miss that!" rejoined the King, just as they took flight.

About an hour later they alighted in a clearing of the Forest, surrounded by hosts of the tiny, colourful birds. Although situated well in the north of greater Faërie and also in the northernmost province of this island of Shee-Mor --- and thus in regions with a climate, as Eli had noted, not unlike France or even Ireland --- this wood was almost tropical. Within its borders, marked principally by huge clumps of towering and swaying bamboos, the air was humid and hot, and many lush, equatorial species of plants and flowers greeted the eye.

The edges of the clearing where they were met by the flocks of red and green parrot-like birds the size of blue-tits, were decorated by hundred of orchids growing on the trunks of various trees: some of these were oaks or other trees common to all the Shee Mor, but most were much more surprising, such as palms and even vines of calabash complete with huge, oval, gourd-like fruits. The flowers of the myriad orchids were of infinite exotic shapes and ranged in colour from piglet-pink to deep claret, with one or two a purple so dark they were nearly black.

Much as the flowers thrilled Eli, the tiny sprites scampering or flying amongst them were even more surprising and wonderful. These were all dark skinned, like the colour of the blackest of the orchids, but dressed in pastel shades of yellows, lime-greens, soft oranges and rosy-mauves. Their wings were the various shapes of the orchid-petals themselves, and all were glistening gold, like brilliant Christmas bows on riotously-gaudy wrapping paper!

When the King and his daughter dismounted, both were immediately surrounded by fluttering birds and whizzing sprites. The birds settled, eventually, on the sandy soil, but most of the black fairies hovered in mid-air (a few sat smugly on the backs of the little birds), and offered delicious treats to their visitors.

Eli and Aulfrin were regaled with titbits of juicy fruits born on cupped petals, while the horses were offered long, curling leaves of speckled grasses --- which they clearly enjoyed as much as Eli did the fruit. Both the birds and the sprites chattered continuously, and Aulfrin tried to translate as much as he could. It seemed to be a mixture of family news, recent births or marriages, an exciting appearance of a novel form of bright pink mushroom at the feet of several of the banyan trees, and inquiries as to the health and business of Jizay and Ferglas, who had paid them a visit not long ago and were fondly remembered by all and sundry.

During all this commotion, a little ebony-black lady-sprite --- rather rotund, seemingly more elderly than the rest and crowned with a sort of turban of twisted petals in garish hues --- flew up close to Eli's face and scrutinised her for a moment. Aulfrin grinned, but Eli felt a bit taken-aback. The aged sprite, only about seven inches in height, her dark face wrinkled like a walnut and not much larger than one, pursed her lips and literally looked Eli up and down, her minuscule arms akimbo over her ample (for her diminutive size) bodice.

In the end, Eli had to grin too. The tiny black fairy's expression was just like a rather domineering but very loving Negro mama of the ol' Deep South in America, about to give a stiff reprimand to her mischievous little boy caught stealing a piece of cornbread behind her back!

Aulfrin whispered in Eli's ear: "This is Mama Ngeza, the mother-elder of all of this community. She is an extremely venerable and very important fairy…"

She spoke in a high-pitched and quite slow voice, but her lilting accents were still those of a language unknown, or unremembered, to Eli. Aulfrin laughed heartily as he nodded, dismissing the tiny 'mama'-sprite graciously. He turned to Eli with his translation.

"She said something along the lines of, and I paraphrase: *So! This is the lady that my sweet-hearted Lord Iolar-Reyse is supposed to be in love with, is it? Well, my, my, but I don't wonder that he's having a difficult time of it! She's as head-strong as a zebu and as wild as a panther, and that fiery hair of hers is surely no lie, either. She looks old enough to have sense enough, but it seems she can't make up that independent mind of hers --- and that dear boy is suffering something terrible. I'll bring her mandrake and orange blossom, perfumed with ambergris from the whale-fathers. That should set her to rights…A good strong dose of my love-potion, and she'll see and understand exactly where her muddled heart ought to lie!"*

"She's bringing me a love potion so that I will accept Reyse's suit?!" quipped Eli, still giggling with her father.

"Seems so," he replied, trying to sound serious, but unable to suppress a chortle. "It would be rude to refuse it. And Reyse is a fine fellow…!"

"Oh dear!" cried Eli, "I'd rather make my own *zebu-headed* decision, if you please. She's quite right about me, I fear!"

Aulfrin was laughing heartily now, but he tried to look more composed as the little black fairy reappeared with half a small calabash gourd ceremoniously but precariously borne on her small, turbaned head. Luckily, Eli was not required to drink the potion there and then, for --- as Aulfrin repeated the instructions for Eli's ears --- it was necessary that Reyse be present, as the effects would be instantaneous. The contents of the gourd, looking to Eli very suspicious indeed, were carefully poured into a hollow bamboo phial and sealed with a gummy substance provided by an attendant humming-bird with a flashy electric-blue throat. Eli bowed her head as politely as she could, and thanked the maternal little black fairy, who buzzed off contentedly.

She stored the phial in her shoulder bag, with Lily's journal and Reyse's white rose, and she and the King mounted their steeds and took to the air once again.

****

As they flew over the eastern half of the Fire-Bird Forest, Eli had a good view of the Scarlet Ribbon, the twisting and turning river that wound from Shooting Star Lake to the Sunder-Stone. It must have been near noon, for the high June sun was streaming down on the tropical woods and also on the swift-running river, making it look more like a golden ribbon than a scarlet one. Even from their height far above the bamboos and the banyans, the blue spruce-trees and assorted pines, Eli could hear the calls of strange birds down below, and the bellowing of larger animals, unseen but judging from their roaring voices not small at all. She wondered if there were elephants and rhinos, lions and tigers and the like, in Faërie --- but her father was too far ahead to ask.

They flew on, perhaps for another hour or so, languidly and gracefully, sometimes indulging in a spiralling loop to descend almost low enough to tickle the topmost leaves beneath them with the slow-motion prancing of their steed's hooves. The land had become somewhat rockier, and Eli could descry a range of hills to the north-east beyond the river and the last of the trees. These were not mountains, but rather softly rounded forms, high but not haughty, inviting rather than imposing. But she was not long tempted to heed their invitation, for before them was the land's end, and the cliffs that looked out onto the great island home of the gulls and kittiwakes.

And in the midst of the long, jagged line of stones and wind-buffeted shrubs, and nearer to the travellers than the ridge of the cliffs, rose the pearly point of the Sunder-Stone, seen from the back. For where the river flowed over --- or perhaps *through* --- the Stone, to tumble into the Kitty-Kyle, its head was thrust far, far up into the sea-breezes. What it must resemble from the other side, Eli could not begin to imagine.

But soon she would know.

Aulfrin flew low, between the first hints of the hills to their right and the excited and swift running loops of the Scarlet Ribbon, nearing the Sunder-Stone, to their left. They passed the pearl-peak, about half-a-mile away, but at least on this its eastern side the vision of the cascade was obscured by rising clouds of spray and mist, beaded with prism-coloured lights which tricked the eye and teased the senses.

Nearly ten miles on they flew, and Eli decided not to even try to look back over her shoulder until they reached their landing place. This her father was indicating with an outstretched hand

and broad smile. A promontory, sloping down into the Kyle on this north-eastern side of the inlet, and ending in a rounded belvedere of flat stone, half as high as the cliffs behind. It offered an awesome view southwards back over another rocky outcrop, much lower than itself, and beyond that to the towering pinnacle of the Sunder-Stone, rising over seven-hundred feet into the skies and dominating the lesser cliffs of the shore-line for several miles to either side, as they diminished in height little by little all along this side of the strait. Twenty or so miles across the strait were the much taller walls of the Kitty-Cliffs, reaching to heights of well over a thousand feet.

Eli had barely landed and had not even slipped from Peronne's back before she caught her breath and her mouth opened in silent shock and wonder. In a trance, she now swung her right leg over the back of her winged mount, and alighted on the smooth, sea-sprayed stone, immediately reaching out to take her father's hand and simply stand and stare.

The Sunder-Stone blazed brilliant white in the June sunshine, laced with softer white mists and garlanded with a rainbow painted amid the fine spray of the waterfall where it thundered into the surging strait at its feet. From the perspective of Eli and the King, it seemed even taller than it was, like a giant's spear of white-ice piercing the heavens. Less than a hundred feet wide at its base, it seemed impossibly slender and delicate as it tapered upwards, smooth and rounded in two vertical columns that were naturally fused into a single spike of marble-like rock. Not single, in fact, for from bottom to top, in the exact centre, ran a vertical fissure --- or so it seemed, for behind the glistening thread of the waterfall it was difficult to be sure if the opening, no more than a foot or two in width, was really so exact and aligned. But judging from the fan of the escaping water, all along the Sunder-Stone's face, the legend spoke the truth.

As if the glory of this natural miracle were not enough, to Eli's dizzy delight, dolphins and basking sharks abounded in the stretch of shimmering blue, white-waved water between the promontory and the Sunder-Stone, *and* on dozens of the larger rocks all along the cliff-feet were *mer-men*, taking the mid-day sun at their leisure or talking together or diving into the waves to play with the huge fishes or lifting immense conch-shells to their bearded faces and blowing vibrating notes like the songs of bull-elephants or the cries of whooping cranes.

"Oh no," Eli laughed to herself, "this is just <u>too</u> incredible!"

Some of the mer-men had noticed the visitors now, and a braying of shell-music echoed back and forth between the two sides of the Kyle to greet and honour the King. Eli could see no mermaids, only men; they seemed to be contented with their masculine and private world, for they were all jolly and smug and robust and radiant.

Aulfrin's arm was over his daughter's shoulders now, and he laughed with her at the beauty and wild-wonder of the place. Blended with the sound of water and wave, and the music of the sea-horns, was also the shrill keening of the gulls and kittiwakes, gannets and fulmars, circling and doing aerial acrobatics overhead. With great difficulty, he turned Eli's gaze from the Sunder-Stone to look out over the Kyle to the opposite cliff-base, where a twin promontory was visible, a little to the west.

"Let's go there for a more *distant* view, but also for a warm welcome. Luncheon awaits, with an artist! Come along!" And with that, the King led Eli back to Peronne and when he too was mounted they leapt off into the sharp wind of the Strait and crossed the waters, flying low and fast, their horses neighing and flicking the crests of the feathery wavelets with their galloping-in-air hooves.

The 'artist', who greeted them as they landed on the facing ledge of rock, was reminiscent of Vintig at Castle Davenia. Like the aged gardener-groom of Demoran's household, this wizened little fairy was smiling and serene, walking slowly and speaking softly, and he wore his wings too! He was small of stature and dressed in a greenish-grey tunic and rather shiny trousers, the fabric of which looked to Eli like leather or even the dried skin of great fishes. She was sure that fairies did not hunt or fish, but perhaps the hides of certain animals were gifted to them after their owners had died a natural death --- rather like the wood of the ancient tree Finnhol-Og that had willed itself to the Prince Finnir to be used to make his harp.

As the little artist-fairy turned and walked before them, leading his visitors and their steeds under a soaring arch of mottled stone that seemed the entrance to a deep cavern at the back of the rock-ledge, Eli had time to admire his wings. These were the same azure blue as this morning's sky and had the form, not of butterfly or dragonfly wings, but of those of flying fishes. They were not long, and did not touch the ground as he walked, but floated peacefully out from his shoulders behind him, waving like delicately patterned medieval flags or standards.

"He keeps his wings always, like Vintig?" whispered Eli as softly as possible to her father as they followed. But even with the constant sound of the wind and water, gulls and horns, the artist heard her question and turned to smile back at Eli over his shoulder.

"Outside always, yes, my Lady," he called, and his musical voice blended with the aquatic sounds so perfectly, it was like a skilled singer's interpretation of sea-song. "I use my wings constantly when I'm with the kitties. Only once inside my scriptorium do I swallow them back into my self-of-selves!" With that, he chuckled, and Eli thought it was like bubbles bursting --- the sound that champagne would surely make, could it laugh out loud!

When they had passed under the high arch, and the horses had wandered off to the left, to an alcove laid with dried algae and straw, the artist showed the King and his daughter to their luncheon table, all fashioned of the same multi-coloured stone as the Kitty Cliffs with seats softened, like his stables, with a layer of faded seaweed and wilted grasses.

While the artist poured a pale blue liquid into their chalices and uncovered large plates of delicacies that Eli was unable to identify, they were so fantastical in shape and hue, she ventured a question to their host.

"You called this dwelling a 'scriptorium'? Are you an artist-writer then, rather than an artist-painter?"

"This gifted and graced artist is both, I suppose one could say, and a craftsman of other genres also," replied Aulfrin, as the little fairy seemed in no hurry to answer. In fact, he seemed in no hurry at all, in any way. Even his movements as he served them their meal --- which Eli discovered had a taste not dissimilar to *buicuri*, but in many variations and with many different textures and forms --- were in slow motion, like the ministrations of one of the monks of the Abbey of Ligugé, going rhythmically about his sacred duties.

Finally, the half-high fairy, now taking a seat with them at the stone table, smiled at Eli so that his happy eyes closed tight and disappeared into the wrinkles of his delightful face. He then said, "Yes, yes, I paint words, my Lady Mélusine. And many decades ago, though you do not re-remember it again yet, you came to study with me the art of such reverent and meditative calligraphy.

"You were a good student," he added thoughtfully, now allowing his bright little eyes, like those of a bird, to open wide and sparkle at Eli. "Indeed, a diligent little apprentice-scribe, if a little impatient to achieve the results you desired." And he laughed his champagne-bubble chuckle once more.

Aulfrin joined in his jocularity. "That would be my Mélusine!" he commented.

"Ah, quite impatient!" continued the artist, "I have been luring words to dance across sea-parchment pages with grace and inner light for two thousand years, and Her lovely Highness would have liked her gull-feather-*plume-pen* to obey her commands with precision and perfection in a week! Ah, it is ever so with my little scribe-children; but depending on the words they trace, slowly oh so very slowly, the wisdom of the lovely letters will end by sinking deep into their very selves, to shine there forever and ever, like unfading stars reflected on the indigo ocean."

Eli smiled with deep joy, listening to his beautiful discourse on the art of lettering. She sighed, and asked another question, or rather suggesting two in tandem:

"And do you compose the texts you write, or copy books written by others? I wish I could recall my classes with you.... I can't even remember your name, I'm afraid."

The wonderful little calligrapher-fairy shook his head with a childlike grin on his face. "Ah, neither can I, neither can I. I must have as many names as the Kitty Kyle or as the shees of Faërie or as the stars in the constellations of the mer-folk and the fishes (very lovely names they are, too, that the sea-dwellers here give to the stars!). But I do not remember them at all, my many names. No matter, though. I have no need of a name, for I know who I am. That is enough.

"But as for my written words, they are mine by birth or mine by adoption, both, but I do not differentiate. And that is the wisest way to be a father," he giggled, winking at the King. Then he resumed, "They are my children, one and all. When I paint them and pen them, they are doubly mine, and wholly their own. A pleasant mystery to observe! You loved to give the breath of pen-life to words, dear Princess. You were a happy mother of many flourished and illuminated children..."

Eli's eyes, so merry as she listened to the artist, had suddenly grown sad, and the compassionate and alert little fairy saw this at once.

"What have I said to sadden you?" he asked, so softly it sounded like the gentle hiss of the receding tide on a fine-sand beach.

Eli felt her heart opening and overflowing to this curious and monk-like fairy-scribe. She bit her lip for an instant as her eyes turned tearful.

She confessed her sorrow, feeling her heart would break with the memory. "I could never have real children, and I longed for them so. I was so devastated to be childless, in my human life I mean. I tried to adopt, also, but I could not go through with it, and so I failed at both forms of motherhood... I suppose I have no children here, either, as a fairy?" She had turned to her father now, and her expression was hopeful, but wholly pathetic.

However, the artist-fairy was smiling with his head on one side, patient and half-amused, while at the same time filled with sympathy. But it was Aulfrin who answered.

"My dear girl, you are a changeling. Changelings *cannot* have children during their human lives; they are sterile by definition. A fairy visiting the realm of men, *as a fairy*, can parent a child --- as I did twice, bringing both Arden --- that is, Finnir --- and Brocéliana into the world. But a changeling cannot; it is not permitted, not unless they return after refusing their fairy-life here and, in the case of a woman, are yet young enough to bear a child. You learned, and accepted that fact before your adventure, I am sure.

"Here, in your true form as the Princess Mélusine," he added, "you are yet young, and unmarried. And so you may, and will I hope, bear children to your fairy-husband. To Reyse, perhaps."

Eli's face was a study in surprise and dawning comprehension and also a huge wave of bitterness and dismay. She had left her Irish husband Colm, when she was sick with depression and weakened by grave illness caused by her grief, because of something that she had known --- *before* her human life --- would be impossible?! Why had she not remembered this, or been told, somehow, by someone? Her confusion and remorse and aggravation were growing into a veritable tidal wave deep within her.

Whether he did so by design, to help her to stem this tide, or whether simply by the blessing and grace of another force, or Life itself coming to Eli's rescue, the pensive artist-fairy looked with a puzzled expression at the King and changed the subject.

"Reyse? Iolar-MacReyse?" he queried, still in his slow sea-song voice. "I recall that good and noble fairy-lord sending love-letters by gull and dove to my little copyist-student here, while she studied with me. She refused them all and very decidedly! Now perhaps Your Highness has had a change of heart, while you have lingered among the grey-ghost daze-dancers of the world..."

Eli's ears pricked up at the term, for it recalled her own youthful prophesy-poem to her.

> ... *here, among grey ghosts*
> *Wandering in a daze-dance*
> *Below the kittenish clouds...*

"But I doubt it, for you were ever a Lady to know your own heart," the wise little fairy-scribe concluded.

"I used those words in a poem! I wrote about the grey ghosts wandering in a daze-dance," Eli murmured. "Did I write *that* poem while I was here, with you?" Her tears abated and her eyes were wider than ever.

"Of course, of course! You were very fond of composing poetry. I recall those lines clearly. Very apt they were!" he chuckled.

Eli was smiling again now, but she returned to the fairy's comment about the husband her father was hoping would be hers. "And you <u>don't</u> think that Reyse and I will marry, when --- if and when I return?"

Aufrin cleared his throat, rather markedly. Eli glanced at him, aware that she was pushing the limits of the conversation too far for his taste, or even for propriety perhaps. But the wizened little fairy was standing to serve his guests further sea-foam arabesque-crackers in twirling, crunchy, colourful forms and he spoke nonchalantly as he filled their leaf-plates.

"Not in the opinion of your grand-mother," he remarked, simply.

There was a short and proverbially pin-dropping pause of complete silence. Eli froze in the midst of nibbling a green-gold biscuit that tasted of salt and lemon-flowers and capsicum. Aulfrin looked piercingly at the artist, but the diminutive fairy was occupied with refilling their chalices now, and so the King's gaze was unnoticed by him. Eli wondered if her father, using the great magical powers that he reputedly possessed, was trying to see into the tiny fairy's thoughts and learn what this strange retort could mean.

Eli took a sip of her blue wine. And so did the King. And, as the artist was offering no clarification of his remark, Aulfrin replaced his chalice gently on the table before him, and addressed the calmly smiling fairy opposite him.

"In the opinion of *my* mother, or of Rhynwanol's, do you mean, if I may ask?"

The artist was small, and frail, and very aged, no doubt. But he seemed to be a match for the King. Fairies, surmised Eli, were surprising, courageous and unpredictable beings. She had the impression, growing more and more within her, now too, that she and this flying-fish-calligrapher had been on quite close terms as apprentice and master. She could not consciously recall being here before and studying the slow and sacred art of writing with him, but she was beginning to rediscover a deep and unforgettable link forged long ago with this fantastical fairy. He caught Eli's eye, just for an instant, before he replied to the King, meeting his royal regard squarely and yet with infinite respect.

"Morliande," he intoned, even more slowly than he had spoken up till now. "The Queen Morliande, *your* noble mother, my King."

"And when did my mother offer this opinion? Has she been here lately?"

"*Late* or *early*, that is a poem-play of words, my Liege," smiled the artist with even greater serenity and even more perceptible respect. "Morliande is a creature of the sea, and all of us who dwell and delight in the shared element of Faërie's ocean-waters move about and exchange news and share our ... *opinions* as freely and continuously, as *late and as early* as blow the winds over those waters. Sometimes we exchange by bird or fish, sometimes by current or breeze, and sometimes the enchanted Queen will swim here to visit me in her seal-form. One or two of the best books in your son's Demoran's library are the transcriptions of her poems. Yes, yes, she loves composing poetry, as much as does her grand-daughter! An excellent poet, as I'm sure Ruilly the rabbit would agree: he relishes her rhymes and is always asking for me to send him more."

Aulfrin sighed, but now he was smiling too. It was impossible not to. Even Eli's tension had turned to amusement and relaxation. The artist's voice was like the massaging of undulating wavelets in a pristine bay of a hidden, paradise cove.

The King sighed yet again, but he shook his head simultaneously, and with his smile broadening. "And Morliande, the poet-silkie grand-mother of my head-strong and heart-strong daughter, has given you what information, precisely, about Mélusine's eventual marriage?"

The little artist folded his hands, long-fingered, white, beautiful hands, on the table before him and he, too, sighed. But it was the sigh of someone reading love-poetry, Eli thought.

"The Queen believes that she is to marry, one day, the King of the Sheep's Head Shee," he said, and there were stars dancing in his eyes. Was he testing or teasing the King, Eli now wondered. Who was the King of that shee?! Could Morliande not have prophesied her marriage to her half-brother, Finnir, thereby somehow making it acceptable to break the rules of such inter-family unions?! In any case, was her grand-mother's opinion so decisive or inescapable? But before she could formulate any of these questions into actual words, Aulfrin laughed.

"I think that very unlikely!" he snickered, but good-naturedly. "I have been able to learn a little something of the family of royal fairies in that strangest of shees. It is become a place of labyrinthine energies, too magical to be governed or guided. My Queen Rhynwanol now resides there, true, in her exile, and her grand-father was a good and wise King by all accounts. But his son after him was as wild as the head-land gorse-bushes and his second son, Rhynwanol's father, removed to the Little Skellig Shee for that reason. The prince-apparent I cannot trace, not by any means that I have found. He is a traveller, much like Reyse in fact; so much is clear. I have even wondered if he has not ventured into the human world, to live out a semi-human life there. Even were he to prove a suitable suitor, I do not believe that Mélusine would give her heart there. All of that clan is descended from her great-grandfather, and so is a part of her blood-line. And Eli has learned, on this Visit home, that it is not lawful for a royal fairy to marry back into her own family."

"Ah," conjectured the artist, weighing this news, "but the King of the Sheep's Head could come from the other royal family, Your Majesty."

"The *other* royal family?" repeated the King.

"When the mad king you spoke of passed into the cradle of death, we have heard --- we of the sea --- that it was not one of his *own* family which took the throne at all. When your own

Queen's father quit the Sheep's Head Shee for the Little Skellig, and his elder brother went a-wandering, another family replaced the line of *his* father. If that is true, the eldest prince of that shee, who will become its king in due time, is *not* of Mélusine's family at all."

"I have not heard this tale, by my beard and my emerald crown! What family is this that has come to power in that shee?"

"I can tell you nothing more to identify them, my dear King. I do not know the name of any member of the clan. They are as nameless or forgetful as I! I only know that the actual king is of no relation to you or to the Queen. They come from another shee altogether, and one that is very far distant. I believe it is the most remote, yes, on the other side of the starry Spiral."

"The Shee of the White Kangaroo?! They come from the clan of fairies we call aborigines, who live between their own shee and the land of the kangaroos?"

"As yes, yes, that's it! Kangaroos! I remember Morliande speaking of those. They are an animal we do not see in this shee, nor any other, I'm sure. They carry their children in their pockets --- well, many a parent has tried to do that! --- but they are always leaping out and hopping off on their own business. Oh my, oh my; that is exactly the way with the son of the new High King of the Sheep's Head. Morliande says that he can't be found, not by guessing or questing, not anywhere! But she still maintains that the one who will come to the throne of the shee where the banished Queen now resides, that one will be the husband of Rhynwanol's daughter. I *suppose* she means Mélusine?"

The King was silent, his lips pursed in resignation and on-going exasperated amusement. And then he said, "It may be Mélusine she is thinking of, yes. Or another. Rhynwanol has had *four* daughters, in fact, my good artist. Mélusine and also Alégondine, and her twins the half-fairies Mowena and Malmaza. I would venture to think it more likely that it will be

Alégondine, for she is well-acquainted with the Sheep's Head Shee already, and may even know more of the whereabouts of the vagrant prince than does my mother.

"No matter for now," he said, and glanced at his daughter beside him. "I hope that Eli, or Mélusine when she returns fully to us, will make the choice that is the highest and noblest and most blessed. But as she is less easy to put into a pocket than even the most unruly little joey, we can only wait and see!"

Obviously more than ready to conclude their discussion, Aulfrin arose and thanked the little scribe-fairy for the lunch and for all his wisdom and words. There was a tingling moment of energy-exchange between the two: the tall, red-haired and red-bearded King, his silver filigree crown of emeralds shiny dully in the scant light of the cavern --- and the ancient calligrapher-fairy, only half as high as the King, inscrutable, peaceful, timeless and nameless. As they stood facing one another across the table, the little fairy's wings silently sprouted from his shoulders, and he rose just slightly into the air to circle the table's end and precede father and daughter out of his 'scriptorium'.

"Look, look," he called back to his visitors as he reached the open air above the platform of dark, wide stone facing out over the Kyle. The King and Eli had been joined by the horses, and were now walking out into the sunshine, ready to remount.

"Look at the shining tongue of the greatest poet, the Sunder-Stone-Singer, the white falls that feather forth from the cloven needle of the insight-sower! Look ...and listen!"

With the little grey-green form of the artist hovering in mid-air like one of the gulls over the sea, Eli and Aulfrin paused to admire the distant and yet ever-impressive form of the Sunder-Stone, twenty miles across the Kyle at the head of the inlet facing them. Whiter even than the slim, towering rock-face was the thread of the glistening cascade, ever-moving, ever-singing. The air was so crisp and clear, that ordinary vision was magnified and clarified into brilliantly precise images of even the most far-off details of the scene before them.

The mer-men were silent now and their horns were laid on their laps as they reclined on dark rocks along the cliff-feet, their iridescent, scaly tails flipping in and out of the lapping waves. One or two dolphins still cavorted in the intervening stretch of water but the gulls and kitties were gone to their nests, high over the heads of the watchers. Only the Sunder-Stone shone and sang, a white finger pointing insistently upwards into the heavens, with its whiter tress of waterfall-hair streaming downwards into the Strait.

Eli did not know if her father heard the poem that came to her ears, but she somehow believed that it was only whispered or chanted for her. The artist hovered still, just above them, but Eli was sure that the words did not come from him. Maybe she had written them herself, long ago --- but she thought not. The idea came into her head that this was a poem of her grandmother, of Morliande, but perhaps it was simply a sea-verse, wafted over the Kyle, which had been born in the white droplets of the Sunder-Stone's feather-fall.

The King's son joined me on my way,
And so I stopped to wed;
A hymn of love was hummed by the Moon
And the Sun had warmed our bed.

We danced and sang, and filled the night
With stars from under the world
And over our heads the waters roared
And the banners were unfurled.

For the King has fled, long live the King!
Now the empty throne is filled
Not only by one, but by lovers two,

The Sunder-Stone of Kitty-Kyle

And by harpers sweetly-skilled!

Play on, play on! Come dance to the Moon
  And sing to the Sun's refrain!
The King and Queen are two and one,
  And the single Peak split in twain.

A sundered steeple, a ribbon of white
  Chanting firm words in soft spray;
Stone or water? 'Tis hard to tell
  And none can truly say.

I soar, I plunge, now rock, now rain,
  Now kin, now king, now mate.
Slowly, slowly, unravel my rhyme,
  But linger not too late.

For sleep is sundered like the stone
  And waking must take its place.
Two halves breed a whole in music's round,
  Half-Moon and Half-Sun face,

Unite and sing and dance and love
  Like the soaring stone and its tears;
Stars stand on their heads and waters whirl
  To laugh at our fleeing fears!

****

A Delicate Balance

Chapter Sixteen:
Rendez-Vous at Castle Davenia

ulfrin and Cynnabar led the way over the rippling Kyle and Eli and Peronne followed willingly, meandering in mid-air over the broad Strait, back and forth before the Sunder-Stone for a long while, and then flying slowly up the northern prong of the antler-shaped Sound for easily eighty miles or so before reaching the open sea.

At last, late in the afternoon, a largish island presented itself to their view, just as they arrived at the furthest point of the Kitty Cliffs: an island of pink granite, or so it appeared, about five miles to the north of the point and facing out into the seemingly infinite and empty expanse of the laurel-green ocean. The horses alighted on the shoreline of its eastern side, a little cove of soft, rose-coloured sand covered with winkles and cockles in pale and dark greys, creamy white and deep blues. Eli thought how lovely the wet colours looked against the unusual pink sand, as if all the little shells had been washed and polished --- although they were mostly in the shade now cast by the higher reaches of the island behind.

When they had dismounted, the winged-horses trotted up the beach to the tide-pools among the rosy stones, searching for tasty seaweed and bits of stubby shore-grass. Eli and her father strolled along the beach, and ended by climbing up the first few steps of a smooth-hewn stairway criss-crossing this side of the rock-face, going at least half-way up its full height of about three-hundred feet. From the first landing of this rocky staircase, Eli could look down into the crystal waters --- partially in shadow now but in places still illuminated by the westering sun at their backs --- and see a huge school of large fishes, metallic blue when they broke the surface of the waves, with undersides as silver as a knight's armour when they executed a deft flip or leap.

Aulfrin explained that they were the great tunas of the warm currents that encircled this strange pink island, and that most of their cousins lived along the western coastlines of Faërie, or far out to sea around the Sea-Serpent Archipelago. The large tunas were sleek and strong and in their swift movements very elegant, and their jubilant athleticism delighted Eli.

"When you studied with the calligrapher-fairy that we visited today --- ah, you must have been about twenty-five or six then, yes, for it was when Reyse began his ardent suit for your love --- you had many friends among the tunas, for they are on good terms with the mer-folk and enjoy their music, especially that of the mermaid-harpers."

"I seem to have spent many centuries, already, refusing Reyse's 'suit', as you call it," remarked Eli rather cynically. "I wonder he persists in courting me!"

"Love is indefatigable," shrugged the King, with a philosophical grin. "And Reyse is yet young and impetuous."

"He is young, Reyse, by fairy-standards? I find you all utterly ageless, even the fairies who seem evidently very ancient. How old is Reyse then?"

"Let's see," considered Aulfrin, fingering his ruddy beard and with eyes squinting a little into the sea-breeze, as if he were looking out into eternity itself. "As I told you on your last Visit, I believe, Reyse would be fifty-eight now. Yes, a youngster. But then, so am I! Reyse was born in the year 800, and I only eighty or so years earlier, in 721. We are really of the same generation. And we are children of the same month, for I was born at Lughnasa, that is the 1st of August, while Reyse was born on the 10th. He is the youngest son of the Eagle Clan of the Half-Moon Horse Lords of his shee, while I am both the oldest and the youngest among my siblings --- for I have none!"

Eli smiled at him, enjoying the lesson in family history and fairy-ages. "You were an *only* child, like me? I mean me as Eli," she giggled. "Oh dear, this is difficult keeping my balance between being in my fifties now as a human, and therefore getting on a bit towards middle-age, and being over six-hundred as a fairy --- counting from my birth in 1357 I believe I've been told it was --- and yet, what with Initiations and age-slowing and the Great Charm, now being…hmm…only thirty-three as the Princess Mélusine. Is that right?! I must be considered quite young for a fairy!"

"Yes, yes," laughed her father, "in a nutshell, that's quite right. Humans live very short lives and fairies live thousands of years. Though my own father was only about two-thousand years old when he left this life and was washed away into the seas from the Great Strand, and I found it very young to be leaving. But my mother, Morliande, was a fair bit older than him, for she was born twelve centuries before Christ… And so, though retired into the life of a reclusive silkie now, she would be considered only 'middle-aged' by fairy standards."

"That's very odd that you use such terms as 'before Christ', and even count years as mankind does, isn't it?" interrupted Eli, noticing for the first time that the dates were in centuries that corresponded to the Judeo-Christian reckoning of the calendar.

"Not at all, my dear girl," replied Aulfrin, unfazed. "We are simply and politely adapting to your culture as a returning changeling, in both language and place-names and dates. Furthermore, we have many dealings with human-kind, so it is not difficult or very unusual for us to use these conventions for our dates, nor a bother to think in terms of human tongues. But in our own fairy-languages and our natural culture, we have not at all the same way of even conceiving of the notion of time, though we do of course count the seasons and years. That said, the appearance on earth of *the Verb* or Christ, of the life-force of God's intentions at the time of creation, that did not go unremarked by the enchanted people in their lives and legends any more than it did by all the other animals, or by the plants and pebbles, mountains and streams in all of their respective mythologies and memories too. So we rather like using the *before Christ* and *anno domini* way of counting centuries.

"But, you know, we are always more interested in certain *days* that return in the cycle of the seasons or in the rhythm of the moon than we are in numbered years or even our own ages. We love special dates, ones that have great importance for us: such as Beltaine and Lughnasa, Samhain and Imbolc, the solstices and equinoxes, and many other days associated with certain fine fairies or even with humans.

"For instance, in three days' time we will be meeting at your brother Demoran's Castle, for a council and discussion, on a date quite auspicious to us. It will be the 17th of June, and we celebrate a charming tale, that of an Irishwoman whom we name Ævnad. She had not a little fairy-blood in her veins, on her mother's side, and was herself the mother of a very wise and saintly boy. This was only a few years before my own birth, so it is not an ancient festival by any account. But it is a lovely story, for the babe was born in a midnight snow-storm, while the mother was fleeing in shame and disgrace because of her illegitimate and unwanted child. Although she had intended to allow him to die, a huge white bird like a giant dove --- I'm sure she believed it was an angel! --- was sent to her from Reyse's shee, the Shee of the Dove, and protected both mother and new-born until dawn, when they were found and guided to more hospitable shelter.

"The little boy, as he grew, enjoyed a great affinity with dogs and wolves as it happened, but most especially with foxes, and that shows the fairy-spirit that was in him. Ævnad's line of fairy ancestors were enamoured of foxes, and for us too --- in this shee --- foxes are almost sacred; above all when we wish to conduct a gathering to discuss great and weighty matters, for they are an animal with unparalleled subtlety of thought and are very quick thinkers in even the tightest of corners."

"What a lovely tale! And will there be foxes joining us at Demoran's invitation? And what will be the theme and the 'tight corners' of this important meeting in Castle Davenia?" ventured Eli.

"Aha!" quipped the still smiling King. "We must all wait and see! But know that all the foxes of the realm will have their ears pricked, whether they are with us in person or not, for the subject is delicate and those fairies invited to our *rendez-vous* will be among the most wily and cunning, perhaps. But as well as tricky foxes, there will be kind doves, so all should go well. Yes, yes, we shall see, we shall see…"

Without further conversation, father and daughter continued up a little higher along the shadowy stairs, to enjoy the view over the mouth of the Kyle and the darkening green seas and also to admire the beauty of the distant cliffs, painted by the sunset glow, on the opposite shore. Then they descended and rejoined the horses to fly on to the headland of Moon-Mad Bay and to the Wonder Wood (where Eli had first met her half-sister, Brocéliana). There they would dine with the deer, and spend the night.

As they flew into the coloured skies, the new moon was truly a lunar-lash, very fine and white and fragile, among the orange and red clouds outlined in gold. Both Eli and Aulfrin were silent and thoughtful, each in their own hearts allowing its souvenirs and symbolism to fill them with wistfulness.

****

The third and final week of Eli's second Visit would thus begin, the following morning, by her awakening under the flowery boughs of the Wonder Wood, in a secluded glade inhabited by

A Delicate Balance

innumerable rabbits and by svelte deer with large, deep black eyes. Aulfrin and she explored together the Wood and bathed in a fresh spring of cool water at mid-day, for it was very warm and windless. They remained in and around the Wood all of that day, and slept again in the same beds that were merely the intertwined vines of the trailing flowers, strung between the boles of trees at the margins of the glade.

Eli continued to reflect upon the utter beauty of this entire enchanted world she had come back to, and to shake her head at the amazing 'fairy-tale' she was living. There was, however, no temptation at any moment to doubt or to question this highly unlikely situation. She was still resonating, in her very soul, the 'yes' that had taken form at the very first hints from the 'winking watcher' and the odd signs and messages she had received.

She read a passage in Lily's notebook, just before sleeping, that recalled words often spoken by her belovèd little moon in her earliest childhood. The entry was near to the beginning of the journal, and Lily had only recently begun to receive her miraculous visits from her 'Sean'.

*Never be _too_ surprised by how incredible Life can be, my dear Eli. It's only ever _fear_ that stops us from expecting it to be extraordinary and amazing at every moment! Life is, from start to finish, **wonderful** --- literally, I mean. It should be filled with unlimited _wonder_ from the first miracle of taking our own personal shape and being born out of the womb of our mother (**what** a fabulous and original idea!) to the last breath of releasing all the unnecessary details of our voyage on this lovely blue star or planet (I really prefer to think of Earth as a star, but I suppose that's not at all scientific!). No, don't fall into the trap of being incredulous or suspicious of the marvellous. Amazing miracles are simply your birth-right.*

When she had written those words in the small, white notebook that Eli now cherished, Lily had already met --- once again --- her departed husband Sean. But she had uttered similar thoughts even before that event had confirmed her unwavering belief in the extraordinary. Indeed, Lily had always been a woman completely and endlessly *impressed* by the surprising miracle of Life, someone who had cultivated and retained a childlike wonder, and also an open and unwavering faith.

Eli was so happy to think that her human 'mother' had learned of her daughter's fairy-nature and had accepted it, just as Eli was now, herself, accepting her duel-reality and at least trying to balance the two worlds she inhabited. She wished that Lily had been able to come here, even just for a visit, to see the amazing country that was Eli's, or Mélusine's, true home. She would have loved it!

Confident in the reality of this glorious realm of Faërie, of her place in it and of who and what she truly was, Eli was nonetheless disturbed by worries and fears. And haunted by her own indecision about whether she would ultimately return here or not.

Her nightmare was still troubling her, and also the remarks that she had found in Lily's journal alluding to her childhood trauma. Then there was what Piv had said of Erreig's desire for her, coupled strangely with his *fear* of her. They all seemed to add up to a dreadful and weighty burden from her past, of violence and intrigue. Had the Dragon-Chieftain ventured into the human world in order to attack her as a child?! What a horrid thought! Was he now hunting her, here in this kingdom of Faërie? Would he follow her back into the human world?

But what an odd thought, to believe that Erreig *himself* had been the perpetrator of the crime, given that her father and others seemed convinced that the Dragon-Lord did not know of her changeling experience at all. What had her vision, in that awful dream, really meant and where had it come from? Was it the truth, or symbolic of something much deeper? When she had beheld Erreig, in the Salley Woods, she had not been able to react with dislike or disgust. He had, rather, somehow touched her heart.

In any case, it seemed certain that she *had* been abused as a little girl in Los Angeles; though Lily's journal did not, in fact, state such a thing outright --- for she had begun to search the entries to find a description of the actual event. She had recognised the sensations and the emotions in her dream-scene, and she clearly had all the psychological symptoms in her human life, what with her many odd and unsettling love affairs, her escapist and non-committal character, and her final brush with domestic violence in her life with Yves.

However, not all her relationships had been coloured by the psychological residue of such a crime in her childhood. There had been that brief affair with Liam, with Reyse in human guise, and that had not been sorrowful or pathological at all. Quite the contrary, it had been pure delight! And her marriage with sweet, gentle Colm: that had been real and deep love, although it had been curtailed by her depression --- which she now knew to have been linked to an 'infertility problem' that was part and parcel of her fairy-nature. Oh, if only she had known *that* at the time...! But it would not have been possible to even guess such a thing.

Thinking of her past lovers, and especially of her joyful interlude with Liam, or Reyse, brought Eli back to another worry, and even to various things that were beginning to anger her.

There seemed to be a good deal of talk about marriage, *her* marriage, and she did not like it. She had the impression that her *fiancé* was being chosen or indicated as part of a formal and contractual betrothal, appropriate for a princess. Yes, it was very like an arranged and almost diplomatic marriage, with various members of her family or entourage discussing what union would be most propitious for her, and for the kingdom. Her father would be very pleased to see his realm united by marriage to Reyse's, or so she had deduced. And now her grandmother, the Queen Morliande, was prophesying a union for her with the next king of the Sheep's Head Shee --- while the little black fairy-mama of the Fire Bird Forest was in agreement with the King's tastes!

Eli felt that she (and all her <u>own</u> desires in regard to love and marriage) were being kept well outside of the negotiations, and even the poem she had heard in the spray of the waterfall from the Sunder-Stone seemed to be requiring her to make some choice or other, as if it were all predestined!

At least as a human, she felt that she had arrived at an age where she could and would decide for herself about such things. Love-potions in little bamboo-phials, indeed! And Reyse turning himself into a human lover and seducing her for a fling of two weeks in Ireland, knowing quite well --- as he did --- that she had refused him in her true fairy life. Romantic and enjoyable, perhaps, but it was also *more* than a bit cheeky; it was downright dishonest of him!

Eli sighed deeply and with a little snort of disgust tried to turn over in her flower-vine hammock, but found that such a manoeuvre would probably result in her falling out of it!

"Calm down, my girl," she said to herself in an almost audible whisper. "Anger is never, never, never the solution to any problem. Lily taught you that, and probably your own mother, Rhynwanol did too, centuries before."

The thought of her true mother, the Queen, now rushed into her mind and filled it with a glowing warmth, like the light from the primitive-looking little stone vase in the Concocting Cell. That love for her fairy-mother --- though the years spent with her were almost entirely lost in forgetfulness as yet --- flooded her heart, and with the picture in her mind of the Queen's Head Vase in the centre of the dim little room smelling of spices and potpourri, she was suddenly no longer alone or in anger. For the images all resolved into one, and it was not Liam or Reyse or Colm or Lily or even the Queen Rhynwanol.

It was Finnir.

Finnir there beside her and speaking with her, in front of the Vase. Finnir standing before her on the shores of the Shooting-Star Lake with Aytel and Brea at his side; sitting opposite her across the table while the King proposed the mission to find Morliande; riding with his blue-cloaked company out of the north-east gate of Fantasie --- mounted upon a white horse and playing gay airs on a small harp.... And last of all, the tale of his funeral-pyre and strange resurrection in the Chapel of Windy Hill as it appeared in a ghostly vision hovering over the Whale Race Sound and then his victory ride out from the caves of the White Cats borne by his unicorn-horse on a pathway strewn with yellow mimosa-blossom.

Faërie might indeed be an extraordinary place, filled with wonders that she --- according to Lily --- should simply accept as her birth-right, like all the miracles of living. But when it came to Finnir, the bounds were exceeded. Everything about him was **too** wonderful to be believed, at least with the head or in any sensible and sober way.

Only the heart could bear such beauty and fantasy. Only a heart in love.

And therein lay her greatest worry and dilemma. For she was heart-breakingly, heart-achingly in love with her half-brother. In this kingdom of her father Aulfrin, their union was forbidden. In the world of humans, should they go there somehow together, just imagine it, as two exiled fairies or as a fairy-lord visiting an aging human woman, their love affair would be cut off from this glorious land and they would remain aliens to it forever. Though Eli glimpsed a tiny ray of hope in such a plan: perhaps *that* could be a resolution to the 'riddle'! But, still, it would not be 'forever' or even for the centuries or millennia of fairy-life; it would be only for a few short and very 'human' years. Or could they voyage back and forth together, between Faërie and the world, playing with time's passage perhaps?!

In any case, Eli did not know if Finner loved *her* (but she found that she believed that he did as surely as she believed in her love for him). And what if, instead, she *did* come back here to Faërie as the Princess Mélusine, and Finnir was willing to live a love-story with her: in that scenario it would have to be entirely clandestine and, what was more, it would rob him of his own magical powers and threaten his role as the next king after their father. She could not do that to the man, or fairy, that she loved.

She could not continue, could not pursue these thoughts any further. They were exhausting her.

She exhaled profoundly and blinked once or twice. It was deep night, but not dark at all, for there were glow-worms on the trees all about her, trees richly scented with their masses of dim flowers, and between the branches and bunches of blossom was a velvet-black sky crowded with incredibly bright stars.

Eli found that she was more than simply tired, she was drained and empty; and in her sleepiness she allowed all her thoughts to float away, even the images of Finnir. She just looked at the stars, and let her spirit and mind waft upwards into their utterly silent beauty.

"*The life-force of God's intentions at the time of creation....*" A soft voice was crooning the words that her father had said earlier. "*The Verb ... the appearance on earth of the Verb...The life-force of God's intentions...*

Eli found that she could look at the stars and not think at all, or nearly so. She could just feel the 'Verb', the pulsating impulse of creation itself. She felt suddenly so calm and at peace that it brought her back to the high, bright, modern church in the Abbey of Ligugé --- but without any inward comment or analysis. She could see it, and be there and here at the same time, praying, but without any words.

Or perhaps --- she accepted with a contented sigh --- all of her words and thoughts had simply turned into stars...

And with that, she fell asleep.

****

"Would you be willing, my dear girl, to fly off early and take our breakfast in the Dog-Delight Hills?"

It was Aulfrin's voice, merrily calling across the glade as Eli awoke, and Peronne and Cynnabar were standing near him, ready for flight.

Eli had slept deeply and well, with no nightmares and not even any dreams that she could recall. Smiling and rubbing her eyes and face gently, she swung out of her flower-vine hammock and wiggled her toes in the dewy grass as she sat for a moment, watching the dozens of rabbits scampering and playing and blinking at her in the morning light.

Her cloak had served as a blanket, and so now she stood up and pulled it 'round her shoulders, walked gingerly through the crazy choreography of rabbit-antics filling the glade, and nodded to her father.

"Wonderful idea!" she said, and she looked for a moment into the depths of his green, twinkling eyes. The same, she thought, the very same that I knew as an infant. When I see them, I can almost hear the notes of his painted-dulcimer or his flute, and see him with his arm about Lily's waist, and both of them laughing together. I may not have too many memories coming back, yet, of my true life here; but I think I can begin to recall more and more of my father from my toddling-days in the Sunset Boulevard canyon. And if that's true, I'm very grateful.

"Do we fly to the same Inn where all the dogs were? Are we to have hearty soup and bone-hard bread for breakfast?" she laughed.

Aulfrin chuckled too. "We're not going quite so far, not this morning. I've had word that Ferglas and Jizay are in the blue hills to the north of that fine establishment, and that they are awaiting us there. We will join them and have some news, perhaps; for they have been talking and listening on my behalf, no doubt, these past days. And then we will all go on to the Dappled Woods."

"Jizay?! Oh, how very nice. I'm ready!" Eli finished securing her long hair with its coral comb, pulled on her soft ankle-boots, and easily hopped up onto Peronne's back. Aulfrin smiled at her, nodding but not speaking his thoughts aloud.

It was less than an hour's ride, high over the grasslands and then the outlying hills of the Dog-Delight's northern limits. Far off to her right, Eli could descry the Sweet-Faced Flower Beds and beyond them the sparkle of the waters of the Whale Race where it joined the open sea. But she could not see Scholar Owl Island, lost in the horizon's mists. Her heart thrilled a little at the idea that she was there also, asleep or in a death-like trance, awaiting the moment of her return and her rediscovery of her own, real body.

Strange to have two bodies, Eli mused; but something deep within had long ago accepted the idea, and so she felt no great incongruity. It's like the two bodies of Finnir, while he was in the Cat Caves and also in the Chapel of Windy Hill. Which is real, and which is phantom? Or can one soul have two bodies at the same time?!

Thunder clouds were looming in the west and as Eli thought these things she stared out over the leagues of Davenia to the dark and distant forms, promising rain. Behind her the sun was rising, and as it did so, a rainbow took shape in the moist morning air, against the backdrop of the massive thunderheads. Banvowha, thought Eli now, she would explain the riddle of having two bodies and the miracle of both being 'me' at the same time. The rainbow-fairy told me that I myself concoct my present reality:

All that you see with your human vision is conjured in your own mind's eye, and you paint pretty, or fearsome, pictures on a white canvas with the brush of your limited perceptions and distorted expectations... You wear the playful glasses of your own projections springing up from all of your life's experiences. But not from the Truth. Not yet.

Soon I will be seeing with my true eyes once again, concluded Eli. I'll know how it was possible and my two selves will become fused into one. Or I wonder if that is how it works...?

Eli's thoughts evaporated, and she flew up beside her father.

"Looks like rain," she enthused.

"Ah! That's a fairy speaking! Yes, yes, I think so. There will be dancing in Davenia this evening, for the thunder-birds are already flying ahead of the cloud-wall. Do you see?"

Eli strained her eyes, but she had not her father's keen vision. No matter, she was content; it was so beautiful to see the arc of the rainbow in the skies beyond the River Ere. And soon she would be reunited with Jizay! Lovely...lovely..."

Their flight ended with a steep upward climb into the warm air and then a short spiralling descent into a high, hidden plateau of the blue-stone mountains. They were in the very midst of the greatest peaks, it seemed to Eli, where four jagged and distinct summits looked down onto a secluded little glen, certainly a thousand feet above the plains at the base of the range.

To her amazement, Eli found herself in a vast vegetable garden! The rather light and almost sandy soil was covered with plants, mixed and muddled but all very vigorous and contented: broccoli and beets, Brussels-sprouts and kale, cauliflower and exuberant cabbages of all colours, and even beautiful sprays of asparagus. As she looked about her in surprise and delight, Aulfrin stooped and drew a couple of large radishes out of the earth, dusted them off, and handed one to Eli. It had deep crimson skin with a halo of white, and its interior was also pink, like a rosé wine.

"I imagine there will be more for lunch," remarked the King, his mouth full --- "I love radishes, but these are not hot enough for my taste; they are very tame and timid yet. Let's see what the hounds have come up with."

They left the horses to browse about the garden while they wandered to the western side of the glen where a group of small but leafy apple-trees grew. Among the abundant mid-green leaves were many chartreuse-green fruits, already ripening. But before she could be tempted to taste one, Eli noticed that the two dogs were also there, under the trees, standing to greet their guests with tails wagging and gentle smiles on their wise and loving faces.

How they had contrived it, Eli was unable to guess; but arranged on several over-sized cabbage-leaves laid on the ground were decorative patterns of various raw vegetables and also a small apple-wood bowl in the centre of the largest leaf containing a sweet, bubbly cider to share. The dogs ate with them, and Eli felt far, far away from all her angers and worries. The mountain air was invigorating --- even for Faërie, where *all* the air was fresh and clean! --- and she thought that she must be becoming more and more fairy-ish now, for the taste of rain-to-come was carried in the tingling air and it made her heart dance already.

But when they had concluded their lunch, Ferglas rose from where he was seated near the King and spoke, wordlessly and without any movement of his mouth, in his rich, sonorous voice which Eli could hear distinctly deep inside her own head.

"Now that Your Highness and Your Majesty have supped on such calming and heart-cheering vegetables, I must speak of very serious and troubling matters. We have been journeying these past days across the white-rabbit ridges at the head of the King's Rise, and back again north to the Bay of Knotty Roots and the Thousand-Toed Trees," he began, "and both rabbit and water-rat have given us tidings, as have the chaffinches, nut-hatches and jays. And the news is not good, my Liege."

Aulfrin was silent, and if he was alarmed it did not register in his fine-boned face or in his deep eyes. Jizay was still lying near Eli's crossed legs, and now placed one paw on her knee and laid his golden head in her lap. Ferglas continued.

"Rabbit and bird have relayed messages from the squirrels of the Hazel-Woods, and the Rat-folk have heard the same accounts from the fishes and from the swallows. Your Highness, I must tell you that Aytel has been killed, and Brea and the Prince Finnir are by all accounts lost in the seas beyond the three islands of Silkie-Seal Bay.

"In panic the fishes, dolphins and whales have sought for them, but no trace could they find. Three of the hounds of brave Brea have also been lost, three others have remained hidden in the shell-shoals at the mouth of the Black Boar River where it empties into the Bay; but the remaining two came north, at great risk and in great haste, through Quillir to Aumelas-Pen. By the messages of our rabbit-couriers we have sent them back to Barrywood, in case further news should come there by the Mauve Dragon or from other sources."

Eli's hand was trembling on Jizay's head, and she was conscious that she must have turned deathly white; she felt as if she had been turned to stone. Finnir was lost? And one of his companions killed?!

While her thoughts were whirling and her eyes glazed with disbelief, Aulfrin stood and spoke.

"We go on to Castle Davenia with all speed. I will entrust Eli to her brother Demoran, and I will return to Fantasie for harp-counsel and to send forth a party of fairies and beasts to the rescue of my son and Brea.

"What creature has killed the noble Aytel?" he added, addressing Ferglas as he pulled Eli to her feet and all began to walk quickly back towards to the horses.

The wolf-hound's shell collar was jingling as he trotted beside the King, and in comparison to its sweet-chiming sound his sombre voice made a sad contrast.

"A dragon, or a great cat, we do not know. His body, carried by a hardy flock of jays back to Mazilun now, bore many vicious wounds. The youngest out-rider of Erreig's elite was seen wheeling low and fast over the River Silverfire, heading south on the evening of the tragedy, and some of the birds believe he and his dragon are to blame. Fair Aytel's death, and the loss of the two other regal fairies, occurred on the night of the newly-born moon, two evenings ago now. But word only reached us yesterday."

Aulfrin glanced down at his great hound as he mounted his winged-horse, having lifted Eli --- still utterly dazed --- onto Peronne's back already.

"That would be the dragon that Peronne chased from the Salley Woods, Tinna-Payst and his rider Tintrac. It was Tinna-Payst that scorched your forelegs, was it not, my gentle Peronne? He is a brash boy who rides him, that dragonling. A good fairy-family, but ever impetuous and thoughtless, the youngest of that clan. Ah, my poor Aytel; it grieves me so to think he has been stilled. He was as beauteous as a birch-tree and as wise as a Scholar-Owl.

"But we must find Brea and the Prince. Come Eli, we fly in haste. Run my dear hounds and we will meet in the Dappled Woods tonight before the storm breaks. I can hear the thunder over the Star-Grazing Fields already. Let us be off!"

Eli was not crying, was not blinking, was barely able to breathe or think. She twined Peronne's long white mane through her fingers, bowed her head to his neck, and clung with her legs as the winged-horse leapt into the skies just behind Cynnabar. Glancing down at the wild vegetable garden beneath them with its pleasant coppice of apple-trees, she could see Jizay and Ferglas careering off through a cleft in the blue mountains behind the little orchard and charging down a narrow pathway into the south-west.

She could summon no clear thought into her head, not at all. Only the pounding of her heart, as if it would explode out of her chest, reminded her that she was alive.

****

Peronne and Cynnabar, flying low like ducks over a lake, sped down the eastern flank of the Crescent Isle and then left the path of the River Ere to cut across vast meadows of geraniums, or so Eli guessed, looking down onto the reaches of rich vermillion colour. But their flight was too swift for her to be sure of the race of plants, her vision blurred by the whistling wind in her squinting eyes.

Over the triple-whorls of Red Triskel Lake they passed and dove into an opening in the forest fringe, between two mighty oaks like sentinels on the lake-shore. The horses landed with grace, like equine ballerinas, and then galloped the remaining two miles or so to the eastern gate of Castle Davenia.

Vintig was awaiting them, and he led the horses away in respectful silence as the King and Eli walked to the steps of the palace. Demoran was coming down them, and hovering above the balustrade was Piv. At the sight of the little pixie, Eli's spirits lifted somewhat, and she almost smiled as he flew to her, alighted at her feet, and reached up to take her hand as they mounted the steps together.

With no formal greeting to his father or to Eli, Demoran laid both his hands on the King's shoulders and met his eye.

"Father, Periwinkle has just arrived, not yet an hour ago, and he has brought word from...from a fairy of Quillir. Aytel lives, he is not dead. His wounds seemed surely to have been mortal, but he has been tended by skilled hands and by... song. And he lives."

Aulfrin and his son were at the foot of the short flight of steps up to the Castle, and Eli and Piv looked back down at them from the landing above. Eli could see her father's eyes blaze with a green light, and then become calm once again. He regarded Demoran's olive-and-gold-speckled eyes now, with questioning intensity, but with relief also.

"He has been healed... *by a Sun-Singer*?" His voice was slow and steady, but filled with many layers of emotion as he spoke.

"Yes, my father. By a Sun-Singer and shape-changer, it seems. One who will be joining us here shortly, even before tomorrow's council --- if your invitation still stands. It was Garo who intercepted the jays in their flight to Barrywood with the broken body of Aytel. He commanded that he be taken to the White Dragon Fortress, and there his suffering was sung from him and he was called back to life. He sleeps there still --- for he has tasted the first hour of death, and come bravely and arduously back. He is very weary, but he will survive. Piv has seen him."

Aulfrin glanced at the pixie, and his eyes were shining now with gratitude and with incomprehension. But his face was still stern.

"You come from the White Dragon Fortress, Periwinkle? And will I learn news of Finnir from this adventure, also?" asked the King in a low voice, now gazing with deference up at Piv where he still stood hand-in-hand with Eli several steps above. The little green-capped head nodded once.

A hint of a smile played at the corner of Aulfrin's mouth, and he mounted the steps smartly, his arm now on Demoran's shoulder.

"Let us go inside, and speak," sighed the monarch, as he and his son passed under the arch of living flowers and into the Castle. Eli and Piv followed, and as they walked Eli whispered, almost inaudibly down to her little friend, the first words she had been able to mutter.

"Is Finnir alive, then, Piv? Has he been found?"

But the pixie had no time to answer, for they had reached the modest dining-room that Eli remembered from her first Visit, and the King beckoned Piv to be seated on the table before him where he sat.

"Now, Periwinkle, I pray you, tell us what you have learned," he said.

Piv hesitated only long enough to draw a deep breath. "I was in the Silver City, listening to what insights I could hear from the mushrooms about the Great Trees, my dearest Aulfrin. There was a murmuring about Erreig having been seen to the north of the Turquoise Mountains, on the borders of Aumelas-Pen, and I was suddenly anxious for my little Eli, for Mélusine. Therefore, I went in the dark near-morning of yester-night, under a moonless sky --- for she had gone to her bed early --- to the Stone Circle.

"There it is that I met Garo, for he studies with the Stones at times, in preparation for the role he must assume so soon now, as the Sage-Hermit to come. He is almost ready, my dear King, to take up that enchanted role; for he sees with many eyes and can hear the rustling of leaves and the flowing of water over many, many miles. He confirmed what I had heard of his father's presence on the margins of the high province, and he was as worried as I was when he knew of it. He walked once around the Source with me, listening to the wisdom of the circular waters.

"It seems that he could feel that his father was not far from Eli, in thought or fear or in actual distance, but he also knew that Erreig was simultaneously seeking news of Finnir or his people. He said that his father was questioning many of the reptiles and insects to learn if the unicorns of Barrywood were come out of their Glens and into the Salley Woods and the Flying Horse Hills, with the intention of crossing the pass at the foot of the Yellow Wren Mountain and thus gaining access to the Dragons' Drink.

"As we made our tour of the Source, Garo stopped, suddenly, in his listening and walking; a bitter cry escaped his lips and he added, *One of Aulfrin's loyal allies is in Quillir, at least one, for I can see him in my heart. He has been wounded by a dragon, but not by Bawn; it is a lesser worm that has attacked him. But why? Birds are bearing his body, and his last breath is ebbing from it. I see where they are. Come with me, Piv, if you wish --- we run like the wind itself to the Pine Forests over-looking Star Island. We must save him if we can!*

"We could feel the dawn drawing back the curtains of the dark sky in the east, when we arrived at the shores of the River Luef, just where it leaves the Silverfire. I had ridden on Garo's back, for he was transformed into a swift white wolf. The stealthy jays had been carrying the body of Aytel through the night, slowly and fearfully for they were very near to Erreig's fortress in the Beldrum Mountains. But when we found them, it was clear that Aytel was already dead.

"Garo changed his form again now, and became a lithe and leathery young dragon. Aytel was laid between his wings by the jays, and I sat astride the grey worm as we flew to the Fortress. When we arrived, Garo kept me hidden under his cloak, for he had swiftly taken his fairy-form once again."

Piv's story was interrupted now, for a sound was heard in the Entrance Hall beyond the door of the dining-room, and Aulfrin stood suddenly.

"He is arrived. I can feel Garo here, but who is with him?"

Demoran answered his father: "I bid Garo come this evening, as soon as I heard Piv's tale an hour or so ago. He was already near to Davenia and I thought you would wish to interrogate him yourself. He has come with another guest whom I have bidden to the meeting tomorrow. That introduction can perhaps wait; but will you see Garo now?"

The King was silent for a moment, as were Piv and Demoran, Eli and the dogs. Even the sounds in the Entrance Hall had ceased entirely. But Aulfrin now nodded with evident pleasure at the arrangements.

"Yes, I will greet him. Invite him in."

Even as the invitation was spoken, Garo appeared at the doorway. His tanned face bore an open and amiable expression, his cobalt-blue eyes were both sparkling and yet filled with compassion, his sandy-yellow hair was loosely gathered into a knot at the back of his head --- all the better to see the glistening sunstones that dangled from his ear-lobes in their tracery nets of thin gold. His right hand was on his breast as he bowed, and as he lowered it the triangular obsidian in its palm shone with a sombre and brooding interior light.

"I owe you my thanks, I believe, Garo," said the King. "You have generously and skilfully worked some very great magic for my servant, Aytel. Be it gift or miracle, I offer you my gratitude."

Garo did not answer immediately, but smiled warmly. Aulfrin returned to his place and as he sat, Demoran gestured for Garo to be seated at the table also. Eli looked with great hope at the confident and composed fairy, longing to ask him if he had news of Finnir as well as Aytel.

"Aytel was grievously hurt, and I feared that he had known much pain. That burden I took upon myself to alleviate, and with what magic --- as you name it --- that I possess, I softened the memory and ensured that, when he awoke, he would no longer bear wounds that would cause such suffering. But as for his awakening, his return from the other side of the threshold of death, that was not *my* sun-singing."

"Which of the Sun-Singers offered this blessing to my brave Aytel?" inquired the King. Eli, remembering Leyano's tale of his own return from death, knew the answer before it left Garo's lips. She watched her father's face as he listened.

"Erreig, my Liege. It was my father who sang over the body of Aytel and urged him back to this life."

Eli had done well to watch, for her father was struck silent as stone and seemed almost disbelieving, but only for an instant.

"*Why?*" whispered Aulfrin, but with richly resonating wonder and appreciation. "Why would Erreig thus save a Moon-Dancer, trespassing --- as he would undoubtedly see it --- into Quillir?"

To her surprise, Garo glanced, just for a split second, in her direction before answering.

"My father is seeking to do good where he has done great harm, among the Moon-Dancers that is. He is convinced that he must use every means he can to recompense his evil with good. This is my reading of the situation, though my father has not put it into those words himself."

Aulfrin, nodding slowly, was surely thinking of Erreig's adulterous affair with his Queen. Eli, on the other hand, was sure that Garo's glance confirmed her own suspicions that Erreig had been *her* attacker, and that he was struggling under the weight of that guilt. But how would Garo know of *that*?

As she was turning this thought over in her mind, Aulfrin now asked the question that was much more vital to Eli.

"Have you, or Aytel, any news of the whereabouts of the Prince Finnir, and of the other fairy-lord of Barrywood, Brea?"

"For my part, no, Your Highness. The Prince Demoran has told me that they are lost, but I have only learned this since my message from him this afternoon. However, if you will permit me, I think that my companion, who has just arrived with me here, may know more."

The King rose, as did the others in the room, and he said, "I was planning to go, with great haste, to the Silver City. There I will have insight from Tree and Stone, and from the voice of my harp; furthermore, from Fantasie I can send swift aid to my son. But if your companion can give me counsel, I will take it before I go. Where is he? Can he be summoned here now?"

"He is, in fact, a *she*," said Garo, gently and with reverence. "And she awaits you in the Council-Chamber upstairs. She would prefer to see you alone, she says. For it has been a very long time since you met, and it would please her to do so in private, before tomorrow's meeting."

Aulfrin's face was ever more and more confused and curious. He did not even need to speak aloud his request for her name, for he closed his eyes for a moment and it was clear that he had sensed her presence.

"*Alégondine is here.* The Princess Alégondine, my little flower, she is here to speak with me?"

The tenderness in her father's voice rippled over Eli's heart, not with any jealousy for her father's favour, but rather with some sort of longing or shared love. She felt so happy for Aulfrin, about to be reunited with that beautiful and mystical fairy-woman, whom he had loved as his own daughter when she was a child. She felt that her father was being granted a sort of blessing or grace; and how grateful she, Eli, would be if her half-sister could indeed give news of Finnir!

Aulfrin went upstairs, and Demoran called for a restorative cup or glass for Eli and Garo and Piv. Eli was slowly coming back to some sort of normal respiration, and her heart was beating a little more slowly.

As they sipped from their blown-glass goblets, she turned to the pixie.

"Do *you*, also, have news of Finnir?" she ventured.

Piv nodded once again, as he had to the King.

"I arrived with Garo an hour ago," Piv remarked, nibbling the corner of a large waffle-like cracker and waiting for the two attendants serving them to depart. Then he added, "But while Garo went to greet his sister, who was walking by the Golden Water, I had another guest to welcome, who had come with Alégondine --- only he won't be staying for tomorrow's meeting, and he won't be seeing the King, not yet." Eli raised her eyebrows, but Piv did not keep her wondering too long, for he could see that she was very anxious for Finnir.

"My dear, golden, wandering Aindel," sighed Piv. "He is as fine a sailor as Alégondine, and perhaps even just that little bit more enchanted. More important, he has the gift of often being in the right place at the right and perfect time: and so he saw Finnir and Brea leaving Silkie Seal Bay. Aytel turned back to deal with the dragon, but Aindel told me that the Prince and Brea, together with three of the beige-bright hounds, in fact have sailed over the inky waters, speckled with star-light, in a strange and beautiful boat like a long, slim canoe as white as bone.

"No sail, no oars; that's what he said! And swept away by a turn in the wind, off into the invisible western seas. But he was alive, my Eli, so don't be worrying for your brother or for Brea and his hounds. They were all alive. And they were not alone."

****

A Delicate Balance

Chapter Seventeen:
The Longings of Far-Flung Fairies

"*Piv*", *Eli whispered* at last, rather nervously fingering the delicate glass goblet before her on the table, "could I see Aindel, do you think?"

But it was her brother who answered her.

"I think he is still in the library, my dear Eli. He, too, had hoped to see you --- before your second Visit came to an end. But what Periwinkle says is right: Aindel is not ready to meet with our father, not yet. He does not wish the King to know that he is here."

Eli looked intently at Demoran. Oh, how beautiful she still found him! Just as when she had stepped through the 'V' formed by the oak tree in the woods of Ligugé and had felt her hand in his --- the spiders singing gloriously all about them --- to guide her down the Fair Stair and into Faërie.

"You *know* Aindel, then, Demoran? He is not a secret kept from you, too?!"

Her lovely, calm, coppery-haired brother smiled warmly at her. "He's not exactly a secret from the King either, in fact. Aulfrin knows him well. But he does not know that he is so often among us here, and he is not aware --- we all believe --- of Aindel's involvement in our negotiations, in the Alliance of the Spiralling Stars. You have been admitted to our meetings and welcomed in our discourses on this Visit, for as Mélusine you were a very central player in the Alliance. But Aindel awaits the right moment to present himself to our father, for it will be a decisive move."

Eli felt perplexed by all of this furtiveness and secrecy. However, the Alliance was not paramount in her thoughts just now; Finnir was.

"May I go to Aindel, while our father is with Alégondine? Is it safe to do so? I would so love to hear if he has more news of... our half-brother, Finnir."

"Across the hall, then, sweet Eli. I will come for you when our father summons us, as I suppose he soon shall. He may wish to introduce you to your half-sister, as he does not know that you have already met Alégondine again, I suppose; unless he guesses the names of the fairies you encountered on Mermaid Island!"

"But Aindel was there, too," Eli recalled to Demoran. "If Aulfrin can guess or somehow perceive their names, he will know that Aindel was at that meeting!"

"Ah," Demoran smiled still more mysteriously, "his insight might have given him the echo of the word 'Aindel', but he does *not* know him by that name."

Eli shook her head and heaved a little sigh, almost amusedly, to show her consternation at all of this. She smiled back at Demoran, and at Piv and Garo too, then rose and walked as silently as she could across the Entrance Hall.

Inside the bright library, with a rich, but stormily intense sunlight streaking in from a great bay window and warming the three or four cats curled-up or stretched-out on comfortable chairs and settees, Aindel stood beside a lectern made of intertwined branches with a large manuscript open upon it. He was turning one of the richly decorated pages: he looked up from the illuminations and the neat, delicate script to grin at Eli.

He beckoned for her to approach, and he whispered almost inaudibly, "Elegant writing, and excellent interlace: look at this frieze! My final Initiation was spent among oak trees and the clever snails who master this art of colourful knotwork are always to be found among that noble race of tree."

"Is this calligraphic book a creation of the artist-fairy who lives in the cave over-looking the Kitty Kyle?" asked Eli, in an equally hushed voice.

"Indeed, indeed," assented Aindel, his tightly curled, pale blond locks jiggling around his lightly freckled face as he nodded his head. His large, violet-blue eyes reminded Eli, once again, of others she had seen in Faërie, perhaps even those of her hazy vision of Queen Rhynwanol herself. In the rays of the late-afternoon sunlight the little points of amber set at the corners of his eyes complemented their colour and glowed richly. "You have met the wondrous calligrapher once again, then, Lady Eli? I'm glad. You were his devoted disciple and almost, one might say, his protégée, long centuries ago now."

"You know quite a lot about me, it seems, Aindel. How is that?"

"I've been keeping an eye on this kingdom, from a distance or in confidential visits, for many-a-year. And I've been in close touch with Finnir very often, and he with Reyse ... and so I hear a good deal of news!"

"Please can you tell me what you know of Finnir, now, dear Aindel? All this stealth and conspiracy aside, I was so worried to hear that he and Brea were lost --- at sea I believe."

Aindel closed the great manuscript reverently, and led Eli to a pillowed bench occupied only by the soft-furred mottled-grey rabbit, snoozing with his head on a much smaller volume, his whiskers twitching and a contented expression on his little face. Sitting beside this comfy creature, Aindel took Eli's hand in his.

"Not lost, not lost at all; but --- yes --- they are at sea. You know that Aulfrin had sent the three fairies, Finnir and Brea and Aytel, to find the Queen Morliande? Well, not surprisingly, she was awaiting them; for the silkies are a highly intuitive race and they moreover have many means of gathering information from various sources, both on land and in the waters. She was in fairy-form, not seal, when they arrived, for she does not like to don her seal-skin when there is no moon, and it was at the time of the new --- or dark --- moon when they met.

"It was early evening, and she was just sailing back from Star Island, with me, in my slender craft of white whale-bone. A gracious whale, once a close friend of Morliande and of the King Aulfrelas, offered his relics to the royal couple a thousand years ago. The Sage-Hermit, which is now --- as you know --- the title of the former King, gave this beautiful and enchanted *currach*-canoe to me, when I turned seventeen and had completed all of my Initiations. I still use it to visit the Hermit, and also Morliande, when I may."

"And it is in that magical boat that Finnir and Brea have left these shores?" enquired Eli, her eyes round and her voice still very low.

"Finnir, Brea, three of the cream-white hounds, and Morliande herself. Yes, they have all gone."

"*Where* have they gone?"

"To the Little Skellig Shee, and from there to the shee of the Sheep's Head. On a diplomatic mission, if you like. But, just as *my* somewhat diplomatic visits here are not, yet, to be revealed to the King, so too this journey of the Prince Finnir and his companions, both fairy and canine, is also to be cloaked in fog, figuratively and also literally! As my bone-boat passed the three islands at the limits of Silkie-Seal Bay, a dense fog enveloped them all. But Morliande will guide the craft, and the whales too I'll warrant."

"How long will Finnir be absent? Will he come back to Faërie soon?"

"He cannot long leave his Portal unguarded, but that is why I am here. I will take his place in Barrywood; though as far as Aulfrin knows, it will be Neya-Voun, Finnir's horse, and others of his most-trusted servants. Our dear friend Reyse will most likely also offer his services when he arrives this evening, and I'm sure the King will accept. But Finnir will be back soon, yes --- in a fortnight, I should think."

Eli's countenance fell. "In two weeks? But I will be gone! I must leave in five day's time."

Aindel saw the despair in Eli's eyes, and he smiled with compassion, or almost with the touching pleasure of seeing her sentimentality. "But you'll come back, Lady Eli, and soon perhaps. You have another Visit left, before you must decide on staying here or remaining a human, have you not?"

Eli sighed, and at the same instant both she and Aindel noticed Demoran at the library door, signalling that Aulfrin had called for them all to go upstairs. All but Aindel, of course.

"Thank you," Eli mouthed in silence. And the violet-eyes flashed their love and blessings to her as she rose and went to the doorway. When she turned back to look once more at the tall fairy, only the rabbit Ruilly was on the bench, for Aindel had already slipped out through the billowing gauze curtains, into the garden.

****

The King was, as Eli had curiously but instinctively expected, alone.

She and Demoran, with Piv flying ahead, had mounted the stairs to the wide Council-Chamber, finding the same tiny many-coloured beetles scurrying over the polished wooden floor of the landing as they walked across it. Eli passed under the arched door and into the now-familiar room. She looked quickly around the airy expanse of the chamber of counsel and even glanced out onto the balconies, but Alégondine was not there.

Aulfrin registered his daughter's disappointment and remarked, "You will meet your half-sister tomorrow, dear Eli. She had urgent business with her brother, Garo. They will both join us for our planned meeting in the morning, on the day of blessed Ævnad."

It was only then that Eli noticed that Garo had not come up the stairs with them. Her thoughts had been so taken up with Finnir, swept away into the foggy seas on a mission which would make it impossible for her to see him again soon, that she had not given a thought to the whereabouts of Garo when she left the library.

"But", continued Aulfrin, "I have some news to comfort you, and us all, regarding your brother and Brea. It seems that they will only be able to meet with my mother, the Queen Morliande, at sea. Alégondine met them in the Bay of Nod and agreed to assist them. She secured the use of a slender but solid boat, and they have set off --- not too long a voyage, it seems --- to find Morliande on one of the silkie-islands a league or so from the three little islands of the seals. A silkie-island is not like those three craggy isles; it is a ghost rock, able to appear where it is bidden by the seal-folk. But it is substantial enough for the fairies Finnir and Brea, and even the pale wolf-hounds, to alight upon it. Aytel was returning to give this report to me, when he was ambushed by Tinna-Payst and Tintrac. After our conclave tomorrow, Garo and Alégondine will go to Quillir to escort Aytel back to Fantasie and I will be able to speak with him when I return to the Silver City."

Eli was quiet for a moment, digesting this tale that Alégondine had told their father, and wondering why the true story --- if indeed Aindel's version was that --- had not been revealed to him. Well, of course, the *diplomatic* nature of the companions' trip to the Shee of the Little Skellig and to that of the Sheep's Head could not be divulged, not as yet (as everyone seemed to be saying of everything, at the moment, she thought!). So, she supposed, it was necessary to invent another story to explain their voyage and their absence of several days.

"Then you will not have to go to Fantasie immediately, and the meeting can take place as planned?" was the only comment she made.

Aulfrin descended the dais where he had presumably sat to speak with Alégondine, and came to Eli's side, placing a hand on both her and his son's shoulder and saying, "Exactly so. So let us relax and await the others, who will be arriving this evening, and in the morning. I believe I heard the merry shell-music of Ferglas coming across the garden, and so he and Jizay are most probably downstairs already. And my dear and loyal Reyse will be here for supper. The two others arrive only for the council, early tomorrow."

He then continued, "Not as exhilarating as a swim in a fresh pool, my dearest Eli, but a hot bath with fragrant herbs and petals can be revitalising too. I suggest you enjoy just that! And now that we know that all the fairies and hounds of the company are alive, we can breathe a sigh of relief."

As in her human life, so here in Faërie, Eli was very happy to indulge in the pleasure of a steaming bath. Demoran called for Calenny to make the preparations, and the exhausted Eli withdrew to her bed-chamber, where a beautiful bathtub of carved white stone, thin-walled and as smooth as moleskin, was set in the centre of the room.

On her way, Piv flew beside her along the corridor. When they reached the door of the bedroom, he brushed his tiny hand over her hair, still rather tousled after her rapid flight and gallop through the Dappled Woods.

"There are no worries, my Eli-een," he piped softly in her ear. "The Lord Reyse will be here soon, and your brother lives. They are both great adventurers, and the Prince Finnir especially is protected by much enchantment. So have no worries!"

"I'm still enough of a human, I think, my darling Piv, to fear greatly when life and death are in the balance."

The pixie looked a little bewildered, and then he shook his head at her as if she were a silly child misunderstanding some simple and logical fact.

"*Life* is never in the balance, as you say my crazy little Eli, with *death*. Don't oppose them like that; it's nonsense! Life and death are not opposites: death can only have *birth* as its opposite --- though even that is wrong --- better to say as its complement, like summer to winter. *Life* can't be in 'the balance' with something else, and it has no opposite at all. It's all there is!"

Eli looked into the round cerulean eyes set in the tiny, rosy-cheeked face beneath its jaunty little green cap. The pixie hovered where he was, and now he grinned from ear to ear and gave her a little kiss on her forehead. He buzzed off again down the corridor as Eli's own eyes overflowed with hot tears.

As Calenny passed out of the door with a gracious inclination of her head, Eli went in. The room was filled with warm, moist mist and flowery perfumes. She had never been so happy to take a long, sweet, meditative and much-needed bath.

****

Too filled with her sentiments and questions to rejoin the others right away, Eli lay on her bed after her bath, with Lily's journal in her hands --- but unopened. She had intended to read a page or two, but she found that it was just the comforting proximity of her little moon that she desired, at least available to her in the form of her notebook. She had never missed Lily so much.

"Strange," she mused, "how for nearly fifty years I missed my father and now that I have him back, I miss my mother! Well, my foster-mother..."

From where Eli lay, she could see out a tall, narrow window into the west. Sunset had passed and the sky was growing darker, a plum-red turning to rich blue. The waxing crescent moon was framed by the slim window, and Eli had to shake her head. "No, not a 'foster-mother' at all: a very real and devoted and true mother. I have a fairy-mother, and I have a human-mother, both. And that's all there is to it."

She rose and went to return Lily's journal to her shoulder-bag, which was lying on the bedside table of inlaid apple-and-cherry-wood studded with tiny silver shells.

"Beauty seems so natural to this place", she added, continuing her interior monologue as she regarded the skilled craftsmanship and simple but harmonious design of the charming table. "Is *this* what it's like to be a princess, a fairy-princess? It's not at all like the definition of that role which I conjured up in my childish head when I was reading stories or watching films in the world! For one thing, there's no money here, so wealth and its luxuries are not a part of this royal life. And I've not really noticed any social distinction between classes, so there isn't a feeling of being an aristocrat or a titled noble --- *everything* seems noble here.

"But beauty and the respect *for* it --- and the appreciation *of* it --- seem to infuse this life in Faërie, for everyone and for everything. I have the feeling that the moon itself knows that she's beautiful, and feels blessed and confident and honoured because of that --- not proud of it or arrogant about it --- just grateful and normal and happy. She seems just naturally *pleased* to be beautiful, to be rising and setting, waxing and waning, coming and going across the paint-box palette of the skies.

"I think I should feel the same. I think that is what Lily would tell me. The only problem is, I really don't know if I'm *coming or going*! Ah, well... I have another few days here this time, and then another Visit. I will know, in the end."

As she went to slip the notebook back into her bag, she took out the white rose that Reyse had offered her --- still fresh and fragrant, and also the little phial of 'love-potion' from the diminutive black fairy. She smiled at both, but more so at the rose, she had to admit.

A warm tingle of anticipation rose into her cheeks and made her eyes shine, thinking that Reyse may have already arrived and she would see him shortly. And then a little counter-charge of irritation flashed into her mind, remembering the resentment she had felt when thinking of his coming into the human world, to Kilkenny, and having a romantic 'interlude' with her when he *knew* that she had rejected his advances in their fairy-life together.

She fingered the little bamboo phial, and wondered if taking a sip of it, when she was with Reyse this evening, would turn her heart in his favour --- and away from Finnir. It would be a solution, that. Already she found that her irritation with her champion and loyal suitor was evaporating as quickly as it had arisen.

Eli now recalled their passionate, but short-lived affair in Ireland when she had been in her twenties. Nearly thirty years ago that was, but in Eli's heart the fire of their little love-story was easily rekindled in memory, and almost in present reality. In her turbulent life of misguided loves and dead-end romances, those two weeks shone out like a miraculous moment of respite, a parenthesis amid the tearful and troubled tales of disappointment and disaster.

Why had it ended? She could not really recall. Liam had simply left one morning and she had travelled back to the States shortly afterwards. When she had found the tiny piece of paper on the pillow, with those lines from Keats, had she felt anguish or abandonment? Had her heart broken with sorrow?

"That's odd," she admitted now, "I can't remember feeling too sad. It was as if I knew that it was to end, but that I also knew that I'd find him again one day. Did he, magically, put that idea into my head, so that I would not be devastated by his departure? Did he play me to sleep that night with a lullaby on his *vielle*, as he did from his alcove in the great room of the seven arched windows in Fantasie, and enchant me so that I would not grieve?"

She looked intently now at the gift from the black fairy, and laughed out loud.

"I hardly need to drink this, I think. I'm nearly in love with Reyse again already!"

Eli replaced the phial in the bag, and opened Lily's journal to tuck the white rose into it. But the page she opened to already had a book-mark: the silver leaf.

Eli stared, and then closed her eyes for a second, almost as if she was trying to listen to a voice deep inside herself. But as soon as her eyes were closed, she could see a dreamy image of a *trompe-l'œil* window in the house of Banvowha. The moon was full, and there was a tiny, prancing unicorn at the margin of the dark woods. And trailing over the painted sill was a branch with delicate silver leaves upon it --- like this one. As her imagination grew more and more real and detailed, one leaf came away from the stem and was now falling, falling, pirouetting in the air as it fell into Eli's outstretched hand.

Coming back to herself with a jolt, Eli opened her eyes.

She rubbed her hands over her flushed face. And then she noticed that she had unwittingly closed the notebook --- and so she gingerly slipped it into the bag without another thought.

Or, if she *did* have a thought, it was not one but several: Where was Finnir now? What had he gone to the two other shees to discuss, and with whom? Who and what was the Queen Morliande, aside from her paternal grand-mother as a fairy? Oh, if only she could see Finnir once more, before she had to leave and go back through the Portal of Mermaid Island…

And forcing herself to silence these thoughts now, Eli turned to leave the room, just as Jizay's dear head appeared at the doorway, with a joyous bark to greet her and invite her to supper.

****

Reyse was there, his handsome face glowing with happiness to see Eli, his deep brown eyes sparkling and his broad shoulders and muscular arms --- beneath a light tunic of brick-red linen the hue of a chaffinch's breast-feathers --- reminding Eli once more of the pleasure of being his lover in a distant time and place. He raised his eyebrow at the look she gave him, so perhaps he guessed her thoughts.

Blushing slightly, Eli accepted the kiss that he bestowed on her hand and then took her seat at the table without meeting his eye again.

Only the three, or five, of them were there for this meal in a cosy, upstairs dining-room: Eli, Reyse and Aulfrin, plus the two dogs. Garo was still with his sister, evidently, and both would only return to Castle Davenia in the morning. And Demoran had been somewhat alarmed by reports brought to him by the two other guests: Muscari and Eochra, who had arrived while Eli was in her bath. There seemed to have been some disturbance in the northern reaches of the Dappled Woods; and therefore the Prince and his two horse-lords (or rather a lord and a lady) had hastily ridden off to take a look.

"The stars will come out after the rain," Aulfrin added, concluding this information, "and so they will have those gentle lights shining among the branches, like celestial lamps to light their way!"

"After the rain?!" inquired Eli. "I missed the rain-storm? I was looking forward to that!"

"I think you bathed and perhaps napped through it," laughed her father. "It was very brief, but quite dramatic and thunderous. All the fairies of Demoran's household were out in the gardens dancing, even aged Vintig --- a merry sight!"

"Oh," sighed Eli, "I wish I'd seen that. But at least I caught a glimpse of the new moon, in a lovely purple sky, just after sunset."

Reyse and the King exchanged glances, and then Aulfrin said softly, "So you were, indeed, napping, my dear Eli. No sunset or moonset to see this evening, for that was when the thunderstorm broke. The rain is only now clearing, and the skies are still partially roofed in dark cloud. But, as I say, the stars will appear again soon. And the riders will be back to give us their report of what they have discovered."

Eli ate in silence, puzzling over her visions and dreams. She seemed to be receiving regular visits from moons that were not there, or at least not visible. Well, she had to admit that she was living a very strange adventure here, and this seemed to be part of the process of coming back to Faërie, especially as she was a *Moon-Dancer* as the Princess Mélusine. Or she was being sent messages from Lily, or from some other source? Or was she quite mad?

Too baffled and at the same time too happy with her amazing situation and home-coming here to be upset, she decided to just let it be. If they were messages, she would finish by understanding them, one would hope. And if she were mad, well, she was a very happy mad-woman and enjoying her folly!

As she smiled, she glanced up and finally caught Reyse's eye. The feeling of being known and loved, for many centuries, flooded over her as the gallant fairy looked deeply into her own eyes. It was not an intrusive 'knowing' --- it was quite pleasant, in fact.

Muscari and Piv appeared as they finished their meal, joining them for a cup of some honeyed herbal-infusion. The lovely blue horse-lady had evidently found Periwinkle still dancing a gay gavotte with several of the smaller sprites and a visiting family of pixies, all around the circular basin of the garden-fountain.

"The little bright-green frogs," confided Piv, "were absolutely delirious with delight, and it was a treat to caper and cavort with them!" Eli laughed, but was now doubly sorry that she had missed the rain-dancing. She hoped there would be another occasion before her Visit was concluded.

Piv wrinkled up his little face in a silent guffaw, his eyes tight closed and his grin as mischievous as a child's. He opened his eyes and kissed Eli's cheek in passing as he flew up to find a place on the table's rim where he could sit and drink his mug of herbal tea.

Eochra and Muscari now entered the dining-room, and greetings were exchanged and chairs drawn up to the table for the new-comers. She was very pleased to meet the two fairies again, and now Demoran rejoined them as well. But their report to the King was, to Eli's ears, as suspicious and elusive as the tale Alégondine had told earlier.

It was clear to *her* that they had been off to a *rendez-vous* of their own; but perhaps, she reflected, she was now inclined to see mystery and half-told truths everywhere, for she felt herself being pulled deeper and deeper into the net of secrecy and hood-winking. Perhaps it was all to a good purpose, but it smacked of deception, to Eli, all the same. And she could feel that she was *expecting* it all around her now, like someone reading a detective story and trying to out-guess the author!

All they told the King was that great flocks of birds had been seen, flying before the storm, and that they had settled in the Dappled Woods. The Horse-Lords of upper Davenia were worried lest they be harbingers of some catastrophe --- for many of the fairies of the Star-Grazing fields still recalled the rebellion and occupation of Erreig and his dragons, and his closing of the Portal of the Fair Stair, and the ensuing panic among the wee-folk throughout the Woods. Many of the frightened fairies had, at that time, rushed into France before the Portal was locked and had found themselves refugees in the human-world for well over a year.

But no, it seemed that the birds were not ill-omens nor bearers of woeful tidings, after all, this time.

"Thunderbirds, no doubt," commented Aulfin as he sipped his beverage.

Eli noticed Muscari and Eochra exchange glances, but Demoran replied candidly.

"Not quite, for the true thunderbirds had long-since crossed the Dog-Delights and were gone to roost in the Woods of the Thousand-Toed Trees. These were Scholar Owls."

"Scholar Owls?" repeated the King, regarding his son with a questioning tilt of his head.

Demoran's calm demeanour held firm, and he nodded thoughtfully. "Yes, a large host. I think they know that Eli is here, and they may also have heard rumours of your anxiety for her safety. They most probably wished to be reassured that she was under no threat from Erreig. I spoke with several members of the flock, telling them that Eli was safe and sound in my Castle, and that seemed to suffice. They have flown north to their Island once more, all but a few."

Aufrin made no reply, but he looked down at Ferglas, reposing at his feet with his fine head lifted and listening intently to the Prince's words. The blue hound cleared his throat, rather pointedly, Eli noted, but said nothing either.

The conversation turned to the time for tomorrow's meeting, and also to that of breakfast (it was Piv who introduced this important subject) and then wishes for a good and peaceful night's sleep were exchanged and the room emptied. Save for Eli and her father, and their two dogs.

After a couple of moments' silence between them, Aulfrin looked at his changeling daughter and laughed with a little shrug.

"Please don't make too much eye contact with me during tomorrow's meeting, my Eli, or I shall surely laugh," he snickered. "They take themselves so seriously, these conspirators, and I really wish they would grant me a little more intelligence. Do they think me an old dotard of a king?! I'm only sixty-five, you know, well, if you don't count in centuries - -- for then I'm one-thousand-two-hundred-and-eighty-nine: but that's still young indeed for a fairy-king!"

Eli had to smile at her father. "I'm sure they *know* that you know more than you say, but they don't know how *much* you know exactly!" They both laughed now, and Aulfrin rose and led Eli towards the door with his arm about her shoulder.

Before they said good-night, Eli decided to ask her father something that had been tickling her mind: "You had *never* seen Alégondine since she was five, before today, father?"

Aulfrin stopped and sighed. He hugged her to him more closely, and Eli could feel --- once again ---- that tingling surge of fairy-energy that had first de-stabilised her so. She was more used to it now, but her father's close contact felt like the warm water of her bath filling her with fragrance and rippling force.

"No, never until today. She is very beautiful, and very like my Queen. You will enjoy meeting her tomorrow."

So, thought Eli, he knows much, but *not* that I have met my half-sister already at Leyano's Castle, *and* seen her at a distance in the Salley Woods. But then another thought struck her, and she could not --- did not wish to --- retain herself.

She said, almost as if it were a confession, "I saw you sailing, as you and Ferglas were coming to rejoin Brocéliana and me and Jizay, on my first Visit, when you brought her crescent-moon boat to the haven-harbour at the mouth of the River Ere. Rapture had taken me to the Point of Vision and looking out over the dark waters, I saw you sailing across the Whale Race. But there were *two* boats that crossed paths there and stopped, side by side, and the other was a great sail-boat. I couldn't see the sailor, but I somehow felt sure that it was Alégondine. She's a famous sailor, is she not? Didn't you speak with her then, when your two boats met one another?"

Aulfrin was very still, and then he led Eli back a little way into the room, and he looked deeply into her eyes. "You had a vision of that? How curious, and how lovely."

Eli was very quiet, for she saw that her father was moved, but she knew he would continue. He seemed to be weeping, but he smiled at the same time.

"That vision," he began slowly, "was shown you, I don't know why, to reveal to you *another* voyage that I had made, in the same wonderful boat as Brocéliana had used on that occasion. It was not when I sailed back to the haven to meet you and your sister a little further along the river. No, it was a voyage I made in that same craft ... last autumn. And the other boat was a very enchanted one indeed, summoned into being by the Lady Ecume for a very special guest to be brought to this my kingdom, a guest that had never before visited the land of Faërie, and who had longed to see it, with me, for just a few days. For just one privileged visit, before she died."

Eli was trembling violently, and also crying, but --- like her father --- she was smiling at the same time. Aulfrin concluded:

"It was our little moon; it was Lily.

"We both knew that she would die in the weeks or months ahead, for she was ready to do so, and she was quite old. An 'old woman' for a human, but as beautiful, or even more so, than she had been in her youth. She asked me if she might see my country, but she could not enter by one of the Portals, as this had been forbidden to her. An interdiction had been laid upon her; it was a kind of 'spell', which we call a *gessa*, and it dated from when I had died as Sean.

"I guessed it had originated with the Sage-Hermit, who has the power to ordain *gessa* --- though others of the Ancient and Great Ones may also do so. Lily's *gessa* was that she could not set foot on the land of my kingdom. But the dear and ingenious mermaid, the Lady Ecume, offered to escort her here by the paths that the mer-folk use to visit human seas. She agreed to fetch her in Bantry Bay, in a fairy-boat --- from which she could have access to our oceans and see much of the coast of Faërie and even sail a little way up one or two of the rivers."

Eli could hardly form her words clearly. "She came here? My dear moon, she really came to Faërie?"

"Yes, and I joined her at that moment you witnessed in your vision, and together, in the mermaid's sail-boat, we travelled in the north and west of my realm for three days and nights. She loved it and was so happy to see where you would one day return, and where her own true child had grown-up. She refused to be presented to her daughter though, and so Brocéliana does not know that her mother was ever here. My dear, dear Lily, she said it would break her heart to even behold our daughter at a distance. She could not do so. And I think she was wise, for both their sakes."

At last Eli found the composure to whisper, "I'm so very glad. I'm so grateful to the marvellous mermaid, and to you. I'm so happy for her."

Aulfrin held his daughter tight and close in a long embrace. His head resting on hers, he finally added, "I loved her, Eli. I loved Lily deeply, and in a part of my heart and soul I still do. I was so glad to allow her to glimpse this world. I longed, at that moment, to hold on to her and keep her here. Impossible, of course! And not even among *her* desires, in fact. She was very content to die a human death; she told me that, for she wanted to enter into the Light that she, as a Christian, had such faith in and so longed to experience. But now, now that she is gone and you are here, coming back to us, now I know in my heart where *my* heart lies.

"I know that I must somehow try to recapture the love of my lost Queen, my wife Rhynwanol, for I have kept her in exile and very far from me, and for much too long. I know I must try. But how to regain such a far-flung love, that is *not* among the things that I know. No, it is not clear to me at all."

****

Eli had returned to her bedroom, happy for her human mother and sorrowful for her fairy one. Having no real idea how the Queen Rhynwanol truly felt, now, about her estranged husband or even about her dragon-chieftain lover, Eli could not guess if the reconciliation of her parents would be likely, or even possible. She was coming to know, and love, her father once again --- but as for her mother, it was a different story. For the time being, Eli had precious little memory of the Queen, save for the glimpses she had been granted in ghostly vision.

But her weariness was enough to outweigh her churning thoughts, on many subjects, and she slept soundly.

The morning dawned bright and golden and, as Piv had asked, breakfast was served on the lawn to the south of the Castle, with its pretty view down through the trees to the short stretch of the river which joined the two Lakes. Beyond the willows which grew all along the banks of that stream, lay the path that Eli had taken, with Demoran, to come to his Castle on that first morning at the very end of April.

Now the company was standing assembled on the rain-washed grass, and Eli was feeling herself to be at ease and very much at home, already, among the folk of Faërie. Her brother, Demoran, stood at her side, sharing a bunch of remarkably sweet gooseberries with her. Alégondine was speaking with the King, with Garo close by but, it seemed, in respectful silence as he broke off pieces of a dark brown loaf to munch thoughtfully or share with Ferglas sitting very regally by his feet. Muscari and Eochra were engaged in cheerful conversation with Reyse, who occasionally flashed his smile in Eli's direction, or gave her a wink. And Piv, an enormous muffin cupped in his tiny hand, was astride Jizay, walking in lazy circles over the lawn; and both were chatting with a large tabby cat who strolled along beside them.

Eli had understood, from the discussion the evening before, that the official 'meeting' which had been convened for today would take place at in the afternoon. It seemed that fairies had a fondness for twilight, and they all wished to conclude their council with the story-telling session to honour the babe born in the snows. But as this was Ævnad's Day, the 17th of June, and therefore a sort of festival for them all, the morning would be spent in music and even dancing (without the need for rain!). As they finished their picnic breakfast on the lawn, musicians began to arrive from the doors of the Castle and out of the woods as well.

Harps and flutes, fiddles and pipes, gently began to infuse the air with their notes. Muscari pulled her tiny whistle from a pocket of her blue robe, and Garo went into the Castle and returned with his *bodhrán*. Attendants appeared from the same great doors, bearing a lute which they handed to the Prince Demoran, and to the Lord Reyse an ornate *vielle*. Eochra slipped away and returned with his little mandolin. Even the King extracted his silver flute from his breast pocket and joined in the music-making. And, to Eli's great joy, late in the morning Alégondine lent her sonorous voice to the concert and sang in some archaic fairy-language airs that brought many other fairies out onto the grass to dance in stately or energetic measure.

Hours seemed to go by without a pause in the music, song or dance; but finally trestle tables were arranged at the top of the lawn, near the Castle-steps, and goblets of clear, fruity wine were poured and wooden or leaf or giant-acorn bowls and plates appeared, placed all down the table and filled with delicacies from Vintig's gardens.

Eli found herself seated between Garo and Alégondine, with Muscari and Eochra facing her. The King's crystal dais elevated his golden-oak throne above the grass at the table's far end. Beside him were Demoran on his right and Reyse on his left. At the other end of the table Periwinkle was perched, with his little legs crossed tailor-fashion, on a comfy cushion of green cloth to match his cap, and beside him --- also on the table --- sat Ruilly the rabbit. The hounds, Jizay and Ferglas, were both seated contentedly beside Eli and the King, respectively. During their meal, many fairies continued to wander over the grass, or among the trees, playing, laughing and singing snatches of song.

When the luncheon was ended, all the guests remained where they were, but the mood of the gathering changed profoundly. The other fairies had all disappeared and the lawn was now very quiet, except for the sounds of nearby bird-song. The sun was bright and warm overhead still, but now moving a little to the west, and the nearby trees were beginning to cast patterns of leaf-and-branch shadows that seemed to cool the air.

Or was it the slight tension regarding the conversation to come, which made the atmosphere seem a bit cooler, and less warm and gay?

Aulfrin's voice was still rich and welcoming, however, as he solemnly invoked the memory of Ævnad and called the meeting to begin.

> *Fleeing from blame and shame and woe,*
> *Chased forth from hearth into the snow,*
> *Ævnad was driven by frail despair*
> *And fear.*
>
> *But what her crime and why her guilt?*
> *Should clan demand that blood be spilt*
> *Of innocent child conceived and born*
> *In love?*
>
> *Yea, here in Ævnad's name I dare*
> *To ask if Love can ever ere:*
> *If seeds be sown in great hearts they*
> *Grow strong.*

A Delicate Balance

Now we too wander in disgrace,
The two halves of my kingdom's face:
For Sun and Moon cannot unite
In fear.

I bring you together to hear my rhyme
And solve the riddle of our time.
For our child-of-the-snow is born of hate,
Not Love.

Fair Ævnad's babe is warmed by wings
Of a mighty Dove who at midnight brings
A fairy-blessing that her babe
Be strong.

Strong in the peace which is nature's part,
Skilled in that language and patient art
To heal and unite and to finally banish
All fear.

Let our snow-child, our conflict, cease,
And welcome the warmth of the dove of peace
Uniting Sun and Moon in one face
Of Love.

Only then shall we see with the eyes
Of the Sun that beholds in the starry skies
The Moon ever-full, ever blessed and
Ever strong.

Aulfrin finished his rhyme, and folded his hands on the table before him. He closed his deep green eyes and the calm hint of a smile settled on his lips.

It was a very unusual way to begin a meeting, Eli thought, at least a meeting intended to address political problems in the kingdom, issues such as division, rivalry and aggression. And it only became stranger, for following Aulfrin's recitation, everyone kept a very, very long silence.

It was not a surprised or affronted silence; it was more like a meditation, similar to the feeling Eli had experienced at the Haven of the Smiling Salmon. Some of the fairies closed their eyes, too. Most smiled. Piv stroked Ruilly's grey fur and seemed to be humming to himself as he swayed gently to and fro. It was only now, as Eli's eye stole around the table to look at each member of the gathering in turn, that she realised they were eleven, not counting Aulfrin. She hazarded a guess that this was done on purpose, symbolic of the eleven shees of the Alliance of the Spiralling Stars, with the King of this shee somehow positioned separately to that count, maybe overseeing the eleven stars from his own vantage point...

Just when she was beginning to wonder if the meeting was simply going to continue this way until night-time, in profound and contemplative silence, Eli noticed that her father had reached for the great pottery jug of wine, right before him on the table, and was pouring some into the goblet nearest to Garo.

"I am very glad to make your acquaintance, Garo of Quillir," he said, as he re-filled his own chalice now too. "May I ask you all to refill your cups, so that we can drink to this auspicious encounter?" And the wine-jug was duly passed around the table.

The King then continued, raising his chalice and saying: "To Garo, who has very kindly relieved the suffering of my servant Aytel with his skilful enchantments, and who is preparing to take up the role of the next Sage-Hermit, in two year's time --- if I am not mistaken? And who has accepted my invitation to meet and discuss the delicate situation which exists between his father and myself, between the land of Quillir and rest of the realm of Faërie. To Garo."

All drank, and there was another --- slightly more tense --- pause in the proceedings. Garo replied, now, to the King's toast.

"Thank you, Your Majesty. I am honoured to be welcomed here, and I share fully your desire to see peace and unity in this great Shee-Mor." He then added, "But I did not know that you were aware of my having been apprenticed to the Sage-Hermit and promised as his successor."

Aulfrin smiled and the light of the sun, twinkling through the high trees nearest to the Castle, made his emerald crown shine out with sudden force. Or *was* it the sunlight? Eli felt unsure, wondering if the gems could glisten of their own will, or in sympathy with the King's very thoughts.

"I know many things, and I learn more each day." Aulfrin spoke slowly, but with no tinge of annoyance or defensiveness in his voice. "I have known for many years now of the bargain your father made with Maelcraig, allowing him to secure a potent charm against my own magical powers and forcing me to abandon my human wife and child, and to return to this my fairy-kingdom."

Eli glanced, as unnoticeably as possible she hoped, around the table at the faces of the others. As she had been told by Broceliana at the gathering on Mermaid Island, the King was still unaware that his own father, the King Aulfrelas, was the present Sage-Hermit. Aulfrin clearly thought that his father had been washed out to sea from the Great Strand and had passed into a fairy's death. Did *all* the others know that this was not the case, save the King? Did Reyse know? Did Demoran?

But Aulfrin was concluding his remarks by adding, "I have much to reproach of your father Erreig, my dear Garo. That counter-charm and, of course, his seduction of my wife the Queen in the year 1367. But his proposal of you as Sage-Hermit I hold to be a boon for this realm. You are poised and placid, I see, and I deem you to be wise and filled with compassion. I understand, also, that you have acquired great skills in shape-changing and obviously you are adept in the healing-arts as well. I will not be sorry to see you replace Maelcraig."

"I am not so pleased by the arrangements as you are, Majesty," was Garo's steady but sincere reply. Eli's heart burned for the plight of Brocéliana, who would lose her beloved Garo when he became the next Hermit. Or possibly even sooner, when she herself became the cause for their separation and her half-sister would be required to return to the human world as the Princess Mélusine re-awakened on Scholar-Owl Island.

"Are you not?" was Aulfrin's only comment, and whether it was said with sympathy or somewhat ironically, Eli could not tell.

The King now addressed Alégondine, and then enlarged his discourse to include all the others present, as his sharp regard and twinkling eye attested.

"And glad in heart am I, also, to once again see and speak with you, Alégondine, once the little flower of my realm and --- so I thought then --- the full-sister to the Princess Mélusine. But now I feel inclined to say, before you all, that the ties and limitations of blood-relationships seem to me less binding than they once did. And it is you, dear Eli, who have brought this wisdom home to me, literally! For I see in you so much of the human woman I wedded and whom you held to be your own mother for fifty years of life. Though she is not of your true family, she has become your beloved mother in your human heart, and she has flooded your open and fearless spirit with her own love and beautiful character. She will never leave your heart now, even though you rediscover the love of your fairy-mother, also deep within your heart and --- I have no doubt --- in hers too.

"And so I feel inclined to say to you all that my own family has grown with Eli's changeling experience. I, too, will keep Lily as a treasure locked in *my* heart, and I will ever consider

Eli's half-sister Brocéliana, the child of Lily, as my own royal-fairy daughter --- as I now welcome Alégondine as a Princess of this my kingdom, although she is the child of my Queen but not of my lineage. She is the off-spring of my petty-rival, Erreig; but I wish to be clear in my words now, to you all, concerning the Dragon-Lord.

"I *never* rose in aggression against Erreig, nor did the desire cross my thoughts, until he rose, first, against me. I am angered, of course, by the ever-deeper division he has wrought between Sun-Singer and Moon-Dancer, though rumours of it had existed in this shee long before his time. Indeed, his power is not *so* great, for he could not have orchestrated such dissention had it not been ripening in the minds and spirits of my subjects long before. Many in this shee have feared our communication and sometime integration with the human lands; and they only needed Erreig to take his stand before me, to face me squarely with their demands that the Portals be closed, once and forever, to all the voyages, back and forth, between fairies and men.

"But I know your opinion on this subject, all of you who have formed an Alliance --- albeit 'behind my back'! --- between the eleven shees of Greater Faërie. And you are right in what you read between the dividing-lines, as it were, of Erreig's policies, born of his own fears. The question is not only if Faërie should remain accessible to humans, and if we should retain our privilege of visiting and oftimes influencing their world. The question is larger than that: should Faërie, all of Faërie, recognise frontiers or boundaries at all?! The Alliance would have us move towards total unification, throughout the world of fairies and with the world of men also; the very opposite of Erreig's egoic designs to make more and more divisions and ever more insulating walls between us --- even between the fairies of this the Shee Mor."

Eli's heart was pounding, with emotion, with pride to be the daughter of Aulfrin, with joy at his words. But his next, and concluding, speech made her catch her breath with sudden concern.

"But you are acting, all of you, rashly and subversively," he said, as if reprimanding a naughty child, Eli thought. "I am the King of this realm, and your Alliance is operating without my authority or even my advice. This angers me also. I think I might have been granted the respect of your confidence and I might have been asked for aid in the accomplishments, or at least the furtherance, of your plans.

"I am King, as I say, and after me my heir will come to the throne of this shee. Seven of the shees of the Eleven Stars are ruled by royal fairies. One is led by a matriarch of holy mien, and three are governed by great clans of noble fairies, though they do not call themselves 'royal'. I would not agree to these eleven islands becoming one confederacy without the compliance of all of these great fairies, and as almost all of you here owe your present allegiance to me, I would suggest that you begin by aiding me in the recovery of Quillir and the unification of this, the Shee Mor. The Portals of this Shee must be securely protected and guarded, but kept open to frequent exchanges, before we begin to weave a single unity out of all the isles of the eleven shees. And this will be *my* task, with your support, and not *yours* without *mine*! I would like to imagine that we may all work together, and at a calm and serene pace, to realise our goals."

Now it was clear that it was not only Eli who was holding her breath. All the guests around the table seemed to have stopped still, with reverence or remorse or at least deep reflection, at Aulfrin's words. All but Piv.

"Your Majesty, my darling King Aulfrin," piped the fluty voice from the far end of the table, "the Prince Finnir is not here, and neither --- really --- is the Princess Mélusine. And there are perhaps other fairies working from their own shees along similar lines. I'm sure there are great voices in the choir which are not singing with us today."

Far from being indignant at the interruption of the tiny voice and his remarks, Aulfrin looked with great respect down the table and nodded slightly.

"And what do you wish to suggest to me, with this reminder, dear Periwinkle? I am very happy, indeed, to hear your wisdom."

"Well, my dear Majesty, it's just this," explained Piv, now standing up on his short and stocky legs, his multi-coloured tunic reaching to his knees, his bright green wings flapping vigorously once and then becoming calm: "It's as you said of the fears of all the fairies of this kingdom, being there --- under the surface, as it were --- for ages before Erreig came along and gathered them under his standard. The fears were there first, and then all the fearful fairies banded together to close the Portals and put up a frontier to make Quillir like a land apart from all the rest. But it's probably the same for our Alliance.

"Many, many fairies must want it, must want us all to be one: the whole of Faërie without borders, and the freedom to mingle with humans and help them more and more. If they didn't, it couldn't have come to the surface in those mighty fairies who offer to lead the way. Fairies such as Finnir and Mélusine, and my sweet Garo here --- among others, they are very important because they are gifted leaders and the hopes of many come together in them. Yes, those hopes and the changes they bring come together, they bubble up to the surface, from deeper down and from far and near --- joining and becoming stronger.

"But that's how it must be, don't you see, as regards all such changes. It will not and cannot come from *you* --- with all due respect --- simply because you *are* the King! It *can't* go from the top down; the changes have to come from the bottom up, from the **everywhere** into the **here and now**. They have to come from us all, drop by drop, and then the kings and queens and noble clans will become drops too, very naturally. Just like it is in nature, in fact. You, even the grandest and the highest, can't *ordain* the changes, and force them to happen. You, the rulers, are like us all: you are each a lovely little-tiny smidgen of new energy that calls forth the new season --- for Faërie and for the humans too. And we're *all* equally as vital and as filled with the power of newness as every drop of rain that tickles springtime out of the earth!"

Eli would have loved Piv to continue forever, for his words glowed inside her as she heard them and made her feel warm and hopeful and happy.

But suddenly his tone changed, and as it did, a dizziness came over her and she slumped to her right. Garo caught her before she fell, and Reyse left his chair and hurried to support her as well. Before she fainted, she heard Piv's chiming voice, though it seemed very far away now.

"Sire!" cried the pixie, pointing up beside the slanted rooftops of the towers of Castle Davenia, where the tall trees grew beside the Entrance Steps, "the Scholar-Owls are there, swooping down in huge flocks --- many, *many* of them... Something has happened to Mélusine on their Island!"

****

A Delicate Balance

Chapter Eighteen:
Turning Fear to Light

Reyse's hand was holding hers when Eli awoke in a fragrant, warm room, dimly lit by several candles and very quiet. She was still a bit confused and had trouble focusing her eyes for several minutes. The room seemed to her to be veiled in mist or fog, but as she recovered a more normal vision, she realised that the bed was hung with diaphanous curtains of white lace spun from usnea-lichen (or Old Man's Beard), as were the windows. At one of these was the faint image of a half-moon, dreamlike and blurry through the drapes.

"Good evening, my Lady Eli," said Reyse, with a very audible sigh of profound relief. "I was afraid you would sleep right up until the end of your Visit and have to be carried back through the Portal of Dawn Rock by a flock of seagulls!"

A smile brought Eli's mouth back to life, and she, too, sighed deeply. And then she murmured a soft "hello".

Continuing to speak slowly and in a very relaxed tone, she asked, "I've been asleep a long time, then, Reyse? I can remember Piv saying that the Scholar-Owls were all around us, or something like that. I'm afraid I brought a sudden curtain down on the King's meeting with his eleven guests. What a pity, it seemed to be a good thing, I thought, that he could address you all as he did, and what Piv said was splendid…"

"You remember a great deal, and even the number of those at table! Good, good. You are come fully back to where you should be, then. I really had no doubt that you would."

He stood and helped Eli to sit up a little in the bed, then he sat again on the edge of the soft mattress, facing her, and offered her a cup of water with a perfume like a bouquet of lilac and sweet-peas. She could now see that Jizay was there too, lying --- with a smile on his uplifted head --- just beside the bed.

"And don't fret at curtailing the *spoken* part of the meeting, my dear Eli," resumed Reyse as she drank. "Most was said between us during the music and dancing, as is usual with fairies. Much was said, much was kept secret, much was suggested… Fairies love such riddling. Did you notice, too, all the perky red heads of the cunning foxes poking out from the bushes beneath the trees?! Ha, there was plenty of fox-play in the air all the day! But Aulfrin *had* to make a speech too --- perhaps almost more for your benefit than for ours."

"But what happened to me, when the Owls arrived?" queried Eli, allowing Reyse to take her hand once again.

"Let us not go too quickly," cautioned her companion. "You've had a rather severe shock, and though you sound clear-headed and yourself again now, I would advise relaxing tonight, and hearing all the news tomorrow. You're still safe and sound in Castle Davenia; and it's only the 19th of June, by the way, so you have all of tomorrow and then your return to the human world on the afternoon of the 21st, from Leyano's Portal. You've been unconscious for two days."

Eli, quite *unlike* her habitual ungovernable and impatient self, accepted Reyse's advice without question, and added only, "And it's the half-moon tonight, how nice. And you're here, a Lord of the Half-Moon Horses…"

Reyse laughed and bent to kiss her forehead.

"Sleep now, but a normal and healthful sleep, little Moon-Dancer," he said. "I am in the adjacent room, and I will play you a slumber-song to bless your rest. We'll talk more, with your father and Demoran, in the morning."

Eli slipped down again onto her pillow and reached her hand over the side of the bed to caress Jizay. The strains of Reyse's *vielle*-music floated out of the room's anti-chamber, beyond further flimsy curtains of white web-like fabric. She was soon asleep.

On the morrow, Jizay awakened her with a kiss on her hand, which in her dreams corresponded to the sensation of another kiss from other lips. Eli emitted a little moan of pleasure, and opened her eyes. As she did so, Calenny came into the room.

"Would you accept my help, Your Highness, for washing and dressing?" asked the gentle, youthful voice.

"I think I can manage, dear Calenny. I feel alright now. Thank you."

Indeed, Eli found it hard to imagine that she had been in a faint, or perhaps even a kind of coma, for two days. She felt strong and rested now. Perhaps it was Reyse's magical music that had helped to restore her to full vigour.

Her face and neck splashed, Eli donned a comfortable gown of yellow, in a velvety fabric as downy as hibiscus petals and patterned like the leaves of variegated lavatera-tree-mallow. She and Jizay were just leaving her bedroom when Reyse appeared at the door, and offered his arm to escort her downstairs.

Demoran rose immediately from his place at the breakfast-table and came swiftly to greet her, with his happy face and his mottled green and golden eyes shining. Aulfrin stood at his place and held a chair ready for Eli to sit beside him.

"I'm sorry I made such a dramatic end to your meeting on Ævnad's Day," began Eli. "I suppose you never got to tell her story in full that evening."

"No matter, no matter," retorted her father, pouring her a generous bowl of tea. "The tale is well-known to us all. You may hear it next year!"

Demoran, still beaming at his sister, remarked, "You resemble...yourself, my dear Eli, very much. You are a very fairy-like human, in fact."

Eli gave him a puzzled look, but Aulfrin laughed. "We had just been saying that we would tell you, this morning, what happened and not conceal the *truly* dramatic nature of the events. The real drama, in fact, was not your fainting at table, my dearest daughter; it was the sleep-walking of your ghost on Scholar-Owl Island.

"My son went with Muscari and Eochra as soon as the Owls gave us the news, and so he has seen your phantom-form. He remarked, as soon as he returned, that he was struck by how you have truly kept her likeness in your human life --- which is not always the case with changelings."

Demoran added, "For a woman coming back from *their* world, you do not look entirely human, my dear sister. Mélusine, as she sleeps again now on the Island of the Owls, is your twin."

Eli glanced quickly around the table at all three of the fairies there. "She *awoke* then --- I mean, *I* awoke?!"

"One could say that you were *awakened*," corrected her father.

"By whom?" asked Eli, not sure at all how her two lives overlapped or co-existed, and how it was that she could be disturbed in her state of limbo.

Demoran announced the answer in a rather hushed tone: "By Erreig."

After a moment, he continued, "Erreig seized his opportunity, knowing --- from what source we are not sure --- that those who might hinder him were well-occupied here and further afield, to visit you in your sacred place of repose. We, Muscari and Eochra and myself, had spoken with the Owls only the day before, as you may recall, for they had felt an uneasiness in the air and were come into the Dappled Woods to seek more information. Unfortunately, we reassured them, and that was very foolish. We had thought, all three of us, that they had heard of the attack on Aytel and also knew that Erreig had been seen, as we then knew as well, north of the Turquoise Mountains --- searching for news of Finnir. We told them that you were safe here in my Castle, for we thought it was for the changeling Eli that they feared."

"It turns out that it was not what they sensed at all, those threats to you *as Eli*," said Reyse, taking up the story. "They had felt that Erreig was about to venture into Davenia. They could feel his intentions in the air, I think. You see, he has finally learned that the *Princess Mélusine* was the changeling babe of Aulfrin in the human world. He did not have this information before, and I myself wonder if it was not extracted from Aytel, weakened in body and perhaps rendered rather vulnerable, and still --- at that time --- detained in the White Dragon Fortress. In any case, Erreig and Bawn arrived on the morning of Ævnad's Day on Scholar Owl Island. I have asked myself if he was not intent on taking the sleeping body of Mélusine from her resting-place; but perhaps he had other plans."

Eli gasped, for somehow imaging herself being kidnapped by Erreig, even in her ghost-form, made shudders of fear and loathing run up her spine.

Aulfrin spoke again now. "What he *did* truly plan, we cannot know exactly. To hold you hostage, or to ransom? To use Mélusine to bargain with the Moon-Dancers as he had intended to do when he captured your two brothers fifty years ago? Or did he have even more sinister ideas? Maybe he thought to find you, like Aytel, at his mercy in your liminal state, and more open to some of his more perverse proposals. We do not know and never shall, perhaps.

"For even sound asleep, it would appear, you are far from weak or malleable! For, just as you had vowed to him once before what you would do, my incredible Princess, you took it upon *yourself* to bring his scheme down in ruins."

"Did I?!" exclaimed Eli. "How did I do that?"

Reyse, she noted, was smiling very proudly at her as Aulfrin replied. "You arose from your bier --- how that is possible, I cannot even imagine myself --- and you confronted him, in your phantom-form. I have never heard tell of such power; I surmise that it is linked to your Great Charm, or perhaps you had the help of one of your protectors and guides. In any case, it is clear that you did not have to do more than show yourself fully awakened and aware; for without any confrontation of words, according to the Owl-guardians, Erreig fled. Now, perhaps you spoke to him in silence. But the Owls that were there heard nothing, and they are normally very skilled in silent speech."

"The Owls were there, but they could not prevent Erreig's entry?" whispered Eli.

"That is what we are trying, still, to understand," conceded Demoran. "They were immobilised and rendered stiff as stone, as I had been --- centuries ago --- when the Sage-Hermit came to the City of Fantasie and lifted the child Alégondine away from my care and company. Was the Sage-Hermit involved in Erreig's penetration of the sealed and hollowed chamber on Scholar-Owl Island? Or has the Dragon-Lord himself mastered such charms? In any case, the Owls could see all that happened, and supposedly could hear as well --- had anything been said by Mélusine --- but they could do nothing to hinder Erreig."

"But you yourself could," interjected Reyse.

"I have told you before, my dearest Eli," said the King with a knowing nod, "Erreig fears you. And whether frightened by your floating form or some perilous utterance that passed from your silent and shrouded figure to his ears only, the Dragon-

Chieftain quailed and fled. At the very door of your vault, he mounted Bawn with a deft leap into the air as she took flight, just as Demoran and his companions arrived on the Island and caught sight of <u>you</u> hovering at the entrance to your cavern-chamber."

"When I reached your bier," concluded Demoran now, "you were already again lying in state --- or, I should say, Mélusine was. But Eli, here at my Castle, had passed into a deathly faint. We were very worried, for if the spectre of the true fairy is somehow fully revived, *prematurely*, the changeling will fade like a withered leaf, only much more quickly. But, as I now read the events, my remarkable little sister, I think you had *planned* for just such an eventuality. Somehow, you had written this response to a 'possible invasion into your vault' into your own transformation, into the contract you had conceived, yourself, for your adventure. Or, perhaps, there was sufficient anger in you at the effrontery of Erreig's intrusion, to stir your heart and spirit to stop him."

"And thereafter, rather than giving chase to Erreig," added Reyse, "the three fairies left the Island and returned here, for you were rendered very fragile indeed by the event, and we have all had two days of grave concern.

"But here you are, and looking as well as ever. I must agree, you are remarkable."

They continued their breakfast, and when they had finished, Eli asked, "And where are the others? Has everyone else left now? Did *anyone* go chasing after Erreig?"

"The Horse-Lords have spent these past two days patrolling Davenia; that is Eochra and his host, and several of the household of Muscari too," explained Demoran. "And Piv went as far as Aumelas-Pen with Garo and Alégondine, where he turned aside to the Silver City and to the Gardens about the Great Trees for what insights they might offer, and Erreig's children went on to Quillir. I will not say that they were 'chasing' their father back, but they will certainly be seeking to learn more of what he was attempting to do. They also arranged for the return of Aytel, not to Barrywood directly, but to Fantasie. He arrived there yesterday, we have learned from the Heron-Fairy, and there --- after your departure, dear Eli --- our father will be able to speak with him as he continues his recovery and convalescence."

Aulfrin added, "And Ferglas and many of his family have gone ahead of us, into the east and along the banks of the Shooting Star Lake, to make certain that no dangers lurk along our route. For we must take you back to Mermaid Island before tomorrow, my dearest Eli. You leave from there on the afternoon of the 21st, your birthday --- as Mélusine." Aulfrin's voice was tinged with a little sorrow, but now his tone became lighter. "But your *next* Visit will be your last, and then you will be evermore here in Faërie as the Princess you are, and your sleeping 'twin' will be able to awaken for good!"

"Do you feel up to riding Peronne back to Sea-Horse Bay, Eli, or would you prefer travelling by land than by air?" Reyse inquired.

She hesitated, and the King said, "No need to decide immediately. Take a walk in the gardens with Jizay and Reyse, if you like, my girl. We should leave later this morning, if possible, or just after lunch at the latest. It is a long route, but if we leave early we will be able to take it at a steady and unhurried pace."

"Thank you, father. I'm sure I'll be alright to go this morning. How long, in all, will our journey take?"

"With the wind at our backs, as it is today, we should make the flight in about five hours, maybe six. Yes, it's a good distance: not far short of four-hundred miles. But Peronne is a fine mount and will bear you smoothly and swiftly. I think flying would be best, and safest. It will afford us the best view of all that passes along the way as well."

His daughter assented to this with a nod, and sipped her tea slowly. And then she looked up, again, at the King.

"Father?" she ventured, almost --- Aulfrin detected --- with a hint of her somewhat cheeky personality shining through, "On my first Visit home, you gave me back Jizay, my hound of joy. And on this one, you gave me Peronne to ride once again. What is left to offer me for my third?!"

The King smiled merrily and his forest-green eyes were dancing. He was clearly extremely glad to see Eli well and come back to herself again. He leaned towards her and whispered in her ear.

"Your own wings, my dearest girl. Your own fairy-wings."

Eli's eyes grew as large as turquoise plums and her expression turned to pure wonder. But she could say nothing, not a word.

****

"Will I see any of the other fairies again, on this Visit, do you know, Reyse?"

Eli's tone was a little sad, as they wandered together about the tidy flower-beds, noisy with the rainbow-striped bees. Jizay conversed with the frogs sitting all around the edges of the central fountain and Vintig pottered happily in a large patch of strawberries further off.

"Whom did you particularly wish to see again?" he rejoined, tightening his grip on her hand, laid on his forearm as they walked arm in arm. "Garo, or Alégondine…or Finnir?"

Eli looked at her yellow-slippered feet, and not at Reyse, for she could feel that the colour was reddening in her cheeks.

"Yes, well, all of them, I suppose. But I was mostly thinking of Piv, in fact."

Reyse seemed relieved by this response, and laughed. "Well, that last personage in the list would not miss saying a farewell to you, and wishing you a Happy Birthday too! He and I have both planned to make the voyage, together, to Mermaid Island, tomorrow morning. I go to the Silver City when you and your father depart from here. I will see Aytel if possible and then Periwinkle and I will ride forth this evening, and most probably travel through the starry night, under the just-past-half-moon, to arrive at Leyano's Golden Sand Castle for your birthday breakfast."

"While you're in Fantasie, will you see Aindel also? Has he returned there?"

"Aindel, of the Sheep's Head?" Reyse appeared to be taken aback by Eli's question. "You know Aindel, my Lady Eli? When and where did you cross paths with that wondrous fairy?!"

Eli hesitated, biting her lip for an instant and then opening her mouth to speak --- but immediately closing it again. "Once, at *The Tipsy Star*," she finally answered, as if she had been trying to recall. "Yes, Jizay and I went there, on our own, during my first Visit, and we chatted a bit. I should like to speak with him again."

She felt absolutely mystified, now, as to who knew what, and whom, even among the members of the Alliance! Did not Reyse *know* that Aindel had been at the meeting on Mermaid Island, nearly three weeks ago? Nor that he had come here, to Castle Davenia, the day before Ævnad's Day?

"I would think that you would indeed, for he is a fine and very delightful fairy," Reyse now said, relieving Eli in her turn, for he did not seem too surprised that they had met in the Silver City after all. "He is often in this shee, but he likes to keep his visits rather secret --- I'm even surprised that he gave you his name. He is of the royal clan of the Sheep's Head Shee and I do not think his father fully approves of his coming here. Why, I am not sure --- but most likely the King of that shee shares the opinion of the Sun-Singers, and is not in sympathy with the abolition of boundaries between the shees, or with comings and goings between them. That would be my guess.

"Aindel has travelled with Finnir and myself, but rarely in this the Shee Mor. Our adventures, ah many and marvellous and as wild as our youthfulness, were to very distant shees and even to the very limits of Faërie's oceans, where the first of the out-lying islands of even more blessed realms may be glimpsed."

Eli now glanced up into Reyse's fair and wise and slightly weathered face. She felt the familiarity of all of its contours and could not help but wonder if she would feel as at home in his arms as she did at his side. Was this love, she ventured to demand of herself.

His own eyes were looking up into the eastern sky, but Eli's could not follow them, for he was looking directly at the sun, climbing now high over the tallest trees of the Dappled Woods which bordered Red Triskel Lake. She recalled that, in her apartment in Saintes, Reyse had also looked out, straight at the sun.

"He is an eagle, indeed," she said to herself. "He is Iolar MacReyse-Roic, the Eagle of the Clan of the Half-Moon Horses. And he loves me. How wonderful that seems to me, at this moment. But I just don't know, yet, if what I feel for Reyse is love, or admiration, or amazement, or just being completely at ease in his presence.

"And I don't think I will know until I come back here, as who I really am," she concluded, still silently unravelling her thoughts.

Reyse now turned his head of long, wavy brown hair and looked back to the northern doors of the Castle. Demoran was walking towards them. Before her brother reached them, Reyse looked deeply into Eli's eyes, now, for just a second.

"I will leave you to take *your* leave of your brother, my Lady. And I will ride back to Fantasie and to our little pixie friend. We will both see you tomorrow morning. My heart is ever turned and attuned to you, Eli, and I remain at your service, pledging you my protection forever."

A Delicate Balance

Eli felt herself beginning to tremble, but she could not make a reply. Reyse withdrew with a smile, as Demoran arrived at her side.

Her brother inclined his head, also with a warm smile, in Reyse's direction, and then turned to his sister.

"You will be leaving my Castle shortly now, my dear Eli, and taking flight with our father for the Portal of Dawn Rock. I will be very glad to welcome you back to Faërie in the weeks ahead, and I hope it will be an occasion of rejoicing for your homecoming as Mélusine."

Eli thanked her handsome brother, and yet her words and tone of voice were rather sorrowful in reply to his gay good-wishes.

"I have been wondering about my third Visit, Demoran. I'm hesitating and I don't really know whom to talk to about it."

Demoran gave her his hand, and led her to a stone seat surrounded by lavender, alive with white butterflies and crazily-coloured bees.

"Tell me," he said simply.

Eli stroked the petal-soft fabric of her lovely yellow dress, and then she fumbled for a moment with the strands of her coppery hair that were falling into her eyes. Jizay came trotting over to her, and laid his head on her lap.

A thought came suddenly to Eli. "Oh, Jizay won't be flying across four-hundred miles of blue sky with us! And I'll warrant he won't be running that distance either. Do I say good-bye to you here, my hound of joy?"

She heard his answer, warm and kind, just as she had always imagined the voice of Laurien, her make-believe dog, in her childhood. "I will await you here in the Dappled Woods, my mistress and my dear companion," he said silently. "I will be here when you return to Faërie."

Eli's eyes were flooding with tears as she bent over slightly and laid her head on Jizay's. He licked her cheeks, and as she straightened up again, he turned and walked, very nobly Eli thought, towards the billowing gauze curtains of the library further along the garden's boundaries.

She turned back to Demoran. He asked her, "What is making you hesitate about coming back to your life here, my dear sister?"

Eli wiped her hand over her wet eyes, and smiled a bit wanly at the fairy beside her. She exhaled deeply. And then she began to speak, but rather quickly.

"Well, if and when I return, Brocéliana will have to leave --- and she is in love with Garo, and I find that very sad. In two years, in any case, he will leave her to become the Sage-Hermit; so maybe I should at least wait those two years. And then there's Erreig, and his hunting of me or fearing me or trying to woo me. It's a very tense situation, and I feel unable to deal with it at all in human-form and during my third Visit it may become dangerous or even deadly, and it frightens me not a little. And...I've met someone here, and I feel so drawn to him, and I know I cannot be with him, and that it's someone *else* whom I *should* love and whom our father wishes me to be with, and even marry --- and I'm afraid that I don't even know if I *ever* want to marry!

"And then, too, I don't know what *good* I can do here in this magical place, living an enchanted and altogether privileged royal-fairy-life, when I see so much that I could maybe do in the world. I've learned such a lot *here*, and it is so very urgent that humans learn these things too --- or that's what I think, what I've come to believe. I feel I could do more good there than here; for here I will only cause problems, I'm afraid."

Demoran was smiling, not at all wanly, but very lovingly. One of his many cats walked by and jumped on his lap; he stroked it slowly and, evidently, just as it most liked --- by the sound of its bombinating purr.

"Fear makes a poor counsellor," he said at last. "And that's a great many fears running about in your head, my sweet Eli.

And it's rather strange, is it not, to use such words together, as you have linked in your statements: *love* and *sadness*, for instance, or even the word *should* coupled with that word *love*. They have little to do with one another.

"May I tell you a little story about fear, which we learn in Faërie when we are children, and that you have alas forgotten, it would seem?

*"An old woodland leprechaun was sitting one day on his toadstool in the sunny woods, but he was ill-at-ease. For he had one great and terrifying <u>fear</u>, and it was very odd for a leprechaun, especially one living in the woods of Faërie. For he was afraid of **spiders** (imagine such a thing!). And just at this moment, he had glanced over at another nearby toadstool and, as he squinted and blinked one eye in the playful light dappling the leaf-mould of the forest-ground, he saw an **enormous** spider sitting on the cap of the giant mushroom near him. He was about to jump right out of his skin with terror, when all of a sudden something tickled his face. Well, he had very long and bushy eyebrows, and from the stiff, curly hairs of the one over his open, but squinting, eye a tiny, tiny spider had descended on its silky thread.*

*"In a flash, he realised that what he had taken to be a **giant** spider a little way off on the other toadstool, was in fact only a trick played by his half-closed eye: for it was this minuscule little spider-een that he had seen right before his eye! He gently took the silken thread between two fingers and held the teeny spider before him to say 'hello'. She was, in fact, just beautiful and almost comical as she dangled there. She was not at all terrifying, of course; and he laughed so heartily at himself that he cured his fear of spiders forever, and thereafter he found them --- and all of his fears --- to be very small and really quite funny and even, sometimes, extremely beautiful things which taught him very profound lessons."*

"Come now," continued Demoran, taking Eli by the hand and --- as she stood --- wiping the tear that was now tickling *her* face, "Vintig is emerging from the stables with Peronne and Cynnabar, and you must begin your flight. And you should change into suitable garments for the trip, too. Your riding gear is laid-out for you in the small dressing-room off the Entrance Hall. Be quick, brave sister of mine!"

When Eli re-appeared a few minutes later, Aulfrin was standing with his son, and the horses were indeed impatiently pawing at the ground where they waited beside Vintig at the doors of the stables.

"May the blessings of the Dappled Woods be upon you, and the silver light of the Moon spread itself before your dancing feet," Demoran said, and then he kissed her cheek. And Eli went with the King to begin their long journey to Sea-Horse Bay.

****

Skirting the southern banks of the Swan's Joy River, perhaps a hundred feet below them, Eli could see the jewel-like colours of the great Rose-Beds. She wondered, once again, if it was among those very roses that she had passed her first Initiation.

Not long after, the purples and pinks of the Rhododendron Woods appeared to their left, and far off to their right, in the south, Eli could just glimpse shining silver towers over the tree-tops, with swirling lights rising behind them: the fair City of Fantasie. She stroked Peronne's broad, arched neck as it rose and fell with his air-stride, and she whispered, "I'll be back, Peronne. I'll ride back here with you. I'll turn again my wind-horse feet to the silver turrets of Fantasie, to the red and yellow banners of my pure beginnings, to my Moon and my Sun."

Peronne whinnied with joy, and Aulfrin turned to look at them both, from where he and Cynnabar glided along a few yards off.

"We'll be making a landing just to the north of Shooting Star Lake," he called, "another hour or so to go before that, though; you're not too tired, are you?"

"Not at all tired, my dear father," Eli called back. "I'm galloping over a road of pure sunshine!"

The King laughed, while he urged the horses into a slightly faster flying-pace as the warm breeze gently pushed them along.

"There's someone here that I'd like you to meet, Eli."

They had just landed in a rich meadow of tall, feathery grasses. The high, swaying bamboos of the Fire-Bird Forest were about ten miles to the north; the broad blue of the starry Lake roughly the same distance to the south. The King asked his daughter to 'relax' her regard and breathe deeply…

As Eli looked around her --- admiring the mix of yellow and greens, off-whites and occasional pinks of the brushy grasses --- she began to discern faces here and there, as she had along the shore of the Lake earlier in her Visit. They faded and then grew clear once again, and they all had wise, bright eyes and some had funny, long noses and many were grinning.

"Continue to look carefully, though in utter relaxation, and the village will come into focus," instructed Aulfrin. Sure enough, a few minutes later the very high stems of wavering grass a little further back, behind the foreground ones, were changing into huts and houses. Soon Eli saw that they were in a village-green, as it were, surrounded by thatched cottages whose walls seemed, also, to be made of grass and straw.

"What a wonderful place!" she enthused. "Where are we?"

"Green Man's Glade, I suppose one could translate the name. Charming, isn't it? Ah, here is the gentleman I wished to present to you, my dear Eli. Garv-Feyar, this is my daughter, Eli, or more correctly the Princess Mélusine."

"My warmest and most respectful greetings, Your Highness," said Garv-Feyar, coming out from among the bristly fronds of feather-grasses, as high as his chest. He bowed to the King, and to Eli, and then ushered them into his straw-cottage.

Eli found herself in a rustic and golden room, where everything was made of hay or straw or grass: table, chairs, cupboards, shelves and even the bowls and boxes *on* the shelves! On the rushy table were chunks of bread, dried fruits and fresh ones, nuts and honey. The only household articles *not* made of grass or straw were the tankards, which appeared to be of turned wood, and which were filled with frothy, amber beer.

It was soon clear why Aulfrin had desired this meeting, and Eli was as fascinated as her father had anticipated.

"Garv-Feyar," explained the King, "will be leaving Faërie in ten days' time, and going back to the human world. He was taken from his cradle seventy years ago, when one of the fairies native to this village chose to become a changeling, just as you did, Eli. He has lived among us since then, but now the fairy in question has completed his three Visits home and has decided to return. And so Garv-Feyar will be returning to his own country."

Eli regarded with curiosity the seventy-year-old fairy, or man in fact; but he looked much younger than she did at fifty. "*You* are a human?" she inquired in awe. "But you look just like a fairy, and very youthful!"

"Aha! That is the way of it here!" giggled the gentleman with hair the colour of hay and eyes almost as blue and clear as Finnir's. "And haven't I enjoyed it! Oh ho, yes! But I'm not sorry, either, to be going back. I've lived here a wondrous long spell, and I've completed my Initiations and then I began to age very slowly, you know, one year for every twenty-five. A fine fairy-trick *that* is! I'm born seventy years ago, as your great and good father the King says, but in fact I was only eighteen when I finished my final Initiation, and so in the past fifty-two years I've only aged two!! Isn't it a lark?! I'm only twenty as a fairy, and I've asked to go back into my human place, or near to it, at that very age. Of course, I won't recall my life here, but I believe that it will cling to me, if you take my meaning, Your good Highness. I'll be a wise and happy twenty-year-old, with no memories of any past to weight upon him and all the music and joy of the fairy-folk hidden somewhere deep inside. Won't it be grand?!" And the wonderful young man chuckled and swigged his delicious beer.

"Where do you go home *to*?" asked Eli. "Where are you from?"

"I was snatched away by fairies from the Portal of Barrywood, for my people came from Inchigeelagh in the west of Ireland, not too far from where the Lee rises in Gougane Barra --- do you know the place, Your Highness?"

Aulfrin glanced, under his red eyebrows, in Eli's direction.

"Yes, yes, I know Gougane Barra. It's a beautiful spot. And what will you do, Garv-Feyar, when you find yourself, well, just suddenly there with no home or people that you know?"

This question seemed to amaze Garv-Feyar. "But the powers-that-be, here in Faërie, aren't they giving me my home to take with me?"

Now it was Eli's turn to be perplexed. "What do you mean, *giving* you your home?"

The merry fairy-man replaced his tankard on the straw table and slapped his two hands on his chest. "My body, my own body. Not quite this one, for the points in my ears with their bright yellow gems in them won't be there no longer, it's true. But they give me a body, just like the human I would have been if I'd growed-up there! And my body is my home, isn't it now? And all the trees and beasts and persons and stars, they'll all be my family. And I can keep, they tell me, all the skills I've learnt here, and that's a mighty haystack of good learning, and will surely see me through. For I can sow and reap, and grow and tend, and talk to bees and turn a fine piece of wood…and I make a good beer, don't you think?"

"Delicious! And I think *that* will surely be held in your favour in West Cork," laughed Eli, joining in the contagious chuckling of Garv-Feyar. "I wish you every good fortune and great happiness in your human life. Maybe we'll meet in Ireland!"

"Ah, but I won't recognise you, Your Highness, for I will have forgotten our meeting today. But you might know me if you spot me; at least I can tell you that I've chosen the name of <u>Brian</u>, though that's common enough there, so it may be of little help..."

"Well, if I'm in Inchigeelagh, I'll look for a happy and very-much-at-home Brian, then!"

Aulfrin looked again, slightly awry, at Eli, but he added nothing to her comments, except to say that it was time they be on their way.

Eli arched one eyebrow, also, as she glanced at her father when they reached the horses. Yes, an interesting choice it was indeed, to present this one of his subjects to her. She shook her head with a grin. Her father's smile flashed, as bright and sunny as the early afternoon.

Well refreshed now, they mounted and trotted lightly up and over the swaying grasses, following the direction of the breeze.

****

How beautiful it was, arriving back at Leyano's island-home.

Eli and Aulfrin had sailed quite slowly over the final long lengths of rolling countryside between the arms of the Queen's Ride River and that of the Jolly Fairy. As they had done so, Eli had had a hazy view of the margins of Barrywood to the south. The immense forest was dark and almost brooding in appearance, or was it almost muttering and sighing, in fact? A sound did indeed seem to rise from the deep green, wavy sea of leafy arms --- akin to the constant song of the Great Trees of Fantasie. Barrywood was clearly a mighty mass of inter-connected 'tree-beings,' so alive --- even from this distance of ten to twenty miles --- that a palpable energy throbbed through the clear air and enveloped Eli as she flew past.

As she had strained to see into the depth of the forest, Eli had noted a glint of silver-blue on the horizon. Far, far beyond the ranks of tall, chanting trees were the wide waters of the Inward Sea. In the midst of that huge body of waterfall-fed liquid enchantment was the Island of Windy Hill. But Eli could not see that far, and could only imagine it, with its white chapel and its exotic mimosa tree.

As they crossed the green waves of Sea-Horse Bay between the stony coast and Mermaid Island, they stepped-up their pace and then slowed again as they came into view of the Sand Castle. Leyano was on the western balcony, high up, overlooking the little cove where Eli and Muscari and Brocéliana had once bathed. He was dressed all in white, but his tunic and summery trousers were dyed by the sunset's first rays so that they appeared a rose-pink, like the flesh of a juicy watermelon, thought Eli! His dark red braids, all six, hung over his shoulders and in them Eli could see spots of bright blue where many turquoise stones glinted. In his ears, high-pointed and set close against his tanned face, gleamed his green peridot-gems. And from the centre of his forehead shone out the light of *Tohtet*, the precious yellow beetle-diamond. It seemed to be mirroring the setting sun, flaming like molten gold or like the searing-hot breath in the gaping jaws of a dragon.

Eli realised that she and her father were now weaving back and forth in the air, just as he and Reyse had done when bringing Peronne to her three weeks ago. As on that occasion, the horses finally spiralled down to the northern lawn of the Castle, and Leyano shortly appeared at the doorway and jogged down the steps to greet them.

Eli embraced her beautiful brother, and looked with deep emotion into his crimson-black eyes. She thought how like Peronne's they looked, for depth and rich hue --- but they had no lilies hidden in them! Only stars sparkling, almost mischievously.

"I will be sorry to leave tomorrow," she confessed, as they regarded on another.

"I will be sorry to see you do so," agreed Leyano. "But tonight you are still here! I have heard some reports, from fish and bird, of all the strange happenings of these past days, but there is surely more to tell. And I have news that may be of great importance, concerning Finnir," he added, speaking very softly now, and only to Eli, as they began to climb the steps together. "Come, we will nibble *buicuri* and sip green sea-wine and share our tidings!"

Her heart racing, Eli passed under the pale driftwood lintel of the doorway with Leyano, both of them following the King --- who was now several strides ahead --- into the wondrous Castle.

Although the Prince had received some accounts of the event, Aulfrin related the details of Mélusine's awakening on Scholar-Owl Island again, very much as he and Demoran and Reyse had told the tale to Eli. But this time he added a titbit of other news.

Aulfrin had deemed this detail which he was now about to reveal would have been too much for Eli to digest right away; and so he had decided to wait until they were here, on the threshold of her departure and far away from both Quillir and Davenia, before sharing it with her.

The greatest of the Owls, their chief and a high-official in the King's intimate circle of nobles, was *not* among those guarding Mélusine's body and so was not rendered still as a statue when Erreig was inside the vault. Instead, he had watched from his perch in one of the huge cedars close-by the resting place of the Princess, as Bawn bore her master away. And he had followed at a safe distance for many miles.

As increasing numbers of bats joined Erreig *en route* for Quillir, the Owl-Chieftain had swept upwards into the high cloud and sped forward until he was just *above* Bawn. He dipped out of the cloud-cover for only a moment, wreaking confusion among the bat-host and diving close beside Erreig, before turning swiftly and returning to his Island. But on his way home, he stopped to bring information of what he had seen to the King.

It appears that Erreig has taken a length of amethyst-mauve drapery from Mélusine's vault. It is a short scarf-like rectangle of almost invisible fabric that had fallen from the Princess's body and slipped to her feet as she stood to confront the intruder --- as was later confirmed by the immobilised Owl-host about her. Before he sped from the sacred cell, the Dragon-Lord had nimbly kicked-up the light-as-air material, and clasped it to his bare breast. The great Owl, noticing that the Dragon-Lord held something as he fled, had therefore followed hard after him, and had thus manoeuvred his flight so as to see it, still hugged against Erreig's dark skin as he sat astride Bawn.

"Is there a special power, some power over *me*, in such a thing?" gasped Eli, her fears rising once again.

Aulfrin shook his head. "I think not. But, of course, there may be. I was not aware of all of the subtleties of your preparations, nor of the charms laid on your mauve draperies at the time of your transformation. But why not put your fear aside, my daughter, and try to look from another angle…"

Attempting to steady her breathing, Eli had the inspiration to return in her thoughts to the children's tale told her by Demoran about the leprechaun frightened of spiders. But where, she wondered, was the beauty or comedy or other changed perspective in this apprehension she now felt: this new fear regarding Erreig being in possession of a piece of her shroud or ghostly-bedding?!

Slowly, as Leyano and the King waited, very calmly and patiently, Eli began to smile, for other thoughts were aringing in her mind, or memory. She spoke in a measured tone.

"I am greater, higher, more noble and more powerful, than Erreig," she commenced, speaking slowly but with growing conviction. "I am more loving and more honest. He may think to have stolen a prize or a sort of talisman that can work some charm of possession over me, but I think it much more likely that I *myself* can use the fabric, which has been in contact with my enchanted form for fifty years, to gain some insight or magical power of surveillance over *him*. He may, in fact, have made a tactical error by indulging in such a theft, for I might very well turn it back upon *him* and see into the depths of the heart against which it is clutched."

Aulfrin nearly cheered. "Now, **that's** my Princess talking! Aha, there you see with the eyes of the heart; you invoke your *own* power and you turn his mischief to your good and true advantage!"

Leyano was smiling very proudly too. "You have seen this, Eli, as our father says, with the eyes of the heart, and thus you begin to dilate the half-face of the Moon to become full at last. For with *the eyes and the heart* of the Sun we shall one day see the Moon ever-full; just as with *the eyes of your own heart* you, Eli, will one day know the fullness of your own power."

The King looked with renewed esteem at his youngest son, as he did at his daughter. As for Eli, she stood and walked to the eastern window, where she stared out at a huge waxing gibbous moon, already high in the darkening sky.

Aulfrin approached her after a moment or two, and with a gentle touch on her shoulder, he bid her enjoy a moment with Leyano while he went to the highest of the towers, where he would find a pearly harp that he kept in this Castle. He sought insight into one or two touchy situations, he told them, and wished to listen, in private, to its wisdom. He would rejoin them shortly.

Eli nodded with a smile, and as their father left the room, she returned to Leyano now standing by the little table and draining his wine-glass. She took another *buicuri* to crunch, knowing she would not be able to taste this delicacy in the human world.

"I'm glad we can have a little time to ourselves, my dear sister," Leyano began, "before you pass through the cleft of Dawn Rock tomorrow afternoon. I have some news that is only for your ears, and tomorrow morning I expect your time will be filled with other fairies and perhaps also with the somewhat bitter-sweet celebrations to honour your fairy-birthday as well as your departure … for a short while."

Eli felt warm and relaxed in Leyano's company. She took a final sip of her own sweet green wine, and they went to a bench beside a south-facing bay-window. At their feet, far below, the sand and stone were darkening in the rich shadows of twilight but they were coated with moonlight as though with white icing. And far off, beyond the Island's coasts, the tiny silver forms of dolphins could be seen, leaping in and out of the wrinkled surface of the sea. Stars were beginning to wink in the skies over Faërie. Eli sighed.

"Your Visit, this time, has been very eventful," Leyano began, his tone not so much philosophic as congratulatory. "That is as it should be. You come here, for three-times-three-weeks, to make the most important decision, perhaps, of your entire life. You *need* to be shaken and challenged in order to do that; it's not just about being shown all the beauties and wonders of this place. But you *have* seen beauty and wonder… and met love and friendship, too, have you not?"

Eli wondered how much Leyano guessed, or was hinting at. She nodded. "So much. So many places and amazing fairies and creatures. And, yes, love…. love of many kinds."

"That's what I wanted to talk to you about, in a way. Love, brotherly love. From our brother Finnir."

Eli felt a thrill as if some energy had entered the room. Something like a wave of silent thunder pulsed through her heart for a split-second and then calmed into a flower-sized nest of light and gentle heat, deep in her chest.

"Finnir has sent a message to you, Eli. He thought you might have been worried about him, and Brea, on their quest. And he wanted you to have word from him before you left, and a greeting for your birthday too. The seal-folk brought it to me yesterday. Oddly, it must have been just as you --- as Eli --- were awakening from your sleep in Castle Davenia, your slumbering on the doorsill between the two worlds, while Mélusine returned to her deep dreams on the Island of the Owls."

"A message from Finnir?! For me? A note, or letter?"

Leyano laughed. "Seals are not too skilful at carrying such missals! No, I'm afraid it's only a few words, relayed by the soft-eyed creatures so beloved of our grand-mother Morliande."

Eli's eyes must have registered her slight disappointment, for her brother laughed again and more amusedly. "Ah, you might have *preferred* an illuminated scroll! Yes, yes, I know that you visited the artist of Kitty Kyle, and I knew that you were, as the Princess, a very skilful calligrapher too. Unfortunately, I do not think that Finnir shares that talent with you!

"But his words should please you, nonetheless, dear Eli. He feared that you might have heard various or even conflicting rumours of his whereabouts, from Aytel or perhaps from Aindel or Alégondine, or even from our father. Therefore, he bid the seals tell you, through me, that he is well-arrived at the Shee of the Little Skellig, and that he shall go from there to the Sheep's Head Shee, and that he will be again in Barrywood earlier than he had presumed --- probably at the full moon: so that would be on the 26th of June. He knows that you will be gone by then, of course, back to the human world. But he asks that, if possible, you go to Gougane Barra in Ireland, early in the autumn --- if you have not returned here to Faërie by then. He will meet you at the entrance to his Portal, with a gift for you."

"Finnir wants me to go to his Portal? To come back with him through it, do you think?"

"That was not his meaning, no, as far as I could tell. He wishes to give you something, at the threshold of his Portal in the woods of Gougane Barra. But it is not for *him* to invite you into Faërie from there. He cannot know if you will return by his doorway, or by another, or *when* for that matter."

Eli hesitated, but she felt so at ease with Leyano that her words escaped her without much circumspection. "I don't know that either, the *when* and the *where* --- but I'm also adding an *if*. I wonder if I should come back at all, Leyano. And though I would love to see Finnir again, I wonder if I ought to risk meeting him as he has asked; for it would no doubt break my heart if I had decided, by then, that I would never be coming back."

Leyano's look was hard to read. He simply asked, "You feel such intense love, for Finnir, for your…brother? And do you believe he feels the same?"

Eli looked rather alarmed now, realising that she had probably said too much.

"You are shocked by that, I suppose, Leyano. Shocked at *my* sentiments, that is. I have no idea about how Finnir feels. But anyway, I know that it's all impossible; our father has told me so. And in any case, he wants me to marry Reyse, as Mélusine I mean…"

"I see that you have, indeed, found a great love here, at least in your own heart. Ah, dear me. Yes, that could be a complication, especially if Finnir is likewise moved…

"As for marrying Reyse," continued Leyano, very slowly, "I would remind you that you are a human still, Eli, and not yet the Princess Mélusine. Let *her* worry about such proposals and about such desires on the part of our father. I imagine that she will know what to do, when the time comes, as regards Reyse. As for you, and Finnir, I think you should also wait, and allow the moon a few more rounds of her dance, as we say.

"I have been thinking about Finnir, a great deal, these past few years," Leyano mused, continuing in his posed and steady voice. "He puzzles me. He is more *fey* than a fairy, if you see what I want to say: he is enchantment itself. I don't wonder that you feel such love for him, especially as you hover between the two worlds at this time. He is Faërie incarnate, for you, in a way, I imagine. I almost see him that way myself. I wonder if we are not, all of us in Faërie, in love with Finnir!

"Paradoxically, I begin to wonder if he could ever be pinned-down to be one of us, really. Or even to enter into a lovers' relationship or a marriage. He is too ethereal, I think. More so even than Aindel, who is a very curious fairy as well."

"Our father does not know Aindel, I have learned recently. Why is that, Leyano?"

"Yes, I wonder about it also. But Aindel is adamant that Aulfrin not be told of his visits. I think it likely that there is some animosity between this Shee Mor and the Sheep's Head, and as Aindel is the elder prince of that shee --- which has for centuries given shelter to the Queen Rhynwanol in her exile and disgrace --- he may feel rather like a trespasser here. Though our mother's own family has left the throne to other more foreign fairies now, she is still perhaps the reason for a certain malcontent, though not out-right aggression, between the two shees. And Aindel, though a great friend of Finnir and of Reyse also, feels therefore perhaps less than welcome --- by Aulfrin --- in this land."

"Yes," considered Eli, "that could explain it. Reyse had a similar explanation for Aindel's mysterious position here. He was, very brielfly, a changeling, like me, you know."

"Was he now? No, I didn't know that. He had a human life, then, and came home? Was this long ago? For I have known of his existence, on visits here, for many centuries, though we are not close friends, I must say."

"Ah, the tale he told me is stranger still, Leyano. He went from his original shee --- though I don't know which one it was --- into Ireland as an infant, but was stolen from the cradle only an hour later by other fairies, from the Sheep's Head Shee! The mother of the human babe he was to replace had out-witted the fairy-folk, and so she kept her own child. And so Aindel became, not a changeling as planned, but the Prince of his new shee; and he said he is very happy there."

Leyano's ink-well eyes shone very strangely as Eli finished.

After a moment he asked, "And the fairies of Aindel's home-shee, what babe did they take away with them, if the human infant was kept by his mother?"

"I don't think they took *a baby* at all. Aindel didn't tell me any more, for our conversation was cut short. Though he did say that a rich gift was given the fairies in compensation for this double-trickery."

Watching her brother's wise face now, Eli saw that some new, *wholly* new idea was taking shape in his thoughts. Trying to guess what he might be seeing, Eli ventured a question.

"Do you think the treasure they received was something very powerful from the Sheep's Head Shee, something similar to the Black Key?"

Leyano came out of his reverie and his face relaxed and warmed as he regarded his sister. "Certainly. It must have been a very great and powerful treasure. And all of the shees have magical marvels, such as the Black Key, of course. So, yes, it may have resembled that.

"Or not..." he added, very softly, his voice trailing off into musing silence.

Aulfrin had just appeared at the arched doorway.

"The moonlight is on the northern reaches of the Bay, my dear children. Let us go and watch the mermaids as they dance in the waves or sit under the stars to play their harp-serenades! The high balcony in the north tower offers a splendid view. Come with me!"

And so they followed the King to the curved balcony high over the lawns where the horses had landed earlier, to watch and listen to the concert and the ballet of the mermaids. Eli looked for the Lady Ecume, but could not discern her from so far away.

She well-recalled, however, that she would be meeting her the next day, on the *inish-beg*, the tiny Island of the Archangel far out in Sea-Horse Bay, to receive a birthday gift from her webbed hands.

****

A Delicate Balance

Chapter Nineteen:
The Offerings of the Summer Solstice

***P**eriwinkle and Reyse* had arrived during the night, and when Eli awoke to the final day of her second Visit, it was to Piv's insistent tugging at the cord of a small hand-bell. He held the bell aloft, like a miniature wind-chime fashioned of sea-shells and pearls, as he flew around the bedroom.

Eli had to laugh as she sat up, seeing the colourful, buzzing pixie making giddy circles and even flying in and out of the wide-open windows.

"Birthday blessings to my little Princess Mélusine today; ah…but she lies sleeping soundly once again, far far away! So I will have to ring my wishes and kisses to you, dearest Eli! Happy Summer Solstice!" he chanted, as he whizzed by her head. On his next tour of the room, he finally came to a halt on Eli's bedside table, and gave the little bell just one more jingle before he placed it at his feet. Then he kissed Eli as she bent over to thank him and wish him a 'good morning'.

"Is that how fairies celebrate birthdays, then, my dear Piv?!"

"Always with bells, yes, my Eli-een. Shell-bells, or blue-bells, hare-bells or fox-gloves, lilies-of-the-valley or campanula, nightshade or fuchsia --- but always we ring bells! Only fairies can hear them, though, so you must be a fairy again now!"

Eli continued to laugh, and then Piv politely turned his back while she hastily dressed.

"I'm not a full-fairy yet, my darling Piv, but I've changed a great deal on this Visit. I can feel it. I'll be more here than there, when I step over the threshold, I'm afraid, and find myself back in Santa Barbara."

Piv looked rather sad when he turned and took Eli's hand, flying along beside her as they went downstairs. But he couldn't stay down-hearted for long, and neither could Eli. Awaiting her for breakfast was Reyse, and of course the King and Leyano.

"A final ride on Peronne this morning, Eli?" proposed her father, cutting her a wedge of some exotic fruit as bright as a cantaloupe but with beads of nectar-filled seeds like a pomegranate. "I thought we might fly down towards Dizzy Dolphin Point --- only take us an hour or so to have it in view. Then early this afternoon you have an appointment, I understand, with a certain mermaid. And then, at the same hour you arrived, you must pass back through Dawn Rock.

"But I am happy, even though you must leave us for a little while, for you have grown stronger in your true nature these past three weeks, and are tugging at the corners of your disguise now, ready to return to yourself. It is shining forth from your eyes!"

Eli smiled, but when she glanced at Leyano she lowered her regard for an instant, thinking of all her confidences to her brother yesterday. Turning to Reyse, she grinned once again --- for his face was glowing with love for her. She could not help but feel her own affection for him rising to colour her cheeks and make her eyes sparkle even more gaily.

The ride over Sea-Horse Bay was more extraordinary than Eli could have imagined. The two great horses, Cynnabar and Peronne, bore their accustomed riders, but this time with the addition of little Piv sitting very proudly just in front of Eli and lifting his face into the wild wind of their flight. But, as well as this, Reyse came with them --- not riding, but flying: his large, elegant brown and white wings nearly transparent in the gleam of the sunlight. Eli could only try to imagine how amazing it would be to fly with her own fairy-wings…

They flew low over the waves at times, and at others climbed high enough to see out to an isolated little island not far to the east. Far off, on that horizon, two other dark and slightly spikey forms indicated another pair of isles. This nearest and most visible one, however, was not at all dark, for its coast was as golden as Leyano's Sand Castle. Its centre, as round as the back of a sleeping cat, was mostly green but seemed flecked with pale yellow and deep orange blooming trees or high bushes. A strange feeling of familiarity stole over Eli as she looked at the island. She could half-picture herself standing upon those shores, and she almost seemed to be remembering something… But as Reyse came into view again, close beside her now, her thoughts blew away on the whistling wind, replaced by other very delightful ones.

When they had flown for about an hour, south-east and keeping about twenty miles from the high cliffs of the mainland coast, Aulfrin gently turned his mount towards a large promontory jutting into the Bay. It was not a long peninsula, but rather a great oval of seaward-sloping meadows, perched on the heads of the cliffs. Landing here, they could look over the remaining eighty-or-so miles to Dizzy Dolphin Point, another somewhat more triangular promontory further along the coast.

"We will not have time to go so far today, my dear Eli," conceded the King. We should turn back, soon now, to Leyano's Castle, for guests will be arriving who wish to see you before you depart. "But it is worth a look, is it not?"

Truly, it was a fantastical sight. The Point was not only triangular in the shape of its horizontal land-mass but also in its perpendicularity. It was a high and very pointed mountain peak, in fact, oddly placed along the line of already imposing cliffs, but looking very independent from all the neighbouring bluffs. Not only was it much, much higher, but it was white-grey: a soft mouse-grey that contrasted with the darker stone all around it.

"The colour," explained Reyse, "is not really that of the rock --- though it is whiter in places than the escarpments all around it. If we were closer, you would be able to see that the soft greyness is constantly moving. It's the goats. The peak is their favourite playground and it is absolutely covered with long-haired, leaping, dancing grey goats!"

"How marvellous," cried Eli. "I wish I could see that! And is that why it's called 'Dizzy Dolphin Point'? Because the goats feel dizzy when they look down from such a height onto the dolphins in the Bay?"

"Nothing makes a goat dizzy!" chuckled Piv. "Or, at least, one could say that they're dizzy already, with fun and frolicking. No, it's the dolphins that get a bit dizzy looking up at the goats, I suppose!"

All four of them laughed at this, and then Periwinkle's little fluty voice continued, "All the land behind, throughout the south-eastern corner of Karijan, is full of goats. All kinds, all sizes, and all as mad with joy as one could imagine. It's called the Dancing Goat Plains. Dear Reyse, he knows the place well…"

"Yes, but I will not speak of that land today, not to Eli, my dear Piv," interjected Reyse, quite abruptly, she felt. She made a mental note to ask him about the place one day, if she got the chance and if he seemed more willing to talk with her about it than he did at the moment. She had a rather instinctive sensation, and perhaps a hazy memory, that her curiosity was linked to something romantic --- perhaps between herself and Reyse in the past. But she swallowed her desire to find out more just now. Instead, she addressed her father.

"You said that guests are expected for lunch? May I know who they are, or is it a surprise party?!"

Aulfrin smiled merrily. "No, I'm afraid it's not planned as that, my dear girl. At least, no more a surprise party than is all of life! I had messages from the pearly harp of the Sand Castle last night, and so I have invited someone who will surely know more about the rumours I heard. That is Garo. And he will not be coming alone, for I have suggested that he accompany Brocéliana in her lovely boat --- as she was to be coming to see you off, in any case."

No, it's not possible, thought Eli. He can't fool me. My father is truly my father and we are too alike for me *not* to know when he is teasing me! For she could see the cheeky wink in his eye that belied his knowledge of more than he was saying. He *must* know of the love between those too; his words were quivering with the mischievous delight of half-saying something, just to see if there would be a reaction from his daughter.

But Eli made no comment, except to say, "How splendid! Well, let's get back then…"

Aulfrin kept his eye fixed on hers for just a moment longer, and then laughed once. They re-mounted and took to the air, Reyse smiling rather knowingly at Eli, too, as he soared up into the sunlight alongside Peronne. Piv settled himself comfortably in his place, gathered a clump of the flying-horse's long white mane into his tiny hands and squeezed his eyes tight shut with a contented sigh. "Ah," he purred, "off we go, back to lunch!"

****

When they arrived at the dining-room of the Sand Castle, music was tumbling out of the open doors to greet them. Garo was tapping his *bodhrán* in intricate and vigorous rhythms, Brocéliana was strumming the lovely painted dulcimer, and Leyano playing his lute --- an instrument a little smaller than that of Demoran's, but just as sweet-voiced. Another musician was also present, whom Eli had not encountered before. This was a tall fairy-woman, quite young, Eli thought, for she appeared to have about the same age as her half-sister. She was stately and merry, sparkling-eyed and serene, all at the same time. Her long black hair hung loose over her azure-blue attire, a dress with a bodice embroidered in dark blue threads and with over-lapping skirts of airy fabric which rippled and waved as she swayed to the music. She played an oboe of clear, bright wood --- very like the colour of Eli's own harp, Clare.

She stood close beside Leyano, and Eli felt that they were a couple before Aulfrin whispered to her, "That is Pallaïs, the betrothed of Leyano, a fairy from the islands to the east, among which is found that of the Archangel, where you will go to meet the Lady Ecume later. And on that subject, I might add that although her Ladyship the wondrous mermaid has informed me of your planned meeting, I do *not* know what she has in mind!" The King added this comment as soon as he saw the question in Eli's eyes, clearly belying that she was wondering just how *much* he knew of the mer-harper's invitation to her.

Now she nodded her acceptance of her father's full complicity in regard to her meeting with the Lady Ecume. At the same time, she continued to look with delight upon Pallaïs.

"My, she is *lovely*. She looks almost oriental to me."

"True, true," assented Aulfrin. "Now that you mention it, I have seen features and colouring akin to hers in the human world, and they were maidens from Asia, indeed. She is, as you say, entirely lovely, and not only in her beauty of face and form. She is a sea-fairy, and gifted with great wisdom. I hope that Leyano will not delay too much longer to set a day for their marriage; but he takes his time, in matters of the heart as in all else."

The music faded to its gentle conclusion, and an amphora of rare, pale orange wine was served to all in thin flutes like champagne glasses, but eccentrically formed in spirals of twisted glass filled with irregularities --- which would have been called 'imperfections' in the human world, Eli thought. But when the orange wine was poured into these flutes, all the little spots and bubbles, crevices and marks in the glass began to dance and gyrate, growing larger and then smaller, even changing position. The wine seemed to bring the glass itself to life!

"If this beverage intoxicates the very glasses and makes them loose all control, what will it do to me?!" she giggled, speaking in a murmur to Reyse at her side. He laughed back at her.

"It will go to your head, I hope, and make you drunk with love --- for me," he whispered, leaning very close to her ear.

Eli's eyes did begin to shine, and her heart felt very light and happy; but she did not attribute this to the wine. She felt filled with life, her fairy-life, and she was savouring every drop of *that* until the last moment when she would have to leave. For the thought was growing, deep within her, that she did not know when, or if, she would return.

But that thought somehow made the joy of the present moment even greater.

They all sat around a beautiful table, shell-studded and inlaid with white and silvery drift-wood and green crystals. Eli felt to be the Princess she was in her life here, rather than the human visitor about to step back into a modern world of mankind with its machinery and money, its wars and greed and destruction and disrespect.

But Eli, being Eli and choosing to see good and beauty rather than pessimism, had also very beautiful images and memories of her human world. Despite its cruelty and lack of harmony, both with nature and between men, Eli loved the earth and its wonders, its varied cultures and its many arts. And she, like Lily, was wont to dwell more on the hope engendered by the millions of deeply 'good' humans than by the contrasting and distressing crowds of more doubtful characters! Moreover her heart was filled to overflowing, now, with the desire to share what she had re-discovered in Faërie with her fellow-humans on the other side of Leyano's Portal. How, she had no clear idea; but she *longed* to bring something of *this* world to that one…

As attendants cleared away the sea-weed-leaf baskets of delicacies, leaving only the last drops of bright wine for the diners to drain from their enchanted glasses, Aulfrin addressed the company.

"We have raised a toast to the Princess Mélusine and her birthday, and feasted and celebrated in fitting style to bid a farewell to Eli Penrohan as she returns to the human world, just once more. And we have all, I think, wished her a hasty return, once again, to Faërie. But now I must broach another subject, asking if Garo --- whom I esteem highly and hold in ever deeper respect --- can tell us what he has learned of his father Erreig."

Of course --- Eli realised as well as all the others --- Garo had been invited here for a purpose. Aulfrin had not spoken with him in private before this, quite probably so that the young dragon-lord would be obliged to give the information he obviously possessed to the King without being elusive or covert in his replies. For here, Garo was in company with fairies very important to him, even loved by him, and the King knew this.

But Garo was not at all put off his stride; he remained tranquil and candid in his regard, a soft smile on his lips, but a strange sorrow in his cobalt-blue eyes.

"As Your Majesty has clearly learned, my father is in danger and difficulty." Garo looked at Aulfrin, frankly and with his own head held high. He then glanced about the table, as if gathering the energies of all of his listeners into his own kind heart before he continued. Reyse and Leyano, Eli and Pallaïs, Piv and also Aulfrin, remained silent, and it seemed certain that each one offered their concern and compassion freely. As for Brocéliana, her own twilight-blue eyes were shining like lamps as she looked at her lover.

"On the Day of Ævnad, four days ago now, my father made a very impetuous decision: to go to the Island of the Scholar Owls and into the vault where the Princess Mélusine is awaiting Eli's decision to return from the human world. How my father knew of the whereabouts of the Princess's body, I cannot tell you, Your Majesty. I cannot even venture a guess as to why his boldness surmounted both his sense and his loyalty to the laws of Faërie. For well he must know that such an intrusion is forbidden by you and by the decency of all our people, be they Sun-Singer or Moon-Dancer." Garo took a deep breath, and added, "But he has paid dearly for his crime, I fear."

Eli grew tense, her stomach contracting in a knot. A sensation, not of fear but of fragility, pervaded her entire being. She moved her hand from her own knee to that of Reyse, sitting close beside her. He took it willingly, as Garo continued once again.

"Yesterday evening, Sire, you sent a swift messenger to seek me and to ask me if I had learned anything more about his theft of a part of the Princess Mélusine's shroud. It was two or three hours before dawn when I received your message, in the protected place where your messenger at last found me. This was not in Quillir though, for I had in fact lingered near to the Stone Circle just south of Fantasie, after having accompanied Aytel back to the gates of the Silver City. I had not had word from or concerning my father since Eli had fainted at Castle Davenia, when I and my sister had departed thence to retrieve Aytel and bear him to Aumelas-Pen. Afterwards, Alégondine had returned to the Beldrum Mountains and her abode in the coastal pine forests, alone.

"I had, as I say, heard no news of Erreig on that journey, for we had not found him at his Fortress, and I was in haste to bear Aytel away to Fantasie. But, once near to the Silver City, the Stones had other tidings for me: I heard the voice of the Sage-Hermit, as I often do when there --- for he is my master and teacher. But now his voice was filled with sorrow and was even a little angry. I have never heard or felt either of those energies from him before. My first desire was to go nearer to the Hermit himself, but this would have served no purpose. For no fairy, save when expressly invited, may set foot on Star Island and live, even myself, the heir to the Hermit. Not until I make the transition to occupy his role, in two years' time, shall I actually be granted the permission to go to his Island sanctuary. And so I waited in the Stone Circle, but all that I heard there has been dark and mournful."

Aulfrin himself now seemed as tense as Eli. "What has he done? What folly has come to Erreig, first to go to Scholar-Owl Island, and now…to do what? I cannot see him with my inner-vision, and the harp I have played here was unable to tell me more."

Garo's voice was grave. "He has taken upon himself to do what no fairy *may* do, as I have just stated. My father took the piece of cloth that he has stolen to Star Island. He has not been seen since."

There was shocked silence all about the table. Even the sound of sea and wind beyond the high windows seemed to have been hushed. Brocéliana's hand had risen to cover her mouth in alarm, and Piv had stood up from his cross-legged position on the table's edge.

"Is he dead?" whispered Eli at last, not able to contain her words any longer. "If no fairy may set foot on the Island of the Sage-Hermit, and Erreig has done so, has he paid… with his life?"

Garo looked deeply into Eli's eyes, and then at the King. "This is what I feared. But I now think otherwise. I think, and this is the strangest intuition I have ever felt, that it was perhaps the Sage-Hermit himself who sent my father on an audacious mission, who required that he find and take a fragment of Mélusine's covering. Why and to what end, I do not know. But, as I say, that is what my intuition tells me. And my father has not returned to his Fortress, and when I asked --- outright --- of the Stones and of the Hermit, I had only this answer: *Erreig is come to Star Island. He has brought the Amethyst Cloth.*"

The silence, this time, was much longer. Eli did not find it at all *meditative*, but anguished or perhaps simply bewildered. But then, she was not yet a fairy once again --- not quite.

After what seemed like an interminable and morbid hiatus, Pallaïs did the most fairy-like thing in such a situation. She began to play music.

The strains of her pale oboe flowed over the table and to Eli it felt as though they passed right through her skin and became confused with the blood flowing in her veins and the white, living bones of her skeleton. When the last note had died away, Pallaïs turned to the King, who slowly opened his eyes --- for they had been softly closed while she played.

"He lives," said the gloriously liquid voice of the sea-fairy. "But whether it was by his design or that of the Hermit that the Amethyst Cloth was stolen, and to affect what strange charm --- if that is the objective --- my instrument does not reveal. But the Dragon-Lord Erreig, it says, is still living and is still on Star Island."

The King relaxed visibly, and Garo also. Reyse squeezed Eli's hand, then he gently opened it and placed it on his thigh, to stroke it soothingly.

Leyano spoke now. "I think it a good thing that Eli is to leave our shores today," he said with a decisive nod, the turquoise pendants in his long braids swinging slightly and the wondrous beetle-shaped diamond in his forehead shining with an interior and pulsating light. "If it is, indeed, a charm which he and also perhaps the Hermit have devised, and by their possession of the Cloth they seek to establish some link to Mélusine in her slumber, I feel that Eli may be safest far from Faërie. At least, until we know more."

"I am not so sure." The rich and strong voice was that of Reyse. "I would be apprehensive for Eli, even in her human life, should any charm disturb the sleep of Mélusine." He looked with gallant consideration at Eli, and then at Aulfrin. "I am happy to go into the world, also, and remain near her, as protector and channel of communication between our two realms."

Eli's heart beat faster, but why, she was not sure. Was she swept-up by the generous vow of her champion to guard her, or was she uncomfortable with the idea that Reyse would be too present and perhaps too persistent in his suit for her affection, and would seek to influence her own pending decisions?

"I thank you, my dear Reyse, but I do not feel that Eli need be kept in custody or under surveillance," said the King solemnly. "Moreover, what with a reinforcement of the guard about the Princess's Island-sanctuary coupled with our determined and immediate efforts to learn more --- even from today and the very moment that Eli takes her leave of us --- we will shortly be in a position to counter *any* dangerous charm that is planned, and at least to understand what this is all about. And though no fairy may go to Star Island, I am the King and it is given to me to communicate with the Sage-Hermit if needs be, or at least to attempt to do so. But this I must do at a closer distance. I will go to Holy Bay this evening. I will also seek out Alégondine, for she may have more details to reveal to me. I now know her to be a far-seeing and very thoughtful fairy; and *perhaps* she is sometimes in close communication with her father."

Reyse bowed his head to Aulfrin. And Eli felt a wave of relief, which puzzled her slightly.

"Do not worry overmuch, my dear Eli," said her father, now rising and coming to place a hand on her shoulder for a moment before walking slowly across the room. His words were quite useless, to Eli's ears, however; for she certainly *was* worried and could not imagine how she could avoid that. She felt the mounting sensation of vulnerability which had swept over her earlier. Only now it was coloured by outright fear.

"*Think of the spider in Demoran's story,*" she told herself, closing her eyes for a moment and trying to straighten her back and relax her shoulders. Her father had moved away, and was looking out the eastern window towards Dawn Rock. "*Think of the spider, and see your fears as exaggerated by your own confusion and out of perspective; see them as very small,*" she repeated, silently, in her thoughts. "*Very small... Oh dear...*"

But her father was speaking again now. "If the Amethyst Cloth is with the Sage-Hermit on Star Island, and the Princess Mélusine has fallen well and truly back into her slumber, then it must be that she no longer feels any threat or aggression. If she did, given her response to its initial theft, I can only guess that she would not be at peace now, and Eli would not be so well as she obviously is. You have revived, my dear daughter, and are not at all fading or languishing; therefore, I think there is no imminent danger. I am inclined to agree with Leyano: it is well that you are leaving Faërie today. You are a human at this time, and safest in the human-world --- until we can learn more. So, be of good courage in your return to those lands, and that will come soon now!

"Only another three hours, and you must pass through the Portal, my girl. Let us go to the Island of the Archangel. I will fly with you, but you will meet the Lady Ecume in private --- as she has requested. Are you ready?"

Eli stood, and looked around the table. She took a moment to gather her wits and calm herself, but then she nodded to her father, and smiled at the company gathered about her.

"Will I see you all again, before I go?" she asked. "Or should I say my farewells now?" Her voice didn't sound as bright as she would have wished; in fact, she would have said that she sounded weak and frail --- and that image did not please her at all.

"The Prince Leyano and the Lord Reyse will be at the Portal," replied her father. But as for the others, yes, you may bid them good-bye here."

A bit tearful now, Eli kissed Piv on his little forehead, and the two friends --- woman and pixie --- looked long and loving at each other. Both smiled, but no words were exchanged --- at least not audibly. Eli then extended her hand to Garo, who kissed it with great courtliness. Brocéliana stood beside Garo, clearly rather overwhelmed by emotion. She extended both her hands to take Eli's, said nothing either, and finally smiled just a little. Eli knew they would both begin to cry if they remained looking at one another or if she tried to put her feelings into sensible or, more likely, sentimental words; and so she smiled again too, and quickly turned away.

Standing a little apart from the others was the sea-fairy, Leyano's love. Eli felt a sudden wave of warmth shine out from the exotically slanted and leaf-shaped eyes of Pallaïs, just before both women bowed their heads slightly. As Eli turned to go, Piv flew over to her suddenly, as if to say something --- but instead he simply stroked her wavy red hair just once, then returned to the table where Garo took his hand.

"I'm ready," Eli said, turning to her father. And they went down the broad stairs to the northern lawn, where their winged-steeds awaited them.

****

One hundred and fifty miles lay between Leyano's Golden Sand Castle and the tiny Island of the Archangel far out at the extreme limits of Sea-Horse Bay. To cover such a distance in the time remaining to Eli, Aulfrin would urge both horses to their swiftest pace, and he told Eli to lean forward onto Peronne's neck and to tighten her knees against his flanks, thus embracing him firmly with both arms and legs. For though there was little or no wind to buffet or destabilise them, still he assured her that this would be an exciting ride!

Joining them in their race, and evidently enjoying it as much as Eli, were great flocks of gulls, kittiwakes and gannets. Among them, too, were several cormorants and Eli also thought she could identify terns and speckled skuas. But there were some smaller birds flying in company with the great sea-dwellers, especially as they neared the larger islands that hid from view the lower mass of rock beyond them. This was the final out-cropping of the group, where the minuscule isle of the Archangel nestled just off its southern coast.

The small birds beside them were mostly flying low over the waves: many were coloured with blue or orange head-feathers or red beaks, or were brightly marked with black and white patterns like petrels. There were countless puffins on the first island, and as they passed over the second one Eli saw that here there were even tiny kingfishers, plunging into the waters at the toes of the coastal rocks where the vegetation seemed to suggest mangroves and halophytes.

The horses slowed their hurried pace as they descended in altitude, and now Eli could lift her head and see, through the billowing strands of Peronne's thick mane, the final island of these three rocky outcrops. Unlike the first two --- which were masses of grey stone thickly covered with vegetation, both bushes and stubby trees --- this third island was entirely formed of deep red rock the colour of a well-aged wine. Eli could see nothing even resembling a tree or a shrub.

It was on this island that the horses came to land, and Eli found that there was a cove of crimson sand tucked into the strange rock formations, facing out towards the little islet two or three miles from the shore.

As she dismounted and felt her soft-booted feet sink into the fine red sand, she noticed that there were, in fact, some plants --- but they, too, were all claret-red. Algae and spiky grass, ground-hugging broad-leafed creepers like pumpkins or melons, and tiny posies of flowers poking through fissures in the rocks, all with ruddy-hued petals and leaves to match.

Aulfrin encouraged his daughter with a nod and a gentle smile, and she followed the direction of his pointing finger to a gnarled and wizened tree-trunk half submerged at the tide's edge. It, too, was a sea-washed version of claret-red, and tied to it was a bobbing raft of --- it seemed --- the same wood.

As she glanced back towards her father and the two horses, Eli thought she could hear words spoken, rather indistinctly mingled with the sound of the waves and the crying of the gulls overhead.

"Untie the raft and let it guide you to your tryst with the greatest of the mermaids, the oldest of the harpers, the most skilled of the healers. Be of good courage, as I perceive that your father the King has advised you, Your Highness, and look *and* listen with the eyes and ears of your heart."

Eli stared for a moment, and then she realised that it had been the unfamiliar voice of Cynnabar, speaking silently to her. Aulfrin nodded once more, and Eli bent to untie the short rope from the drift-wood tree-trunk as she climbed aboard the swaying raft.

Of its own accord, the tiny raft wobbled over the turquoise wavelets straight towards the miniature island. As it came into clearer view, Eli saw that the Isle of the Archangel was red also, but of a much deeper hue than the main island, almost a burgundy-purple. It was made of a knobbly and pocked stone, mounded into a soft hillock. As the raft landed smoothly against a pier of rock shaped like a cupped hand --- which then dipped below the surface of the water to allow raft and rider into the hollow of its palm --- Eli noted that all of the rocks were covered with moss like cottony, deep violet-red algae or lichen. Before she stepped out of the raft and onto these carpeted stones, she clearly heard the instruction, deep within her own chest, to take off her boots and leave them on the raft.

The Offerings of the Summer Solstice

The very air seemed to be charged with mystical and ancient music and tingling, tickling points of energy like icy snowflakes touching the face and arms. Eli walked up and over the hill of cushioned stones: she had the impression of walking on felt or foam. When she reached the summit and could look down to the southern edge of the Isle, she at last saw the Lady Ecume.

The mermaid was sitting on the rocks just at the water's edge, her long blue and green-scaled tail curled just below the surface and clearly visible through the crystal currents. Her torso was naked, and Eli noticed a mark on the back of her right shoulder, like a tattoo of a finely-drawn Celtic triskel in pale blue ink. Her long hair was blowing in the breeze behind her --- and it was not hair at all, but a mass of slender white feathers lined here and there with pale sea-green or sky-blue streaks. Huge pearls were set into the lobes of her pointed ears, and the finger-tips of her webbed hands were either naturally coloured or decorated with shiny red enamel on the nails, the same colour as the stones.

But most startling and beautiful and strange was the harp she played.

The mermaid, eyes closed but with a serene smile on her exquisite face, continued to pluck the cords as Eli approached. The highest point of the fore-pillar of the little lap harp was embellished with a golden sea-horse, its long tail entwined about the pillar, which was painted with spirals and swirls of pistachio-green arabesques. The harp itself was perhaps also made of gold, or of a wood so fair and so polished that it shone like precious metal. Along its top-curve were designs of interlaced knotwork in white, with pearls and aquamarines studded among the painted lines. The sound-box of the harp was likewise painted in flourishes of white and green lines, seemingly a form of marketry or inlaid veneer. All down the sides of the harp's table, on either side, were rows of green chrysoberyl cat's-eye gem-stones.

As Eli came up, right beside the mermaid, the Lady Ecume concluded the air she was playing with a last, rippling glissando, and then laid the harp across her lap, where the scales of her long tail began. Eli felt an unspoken greeting of welcome, and she sat beside the wondrous harper. She now noticed that the two eyes of the seahorse were regarding her. They were bright and alive and yet after a second or two they seemed to cloud and grow stony, now simply resembling points of jade set into the golden metalwork of the creature.

"You carry the writings of Maelys, of Lily, with you on your travels?" The Lady Ecume's voice was warm and watery, very deep and very musical.

"Yes," replied Eli, "I have her journal here in my shoulder-bag. And a white rose from Reyse, and a phial of love-potion from a little black sprite in the Fire-Bird Forest."

"The rose will never fade, but you will not always carry it with you. The love-potion, powerful charm of the whale-fathers, will not be wasted. But of *great* importance is the book written by your mother. Yes," added the mermaid, obviously noting --- without turning her head --- a sudden straightening of Eli's back, "I call her your *mother*. She did not bear you, but she tended you as though you were an extremely precious flower in the garden of her heart, and there is great love between you two, even still."

Eli nodded, and smiled. She could almost feel Lily beside them, so that all three of them were sitting together on the mossy red stones, surrounded by the eternal blue of the sea and sky of Faërie. She had a great desire to ask more of the mermaid regarding the visit that Lily had made to this realm in the enchanted boat that she had seen from the Point of Vision. But something stopped her question before it was formed, and she kept a respectful silence as the Lady Ecume now continued.

"It is good that you keep her book, and that you read of her adventures and her insights. But not all is to be found there. You have much to discover and to learn, before the end. And you go now into a season of storm and dense fog, of wild waves and of hidden rocks that will threaten to ship-wreck you as you voyage. Dangers, yes, Mélusine, are part of the gifts that your life will offer to you on this the six-hundred-and-fifty-third anniversary of your birth. I see the dangers, and so does your mother the Queen Rhynwanol, and so does your grandmother: the mother of your father, the Queen Morliande. Both of these great fairies, at this time, join with me to offer you our protection and guidance."

The mermaid stopped, and now turned to look Eli straight in the eye. The charge of power and unhindered regard into her very soul took Eli's breath away. She tried to swallow, she even tried to move, but could do neither. Slowly, however, her breath came into her lungs once more, as if the sky itself --- or perhaps the Archangel of this Isle --- had sent her a waft of sea-breeze to renew her respiration and stop her from drowning in the mermaid's gaze.

Were those piercing eyes blue, or sea-weed green, or maybe mauve? Eli would never be able to recall. In fact, she wondered afterwards if they were not bright red, like the harper's painted finger-nails and the strange rocks. But she could never remember.

"Good, good," said the Lady Ecume, turning her gaze away from Eli. "You are very strong. You will not drown, when the time comes. Remember that you have been submerged, and yet that breath came back to you. Don't forget this moment, when --- as I say --- the time comes.

"Now, I will give you the gift of your three protectors and guides, the gift that comes through me, but ultimately from the three who love you deeply, among them two Queens of Faërie, Morliande and Rhynwanol,."

"Is it the Black Key?" whispered Eli, unable to retain her curiosity, but immediately afraid that she had spoken foolishly or insolently, and that somehow it was forbidden for her to speak of the Key.

But the mermaid smiled indulgently.

"I have returned the amber-token to the King of this great shee, the Shee Mor of Faërie, and he alone has the right to give that token into the hands of another. The Black Key is hidden, by me, in its sacred place. It may well be that it will come to you, one day, Mélusine. It is not unimaginable. But it is not the only way to pass by the Fourth Portal, nor to conjure life from the fires --- or waters --- of so-called 'death'. We, the women of the seas of Faërie, we have many marvels at our fingertips! But, indeed, it may be that --- some day --- the Black Key will be called forth by you, and used. But that is not the gift that I give you today."

Eli's heart was beating quickly now, and her eyes were shining with the thrill of belonging to this enchanted world, and also with the apprehension linked to the perils which lay ahead, according to this wise and mysterious mermaid.

The Lady Ecume reached her hand around to the left side of her head, which was hidden from Eli's view, and she seemed to undo something from her ear on that side. When her hand reappeared it was closed around a small object, and she now extended that hand to Eli. Slowly, she unfolded the webbed fingers of her hand.

"It is, in fact, three gifts in one," she commented, as Eli received the tiny article. "For it will bring you a power to heal others, and it will also protect you from the dangers which will shortly be unleashed. But, as well as these properties, it is imbued with another and mightier charm. It will open a passage for you, when you shall seek it, which will bring you through the red waters, through the Garnet Vortex, back into Faërie --- by the Fourth Portal.

"You must, before you leave me today, bind yourself to the promise that *you* will neither speak of nor reveal these triple-powers to any other fairy. Save two. When the time is fulfilled, and you are called to use the greatest power of this gift, you will show it to a fairy named Barrimilla, and another fairy will be at your side, and will know of this gift also, and understand its properties. Aside from these two, you must keep it secret from all the creatures of Faërie, pixies and hounds, birds and horses, fairies of land or sea, even trees and mushrooms. Three give it; and likewise you are three to learn of it, yourself and these two others. And that is all. Do you promise?"

"Of course, yes, I promise," said Eli, very slowly and gravely. She looked at the tiny gift, lying now in the palm of her own hand. It seemed to be an ear-ring: hung from a silver hook was a right-hand sickle-moon, fashioned also of rather dark silver. It had a profile face whose single visible eye was either blank or closed for no pupil was to be seen, and a tiny hint of a smile was on its lips. All about the outside of its rounded form were silver petal-shapes, like flickering flames.

The Lady Ecume added, "Wear it on the left of your head, as I have done, in the ear-lobe where, as the Princess, you bear a garnet. Wear it always, now, until the time comes to give it to Barrimilla."

"Who, and what, and *where* is Barrimilla?" asked Eli, mystified.

"You will find him when you need him," was the simple reply.

"Now I wish you well in your return to the human-world, and I charge you to make *good* use of the *powers for good* that you will feel in your fingers, for this token has been filled by the music of the Harp of Seven Eyes, and it will sing forth that music through you, where it is most needed.

"And I will say to you this, in conclusion, my beloved Mélusine: *counter fear with **joy**, always*, and sing forth your music and play with conviction and confidence when the darkness comes about you. I remind you: *before* your human life you were a fairy, and *after it* you will be one once again; but do not forget that between these two --- between past and future --- there lies *the present*, and that there, without a doubt, you are *also* a fairy, whatever else you might be!"

Eli smiled as the mermaid took up her harp and began, again, to play softly and sweetly, the white strings of the Harp of Seven Eyes vibrating and twinkling like sunlight on the water.

Eli reached up to her left ear and felt for the mark of the tiny hole where, in the human world, she often wore an ear-ring. She had not done so here in Faërie on either of her Visits. She now slipped-on the fiery silver sickle-moon, and it seemed to hum for a moment, as if in unison with the chords played by the Lady Ecume.

Bowing her head to the mermaid, who did not look at her again, Eli rose and returned to the cupped hand of red rock, which opened to let her little raft pass out into the sea once more. She floated directly over the short stretch of water to where her father and the two horses were waiting, to fly swiftly together back to the Portal of Dawn Rock.

****

None of them, not Reyse nor Leyano nor the King, seemed to notice the Flaming-Moon pendant hung from her left ear-lobe; or if they did, they made no comment on it. Eli stroked some loose strands of her thick red hair over her ear, just to hide it, in case.

The rest of her long hair was caught-up at the back of her neck, held by the coral comb that Leyano had given her. Her shoulder-bag, containing the bamboo phial, the white rose and Lily's notebook with its silver-leaf bookmark, was hung over her shoulder and rested against her side, under her long cloak. She had changed back into her human clothes, stepping modestly behind the nearby boulders, when she and Aulfrin had arrived here --- for Leyano had brought her belongings to her from his Castle.

She was ready to step through the Portal.

The high pinnacles of Dawn Rock were lit by the sun (now far in the western sky and just beginning to sink towards its setting) and they glowed silver and gold as if they wished to impress Eli with their beauty before she left. The twisted and ancient pine trees around them, as well as the huge boulders, all seemed to be watching her tenderly, bidding her farewell. With a fairy's spirit colouring her perceptions more and more, Eli found that all of nature was vibrantly alive and attentive to her every move, every thought. She wondered if it would feel the same on the other side of the threshold.

Leyano and Aulfrin stood either side of the cave-mouth, the slim crevice leading into the heart of the Rock and the gentle slope descending to the doorway, hidden and invisible to human eyes among the ravines and rocks and pools of Seven Falls, near Santa Barbara. Eli followed as Leyano turned and entered the cave, stopping before her father as she arrived under the shadow of the rugged archway.

He kissed her forehead, his two strong hands upon her shoulders. His eyes were bright, but with pride or hope or tears, Eli could not tell.

"Play your harp, Clare, soon my dear child, asking her to instruct you in your choice of date and place for your final home-coming. I am impatient, now, to have you return!"

Eli smiled, but could not find any words other than, "Thank you, thank you for everything and for all of this. I will miss you so."

"Don't miss me, or Faërie, for too long then! May the light of the Moon and the blessings of her Dancers be always with you, my dearest Eli, my Mélusine. And do not fear anything about all of these strange tidings, of Dragon-Lords and Sage-Hermits. I go to Quillir this very night, and will meet with Alégondine and I will also have news, when I return to Fantasie, from Aytel and from the Great Trees and the Stones too. All will be set to rights before your final Visit, I am sure."

And now Reyse, who had been standing a little way behind the King, came forward.

Love, thought Eli, is a powerful and magical thing, for it gives insight beyond words, into one's very thoughts. This was clear to her, looking into Reyse's hazel-brown eyes, for they seemed capable of piercing all of the veils of her secrets and gazing directly at her fears and doubts, just as they could look unblinking into the sun. She felt naked in the light of those eyes: her misgivings and hesitations all revealed and easily readable to this noble and loyal fairy-lord.

But Reyse did not speak. He only took her hand and lifted it slowly to his lips.

As she drew her hand away, and brought it to her heart to incline her head to him in farewell, she felt something. There, hung about her neck, under her clothes, was a soft, thin cord with a jewel dangling from it, right over her heart. Reyse's eyes flashed, and she heard, unspoken and utterly silent but as rich and warm as his audible voice, the words "Happy Birthday, my Princess." He lowered his eyes, and turned away.

Eli entered the cave-mouth and followed Leyano down the dimly-lit slope. She could hear running water and also the cries of gulls on the other side of the smooth rock-face before her.

She unbuttoned her fairy-cloak now, and handed it to Leyano. He placed his long-fingered and graceful hand on her cheek for an instant and Eli could feel his smile, even in the dimity of the cave. He then reached his hand up to a small hole, like a bird's or bat's dwelling in a niche of the cool stone, and Eli heard a sound like the turn of a key.

The rock-face before her was there no more; it was behind her, smooth and solid. Far out over the foothills she could see to the coast, and the crimson sunset clouds, and the wide Pacific. She breathed deeply, and blinked in the hazy light --- for none of the rocks or trees seemed quite so clear or crisp or alive as they had on the other side of the Portal. In her heart, she murmured a word of farewell to her brother, on the far side of the rocky wall; for she was sure that he could hear her. Then other words came to her.

"Between the past and future, there lies the present, and there, without a doubt, you are also a fairy." The words of the mysterious mermaid floated in her mind like an invigorating and yet soothing balm. Little by little, the natural world seemed to come more to life, and Eli even fancied that she could hear harp music singing in the waterfalls and played by the wind among the boulders and trees. She smiled, clasped her shoulder-bag closer to her and touched the necklace hanging over her heart. Then she reached up and fingered, for a moment, the flaming moon ear-ring.

Her B&B awaited her in the town, and tomorrow she would go to make music with the healing harpist whom she had contacted from France.

Her three hours beyond the rocks in the realm of Faërie were ended, and her hike to the Seven Falls on the afternoon and evening of the 1st of June was over too. Eli climbed down the path and when she reached the town again, the hills behind her were dyed rosy-pink by the rays of the departing sun.

Late that night, looking back up from her bedroom's window towards the place where the Portal was hidden, Eli saw the slightly oval waning gibbous moon rising into the starry Californian sky.

"June the 1st," she murmured to herself. "June the 1st once again, or still, for I'm in the same day that I started and it's not yet the Summer Solstice and my birthday as the Princess Mélusine! How will I ever learn to keep my balance between here and there, sun and moon, my loves and my destiny and my family... my longings and my fears?"

Eli touched again the gift from Reyse, now hanging outside of her shirt. She had discovered it to be a moonstone, like a teardrop, and she recognised that its symbolism and significance were bound up with the moonstones he wore in his ears and the one that the rainbow-fairy had told her she wore, embedded in the skin over her heart. Surely, there were sweet and profoundly poetic messages to be comprehended in this lunar and literally 'heart-touching' gift, from the lovely and devoted Reyse.

She left the window open, for it was warm and summery; thus she could watch the moon continue to rise ever so slowly, as she lay on her bed. Until she fell into a deep sleep.

****

Hic finitur liber secundus

This is the end of **A Delicate Balance**,
Book Two in the trilogy *Return to Faërie*.

Index of Characters

Moonrise

Aindel	301		Lady Ecume	89
Alégondine	53		Laurien	119
Annick	3		Leyano	52
Ardan	328		Liam	6
Aulf	239		Lord Hwittir	284
Aulfrelas	66		Maelcraig	232
Aulfrin	50		Maelys/Lily	14
Bawn	213		Mélusine	31
Belfina & Begneta	300		Morvan/Uncle Mor	43/105
Brocéliana	62			
Calenny	129		Muscari	246
Ceoleen	251		Mushroom Lord	239
Clare	58		Peronne	28
Colm	102		Piv/Periwinkle	261
Corr-Seylestar	269		Rapture	140
Daireen	328		Reyse	195
Demoran	34		Rhynwanol	64
Elfhea & Everil	321		Ruilly	133
Eli Penrohan	1		Sage-Hermit	53
Eochra	246		Sean Penrohan	14
Erreig	66		Sinéad	110
Ferglas	132		Timair	327
Fiach	140		Vanzelle	279
Finnir	52		Vintig	136
Garo	269		Violette	186
Gnome	282		Yann	42
Heron-Fairy	149		Yves	107
Hygga	283			
Jizay	29			
Kirik	211			

A Delicate Balance

Ævnad	376
Artist of Kitty Kyle	359
Aytel	182
Ban-Cocoilleen	343
Banvowha	132
Barrimilla	478
Bram	259
Brea	182
Camiade (M & Mme)	40
Cynnabar	156
Dinnagorm	161
Emile	10
Finnhol-Og	343
Gaëtanne	262
Garv-Feyar	444
Janet	50
King Isck	168
Mama Ngeza	355
Mauve Dragon	290
Morliande	218
Mowena & Malmaza	215
Neya-Voun	187
Pallaïs	464
Rhadeg	259
Tinna Payst & Tintrac	389
Wineberry	233

Maps

Due to the limitations imposed by the printing of this first edition, the following maps are presented only in black & white.

Map of Faërie – full

Detail north-east quarter
Detail south-east quarter
Detail north-west quarter
Detail south-west quarter

Map of the City of Fantasie

The full versions of the two maps in b&w are available for free download at www. return-to-faerie.com

Full-colour reproductions of the Map of Faërie and also the Map of the City of Fantasie are available to order from the **Return to Faërie** on-line shop:

https://www.zazzle.com/store/return_to_faerie

(please note that in this web-address the "e" of *faerie* has no umlaut !)

Other products and gift items associated with this book can also be found at the above address.

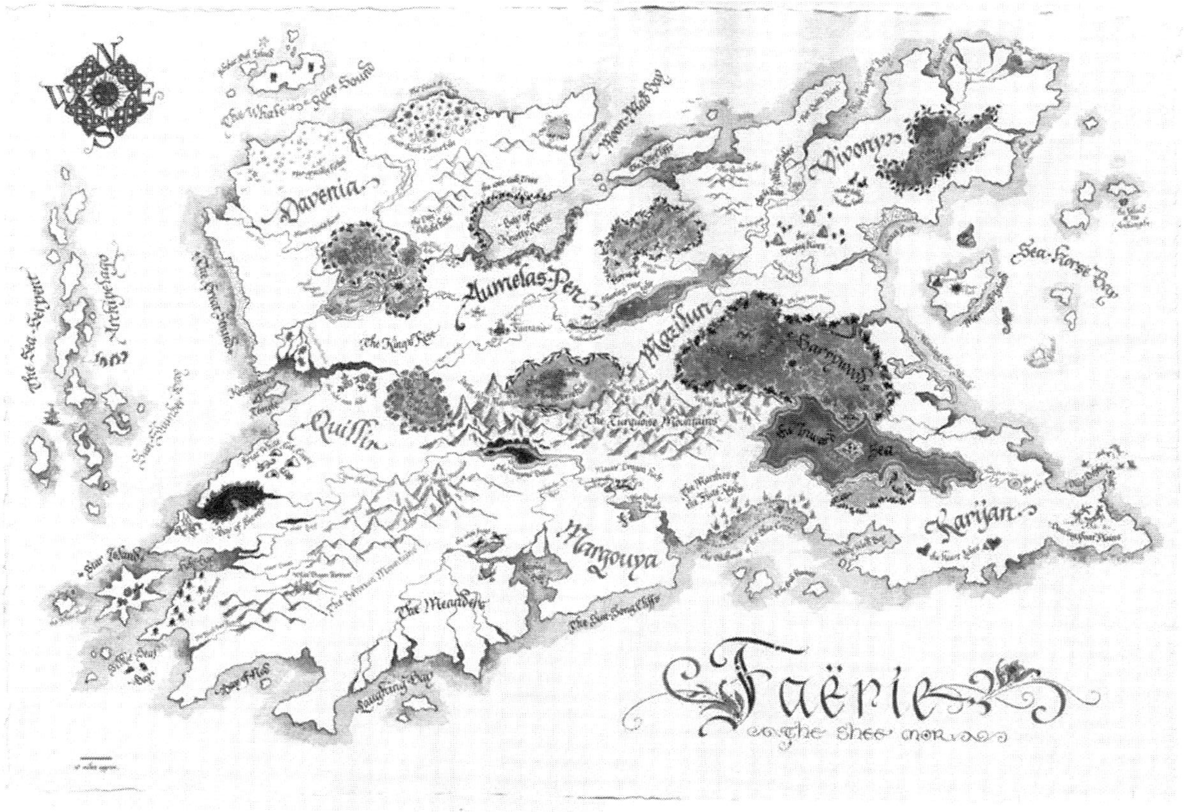
N
W
E
S
Davenia
Aumelas-Pen
Mazilun
Vivonye
Karijan
Quillix
Mangouya
The Meadows
Laughing Bay
The Sea-Serpent
Archipelago
The Great Sound
The King's Rest
The Turquoise Mountains
Sea-Horse Bay
The Sun-Song Cliffs
Star Islands
Faërie
the Shee Mor

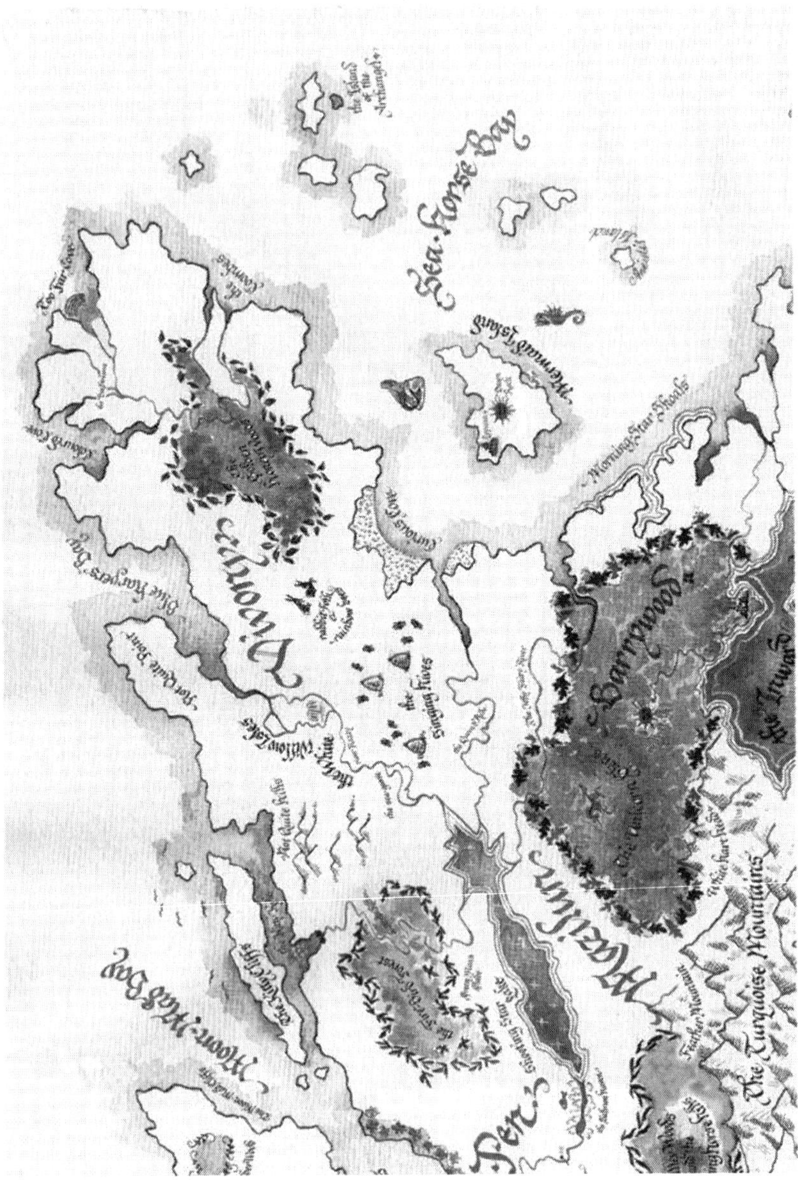

The Turquoise Mountains
White Hart Reeds
The Inward Sea
Windy Hill
Mauve Dragon Rush
Blue Lizard Island
The Marshes of the Flute Reeds
Margouya
the Shallows of the Blue Crabs
The Crab Havens
Windy Word Bay
Karijan
the Heart Lakes
the Pearl
Dizzy Dolphin Point
Dancing Goat Plains
The Sun-Song Cliffs
Faërie
The Shee Mor

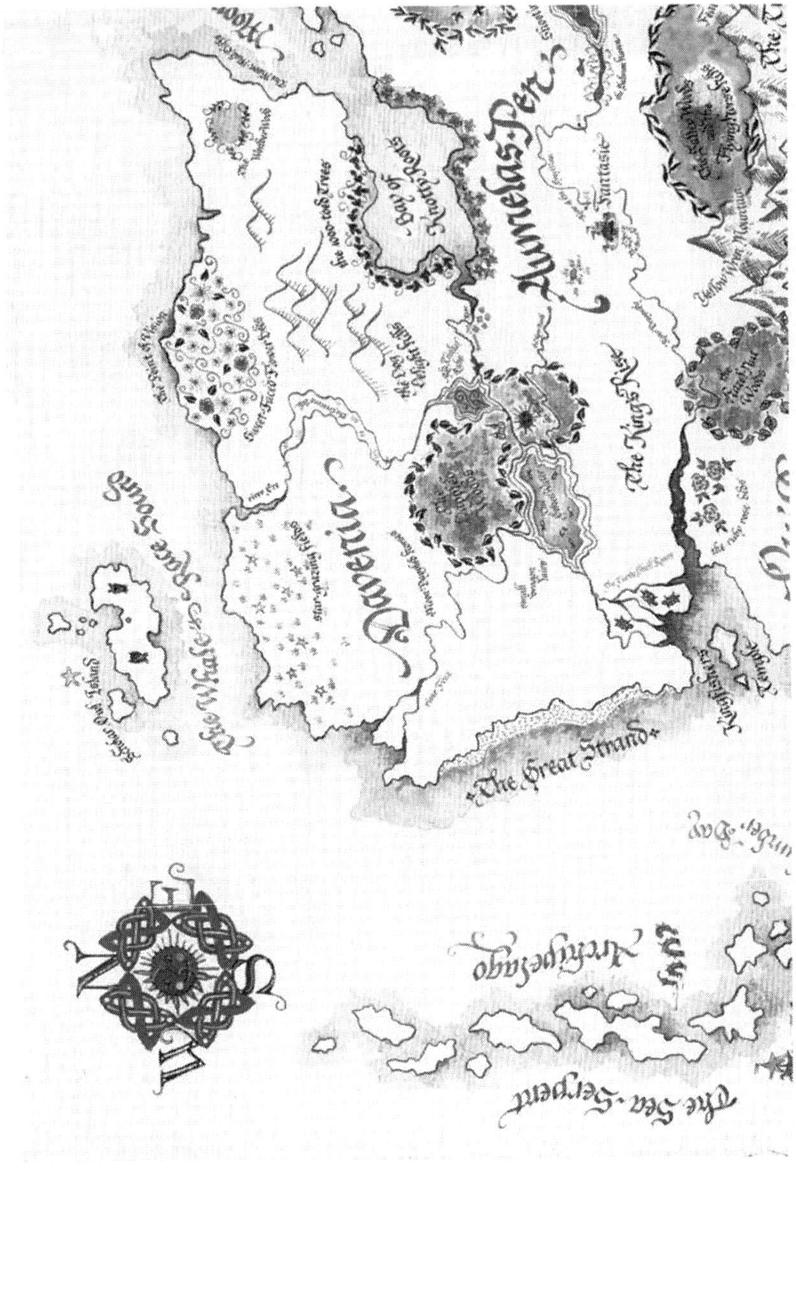

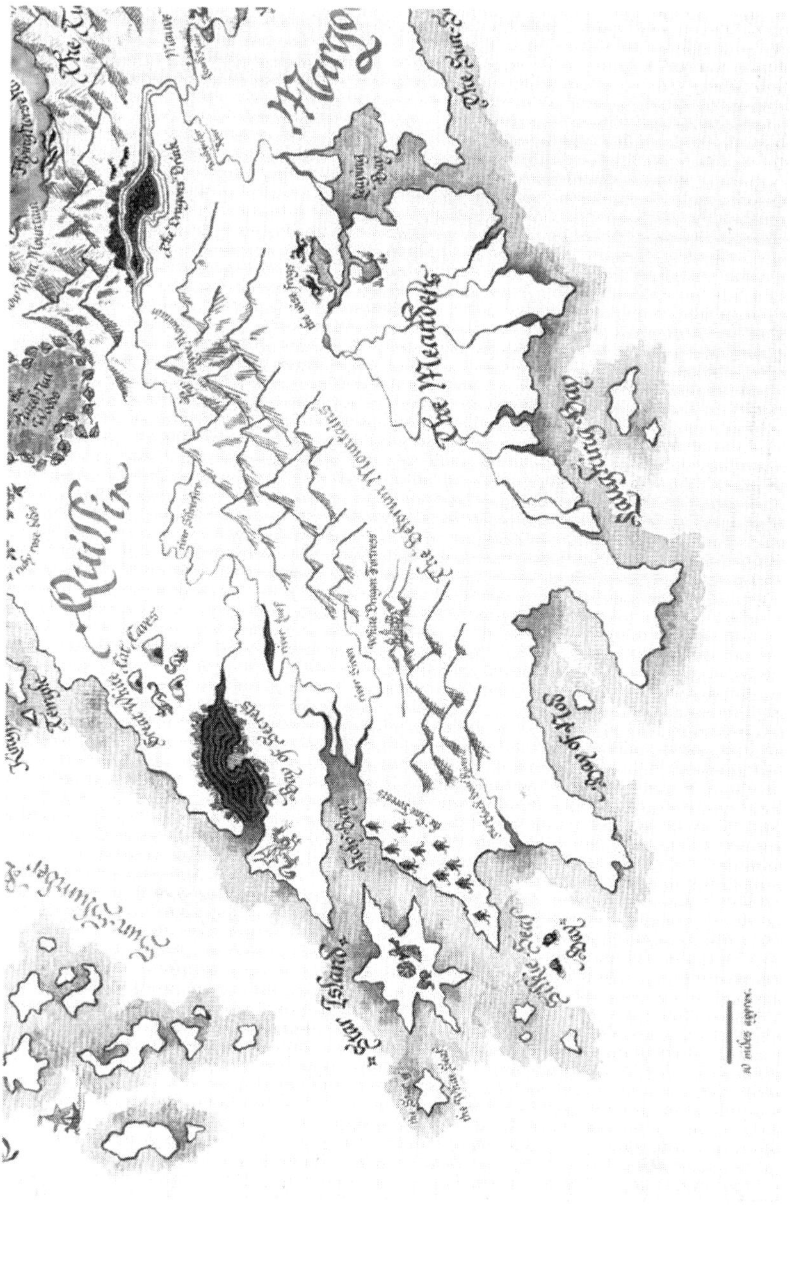
Quillix
The Meanders
Star Island
Bay of Secrets
Great White Cat Caves
The Dragons' Drink
Bay of Toys
Sauntering Bay
Leaping Bay
White Dragon Fortress
10 miles approx.

N
W
E
S
The King's Moon Tower
Lymeril
Lyathel
The Gardens of the Great Trees
Lysandel
The Great Gates
7 Moon Towers
11 Star Towers 7 Gates
= 1 mile approx.
The Silver City of
Fantasie

Printed in Great Britain
by Amazon